Frey Dreams an Imprint of Nikki A Lamers

ISBN 978-0-9970159-8-0 (paperback)
ISBN 978-0-9970159-9-7 (ebook)

W0010873

Table of Contents

Prologue

My heart sinks as I glance into my empty mailbox. I'm not really expecting anything yet, but at the same time, every day I walk to the mailbox with the same hopeful feeling in my chest while swirls of anticipation spin around in my stomach. I turn as my shoulders instantly slouch in defeat. I carefully tiptoe back up my blacktop driveway in an attempt to keep my grey and purple slippers dry. I wince and quickly hop onto my left foot as I feel my right toes dampen with cold from the melted snow, accidentally putting my planted foot into an ice cold puddle. I laugh and shake my head at my clumsiness as I trudge the rest of the way up the two old wooden front porch steps to the matching large oak front door. I push the door open and immediately kick off my now wet slippers. I sigh as I slam the door behind me. I walk over to the soft, brown, ribbed couch and flop down, pulling the grey blanket over me to rid myself of the chill from outside.

I'm anxiously waiting for adoption papers I sent in nearly two months ago, hoping to find out who my birth parents might be. I've always known I was adopted when I was a baby. My parents couldn't have kids of their own and waited a long time for the opportunity to adopt me. I knew before I understood what it really meant to be adopted. I used to think being adopted was the same thing as someone saying I'm Irish or Italian. Once I realized the real meaning of being adopted, I claimed it as another unique thing about me. How could I not when I had such amazing parents? They never stopped reminding me I was the best gift they ever received.

When I turned 18 and graduated from high school, my parents gave me forms from The Wisconsin Department of Children and Families to fill out if and when I was ready to find out more about where I came from. At the time, I hugged my mom and dad and thanked them. I couldn't help but think about all my friends from our adoption group who were also adopted and how differently we all feel, depending on the situation behind our adoption. The questions are endless and the answers terrifying, but with one glance at my mom and dad, I know I'm grateful for this life. I put the papers away in my desk, intending to focus on enjoying my last summer with my boyfriend, my friends and my mom and dad. My parents told me they would support me and help me any way they could if and when I was ever ready. I don't believe I could've asked for better parents.

I rub my chest as the familiar ache begins to take over my heart, climb up my throat and slowly spread throughout the rest of my body like a virus. I take a deep breath, reminding myself that it has only been a year and a half since my parents died in the plane crash. I wish it didn't still hurt so much. I close my eyes, trying to shove away the memory from the month after I left for college. Mom and Dad took off for a well-deserved vacation in Hawaii. I just wish they never got on that small plane to go island hopping. Then they wouldn't have been on it when the plane had engine failure. I hate thinking about the specifics. It hurts too much.

I can't help but think of what I was doing when I got the phone call from my Uncle Tim. I flinch at the memory of sitting in my dorm room laughing with my new roommate, Krissy, while my parents just lost their life. I only knew Krissy for a month, but I will never forget her or anything about that night up to that point. I was wearing a little black dress with short sleeves that hung loose around my full curves. The same dress I later wore to my parents' funeral. Krissy helped me get ready for the party that night, making my long brown curls appear elegant, my thin eyelashes look fuller and my caramel colored brown eyes sparkle. Krissy looked fantastic, her black silky hair appearing just brushed, her perfect chocolate skin covered in the red dress she wore to the party we just came from, her dark brown eyes sparkling with mischief and the beautiful smile she wore right before the world I knew ceased to exist. Then with one phone call, everything instantly felt surreal. Krissy suddenly felt so far away while trying to talk to me, sounding muffled as if I were underwater. Her eyes were drawn together in concern as I frantically began packing up as many things as I could fit in my duffle bag without passing out. I ran out with my bag in hand, barely whimpering an explanation, "My Mom and Dad."

I drove home on autopilot. When I trudged into my parents' empty house, the same house that's now mine, I almost expected them to be standing there waiting for me. "Mom, Dad," I called desperately, but no one answered. I stood in the middle of my living room, staring blankly and feeling lost until my Uncle Tim and his family arrived to help with arrangements. With their support, I let my mind go blank, trying not to feel the overwhelming pain. The wake and funeral services are still a blur. Besides an endless sea of faces leaving me food and telling me, "I'm so sorry," over and over again, I don't remember anything. A week after the funeral, I couldn't stop my tears or make my pain fade away and I knew what I had to do. I withdrew from college and never looked back. Krissy and I still text once in a while and we keep up to date with one another on Instagram (although my life is boring), but just seeing her name on my phone reminds me of what I no longer have. At the time, college didn't seem important, not when I'd lost so much.

I've been numb for so long that waiting for these papers is putting me on edge. I feel as if my emotions are much stronger now than they almost ever were and I'm not quite sure how to deal with it. I haven't felt this much since my parents died. I didn't even feel anything but betrayal and acceptance when I caught my ex-boyfriend Paul cheating on me with my ex-best friend Taylor. The shock of seeing them all over each other at a party during their Christmas break is what pushed me over the edge to finally fill out the basic questions on the adoption papers and send them in the next day. I believe I was holding tightly on to anything and anyone I had before I lost my parents. I wanted everything familiar around me, but I was obviously trying to keep the wrong things. I emotionally checked out of my relationship with Paul long before I saw him with Taylor. I grimace as I glance over at the cliché long stem red roses Paul sent me yesterday for Valentine's Day with a note begging for me to forgive him and take him back. I shake my head in annoyance, remembering how my dad would always find a way to make gifts and moments special for my mom by making things personal and roses are the opposite of personal to me.

The doorbell rings, startling me out of my thoughts. I grimace as I look over at the door, hoping it's not something else from Paul, or Paul himself. I'm sick of avoiding him, but I can't listen to his excuses or begging anymore in any form. Besides, I'm getting really good at evading him. Of course since he went back to college nearly an hour away, he's made it much easier. His efforts have definitely lessened, but he hasn't completely given up. I peak out the window to see our gray haired mailman standing on the front porch. I breathe a sigh of relief and open the door with a friendly smile, "Hi."

"I have too much for the mailbox with this package today," he informs me, holding up a large stack of mail.

"Thank you," I tell him as I take the pile from him. I shut the door as soon as he turns around and begin weeding through the mail as I walk back towards the couch. When I reach the package he mentioned, I turn it over in my hands to read the return address. My heart stops and my hands instantly begin shaking. "Wisconsin Department of Children and Families," I mumble. I drop to the couch, suddenly feeling weak as all the other mail falls to the floor. I gasp for breath as tears begin rolling down my face without even knowing what's inside.

My whole body trembles as all the "what ifs" consume my brain. I convinced myself I was okay with any scenario I could imagine, but am I really? What if there's something I didn't think of? Sobs begin to wrack my body as I cry harder, curling myself into a ball, attempting to protect myself from the package in my hands. I wonder what's inside this massive envelope, but I'm too scared to open it. I'm not looking to find other parents or another family, my mom and dad always gave me so much. I think that's one of the reasons I'm struggling with this so much. They always said they support me, but would the reality be too hard with them gone? I have other family like my two cousins, one I'm really close to. I've always been surrounded with so much love. I would take my overprotective parents back if I could, but I don't know if I can handle the unknown. Am I brave enough or do I even want to be? I don't need another reason to hurt. How am I supposed to know if opening this package is worth it?

Questions start running through my mind on overdrive. What if they don't want to have anything to do with me? What if they do? What are they like and what kind of life do they have now? What if they have separate families that don't know about me? What did I do to their lives by even sending this paperwork in? What if they've already died? How would my mom and dad really feel about it? The last thing I would want to do is hurt them. I wouldn't ever want them to think I'm replacing them because that's impossible! Even though they're gone, they'll always be my parents. I want them to be happy with my decisions even if they're not here to see them. "I can't disappoint them," I murmur.

I don't know how long I sit, nearly motionless, but I realize it's been quite a while when my stomach growls hungrily, encouraging me to start moving again. My whole body aches from my clenched muscles and nerves. "You're being ridiculous, Samantha!" I scold myself. I slowly take a deep breath, hoping to calm my anxiety enough to move forward. I push myself up until I'm sitting with the package in my lap that seems to be the size of "War and Peace".

"I have the power of possibility at my fingertips," I murmur. I take a deep breath and hold it in while I tear the supersized envelope open with trembling fingers. I slowly pull the thick stack out of the envelope and blink, attempting to focus on the first page as my heart pounds out of control. My chest aches and I hear the blood rushing through my ears. I'm keenly aware of two things as the papers slowly come into focus. My mother's name is Catherine and she just died on October 26 of this past year. I gasp, trying to hold back another sob as an overwhelming sense of grief overtakes me and I weep for a woman I never really knew.

I glance around my living room, looking for a source of strength and my eyes fall on a picture of my parents and me at one of my tennis matches. They were always so supportive and if they were here, I know they would be now. "I think those Hallmark movies put me over the edge," I attempt to joke as I look at their picture. "I miss you both so much," I whimper painfully. "I don't know what I'm doing, but I know I need to do something. I thought this should be it, but..." I trail off as I glance at the now tear-stained skewed stack of papers in my lap. I take a deep breath and mumble, "I'm a mess."

I groan and attempt to refocus my attention on the papers in front of me, searching for information. Included are court papers, medical papers, various documents from when she was pregnant with me and even after my birth, but everywhere my birth father's name is written, it's blacked out with a marker or something. My eyebrows scrunch together in confusion. I wonder if he didn't want me to have any of his information. Why wouldn't it tell me one way or another?

I suddenly recall a phone call last month when the Department of Children and Families contacted me because they had more questions for me to complete their search. The guy I spoke to said he was in charge of my case. I run to my room and pull out the notepad I had written on to find his name and number and quickly dial. "Wisconsin Department of Children and Families, this is Chase, can I help you?"

I clear my throat, attempting to steady my voice, "Hi Chase, my name is Samantha Voss. I spoke to you last month regarding a search for my birth parents?"

"Yes, Hi Samantha. I remember you. You live in Illinois, right?"

I force a laugh to relax my nerves, "Uh, yeah. Um, I just have a quick question..." I trail off and wait for some type of response.

"Well, then I'm glad you caught me. I was just about to leave for the day. What can I do for you?" he questions.

"Well, um, I received all my information from you today and I was wondering if you could tell me why I didn't get any information on my birth father? I mean there's some, but his name is blacked out in all the papers. Does that mean he doesn't want me to contact him?" I ramble uncomfortably. These aren't the types of questions that are easy to ask, let alone having to ask them of a stranger.

"Not necessarily, let me take a look. I think I remember," he mumbles as I listen to him shuffling some papers around then clicking from typing into a computer. "Yes, here it is. We actually couldn't provide you with that information legally because there was never any DNA test provided for the courts to prove he was your father. I'm not sure why. So even though both your birth parents signed these adoption papers and it was acknowledged that he was the father, the courts don't recognize him as the birth father."

"I don't understand," I blurt.

He sighs in understanding, "I'm sorry, but maybe there's some more information for you in all those letters from your birth mother. It says she came here to sign the affidavit of consent for the release of her information to you almost two years ago. I guess it was after you turned 18. She also left the letters with your file to be released with all the information if you ever tried to search for her."

"Letters? What letters?" I ask frantically.

"It says here there are 20 letters included with your documents from the birth mother. They should all be there. I remember your case. I packaged everything myself," he informs me not sounding at all concerned.

I run back to the living room and my eyes frantically search where I was reading the papers. I get down on my hands and knees and look under the couch and when I move towards the chair, I spy a bundle of letters along with a couple loose papers between the furniture. I must've dropped them when I lost it. I pick them up and pull them to my chest, breathing a sigh of relief. "I found them," I whisper.

"Good," he replies.

"Thank you Chase."

"Of course. Is there anything else I can help you with?" he asks.

"No thank you," I reply regretfully, still wishing he could give me more. "I'll let you go home now."

He chuckles, "Feel free to call me again if you have any questions or need anything else Samantha. Don't forget, we can also provide you with a copy of your original birth certificate if you'd like for a small fee. Good luck."

"Thank you. Goodbye," I tell him and end the call before he has a chance to say anything else. I'm having a hard enough time processing all of this.

I sit down on the couch and curl my legs up underneath me. I hold the letters tightly in my hands, my fingers feeling like they're burning. I close my eyes for a moment to try to gather my strength. I slowly open my eyes and nervously pull the first one out. I let my eyes roam over the soft handwriting and run my fingers over it reverently. My birth mother wrote me these letters by hand. I guess it's the only thing I'll ever have of hers. Tears flood my eyes and I attempt to gulp down the lump in my throat. I take another deep breath and begin to read.

To My Unborn Child,

I don't even know where to begin. I guess I can begin with the fact that I'm 5 months pregnant. I don't know if you'll be a boy or a girl, but either way you will be coming, just not to me, not exactly anyway. I'm sorry, but I can't be your Mom. I wish things were different, but they aren't, so I wanted to at least leave you with some of my reasons.

I'm 18 years old and barely out of high school. I moved out of my parents' house as soon as I finished school, roaming from place to place with some friends. We stayed in hostels or crashed with friends. Then when I got pregnant with you I tried to change all of that, but I've found I'm not ready to care for anyone else when I can barely take care of myself. I know I wouldn't be the best thing for you, but I also know I love you and I want you to be happy.

I met your father the summer after I graduated from high school at a weekend music festival. We were both single at the time and we spent the weekend together. We parted ways, expecting to never see each other again. He left to go back to college and I wanted to travel the world, but I didn't get too far. I showed up on his front stoop today, after searching for him to tell him about you. To say he was shocked to see me is an understatement. Well I'm sure a lot of it had to do with my swollen belly. Not long after we were together, he met someone and it became serious very quickly. They just found out she's pregnant. She's only about two months along. He plans on proposing to her and starting a life with her. I guess there will only be a few months between you and your half-sibling, but who knows if you'll ever meet.

He offered to do everything he could to help you, but he's trying to pay for college and support himself and his new family. He sounded so lost when we talked about our options for you at this point. He would never be able to do

all of that and support us, so I suggested adoption.
Although we both wish things could be different, neither of
us can care for you right now. We want you to have
opportunities we know we can't give you at this time.

I know in my heart you will be better off without me.
You will have both a mom and dad who will care for you
and love you. This is my way of trying to let you know I love
you with my whole heart and soul. I'm sorry I can't be the
mother you deserve right now. I hope some day you'll be
able to understand our choice. Every single day I'll pray for
you to have love, happiness, courage and a life full of
wonderful adventures. If you're anything like me, maybe
one day you will use your strength and courage to come
find me. If you do, I hope you can forgive me for not being
enough for you in this moment.

I will always love you.
Your Mother for now,
Catherine Schepp

I wipe my tears away, yet again, as I imagine what
she may have felt at the time. What did either of them
feel like when they found out she was pregnant. I'm only
a year older than she was when she had me. What if Paul
and I had gotten pregnant and then I walked in on what I
did over Christmas break? What would I do? We were
careful, but we did have sex. I grimace, hating to even
think about that kind of fate. I don't know what I
would've done, which makes me think I can't blame her
for what she did.

I'm not sure how I feel about him though. My
stomach churns at the thought that I have a brother or
sister out there somewhere who's nearly the same age as
me. It's not that he didn't want a child, it's that he didn't
want me. I close my eyes and try to reign in my thoughts
as I feel myself beginning to panic. I take another deep

breath and slowly open my eyes. I immediately pull out
the second letter, suddenly needing to learn everything I
possibly can about my birth family. I notice my birthday
is written on the front of the envelope and the one right
behind it has the same. I flip through the envelopes to
find each one has only my birthday on the front. "Did she
write me on every birthday?" I question quietly, my heart
suddenly pounding erratically in my chest. I again reach
for the second letter and begin reading.

June 12 – the day of your birth
To My Beautiful Baby Girl,
I don't know what your name will be, but I do know
that you are the most beautiful thing I've ever seen or
touched. They let me cradle your little body in my arms to
say goodbye. I took a deep breath, inhaling your sweet
baby scent and trying to commit it to memory. I examined
every little piece of you as you squirmed, looking for a
comfortable spot in my arms. My heart broke as your tiny
hand wrapped tightly around my pointer finger as if you
were clinging with the knowledge that our time would be
fleeting. You're so tiny and vulnerable with your long thin
body that I can hold in my hands. You came out screaming,
letting me know you will be a fighter and you will be just
fine. At least that's what I'm telling myself. Your hair
appears brown and your eyes blue, but I wonder if they will
stay that way. I'm told those things may change, but I
won't be there to see any of those changes, although I'll be
thinking of you every day. I will always cherish the first few
moments of your life when you were in my arms.
I nearly couldn't let you go, but I knew I needed to
do the right thing for you. I'm now a 19-year-old girl who
can't even take care of herself. I placed a kiss on your soft
little head and let you go as tears ran down my cheeks. I
struggled to breathe as I told you it would be okay, praying

my words to be true. Then I handed you over to the nurse who placed you in a clear bassinette and rolled you back to the nursery. Your father is in there now to see you and sign your birth certificate, but the adoption won't be finalized until after I'm released from the hospital.

They promised me you were going to a good family. It's a closed adoption, so I'll never know who is raising you. It's the best thing for all of us. They told me your new parents desperately want children to love and can't have any of their own. They have good jobs and a nice home in a safe neighborhood for you to grow up. I believe with all my heart and soul that this unknown family will take wonderful care of you. If I didn't, I would have never been able to give you away. I hope you understand.

Letting you go today was one of the hardest things I've ever had to do. I know I can't take care of you now, but I wish I had done things differently so I could. I realize things don't always work out the way I want them to, but as I get my last look at you, I already have so many regrets. Someday if you want to find me, I'll be here waiting. You'll never leave my heart even though you have to leave my arms. I never imagined that the best day of my life would also be my worst. I'm so sorry.

With Love…
Catherine Schepp

I swallow down the lump in my throat, hating that I'm too late. If I had just looked for her when my parents gave me the papers, I would've had the chance to meet her and get to know her. Now I'll never have that chance. For the first time I feel the loss of hope inside me. "I guess I did have something else to lose," I grumble regretfully. I shake my head to keep the tears at bay. I don't think I have the strength to read all of these right now, but maybe I can find more on my biological father. I quickly pull out the last letter in the pile hoping it will give me the answers I'm looking for, like when I read the last few pages of a book. I refocus and begin to read.

June 12 – Your 18th Birthday
To My Beautiful Baby Girl,
Happy 18th Birthday! I hope you're doing something fun to celebrate today. I assume you're probably graduating from high school sometime this month, so I'm going to congratulate you too. I realize you're not a baby anymore, in fact you're now the same age I was when I was pregnant with you, but I know in my heart you're beautiful, smart, talented and strong. Unfortunately, my time may be limited and I don't know if I'll ever have the opportunity to see any of that for myself. I hate that I may never be able to see how wonderful you've become, but I do believe that's exactly what you are. I have to. It's crazy to think I may have seen you at the grocery store or passing by me on the street, but I may never know. I've looked at so many girls over the years, wondering if they might be you.

I'm not sure if you'll come looking for me, but I wanted to make sure you had what you needed when you did, especially if I'm already gone. I want to let you know your father is a good man. He may not have been able to care for you when you were brought into this world, but I wouldn't be able to say that today. He's done well for himself in his career and with his family, but I'll leave that to him to share with you when you're ready.

In all these letters, there's something I've never told you, although I believe now is the time. You may already know from your parents through my basic medical records, but I still need to tell you myself. When I was a very young child, I was diagnosed with cystic fibrosis. It is one of the reasons I believed I would never have children because I didn't think I would be able to care for anyone long term when many times I struggle to take care of myself. Then you unexpectedly came along. I knew I wasn't the right person to raise you between my instability and my sickness, but since your father doesn't have cystic fibrosis in his family history, I knew it couldn't be passed on to you, although you could be a carrier. I would advise you to have genetic testing done to find out for sure. Although, keep in mind, it takes two carriers to have a possibility of passing it on to your own children.

Recently I've had a very difficult time with my sickness. So I went to your father to let him know about the letters in case you search for us. When I called to ask about signing the affidavit and leaving the letters for you, I found that they wouldn't be able to provide you with your father's information, so we both decided that I would. Your father's name is Lincoln Scott. He lives at 1174 Hawks Rd in Chance, WI. It's a small town just outside of Madison. He works at Hometown in Chance. It's a home store with a little of everything. If and when you're ready, he's waiting to talk with you, meet you and know you.

I'm not going to give you advice or tell you what to do. I realize you have parents for that job. I am going to tell you I hope you follow your heart and do what makes you happy. Life is too short to be filled with regret. (Well, maybe a little advice...) I may no longer be here when you find me, but I'll always watch over you and pray for the best for you. I need you to know, I never stopped loving you.

With Love...
Catherine Schepp

I shakily fold up the letter and put it back in the envelope as my mind begins racing with so many questions. Ironically, I suddenly know exactly what I need to do and it doesn't include staying here in Illinois. Maybe I should thank Paul and Taylor for pushing me to make this decision. Maybe this will help me find out who I am.

Chapter 1

"What the hell do you think you're doing Samantha?" I mumble to myself as I stand outside a small blue apartment building staring at the bright yellow front door. I'm starting to second-guess my decision to immediately pack up some of my things and search on-line ads for roommates wanted in Chance, Wisconsin so quickly after getting my adoption papers. The girl I responded to seemed pretty normal, but how the hell do I know for sure when we only met on-line? Nobody would even know to come looking for me if something happened. I forwarded my mail and told the neighbors I'd be gone for a while, but I never bothered to tell anyone where I was going. I used Krissy and an old teacher for references. I didn't even call Uncle Tim or my cousins to tell them. I guess the post office is the only one who knows where to find me, but besides being able to deliver my mail, why would they care? I grimace, knowing I'm being unfair to my family. Now that I'm here though, reality is catching up with me and I'm beginning to feel the panic burning a hole in my gut.

I glance around the quiet neighborhood, but the calm could be because it's March, and absolutely freezing outside. A few inches of snow still covers the ground from the latest snowfall, but the sidewalks and driveways have been shoveled clear. Looking at my surroundings, I almost feel peaceful, but my quivering insides cling to a different story. I can't believe I've done something so stupid. I cringe, knowing my parents wouldn't be happy with me. I can practically hear the lecture and I wouldn't be able to argue because they'd be right. "I think I've completely lost my mind," I sigh in exasperation as I contemplate turning around and going back to Illinois.

"Well since I don't know you, I can't really tell, but signs point to yes since you're standing out in the cold talking to yourself." I squeak startled and spin towards the sound of the low gravelly voice that just sent chills down my spine. My eyes widen as they land on the owner of the sexy voice. My breath catches in my throat at the sight of the guy standing in front of me. He has dark brown hair sticking out from underneath a grey beanie hat and shockingly bright blue eyes that appear to be laughing at me. He's taller than me by probably half a foot, causing me to lift my chin up to look at him. I nervously let my eyes drift down to his sexy smirk as he assesses me, showing off a deep dimple in his left cheek underneath his light stubble. I bite my lip to hold back a moan. His arms are crossed over his broad chest, which appears huge even in his black winter coat. He has to be too good to be true. I force my eyes to return to his face as I grimace at my wayward thoughts.

"Um, Hi. I'm just..." I trail off realizing I don't owe this gorgeous stranger any explanation.

His eyebrows rise in question, as his smirk grows causing my stomach to flip at the sight. "Are you looking for someone or something? I could help," he offers.

"Yes, I mean no...er yeah," I stutter, making him chuckle. I sigh in annoyance and narrow my eyes on him. "Yes," I declare suddenly confident. "I was looking for Cory, but I think I changed my mind."

He chuckles again, "Are you the new roommate she mentioned? She's been waiting for you."

I shake my head, "No, this was a mistake."

"Wait a minute," he pleads. He reaches for my arm, igniting me with his touch even through my thick, ivory winter coat. I take a slow, controlled breath, attempting to suppress a shiver before my eyes move to his hand, still resting on my arm. He instantly drops it when my gaze doesn't waver from his hand. "Sorry," he grumbles and stuffs his hands into his jean pockets. "A mistake?" he questions. "Can I help you?" he asks sounding hopeful.

I shake my head, "No. I just..." I turn and glance at the blue building behind us before I return my focus back to him. I shrug and sigh in resignation. "I just don't know her at all. We've never met. I've talked to her endlessly on-line the past few weeks and checked out her profiles on social media, but I don't know if this is a good idea. How can I move in with someone I've never met?" I blurt out nervously.

His shoulders noticeably relax as his smirk transforms into an easy smile. "I get it, but that's what happens if you move into a dorm in college. It's the same idea right?" I purse my lips, still doubtful. He adds, "Besides, being worried about having Cory as a roommate is laughable. She's like a little ball of sunshine."

My lips twitch as I fight to keep the smile off my lips, "And how do I know I can trust you? I don't know you either," I remind him.

He grins, puffing up his chest and juts out his hand in greeting. I willingly place my small, cold hand in his large, warm one, as I watch his eyes sparkle with mischief. "Hi. I'm Brady Williams. I live here," he gestures with his eyes to the building behind us, "next door to Cory and hopefully after today, you," he explains. He looks at me expectantly, continuing to hold my hand, causing my whole body to warm from his touch. His lips twitch in amusement as he prompts, "And you are?"

I blush easily and shake my head at myself, "I'm sorry, it's been a long...week." He chuckles and I can't help but grin up at him, "I'm Samantha, Samantha Voss."

"Samantha," he whispers my name giving me chills. I force myself to breathe slowly and jerk my hand away, stuffing it into my coat pocket. He clears his throat, then grins widely and informs me, "Now that we're friends, I'd be offended if you didn't take my advice. At least come meet Cory. I promise, you won't regret it."

I don't bother fighting my own smile in response. "Well, I guess I could at least meet her...for you. After all, we are friends and she's a friend of yours, so I'm sure we'll get along fantastic," I reply, my voice dripping with polite sarcasm.

His whole face lights up, taking my breath away. He overtly gestures for me to go in front of him, "Well then, after you Sam." He hesitates before asking, "Is it okay if I call you Sam?"

I grin as I step in front of him, "Well that is what my friends call me." I stop when we get to the front door. I realize my hands are shaking as I slowly reach for the handle. I have a nearly overwhelming feeling that everything is about to change. Hopefully it will finally change for the better. My heart pounds erratically in my chest as he reaches around me, enveloping me with his masculine scent as he pushes the door open for us. "Thank you," I murmur breathlessly still facing the door.

"You're welcome," he replies softly as I step inside.

He takes a deep breath and steps slightly around me, his hand landing on the small of my back for guidance. I pinch my lips closed to hide my gasp and attempt to focus on taking in my surroundings instead. I look around at the dark slate tile floors, white walls and white doors for every apartment. In front of me to the left stands a tall narrow staircase with the steps painted a blue that matches the front of the house along with a white handrail. "He must like blue," I mumble. Brady laughs and the light-hearted sound sends my heart racing.

I turn towards him and he flashes me another heart-melting smile, "You got that right." He gestures towards his left where a little over a dozen gold mailboxes are built into the wall, "You get your mail here. If you have a package, you'll receive a slip and have to pick it up from the Super." He points at the door behind him. "He goes by Mr. K and he lives there in 101. He seems okay and he's around most of the time if you need something fixed." I nod in understanding as he continues to provide me with the information I need if I stay. "The building has four apartments per floor, except this one only has three, so there's fifteen apartments total. The door to the left of the mailboxes leads to the basement. The only thing down there is washers and dryers and a few uncomfortable chairs. The elevator," he gestures to the right of the mailboxes, "is old and doesn't always work, so if you're in a hurry take the stairs," he suggests jokingly. I cringe at the thought of getting stuck in the small elevator. He laughs and points towards the elevator, "So do you want to take your chances with me to the top, or should we hike the stairs to the fourth floor?"

"I'll take my chances," I reply with my own smirk. I'm not about to attempt to walk up four flights of stairs when my legs are shaking so badly. It may be from my nerves, but that doesn't mean they won't give out on me and I definitely don't want to make a fool out of myself in front of this beautiful man.

He pushes the button for the elevator and mumbles almost inaudibly, "I sure hope so."

"What was that?" I ask with raised brows.

He shakes his head and gives me a crooked smile, "Nothing, just thinking." I nod my head as the doors screech open. I take a step in and lean against the worn white paneled wall. He steps in behind me and pushes the button for the fourth floor before leaning against the opposite wall. He bends his left knee and places his foot against the elevator wall as the doors squeak closed. He pulls off his hat and runs his fingers through his messy hair, having no chance of making it right. I bite my bottom lip to keep myself from saying something stupid to this sexy man. He sighs and raises his eyes to meet mine. Caught staring, I refuse to let my eyes waver and continue to hold his gaze. Eventually he clears his throat and asks, "So where are you from Sam?"

"Illinois," I answer vaguely.

He smirks knowingly, "And you're moving to Wisconsin? No wonder you're here alone," he jokes of the common friendly rivalry.

A lump immediately forms in my throat and pinpricks attack my heart and stomach. I feel my eyes well up involuntarily and I tear my gaze away from his without saying a word. He quickly takes two steps across the small elevator invading my space. "I'm sorry. I was just kidding. I have family outside Chicago. I didn't mean anything by it," he explains appearing slightly confused.

I nod my head and rasp, "I know."

He sighs, "I'm sorry. Here I am trying to convince you to move in and instead I stick my foot in my mouth and make you cry."

I shake my head and take a deep steadying breath, "No, it's okay Brady. I'm fine. It's not you, I just have a lot on my mind," I explain trying to brush it off.

He nods like he understands, but looks at me like he wants to know more. He lightly runs his fingers down my arm until he reaches my hand and gives it a light squeeze, attempting to comfort me, but only succeeding in covering my body in goose bumps instead. I can't help but feel an overwhelming urge to ask him to hold me, but I won't. Then he'd really think I'm crazy. He clears his throat and waits until I meet his eyes. "I know you don't know me, but if you ever need anything..." he trails off before adding, "I'm a great listener."

He doesn't let go of my fingers as I whisper, "Thank you." He continues to look at me like he's searching for answers I'm not ready to give a complete stranger as the elevator makes its noisy ascent. Suddenly the doors creak loudly open, breaking our moment. He drops my hand and clears his throat again as he steps into the hallway. He reaches for the doors and holds them back while I step out.

He gestures down the short hall and stops in front of the door with 401 written on the front of the white door in blue. He points to the door labeled 403 to the right, "That's my apartment with my roommate Cody." He continues to turn in a circle as he points out the two apartments across the hall, "Kyla and Mia live in 404 and Seth and Logan are across from you in 402."

"I didn't say I was staying," I remind him, my lips twitching in amusement.

"You will," he answers confidently before knocking loudly on the door we're standing in front of.

Behind the door we hear a muffled squeal followed by footsteps quickly approaching the door. Suddenly something that sounds like someone crashing into the door followed by a loud thud makes us both laugh before the door is thrown open. A girl about the same height as me with warm hazel eyes, blonde hair and a bright smile greets us excitedly. "Hi!" she exclaims. Then her eyes land on Brady and her face noticeably falls. "Oh, Hi Brady. What's up?"

He bursts out laughing, struggling to answer her. She crosses her arms over her chest and glares at him. "Don't be so happy to see me," he grins when he catches his breath and steps past her into the apartment.

She rolls her eyes at him and replies, "You know I'm waiting for my new roommate. I thought you were her," she whines. "I'm just really excited to meet her."

She turns towards me and holds out her hand to greet me with a friendly smile. "Hi, I'm Cory, a friend and obviously neighbor of Brady's."

Brady's grin grows and he tries to muffle his laughter as he watches us. I reach out my hand towards her and introduce myself. "Hi Cory, I'm Samantha, your new roommate."

Her eyes widen and she squeals excitedly before tugging me into the apartment and into her arms for a tight hug. I pat her on the back awkwardly until she lets go and takes a step back. "I'm so sorry. I thought you were one of Brady's girls," she informs me.

I shake my head and smile stiffly at the awkward flip of my stomach. I grimace and quickly shake it off, hating myself for feeling jealous of Brady's unknown girls when I've known him all of five minutes.

Brady steps over to me and throws his arm over my shoulders surprising me. I glance up at him and he explains, "Sam and I go way back." Cory's eyebrows draw together in confusion. Brady continues, "Well, back about five minutes anyway, but it has been a memorable five minutes." My chest tightens with his flirtatious comment as he smiles down at me. I glance over at my new roommate. She has her own questioning smile on her face as she looks between the two of us before her eyes narrow on Brady.

I suddenly feel the need to move and I make a quick decision. "I wanted to come up and meet you before I started bringing my stuff in. I should probably get going since it still gets dark so early. I don't want to be unloading everything in the dark."

"So I guess that means you're staying?" Brady questions.

"For now," I joke.

He grins, "I'll help you with your stuff," Brady offers.

I shake my head ready to refuse his help, but he walks out the door without another word before I have the chance to stop him. "I'll help too," Cory adds. "I just want to show you your room first so you know where your stuff is going."

I smile at Cory and exhale slowly finally feeling a little relief. "Thank you," I murmur.

I quickly glance around the small living room with a tan and rose floral couch and two matching armchairs set up around a TV that rests on a small white entertainment center. "The living room, the kitchen," she adds pointing towards the left. The small kitchen has white appliances, a blue-gray Formica countertop and whitewashed cabinets. A small table with a curved booth is built-in to the corner of the room. The floor is covered with the same tile as in the hallway. Cory practically skips down the short hallway and points to the left doorway, "This is my room." With a quick glance, I notice that although the walls are white, her room is decorated in pink and white with splashes of purple, making it appear frilly and feminine. "Straight ahead is the bathroom we share and this is your room." She pushes open the door to a room filled with nothing but a box spring and mattress. She grimaces, "I know white is boring, but we're not allowed to paint. We can put pictures up though," she tells me. I nod in understanding. "Did you bring any furniture with you?"

I shake my head, "Not really, just a nightstand. I'll have to go back to get more of my stuff eventually," I inform her.

She nods, "Well, whatever I can help you with, let me know."

"Cory?" an unfamiliar male voice calls through the small apartment.

"We're coming," she calls. She walks out the door and I follow behind her to the living room. Brady and another guy a couple inches taller than him are standing just inside the door when we walk into the living room. Cory walks up to the guy and wraps her tiny arms around his hard, broad middle. He pulls her close and her head tucks right underneath his chin. "Thank you for coming," she tells him. He has short blonde hair, a little longer on the top, hazel eyes and a strong jaw. He releases Cory and turns towards me with a crooked smile. "This is my twin brother Cody, also Brady's roommate," she introduces him to me. Their family resemblance is instantly obvious. "Cody, this is Samantha," she gestures to me proudly, like I'm a prize and she's known me forever.

I blush, not knowing quite why as Cody steps over to me. "You guys can call me Sam," I inform them as I hold my hand out to Cody.

He steps past my hand and picks me up in a bear hug, lifting me off my feet and making me squeal in surprise. "I like hugs from gorgeous women much better than handshakes." He sets me down, chuckling as he releases me.

"Ignore him, he's a flirt. He's just here to help," Cory tells me glaring at her brother. I nod feeling flushed. I can't help but notice Brady's stiff posture as Cory grabs her coat off a coatrack in the corner and then pulls me out the door. She pushes the button for the elevator and I turn to look back at the boys behind us. Brady steps in front of Cody as he pulls the door shut and whispers something in his ear. Cody laughs loudly and slaps Brady on the back, while Brady continues to glare at him. They step over to us just as the creaky doors of the elevator open. We all quickly pile in and Brady slides next to me, crossing his arms over his chest.

"Thank you all for helping me," I tell them sincerely. I feel my nerves beginning to dissipate as I look at each of their accepting faces. I may not know who I am or what I'm doing, but I think being here is the right decision. Now I just have to figure out what I'm going to do next. I instantly stop my mind from drifting into emotional territory and attempt to focus on moving all the bags and boxes from my car into my new apartment. "I think I just might stick around," I mumble so only Brady hears. I feel his whole body relax as his laughter fills the small space. Focusing on the guy standing next to me could help to keep my mind off of everything. I smile timidly up at him and he grins down at me, giving me goose bumps. Maybe this is where I'm supposed to be.

Chapter 2

I flop down in the middle of the couch feeling completely exhausted. Cory giggles and I look up at her as she curls her legs under her and sits down in one of the chairs. "Are you all unpacked?" she asks sweetly.

I shake my head with a laugh, "Not even close! I don't know how I've spent nearly the past 24 hours unpacking and I'm not done. I still have a ton of stuff in Illinois too. Then again, the only thing I felt like doing last night after we brought everything in was find my pajamas and my toothbrush. I did make my bed though, so at least I had a place to sleep last night." She laughs. "Thank you again for helping me," I tell her appreciatively.

She opens her mouth to say something when the door to our apartment flies open. She jumps out of her chair startled at the sight of her brother striding into the room in jeans and a long sleeved navy blue graphic t-shirt. "Cody!" she yells at her brother. "You can't just storm in here whenever you feel like it. I'm not the only one who lives here anymore," she reminds him.

He glances at me looking sheepish, "I'm sorry, but I brought pizza," he offers, raising his eyebrows.

She grimaces and sighs, agreeing reluctantly with a stiff nod and making me laugh. "Fine!" she grumbles. "I'll grab plates and soda."

"You mean pop?" I ask grinning.

"Oh that's right, Cory said you're from Illinois," Cody says laughing. He walks over and sets the pizzas on the coffee table in front of me. He sits down next to me and asks, "So Sam, why did you move here?" he asks innocently.

I feel my face begin to heat up as I try to come up with an answer I'm comfortable telling him. "Umm..." I murmur. I really should've thought more about what I would say to this basic question.

I'm saved from answering when Cory walks back in and hands paper plates to Cody before offering me a drink. "I don't know what you like, but we don't have too much anyway. It's Water, Coke or Diet Coke."

"Thanks, I'll take a diet," I grin appreciatively.

"Pepperoni or sausage?" Cody questions holding out two plates to me.

"Either is good," I answer grabbing the closest plate, which happens to be sausage. "Thank you."

"You're welcome," he grins as he hands a plate to his sister before grabbing two slices for himself. He leans back and looks over at me curiously. His smile grows when there's a knock at the door, "Must be Brady," he mumbles.

"Who is it?" Cory yells, none of us wanting to move.

"Brady," he calls back through the door. My nerves instantly go on high alert.

"Come in," she yells back at the same time her brother yells, "Go away!"

Brady walks in wearing a light grey Henley, dark jeans and black converse. His hair is wet and his face is clean-shaven, making his jaw look even stronger and his dimple obvious even without his smile. I gulp down the lump in my throat and attempt to force myself to at least appear calm. He crosses his arms over his chest, causing his biceps to bulge, and glares at Cody, "What the hell man? You could've at least told me the pizza was here before you stole it."

"I didn't steal it, I paid for it when the delivery guy came," he defends himself.

"With my money," Brady glares. He reaches for a plate and a slice of pizza while Cody chuckles and I can't help but join him. Brady turns towards me as his eyebrows rise in question, making my heart skip a beat. "You think that's funny?" he asks, fighting a smile.

I shake my head, "Not exactly. I think you guys are funny. All of you," I clarify gesturing to the three of them. I shrug, "I didn't grow up with any brothers or sisters, but that's exactly what you guys remind me of by the way you're acting. You're entertaining."

Brady's lips twitch in amusement, but then he glances over at Cody before focusing back on me, no longer appearing pleased. He sits down on my other side and my body instantly heats as the couch dips from his weight.

"So what brought you to our small town?" Cody questions, trying again.

I feel myself flinch, still not ready to answer him. "Umm, I'm not quite sure yet. I guess it's kind of complicated. I umm..." I trail off.

Brady steps in to save me, "She's had a long couple days. How about we let her relax and we can tell her about what there is to do around here." I sigh in relief and offer him a grateful smile. "This is a really small town, but there's actually quite a few people our age living here from some of the Madison schools. It's close, but the rent is much cheaper if you don't mind the commute. You'll find that in a lot of the towns around here. Do you go to school?" he asks without judgment.

I shake my head, "No, I tried. It just wasn't for me," I reply. It's the same answer I give everyone, although it's only a partial truth.

"I get it," Cory adds. "College wasn't for me either. I went to beauty school and now I have my own chair at the salon in town," she informs me. "Like I told you before, if you ever need your hair or make-up done, I'm your girl," she grins.

"It's no big deal Sam. I went to vocational school for web development and now I work from home whenever I feel like it," Cody tells me with a satisfied grin. "You'll figure it out," he adds with encouragement. I smile, not feeling quite so alone. "Brady is the only one of us who will have his college degree soon."

My eyes turn to Brady as he finishes the slice of pizza in his hand. He reaches for another slice without saying a word and I ask, "What are you going to school for?"

"Business Management," he mumbles.

I watch him curiously as he takes another bite of his pizza. I can't figure out if school is something he doesn't like to talk about or if it's something else. I decide if he doesn't want to answer me, he doesn't have to, but I want to know more about him. "You're almost done?" I question. "When are you graduating?"

"May," he replies simply.

"Then what?" I ask curiously.

He sighs in resignation and drops his pizza crust onto his plate. He reaches for a Coke and opens it as he stares at a spot on the floor in front of him. He takes a long drink before he finally turns to me with his answer. "My parents own a restaurant and bar on the edge of town and they want me to run the place when I graduate."

Cody and Cory laugh, "You make it sound like a tiny family owned restaurant. It's huge!" Cody exclaims. "There's even a gigantic catering hall for weddings and special events."

Brady winces and I ask, "Is that what you want to do?" His eyes soften as they land on me. I feel my heart pick up its pace again as I stare into his blue eyes feeling heated to my core, but he doesn't even bother opening his mouth to answer.

Cody tosses his plate onto the coffee table and suggests, "Why don't we all go out tonight? We could go down to Mae's for a drink."

I grimace and inform them, "I can't go to a bar."

Cory's eyes widen and she comments, "I didn't think to ask how old you were."

Cody laughs, "So what if she was 75?"

Cory glares at him, "She seemed like a very nice and young looking 75 year-old then. Thanks to social media," she adds sarcastically.

Brady asks quietly, "So how old are you?"

"Almost twenty," I tell them nervously.

"So I'm assuming you don't have a fake ID and we have to wait over a year for you to go out with us?" Cody questions, sounding frustrated.

I shrug and Cory rolls her eyes at her brother, "Like you're so much older. We've only been 21 for a few months and Brady just turned 22 last month."

"Happy Birthday," I whisper to Brady, appreciating his sexy grin in response.

"I want to stay here and get to know my roommate anyway, so I'm out too," Cory informs them.

"We can stay here and hang out with you guys," Brady suggests.

"No!" Cory declares. "You're leaving. I'm keeping Sam to myself the rest of the night. You guys go out and we'll see you tomorrow I'm sure."

"No thanks for the pizza?" Cody whines.

"Thank you Brady," Cory replies sweetly.

"Hey!" Cody argues.

Cory stands and begins to push her brother backwards towards the door. "Thank you Cody," she laughs.

"Much better Sis," he grins and pulls her into a bear hug, quickly messing up her hair until she twists away with both of them laughing.

"You too Brady, get out," she demands.

"You're kicking me out?" he asks sounding surprised, but stands anyway.

"Yup!" she smiles and points to the door. "Go, have fun guys but not too much fun." Both of the boys raise their eyebrows in question and Cory clarifies, "Don't you dare bring any girls home tonight. Sam shouldn't have to listen to that on her first night here," she teases them.

My eyes drop to my lap as my stomach flips anxiously with her words. I know I have no right to feel jealous of a guy I just met, but my brain hasn't caught up to reality yet or maybe I'm just tired. "I could just skip going out and bring Sam back to my room. Then it wouldn't matter," Cody jokes. My eyes widen and snap over to him. He winks at me just as Cory smacks him in the back of the head, making him flinch. She glares at him and he holds his hands up grinning, but not retracting his statement. Brady crosses his arms over his chest and stands rigid. Cody laughs and walks out the door. "I'll come find you later Sam," he calls over his shoulder.

Brady sits back down next to me and remains quiet until I turn my head towards him. "It really was memorable meeting you," he tells me holding my gaze. "I wasn't just saying that Sam. I'm really glad you decided to stay." I smile up at him suddenly feeling shy. "I'll see you tomorrow?"

I shrug, forcing myself to appear nonchalant. "If you're around. I'll probably just try to finish unpacking."

He smiles giving me chills, "Then I'll see you tomorrow Sam." He hesitates before he stands and walks towards the door. He gives me one last look before he says, "Bye."

He closes the door behind him and Cory bursts out laughing. I watch her curiously as she moves towards the chair she was just sitting in and drops back into it with a bottle of water in her hand. "You just got here and they're both already entertaining me."

"What?" I question as my heart flutters.

"My brother and Brady," she grins. I continue to look at her blankly and she explains, "They both obviously think you're hot, which you are by the way, even when you've been working hard all day. It's just not fair," she whines teasingly. "You have gorgeous hair!" she adds and my face heats with her comment. "Anyway, Brady is already acting a little territorial and I can't tell if Cody is messing with him or wants to date you too." She laughs and shrugs, "I guess we'll find out soon enough. They're my built-in entertainment."

I gulp down the lump in my throat, suddenly feeling nervous again. "Umm, what?" I stammer.

She looks at me and her eyes widen as she takes in my reaction, "I just mean they like to give each other a hard time. My brother was flirting with you big time and it's obvious Brady is interested. That may be new, but definitely apparent." I want to know what she means, but I don't ask. Instead I slowly take a deep breath, attempting to quell my anxiety. She adds, "Brady is a good guy. I've known him my whole life." When I remain quiet she asks, "Do you at least think he's cute?" I look at her with doubt, surprised by her question. "If you say no, I won't believe you because we both know he's a lot more than cute."

"If you think he's so hot, why aren't you two together?" I ask instead of answering her question.

She grimaces, "I could never date Brady. He's like a brother to me. Back in high school, he tried to kiss me once to get some girl off his back and it was just gross," she makes a face and sticks her tongue out to prove her point. "I think I just threw up in my mouth thinking about it," she adds. "The girl just thought I was a pissed off girlfriend though by my reaction, so it worked anyway."

I laugh, "Brady is right. You're like a little ball of sunshine."

She giggles. "So you can admit you think he's hot?"

I smile sheepishly, "Like you said, I'd be lying if I didn't."

She squeals excitedly, "I knew it." I shake my head laughing. She changes the subject as she picks up the paper plates and pizza boxes from the coffee table. "Do you want to hang out tomorrow? I can help you hang some pictures or something and maybe introduce you to the rest of our neighbors," she suggests. "Or maybe I can show you around town?"

"Sure, I would love that," I answer sincerely. "Thank you."

Chapter 3

Brady

Cody and I walk through the door at Mae's. My eyes take a quick sweep of the place with it's worn down pale tan wood floors and a wood paneled bar with a wood top covered in different bottle tops from beer companies all over the world and then sealed over to make a smooth surface. Although it's not crowded tonight, it can get that way with the wide age range that patronizes this place. Plus it's the only bar besides my parents place in a five mile radius, although it's only a little farther into Madison with plenty of places to go. Cody lifts his hand in a wave to a few of our friends in the back corner playing both pool and darts while I nod in acknowledgement. I head for an empty stool at the bar, not feeling very social at the moment. "Hey Logan," I greet the bartender as I sit. "Can I get 2 of whatever you have on tap tonight?"

"Sure thing Brady. Start a tab?" he questions. Logan gives a nod of acknowledgement to Cody as he slides onto the stool next to me.

I nod in agreement, "Yeah, thanks."

Logan slides the beers in front of Cody and me, "I assume the other one is for this asshole?" I chuckle in response. "Where's Cory?" he questions.

"Not here," Cody grimaces.

Logan and I laugh at his response and I reply honestly, "She kicked us out. She wants to hang out with her new roommate without us around," I grimace.

Logan laughs, "So I guess that means her new roommate is hot and she didn't want to watch you guys hitting on her. So if you don't bring her in so I can meet her, I'll have to walk across the hall and introduce myself."

I glare at Logan and he laughs harder as he takes in my reaction. "For real?" he asks in surprise.

Cody smirks and jerks his thumb towards me, "He seems to think he can tell me to back off already."

I reach for the pint of beer and take three large gulps before setting it back on the bar and focusing on Cody. "Is it really so hard to stay away from one girl? I don't think I've ever asked that of you before."

He stays quiet for a moment, thinking. "You haven't, but she's fucking hot and we don't have girls like her in this town," Cody grumbles. "Besides, you can't call dibs before I even had a chance to meet her," Cody complains. "How is that even fair? I don't have a chance that way!" I raise my eyebrows and grin mocking him. Cody glares, "Fuck you."

Logan and I both chuckle at Cody's expense. Logan strides to the other side of the bar to help another customer grinning. I turn back towards Cody and ask, "What about Olive then? Does that mean I can ask her out if you're interested in Sam?"

"Ask her out and you'll see what happens," Cody taunts narrowing his eyes on me, "I fucking dare you."

I chuckle and raise my hands up in defeat. "Then back off Sam," I challenge him. "There's just something about her and I need to figure out what it is." I pinch my lips shut, not wanting to give too much away because I know Cody would give me more shit than he already is and I don't want to deal with that Cody. He's right though; she's so beautiful she knocked the air right out of me when I first saw her. Then when she turned and looked at me on the street, her face and eyes expressed so much. I saw fear, confidence and determination. I want to find out why. I want to know more. Then when she started crying in the elevator, I had the strongest urge to tuck her petite, curvy body into my arms to comfort her, which is insane since I barely know her. Besides the fact I was ready to kick my own ass to protect her. It's almost like she's vulnerable and strong in the same breath. I don't know how else to explain it, but I need to know more about her. I'll even admit to myself that I want to know everything.

"Yeah, I already said it, she's hot," Cody smirks.

I elbow him in the gut and grin at his answering grunt. "Besides that Cody," I tell him in exasperation. "When I saw her in front of our building, yeah she's obviously gorgeous, but then I started talking to her..."

"Who were you talking to?" comes a high-pitched voice from over my right shoulder.

I try to hide my cringe by taking another gulp of my beer before I slowly turn around to face her. I stand and lean back against the bar as I take in her straight long blonde hair, short black skirt barely covering her ass and white button down tied at her waist and open to show a black lacy bra and enough cleavage that leaves little to anyone's imagination. "Hi Jackie. What are you doing here?" I question with disinterest.

"I guess they're letting all the underage trash in here nowadays," Cody grumbles as he turns around with his beer in hand and leans back against the bar.

Jackie turns her glare on Cody, "I have an ID."

"A fake one," he grumbles under his breath.

"Don't be an ass because I won't waste my time on you!"

He snorts in amusement, "Are you for real?"

She cringes at his reaction and I try to hide my laughter behind my beer as she turns to face me instead. "Why do you hang out with him?" she asks with her manicured hand resting impatiently on her all too thin waist.

I grind my jaw and chug the rest of my beer before setting it behind me on the bar. I cross my arms defensively over my chest and ignore her question. I don't want to deal with her right now, so I prompt her again, "What's up Jackie?"

She sighs in resignation and steps into me. I leave my arms crossed blocking her from getting too close. She grimaces before schooling her features as she bats her eyelashes up at me. "I was actually hoping you'd be here tonight Brady. I miss you," she adds quietly as she rests her hand on my forearm.

I close my eyes briefly to control my breathing and force myself to relax. Then I open them to focus back on her. "Jackie," I begin tentatively as Cody bursts out laughing at my side. She glares at him and I fight my smile attempting to ignore him, "If you need me, let me know, but like I've told you before, we just don't work as anything but friends."

"We could though Brady. You haven't tried since..." she trails off.

I grimace, "I haven't tried because there isn't anything between us anymore and there hasn't been for a long time. We're friends. I'll keep my promise to you, but I can't go back to how we were in high school. I'm not that guy anymore," I insist.

"And I'm not that girl anymore either. You would know if you did more than swoop in to save me. Friends do more than that," she reminds me.

I cringe, "You're right. I'm sorry, but I can't do more than that right now Jackie. It won't work."

She nods stiffly and leans in placing a kiss on my cheek. She pats my chest placating me and whispers "Okay Brady." She leans over me and I turn my head to the side to get out of her way. "Can I please get a couple shots of tequila over here?" she calls to Logan.

I grimace, "You think that's a good idea?"

She turns to me with a mischievous smile, "As you love to keep reminding me, you're not my keeper Brady." I flinch. I'm almost positive I know what she's trying to do. I shake my head disapprovingly as I watch her do two shots of tequila and then wrap her hand around a glass of whiskey sour. She pushes her chest out in front of me as she stands up straight and winks at me before she saunters off to a couple of her friends on the other side of the bar. She raises her arms in the air and begins dancing by herself for a few beats, but one of the guys near her grips her hips and begins dancing with her. She grins triumphantly and steals a glance over towards me. I shake my head in disgust. I'm not saving her when she's being a bitch.

"Why the fuck do you still put up with her shit? She hasn't been your girlfriend for over four years!" Cody questions.

I sigh and run my hand through my hair in frustration, "You know why Cody."

"That wasn't your fault! You can't blame yourself, especially when she's the one that keeps putting herself in these situations. She's a bitch Brady! Let her deal with her own shit," he demands. "As it is you know she's going to twist what you said in her mind," he tells me like I should know what he's talking about. I glance at him in confusion. He groans and looks at me like I've lost my mind, "Seriously?"

"What?" I ask irritated.

"You always try to be the good guy and let her down easy. That's why she never gives in. You said you can't do more than that *right now*. That's when she gave in for tonight and started her other bullshit trying to make you jealous or come to her rescue or some other crap. I swear you dig your own fucking grave with her. You're always there when she asks, how can she not believe you won't eventually come back to her. You've never done that for any other girl, only her," he reminds me causing me to flinch.

"I know, but you know why!" I defend myself, grinding my jaw in frustration.

He nods, "Yeah, but it doesn't matter in her mind. You have to stop being the one to save her!"

"I don't know if I can," I admit with a sigh. "If something happened again," I begin my stomach queasy with the reminder.

Cody turns towards me and remains quiet. I turn to look at him to read his face and he catches my eyes with a sudden look of determination. "What about Sam?" My chest tightens and a knot forms in my throat at just the mention of her name. "I know you've only known her for 24 hours, but I can honestly say that she's the first girl I've seen you show real interest in since Jackie and even that wasn't anything like this. That was just a small town and teenage hormones," he jokes. "Then there's all the girls you've dated briefly since then, but I already see it in your face that you think she's different. I know you," he declares. "Besides, she's my sister's roommate, so you know Cory would kick your ass if you hit on her if she was just another girl to you. We both know going into it, you'd hold back if you just wanted to fuck her."

I open my mouth to ask why he's going after her then, but he stops me. "I know what you're going to say. I was just giving you shit. Yeah, I'd probably ask her out if I didn't see how you looked at her, but you're already looking at her like you're ready to jump in deep," he explains. "Which is certifiably insane, but if you spend some time with her and you really do like her Brady, you can't do this shit with Jackie. I realize it's not about that, but no girl will understand why you're leaving her to go save your ex from herself and she shouldn't have to. It's not normal."

My whole body sags in defeat knowing he's right. "Shit," I mumble. I have no idea how I'm going to deal with Jackie, but I better figure it out quick.

"She can find someone else to jump whenever she calls," he grumbles. "Okay, enough of this girly shit, I need another beer," he states and raises his hand up for the bartender.

"How long do we have to stay gone?" I grumble annoyed.

Cody chuckles, "You can give my sister and Sam tonight while you hang out with your kick-ass best friend."

I groan and Cody laughs, holding up his empty glass towards Logan to ask for a refill. "Then how about I kick your ass in darts while we waste our time?" I ask reluctantly, giving in.

Cody laughs, "You're funny. You can't kick my ass in anything."

I laugh and slap him on the back, "Keep dreaming." We grab our beers from Logan and I stop Cody before we walk towards the back where a few of our friends are still playing pool. He looks at me expectantly and I tell him quietly, "Thanks. I don't know what the hell I'm going to do, but thanks."

He nods in acceptance and turns towards the back, "Alright ladies, who wants to watch the master at darts?" I chuckle and shake my head as I follow him to the back.

Chapter 4

Samantha

"Okay, we'll see you later then," Cory says just before she hangs up her cell phone. She glances over at me sitting in her yellow Volkswagen Bug and smiles. "That was my brother. He and Brady are going to come meet up with us in a little while at the Pit Stop."

My eyes go wide and I begin fidgeting, my nerves going a little haywire at the thought of seeing Brady again. Cory giggles as I take a deep breath and mentally prepare myself to focus back on where we're parked in downtown Chance. "What?" I ask her.

She shakes her head and shrugs her shoulders grinning, "Nothing." I purse my lips, but before I have a chance to reply, Cory says excitedly, "Come on! All we have left is Main Street." I nod and feel my heart begin to beat erratically, knowing my biological father's store is somewhere on this street. Cory already drove me by the schools, parks and a couple restaurants. Now we're in the center of town in front of a white building with Town Hall and Community Center written above the doors on a small sign.

I step out of the car and cautiously look up and down the street as Cory energetically bounds to my side. "I know it's not very big, but I like it," she tells me apologetically.

I attempt to smile back reassuringly, but I'm afraid it looks more like a grimace with my anxiety. "It's great Cory. Thank you for showing me around," I emphasize appreciatively.

We begin walking down the sidewalk with a few people scattered around going in and out of stores, before quickly rushing back to the warmth of their cars. She points out the post office, the only bank, a small grocery store, a flower shop, a bakery, a pharmacy, a coffee and ice cream shop, a pizza parlor, the beauty parlor where she works, a bookstore and a family restaurant similar to an east coast diner. Then we step in front of "Hometown" and I freeze mid-step. I stare at the glass door, my breathing ragged, while I'm blind to everything inside. Instead, I picture a faceless man with his happy family until they catch sight of me. The smiles turn to glares of hatred and demand for me to get out. I gasp for air, releasing the breath I didn't know I was holding.

"Are you okay Sam?" Cory asks standing in front of me, her brow furrowed with concern.

I realize she may have been trying to get my attention more than once and force myself to pull out of my nightmare. I shake my head and attempt to control my breathing. I hoarsely whisper, "I'm sorry. I'm okay. Sometimes something just reminds me of my parents," I explain with a half-truth. Last night when we were talking, I told her about my mom and dad's accident, but I didn't tell her I was here looking for my birth father. She nods sadly and pats my arm gently in comfort, causing me to notice my hand clutched tightly in my coat. I force myself to release it and drop my hand before forcing a smile towards her. "I'm fine, I promise." I'm just not ready, I add to myself quietly.

She nods reluctantly, "Okay." She points to the store behind her that still holds my unwanted attention. "This place is great. It has a little bit of everything. Do you want to go in and check it out?" she asks innocently.

"Um, maybe next time. My toes are getting cold, but I think I just want to sit down," I voice my lame excuse.

She shrugs like it doesn't matter and to her I'm sure it doesn't, but I don't have the nerve to walk through that door right now. He may not be there, but if he were, how would I know if it was him? What would I say? 'Hi, I'm your daughter. Nice to meet you.' I grimace and shake my head at the ridiculousness of it all.

"Okay," she relents. "Cody and Brady will be here soon. We can head over to the Pit Stop and wait for them," she suggests.

I swallow down the lump in my throat and sigh with relief. I nod in agreement, "That sounds perfect."

"Besides the only thing left really is the gas station, which is also a garage and then some office and medical buildings," she informs me. "Anytime we need anything else, we just drive into Madison since it's so close."

I notice the sign on the front of the building as we walk quietly into the restaurant. I reread it thinking I looked wrong, but it just says, "The Family Restaurant". I turn towards Cory and ask, "You said the Pit Stop?"

She laughs, "Yeah, sorry. Everyone around here calls this place the Pit Stop. No idea how it got started, but it's much better than the boring name it's saddled with don't you think?"

I shrug and focus my attention on my surroundings. I take in the black and white tile floors as we walk to a booth. Cory sits down and I slide into the black leather booth with a white and gray speckled Formica tabletop across from her. There's a long countertop that curves around near the kitchen with a small opening where it appears the wait staff places the orders and the cooks put the orders for pick-up. At the far end of the restaurant sits an old-fashioned jukebox and I can't help but smile. My mom used to get so excited anytime we would see one of those things. She would try to get my dad to dance with her and if not him, I would dance with her. I smile at the memory and glance around at the black and white pictures on the walls. "All the pictures are from somewhere in town. Most of them are from when the town was just being built," Cory informs me.

"That's really cool," I tell her sincerely.

I startle suddenly when a happy screech spins me around in my seat, "Cory!" A waitress with a short black skirt, white button-up shirt and a black apron jumps in front of our table as I continue to take it all in. "What are you up to?"

"Hi Olive. We're meeting Brady and my brother for something to eat," she explains with a smile. "How are you?" she asks genuinely interested.

"Cody is coming here tonight?" she asks blushing. She swiftly straightens her blonde ponytail tied with a red ribbon.

Cory laughs heartily and nods her head, "Yup." Then she turns to me and proudly announces, "This is my new roommate, Samantha."

I smile shyly, "Hi Olive. It's nice to meet you."

She grins, "It's great to meet you too! You seem to be exactly what Cory said you were." My eyes scrunch together in confusion and she shrugs, "You never know what kind of crazy roommate you might find on-line."

I laugh, remembering telling Brady the same thing. "I know exactly what you mean," I say honestly. "Then again, we've only been roommates for three days. How do you know I'm not crazy?" I joke and everyone laughs obligingly.

"So can I get you guys something to drink while you wait so I look like I'm doing something?" she asks with laughter in her voice.

"Sure," Cory tells her. "I'll just have a Diet Coke and you might as well grab Cokes for Cody and Brady too."

She glances at me and I add, "I'll just have a Coke too. Thank you."

Cory calls, "Thanks," as Olive spins away.

"Do you know everyone?" I ask incredulously. Cory glances at me with confusion. I lean towards her, placing my elbows on the table and clarify, "I just mean that I've seen you wave or say Hi to every single person that's been in our eyesight today. You seem to know everyone around here."

She giggles and nods her head in understanding. "Yeah, I guess you could say that. Everyone knows everyone around here. It's kind of a small town thing," she shrugs. "There were less than four hundred people in our high school, so less than one hundred per class. In fact our graduating class had 93 kids and we were considered a big class. Even if you don't know someone, they probably know you or your parents." She smirks, "So I guess I do know nearly everyone, but not everyone can say the same because most of them don't know my awesome roommate yet." I roll my eyes and she laughs as she waves at someone behind me.

I jump slightly as Brady slides into the booth next to me, knocking his legs into mine. Cody sits down next to his sister and grins at me before glancing at Brady. "You stole my seat," Cody accuses with a smirk. My heart speeds up and I feel my face warm with Brady so close. I smile at Cody and turn to acknowledge Brady.

Brady ignores his friend and turns towards me with a wide smile, exposing his dimple. He pulls his gray beanie off of his head and runs his hand through his hair. His dark brown hair goes in every direction, but it only adds to his sexiness. "How was your ten minute tour of

Chance?" he asks. I nod my head and stare into his seemingly endless blue eyes feeling mesmerized by him. He chuckles and prompts, "Sam?"

I mentally shake myself out of my stupor to answer, knowing my face is beat red. "Um, it was fine, good, great," I stammer. "Cory is a great tour guide."

"I can do better than my sister," Cody teases, pulling my attention to him. "How about I show you a few places outside of town next weekend," he suggests flirtatiously.

"Or I could take you tomorrow since I'm on break this week," Brady interrupts just as Olive sets our drinks down in front of us. "Thank you Olive!" Brady overemphasizes grinning appreciatively up at her. "You know exactly what we like."

Cody drops his teasing tone and turns shyly towards Olive, shocking me by his somewhat timid demeanor. "Hi, Olive. Thank you."

"You're welcome," she grins coyly.

"Are you working tomorrow?" he asks.

"Yeah, I have breakfast and lunch tomorrow," she informs him appearing sad by the admission.

"Maybe we could get together after work?" he asks.

Her eyes light up as she admits, "I'd like that. I'm done at 3 tomorrow, I'll text you when I get home."

He nods in agreement, grinning widely up at her. Olive turns to walk away before she spins back around blushing deeply. "So are you guys ready to order?"

I glance over at Cory who's hiding behind her hands, obviously trying to conceal her laugh. "I'll just have a turkey club with fries," I answer her, attempting to put her at ease.

Behind her hands, Cory adds, "I'll have the same."

Brady orders quickly, "A burger, medium rare please."

"I'll have a burger, medium. Thanks Olive," Cody smiles and watches her walk away. The laughter finally gets him to turn towards us. "What?" he demands.

Cory just laughs harder before answering, "I need Olive around more often when I need you to be serious. She works wonders in seconds!"

He glares at his sister as Brady agrees, "And you finally asked her out! Was it because you were afraid she heard you baiting me or because you finally got the balls to do it?"

Cody relaxes at Brady's words and leans back in the booth, throwing his arm over the back with a playful smirk. "Now why would you think I was baiting you Brady? What could I possibly be baiting you for?" he asks sarcastically. "I thought I was just helping to welcome the new girl, our new neighbor, my sister's new roommate."

Brady stiffens momentarily and my whole body instantly heats with embarrassment. Does that mean he might want to get to know me too? I force myself to mentally dismiss my own question. It's not a good idea right now. But out of the corner of my eye, I notice Brady relax before he answers with confidence. "Well, maybe I'm already watching out for the new girl and know better than to let her near the likes of you," he teases. I can't stop the feelings of both excitement that he's watching out for me and disappointment that may be all it is.

"The new girl has a name guys!" Cory interrupts their stare down making me laugh. "It's Samantha and she's sitting right here."

"I'm sorry Sam," Brady and Cody apologize in unison both with huge grins. Obviously neither are very sorry at all.

I blush under Brady's gaze, but I don't let myself look away. A high-pitched perky voice interrupts his hold on me, "Brady!" A tall thin girl with straight, but thick dark blonde hair and golden eyes bounces up to our table and throws her arms around Brady's neck, nearly falling into his lap. I glance at Cory anxiously and notice her openly glaring at the girl. I move my gaze over to Cody whose eyes only show amusement. I'm not sure what to think.

"Hi Jackie," Brady mumbles as he subtly pushes out of her embrace. "What's going on?" he asks cautiously.

She stands to her full height in a short pale pink skirt and a tight chocolate brown knit sweater and pushes out her chest, currently at Brady's eye level. "You disappeared last night. I've been looking all over for you," she states, pushing out her lower lip just the right amount. I don't miss the roll of Cory's eyes and try to hold back my own laugh. At the same time I don't like the feeling of jealousy overwhelming me because of this beautiful girl. I just met Brady. He's definitely not mine to be jealous over. I grimace at my internal battle and try to focus on their conversation instead.

"You could've texted me if you needed something," he reminds her. Cory laughs outright at his comment, bringing Jackie's unwanted attention to her.

"Hi Cory. I saw your ex a couple nights ago at Glen's party," she tells her suggestively. "He seemed to be having a very good time without you."

Cory grimaces, but doesn't say a word in response. Cody jumps in to defend her instead, gritting the words out between his teeth, "Watch it Jackie!"

"What do you want?" Brady questions irritably, trying to stop the rising tension.

Her eyes snap back to Brady, instantly softening when they land on him. "I need your help with something," she informs him. He hesitates and her eyes drift over to me. She swiftly looks me up and down before pursing her lips with distaste. "Please Brady, it's really important. After our talk last night, I wouldn't ask you otherwise," she pleads with her eyes back on him. "I really need you."

He sighs in resignation before turning to me, "I'm sorry Sam. I'll be right back," he informs me apologetically.

"You've gotta' be fucking kidding me," Cody complains sounding pissed off. Brady turns his eyes towards him, his jaw tense and holds his stare. Cody sighs in resignation and holds his hands up in the air telling Brady he's backing off, although he's obviously not happy with him. "Do what *you think* you've gotta' do Brady," he tells him before shaking his head disapprovingly.

Brady anxiously glances at me one more time. Then he sighs as he pushes up out of the booth. Jackie sneaks a peek at me, giving me a victorious smile as I watch him walk across the restaurant with her. I hate the knots forming in my stomach and tell myself to get over it.

Cody slams a fist on the table, snapping my attention back to him. "Relax Cody," Cory sooths her brother.

"I fucking hate that bitch," he declares viciously.

"Who is she?" I ask hesitantly.

Cody looks at me with pity in his eyes, only succeeding in making me feel worse. My heart drops into my stomach, increasing my nausea. I look down at the table and continue to wait for an answer. "She's Brady's ex-girlfriend. They dated way back in high school. For reasons I can't really explain, he believes it's his responsibility to look out for her or help her when she needs it, no matter what it is. She loves to take full advantage of him," he murmurs snidely.

"She is beautiful," I mumble as my chest tightens.

Cory laughs humorlessly, "Yeah, but that's not why."

My eyebrows scrunch together in confusion by the tone of her voice. I know there's something she's not telling me. "What do you mean?" I ask.

She sighs appearing to struggle with what to tell me. She hesitantly begins, "Let's just say he feels guilty for not being there for her when something bad happened. He also blames himself for some things that happened to her after they broke up. He should really tell you the rest of the story."

"She's always been a bitch though," Cody states.

Olive steps up to our table balancing a tray full of food on her right hand. She sets our plates in front of us before Cody whispers thoughtfully, "Thank you Olive."

She smiles sweetly, "Can I do anything else for you?"

He gestures to Brady's plate and asks, "Can you let the jackass know I'm going to take what's his if he doesn't claim it soon?"

She laughs before glancing over her shoulder to where he's sitting with Jackie. She grimaces and nods in agreement before turning away.

We all sit quietly and begin eating, although I mostly pick at my food. Brady slides in next to me and brushes his finger softly on my bicep to get my attention. I reluctantly turn my head towards his and meet his apologetic eyes. "I'm sorry," he begins.

I shake my head, not wanting to hear it. "It doesn't matter Brady. It's not like we're on a date. I just met you. You don't need to apologize to me."

"But I want to Sam because honestly I would like to go out with you. I want to get to know you," he tells me sincerely, causing my heart to skip a beat.

I have the urge to tell him I'd like to go out with him too, but he's obviously too wrapped up in something with his ex. I don't think I can deal with something like that when I'm already trying to figure out how to get the courage to introduce myself to my father and his family if it ever goes that far. I don't need to put myself in a situation where there's another Paul and Taylor. I need to be smart and stop this before it starts. I sigh, feeling defeated and meet his hopeful stare. I try to push away the flutter I feel when I look at him. "I don't know if that's a good idea," I tell him truthfully. "You seem to have enough on your plate with your ex and I have some things I have to do too."

"There's nothing going on with Jackie and me," he declares. "I don't have a girlfriend. I'm single Sam."

I nod my head in understanding as I fight the tingling in my throat. I have a feeling Jackie is the last person around here I want to piss off. "I don't think that's really any of my business," I tell him instead.

He sighs in frustration and runs his fingers through his hair before pulling his beanie on top of his head. I notice a look pass between him and Cody as I try to focus on the food in front of me. We all finish the rest of our meal in silence. Brady continues to steal glances in my direction as I attempt to ignore him.

Olive arrives with the bill and I pull out my wallet to chip in. "How much do I owe?" I ask as Brady picks it up.

He shakes his head, "I've got it. I ruined dinner. I'll pay," he declares.

"It's the least you can do," Cody grumbles.

I open my mouth to argue and Cory shakes her head and mouths, "Let him." I reluctantly let my hand drop as he tosses money on the table to pay for all of us.

"Are you guys headed back to the apartment?" Brady asks.

I nod my head as Cory answers for both of us, "Yeah."

"Okay, I guess we'll see you guys later." Brady looks at me as if he wants to say something else before he stuffs his hands into his pockets and drops his head down in resignation as he walks to the door.

"I told you asshole. What the fuck did she want this time?" I hear Cody ask Brady as we turn in opposite directions towards our cars.

I sigh, hating that I feel so let down. I need to focus on the reason I came here in the first place anyway. I don't need a distraction like Brady Williams. I climb into the passenger seat of Cory's car and buckle my seat belt. "Brady really is a good guy. I think in a way how nice he is to Jackie sort of proves that," she tells me. "Don't jump to conclusions about him. They really aren't together. It's just I don't like to gossip and I think he should be the one to tell you about what happened." She hesitates before adding, "Please just think about giving him a chance. I can tell he really likes you."

I sigh and look out the window, holding my comments to myself. She makes a U-turn and I question what I'm doing as we pass Hometown. Brady may have gotten my attention when I least expected it, but if tonight is any indication of the drama following him when we weren't even on a date, I need to keep my focus on my real reason for being here and away from him.

Chapter 5

I stumble out to the kitchen for a cup of coffee and notice a small yellow sheet of paper with a childlike sketch of a smiling sun next to a full pot of coffee. I pick up the paper with a grin, "Hi Roomie! I had so much fun with you yesterday. I'm really glad you're here! I work until 8pm tonight. If you need anything text or stop in at the shop. Have a great day and enjoy the quiet! – Cory." Brady is right. She really is so sweet. I grimace, realizing Cory's thoughtful note only brought my attention back to Brady.

I mentally shake him out of my head and pour myself a cup of coffee. I wrap my hands around the cup to feel the heat and wander back into my new bedroom. I close my eyes and put my nose in the cup, then take a deep breath to smell the strong aroma, urging myself awake. I slowly sit on my bed and open my eyes to take in my surroundings. I grimace at the last box I still need to unpack. With how long it's taking me to unpack, you'd think I moved my whole house. I sigh relenting, "I guess now is better than never."

I set my coffee cup on my nightstand and pull my hair up into a ponytail, not bothering to change out of my gray and violet checked pajama pants and matching violet tank top. I stand and anxiously walk over to the last box. I flip the top open with determination. My eyes land on a picture of me with my mom and dad the day of my high school graduation. We all look so happy. I knew what was in the box, but I struggle to get the lump out of my throat at the sight anyway. I don't know if I can remember the last time I really felt happy like that. I close my eyes and let a few tears slip onto my cheeks as I hug the frame to my chest. "I'm scared," I whisper into the empty room. "I just wish you were here with me," I admit, feeling overwhelmed with emotion. I hold onto the picture tightly, wishing it were my parents holding me as I stumble back to my bed. I gently place the picture on my nightstand and whisper, "I love you." I curl up on my side, pulling my knees close to my chest and imagine I hear the same words back from them.

A loud knock at the door pulls me out of my reverie. I wipe my face and reach for a Kleenex to dry my tears and blow my nose. I toss the Kleenex in the garbage when another knock sounds at the door. I groan and turn towards the front of the apartment, wondering whom it could be. The knocking becomes insistent as soon as I step out of my bedroom. "I'm coming!" I yell hoarsely. I throw open the door feeling irritated and unsettled. I scream, "What?" before I come face to face with a wide-eyed Brady.

His eyes quickly drift down my body. He takes a step back before he stammers, "Um, hi. I'm sorry. Did I wake you?" he asks but doesn't wait for my answer. "I just thought I'd bring you some donuts from the bakery. I wanted to say I'm sorry for being such an ass last night," he blurts holding out a bakery bag for me to see.

I shake my head, "No, I was up. I was just trying to finish unpacking. Besides, you weren't an ass last night," I pause. "You didn't have to do that," I tell him gesturing to the bag in his hand.

He grins broadly, showing his dimple and giving me chills. "You won't say that after you try one of these. They're addictive. Plus I really am sorry."

I offer him a shaky smile and look up at him with determination, "There's nothing to apologize for."

He frowns and his eyebrows scrunch together, although I'm not sure if it's in concern or frustration. He cautiously takes a step into me, assessing me closely. "Are you okay Sam?" he asks softly.

My breath hitches as his chest brushes against mine, instantly making me aware that I'm still in my pajamas and I'm not wearing a bra. I can only imagine what my body is telling him when his stupid dimple alone gives me goose bumps. I blush and take a step away from him, crossing my arms awkwardly over my chest. "Um, yeah, I'm uh fine," I stammer. "Let me go throw some clothes on," I tell him. I turn and practically run towards my room without waiting for a response from him.

I quickly peel my pajamas off and toss them in the wicker hamper in my closet. I slip a black lacy bra with matching bikini underwear on to help me feel a little sexy, at the same time trying not to question why I feel the need to put them on in the first place. Then I pull a fitted purple half zip sweatshirt over my head and some black yoga pants. I pull the rubber band out of my hair as I walk back into the living room before rewrapping it around my ponytail. I stop when I hear a clang of dishes in the kitchen and turn towards the sound instead. I step into the kitchen just as Brady finishes pouring himself a cup of coffee. "Go ahead, help yourself," I smirk at him.

He turns around and leans back against the counter, slowly lifting his eyes until they meet mine. "I will, thank you," he grins.

I can't help the giggle that escapes before I cover my mouth. I'm grateful he doesn't say anything since my emotions seem to be all over the place. I notice the large platter of donuts sitting on the table in the corner booth and I laugh outright, "Hungry?"

He smiles sheepishly and admits, "I didn't know what you would like."

I reach for a plate and grab a jelly donut before I whisper, "Thank you." He gives me a small nod before he slides into the booth. He sets a plate down next to him and places two donuts on the on it before glancing up at me. I smirk, "You're welcome to stay." He chuckles in response, his blue eyes sparkling before he takes a bite of a glazed donut. I laugh and slide in on the opposite side of the curved booth, our knees bumping under the table. I keep my eyes focused on the donut in my hand, trying to hide my reaction to him. I take a bite of the donut, enjoying the taste as the raspberry jelly oozes into my mouth along with the sugarcoated dough. I close my eyes and moan in satisfaction, "Oh my gosh this is so good. I haven't had one of these in forever."

I swallow the goodness and slowly open my eyes to find Brady's blue eyes staring intently at me. I watch as his Adam's apple bobs up and down seeming dazed. He suddenly clears his throat and lightly shakes his head. "Um, I asked if you were okay before," he begins, "you look like you're upset."

I feel my body heat with embarrassment and I set the donut down on the plate with a sigh. "I'm fine. I was just thinking about my mom and dad," I admit honestly, surprising myself.

"Do you miss them?" he asks innocently.

I flinch and close my eyes, fighting to keep the tears at bay. Brady grumbles, "Damn it." He scoots closer and wraps me in his strong arms. Any thoughts of pulling away from him went out the window the second the warmth of his body encased mine. He gently pulls me into his chest and I let my head rest over his rapidly beating heart. I relax into the comfort of his embrace as a few tears slide down my cheeks. "I'm sorry," he whispers. I shake my head, not wanting to hear another apology. "I've only known you for a few days and I keep making you cry. I'm such an asshole," he grumbles into my hair.

I laugh through my tears as I enjoy the soothing circles he draws with his hands on my back. I sigh, "It's not your fault."

"Can I ask you something?" he whispers hesitantly.

"Mm-hmm," I nod my head, not lifting it from his chest.

"Why are you so far from your family when you obviously miss them so much?" he inquires softly, making me take notice of my heartache.

I take a deep steadying breath and answer him truthfully, feeling a need to share my mom and dad with him. "My parents aren't there anymore and I'm an only child," I whimper. I take another deep breath and rush out the words that still cause my whole body to ache with pain. "Just over a year and a half ago, my parents died in a small plane crash when they were supposed to be on vacation."

I feel his quick intake of breath and the sudden tension in his body as his heartbeat quickens. Then he slowly releases his breath and pulls me into him a little tighter, giving me a comfort I haven't felt since my mom and dad's accident. I don't want to let it go. I'm not sure how long I'm sitting in his arms when he finally whispers with his voice full of emotion, "I know these words don't really mean anything, but I'm so sorry Samantha."

I nod my head, feeling his genuine empathy for me deep in my soul. My emotions begin to overwhelm me as my anxiety begins churning in my gut. I gently push away from his chest, feeling the need to do something, but I don't get up. I wipe my eyes and change the subject murmuring, "I should finish unpacking."

"What can I do to help?" he asks.

I shake my head, "Nothing really, I'm just kind of trying to put things where they belong in my room. Cory helped me with everything else over the weekend, but I didn't do much of anything yesterday. I don't really have a lot here. I didn't bring all my stuff. I wasn't sure..." I trail off with a shrug.

"Well, I'm here to help you this week, so you might want to find something for me to do or I might just drive you crazy," he jokes.

I laugh feeling a little lighter, "You don't have to do that, Brady." I smile up at him in appreciation for trying to lighten the mood.

He nods, "You're right, I don't have to do anything. I want to help you." He pauses and smirks, "Besides, the faster you finish unpacking, the more time you'll have to hang out with me this week," he teases.

"Who said I was going to hang out with you when I'm done?" I smirk.

"I did," he answers grinning.

I can't help the smile that covers my face with his response. I don't understand how he can make me feel better so quickly or even why I'm letting him, but I do. "How about this," I propose, "How about I finish with my room, since you wouldn't know where to put anything anyway?"

"Well that doesn't sound like much of a compromise," he grumbles.

I laugh at the boyish pout on his slightly scruffy and manly face. I can't help but wonder how much he got away with as a child with that same adorable look. I grin up at him and continue, "Then when I'm done later, we can hang out for a little while?"

He tilts his head to the side and purses his lips like he's pondering my suggestion. "You can finish today?" he questions with his eyebrows raised. I nod my head and his lips twitch in amusement. He chuckles and releases his smile, "Okay, it's a date."

"I didn't say it was a date," I remind him.

"You don't have to when you were just begging to hang out with me," he grins playfully and I burst out laughing. "See, you can't even deny it," he teases.

I let my laughter subside and I release a content breath, feeling peaceful for now. I honestly don't remember the last time I felt this way. It's almost like he knew exactly what I needed, but I have no idea how when I don't even know most of the time. I lift my eyes to his and my heart clenches gratefully for him in this moment. "Thank you," I tell him sincerely.

He reaches towards me, his eyes never leaving mine. His fingers touch my bicep and slide gently down my arm until he finds my hand and entwines our fingers together. He gives my hand a gentle, reassuring squeeze and whispers, "Anything you need Sam, I'm happy to help."

My body heats and my stomach ties itself into knots as I stare at him at a loss for words. I've known him for three days and yet it seems he already has the power to make me laugh as well as bring me comfort and peace. Then all I have to do is look at him and I admit to myself how incredibly gorgeous he is. I'd be lying if I didn't. He feels perfect, almost too perfect. He slowly leans towards me and glances down at my lips to make his intentions known. My heart hammers inside my chest and my breathing picks up in anticipation. I want to feel his lips on mine. I taste his warm minty breath mingle with mine when suddenly his ex Jackie pops into my mind out of nowhere. I quickly turn my head to avert his kiss at the sudden reminder.

I feel his hard exhale on my cheek, "I'm sorry."

Instead of responding, I slip my hand out of his, instantly feeling cold. I slide out of the booth and stand nervously. I look away from him and gesture in the direction of my room, "I um, I'm going to get to work. Thank you for the donuts and..."

He stands directly in front of me without saying a word. My hands begin shaking from nerves and I slowly look up to meet his eyes. He searches my face like he's trying to solve a puzzle. He finally opens his mouth and rasps, "Anything Sam." He stares at me, willing me to believe the truth in his simple statement. "Text me when you're done."

"I don't know if..." I begin.

He cuts me off and informs me with a smirk, "If I don't hear from you by 6, I'll be over anyway." His hand twitches at his side like he's struggling to hold it back just before he turns to walk away. "I'm looking forward to tonight," he calls cheerfully just before I hear the front door of my apartment slam shut.

I smile to myself and shake my head at his confidence. I don't know if he's really the best thing for me right now, but I can't help but love the way I already feel around him. Maybe this thing with his ex will be nothing, but it could also be everything. I don't know what to do, but I guess I don't need to decide right this minute. I sigh and walk back to my room feeling on edge. I mumble sarcastically, "At least getting organized will be a distraction from my distraction."

Chapter 6

Brady

I walk back into my apartment and drop down on the couch. I run my hands through my hair before dropping my head back and staring at the ceiling. I can't believe she's alone. I guess she didn't really say she was alone, but she's an only child and her parents are gone. Then she moves here by herself. It seems to me to be the same thing. I've never had such an overwhelming urge to protect someone. Then she tells me about her parents and my feelings more than doubled instantaneously, completely overwhelming me. I could barely catch my breath. I pulled myself together as quickly as possible, but I'm sure she felt it. I just can't decide if that's a good thing or a bad one. It was obvious she wanted to push away from me, especially after all the bullshit with Jackie, but I couldn't let her do that. I don't understand why, but I just can't. It's almost like I need her or need to be there for her, but that's fucking ridiculous because we've barely just met.

I take a deep breath and try to get my head straight. Sam is unbelievably gorgeous and it's obvious I want her. I feel the chemistry boiling between us when we're in the same room, but I don't think that's all it is. It's like I feel something pulling me towards her, but do I just feel bad for her? Then again, I didn't know about her parents until a few minutes ago.

I have a lot of friends whose parents are divorced or not together. I have some friends who don't have anything to do with their parents, but it's their choice in some way. I even have friends who have lost a parent, but not both parents. Besides, I always have my sister too. Sam is an only child. I can't even imagine what it would be like to lose my family in an accident like that.

I may not have the best relationship with my parents lately, but it's not the worst either. I feel smothered more than anything with them on my back about everything. I'll even admit I hate my parents sometimes, especially lately. I fight with them a lot about what my life will be after I graduate this spring. I can't stand that they're trying to push my life in a certain direction when I don't even know what I want. Unfortunately, I'm an asshole and I make sure to let them know it. I cringe just thinking about some of my recent conversations with them. But to not have them in my life at all? I exhale harshly and run my hands through my hair, gripping the ends tightly in frustration before letting them go. I suddenly feel selfish for taking them for granted.

Sam seems so incredibly strong and vulnerable at the same time. Her life was completely turned upside down and she's here now, trying to move on. I can see how hard it is on her and I want to help her. I want to make her laugh. I want to make her smile. I shake my head gently. It's not just that. I sigh and admit to myself that I want to be there for her, I want to protect her. Which means I should probably hold back on trying to fuck her, I grimace. I don't want her to be just another girl. I want her to be more and I can even admit I want to be more to her. Hopefully she wants the same thing. If not, I'll just have to work to prove that I'm what she wants. I chuckle lightly at myself. How the hell does a girl I just met fuck with my head so thoroughly?

A pillow smashes into the back of my head, startling me. I grip it and twist around hurtling it back at Cody before he realizes it's coming. I smirk as it hits him in the face. "What the hell Brady?" he asks holding his arms out like he's innocent. I just roll my eyes in response and he chuckles. "What are you doing today?" he asks as he walks towards the kitchen.

I stand and follow him. I lean against the doorframe and watch him fill his coffee cup. "I have no fucking idea. I have to waste a bunch of time until later I guess," I shrug, glancing at the time on my phone.

"Want to help me test out a new app?" he asks. He turns around sluggishly and leans against the counter as he takes a sip of his coffee. His eyes draw down in confusion, "Do you have something going on later that you didn't tell me about?"

I chuckle and cross my arms over my chest. "You're a bit slow this morning I see," I smirk.

"Fuck you," he responds reflexively, keeping his curious eyes locked on me. "What 21 year old on spring break do you know that's this wide awake at 11 in the morning?"

"You're not on spring break," I remind him.

He shrugs, "And?" I laugh. "Why didn't you go anywhere fun this year and take me with you anyway? We had such a blast last year...I think," he grins.

I shake my head, "I just couldn't do it this year and I'm really glad I didn't."

He smirks, "So you can hang out with me right?"

I ignore his comment and tell him, "I had to go to the bakery this morning."

He pauses and quickly scans the kitchen. "Did you go yet?" I nod my head slowly as he continues to look around the room. "Where is everything? You know you can't go to the bakery without getting something for me unless you want me to kick you out on your ass," he states accusingly. "Or just kick your ass," he mumbles.

I raise my eyebrows, daring him. He sets his coffee down and crosses his arms across his chest before stepping closer to me. I laugh, enjoying torturing him by making him wait. I finally admit, "I brought everything over to Sam to apologize for the mess I made of last night."

He smiles broadly, "I get to start my day by having breakfast with Sam?" My eyes narrow and I feel my body get tight. He laughs in amusement at my reaction. "You did kind of fuck up. You have to stay away from Jackie," he advises again.

I nod, "I know, but it's easier said than done."

He shakes his head, "No it's actually very simple. Just tell her to fuck off."

I grimace and ignore his unsolicited advice. I don't want to talk about Jackie and ruin the morning. I take a deep breath and release it slowly. I reluctantly admit, "I have a date with Sam later."

He grins mischievously, "A date? Does she know about this date? She told me she would hang out with me tonight."

I shake my head, "Sure she did." He laughs in response. I fight my smile as I admit, "Yeah. I kind of made it impossible for her to say no."

He laughs nearly spilling his coffee, "I just bet you did."

I shake my head at wherever his dirty mind is going. "I just have to figure out a way that she doesn't back out," I admit. Cody laughs. "Well, I need her to forget about last night and focus on tonight," I grin. "I just need to figure out how to help her do that," I smirk, making Cody laugh harder.

When he stops laughing he asks, "Is she around now? I can help you come up with something, but I need something in my stomach to do that."

I laugh, "Yeah she's home. She wants to finish getting unpacked and organized today. I offered to help her with whatever she needed, but..." I trail off suppressing a sigh. "I got a lot of donuts," I shrug. "I didn't know what she would like," I confess sheepishly. "There's even more than enough for you," I inform him.

He flips me his middle finger as he strides for the front door. I sigh and close my eyes, leaning back against the doorframe picturing Samantha in her door this morning. I wasn't expecting to walk in on her looking so incredible in that damn tank top. I couldn't tear my eyes away from her. I would love to wake her up like that every morning, minus the pain I saw in her shimmering caramel brown eyes. I had to fist my hands at my sides so I wouldn't reach out and pull her into my arms to comfort her or just touch her. I've never had such a strong reaction to someone like that before.

The front door flies open and Cody walks in with a donut in his mouth and two more in his hand. He kicks the door shut with his foot and strides towards me. He steps past me into the kitchen and grabs a plate, immediately dropping the two donuts in his hand. He pulls the one in his mouth out and informs me, "You no longer have a date tonight."

"Sure," I mumble.

He takes another large bite, "Seriously. She agreed to go out to dinner with me."

I pause, knowing I shouldn't believe him. "I guess I'll just have to beat you to it then."

"Or I could just join you," he smirks.

"Only if you want to worry that I'll sneak into your room at night and take embarrassing pictures of you," I joke. "I could put together a hilarious story for Snapchat!"

He grins, "There's nothing embarrassing about me."

I chuckle and shake my head. "Seriously Cody, she's different. I don't have any idea how I know, I just do. Please back the fuck off," I insist grinding my teeth.

He slowly assesses me as he finishes the first donut and reaches for another. "Relax! I'm just giving you shit Brady. Just like I always do," he reminds me. "If I didn't already know by now how you feel, you just confirmed it for me," he declares smirking. "Besides, you know I would never go after anyone you're really interested in. Beyond all the bullshit, you're my brother."

"Thanks," I murmur quietly.

"Since we're brothers, you're going to have to continue putting up with me and my crap," he grins and I chuckle. "As for tonight, I would suggest making it simple. She already looks tired as hell and it's barely noon."

"You know Cody, that's actually a really good idea," I tell him.

He grins, "Don't be so surprised, I'm full of good ideas."

"Full of something anyway," I taunt.

He shakes his head, "Watch it, or I'll hijack your date."

I smirk, "You couldn't even if you tried."

He waggles his eyebrows, "Wanna' bet?"

"Not even a little bit," I grin. "I'm going to go to the grocery store. Do we need anything?" I ask.

"Beer," he says automatically.

"I mean food," I say with slight exasperation.

"No clue," he grins. I shake my head making him laugh. "What's your plan?" he asks curiously.

"I think I'll make her dinner and I'm still figuring the rest out. If you're good I may let you know afterwards," I grin.

He stuffs the last of his third donut in his mouth and reaches for a bottle of water as he waves with his other hand. "I have to get some work done. Have fun at the store," he jokes as he walks past me and back towards his room.

With my parents owning a restaurant, you'd think I could cook a lot of different things or at least a few things really well. Unfortunately, that's probably the reason I don't know how to make much. I used to eat at the restaurant a lot of nights when my parents were working. When I was younger, my mom would put Becca and me in a corner booth to keep us out of the way. We would color or play with the few toys we were allowed to bring. Of course I would always grab Becca's toys just to annoy her. I needed some kind of entertainment. As I got older I did homework or played games on my Nintendo DS. I'm sure I wasn't the only one who was thankful when I was old enough to either help or stay home.

Hopefully Sam will be okay with Italian. Things have to go well tonight. I definitely need things to go better than they did last night if I want a chance with her. I reach for my keys and wallet, quickly stuffing them into my pocket. Then I grab my phone, noticing a few missed text messages and notifications from my social media accounts. I grimace and slide my phone into my front pocket, not wanting to deal with any of that right now. "Later," I yell over my shoulder towards Cody's room as I stride for the door.

Chapter 7

Samantha

I glance at my phone, still ignoring the numerous texts from Paul and answering the one I know I should, my Uncle Tim. "I'm ok. I promise. You'll like my new roommate." I texted my Uncle last night knowing I should've already told him where I was so someone would know. I guess I'm kind of a chicken for texting instead of calling, but it's the best I could do for now. I couldn't deal with all the questions he would have for me, not yet.

I never texted Brady, but from what he said earlier, I'm sure he'll be here any minute anyway. I can't help but wonder again why I agreed to this. I definitely don't need any drama in my life right now, but there's something that draws me to him. I just want to be around him. I should probably ask him about Jackie. Maybe he'll tell me their situation and then I can decide what I want to do. Well that's if he wants to hang out with me after tonight. I just know I can't do what Taylor did to me to anyone, even someone I don't know or don't really like for that matter. I realize now that Paul and I should've broken up long before anything happened, but I don't believe that's a valid excuse for what they did. I shake my head at myself and grumble, "You're thinking like Brady is your boyfriend. This is just a date. A date I didn't exactly agree to," I add sarcastically.

I walk over to the bathroom to glance in a bigger mirror. I add a long mirror for the back of my door to my mental list of things I need for my room. My long brown curls hang loosely over my shoulders. I'm glance at the loose-fitting gray knit top that hangs slightly off my shoulders, but tightens just below my waist. My eyes move down my body to the black leggings and tall black boots with a silver buckle on the outside of both ankles. I reach for a tube of pink lip-gloss and swiftly roll it over my lips, happy with my light make-up. I don't want to look like I'm trying too hard, especially when he knows what my plans were for the day.

A loud knock on the door sends butterflies flying through my stomach in anticipation. I slip my lip-gloss into the drawer on the bottom right and stride for the front door. I pull the door open to a clean-shaven Brady smiling down at me with his deep dimple on display, knocking the air out of my lungs. I can't stop my eyes from wandering quickly down his chest, covered in a long sleeve light blue t-shirt with a picture of a fish where the pocket would be. His shirt hangs loose over a pair of faded blue jeans and his toes stick out of the bottom of his pants in black flip flops, pulling a smile from my lips. I meet his eyes finding his eyebrows arched in question, "You look beautiful, but are you going to let me come in?"

I blush a deep shade of red, belatedly noticing the green bags he's carrying. I step back and try to reach for one, "I'm sorry. Can I help you?"

He steps out of my reach chuckling, "I got it." He strides towards the kitchen. I shut the door and quickly follow after him.

"What is all that?" I ask already knowing the answer as a heavenly smell of garlic and tomatoes hits my nose.

"I made us dinner," he confesses with a shrug.

"You didn't have to do that," I tell him.

He smirks, "Well, I figured if I brought the date to you, there would be less of a chance that you would back out on me at the last minute because you were too tired or some other lame excuse."

I laugh, "Well I would've come to you then. It's not like you live too far away."

"Good to know," he grins chuckling. I blush and he continues, "Besides, I made dinner for you, not for Cody." I laugh again and his smile drops off his lips as he stares seriously at me. "He would've eaten everything and tried to steal all of your attention. I want you all to myself tonight for our first date," he admits.

I blush a deeper shade of red making him smile as he turns away. He begins emptying all the food out of the bags as I take the moment to pull myself together. I clear my throat, "Everything smells so good."

He grins and admits, "I hope you like it." His eyes widen and he puts his finger up, "I forgot something. I'll be right back." I watch him as he walks back towards the door and pulls it open, only to stop when he finds Cody standing on the other side holding a small bouquet of pink, yellow and white daisy-like flowers. Brady takes the flowers from Cody and says, "Thanks," before attempting to shut the door on him. Cody laughs and sticks his foot in the door and places his hand up higher to stop the momentum.

"If I'm bringing flowers for Sam, I should at least be able to say Hi to our girl," Cody grins over at me.

Brady sighs in resignation, "Fine."

Cody steps inside and takes two long strides over to me, lifting me up in his arms, "Hi my sexy neighbor." He chuckles before gently setting me back on my feet.

"Hi Cody," I grin blushing, at the same time, holding back my laughter.

"I'm sorry I can't stay for dinner," he apologizes like I invited him. Then again, I didn't exactly invite Brady either. "I'll make it up to you," he jokes and Brady groans in exasperation.

I giggle in response, enjoying their banter. He stands to his full height as he stares at Brady, "Be good to her. My sister will be home soon to check on you."

Brady shakes his head like he's annoyed with Cody, but his lips curve up like he's holding back his laughter. He follows him to the door and shoves him out making Cody chuckle. "Bye!"

I wave and Cody yells, "Bye Sam," as the door swings shut.

I laugh, "You two are funny. It's almost like you're related or something."

The corners of his lips twitch up, "Yeah, we've been friends for a long time. He's like a brother to me, just as Cory's like a sister. We've always given each other a lot of shit," he admits. He takes a step towards me and holds out the flowers, "These are for you."

"Thank you," I tell him, "they're beautiful." I reach for the flowers and gasp as a shock of tingles shoot up my arm when he brushes his fingers against mine. "I should put them in water," I tell him nervously and quickly turn back towards the kitchen. I stop abruptly, "I don't have a vase."

He steps up close to me and places his hand on the small of my back causing a quick intake of my breath. "Cory has a couple under the sink in here," he informs me. His warm breath on my ear sends shivers down my spine. "She loves fresh flowers. When she visits her parents in the warmer months, she cuts some at their house to bring here. The rest of the year she just buys them for herself," he smirks.

I gulp down the lump in my throat and stumble towards the kitchen sink, feeling breathless. I crouch down to find two large clear vases and one small crystal vase under the sink. I pull out one of the larger ones and fill it with water before I slip the flowers in it and set it down on the counter. I take a deep breath and turn to face him, finally uttering, "Thank you."

He grins, "You're welcome." He stares into my eyes momentarily before he breaks our connection. "We should eat before the food gets cold," he reminds me. "Do you want to grab a couple plates and glasses?" he asks.

I open the cabinet behind him and pull out two blue and white ceramic plates. I set them on the counter next to him. "What do you want to drink?" I ask reaching for two glasses.

"I'll just have water for now," he tells me. I pull a pitcher out of the refrigerator with filtered water and pour us each a glass before setting it down on the corner booth table. "I hope you're not a vegetarian," he says with raised eyebrows.

"No, not me," I smile.

He breathes a sigh of relief, "Good. Then I also hope you like Italian. I made spaghetti and meatballs."

I grin, "Anyone who says they don't is lying."

He chuckles and grins broadly, "Good, cause there's not too much I can make, but this is my specialty."

I laugh and slide into the booth. He sets two plates down on the table filled with spaghetti and meatballs and a slice of garlic bread. "Well, thank you for making dinner. You didn't have to do that." He slides in right next to me, his knee gently bouncing against mine and leaves it resting there. I spin some noodles onto my fork and take a bite, enjoying the sweetness of the sauce.

He doesn't comment. Instead he asks, "So how are you liking it here so far?" He takes a bite of his own dinner as he awaits my response.

I shrug, "Well, I have nice neighbors." He laughs, but the truth is, I haven't really had the chance to experience much more than that here. I cut into my oversized meatball with my fork and my mouth begins watering from the flavors the moment it hits my tongue. I groan in appreciation, "Oh my gosh these are so good! Did you make these from scratch?" I question, knowing they couldn't be store bought.

"Yeah," he answers, his voice sounding strained.

I take another bite and look up at him, attempting to assess his look. I give up and ask, "So what do you do besides go to school, harass your roommate and make spaghetti and meatballs for your new neighbor?"

He throws his head back and laughs; the husky sound sending chills right through me. "Well, if I'm harassing Cody he probably deserves it. As for dinner, do I need to remind you again this is a date? I don't bring Cody on my dates," he teases me.

I flush at his response and with the sudden reminder of what I want to ask him. "I realize that, but I have to ask..." I begin hesitantly as I twist my fork repeatedly in my hand. "Are you really free to be able to go on dates with other girls?" He sighs and sets his fork down on his plate. "I'm sorry maybe I shouldn't have asked," I blurt out, attempting to backtrack.

He shakes his head and emphasizes, "No, you have every right to ask since I do consider this a date." I nervously glance up at him, wanting to look into his eyes for the truth when he speaks. "You mean Jackie?" he clarifies his jaw tight. I nod my head stiffly. "Jackie and I are just friends. We briefly dated back in high school, over four years ago," he emphasizes. "Then after we broke up she went a little wild and," he sighs and runs his hand through his hair. "She went through some stuff. We both did. I guess I feel like I should look out for her." I watch as guilt passes through his eyes.

"Why did you guys break up?" I ask him.

He shrugs, but won't meet my eyes. He heavily sighs again, "Honestly, I broke up with her towards the end of my senior year. We didn't really have much in common. We just weren't right for each other. She didn't see it that way though and wanted more from me. At the time all I wanted was to have fun and go out with other girls," he admits sheepishly.

"But why do you feel responsible for her?" I press him for more answers trying to better understand. He sighs again and runs his hands through his hair. "I'm sorry I keep pushing you, forget I asked," I blurt nervously.

"Sam," he attempts.

I shake my head, "No, I'm sorry. Maybe we'll talk about it another time and maybe we won't. I've known you less than a week. I'm not ready to hear your answers to questions that are none of my business." He closes his mouth appearing conflicted before he reluctantly gives in and takes another bite of dinner. "So did you play any sports in high school or college?" I ask, trying to change the subject.

He quietly searches my face, but I'm not quite sure what he's looking for. He finally answers with a nod, "Yeah. I did football, basketball and baseball in high school, but baseball is really my sport. I played my freshman year," he admits, "But it was way too much of a commitment with school and family and basically anything else."

"Do you miss it?" I ask.

He shrugs and confesses, "Sometimes, but I don't regret quitting. It was the right thing for me. What about you?"

I grimace, "I was a cheerleader and I ran hurdles in track."

He laughs, "What did you not like it or something?" I must look confused because he clarifies, "You don't look happy about it."

I sigh and acknowledge, "I guess when I think about it now, I think about things I don't want to think about anymore, like my parents being at my competitions, games or meets."

He gives me a look filled with so much compassion and understanding, but not the pity I'm used to seeing. He reaches up and tucks one of my curls behind my ear and lets his thumb slide down my jawline leaving goose bumps in its wake. He leans slightly towards me and hesitates just before lightly pressing his lips to mine. I gasp at the warm gentleness of his kiss and nearly whimper when he pulls away just as quickly. "I've wanted to do that since I laid eyes on you outside the building," he admits. He grins sheepishly, "I couldn't wait any longer."

"I should go brush my teeth. I smell like garlic," I tell him and scrunch up my nose in disgust.

He laughs hard, his eyes sparkling like diamonds. "Both of us do. I can't eat spaghetti without garlic in the sauce or without garlic bread. I just made sure you have as much garlic on your plate as me," he teases. I laugh along with him, feeling myself blush. "Do you want to watch a movie or something? I think you deserve to take it easy after all your hard work moving this week."

I smile shyly up at him, "Okay. That sounds perfect."

We stand and he cleans up the food, while I rinse the dishes and put them in the dishwasher. "So what types of movies do you like to watch? And please don't say romance," he pleads jokingly.

I cup my hands under the water and attempt to splash it at him, "What's wrong with romance?"

He grumbles, "Hey," just before he charges me. I squeal as he wraps his muscled arms around me, pinning my arms to my sides. He adjusts and grips me in one hand as he splashes me with the other laughing, "I'm pretty sure I'll win this kind of argument every time."

"Stop!" I screech. "Please, Brady," I plead laughing. He turns the water off and lets me wiggle out of his arms. I spin around to face him with a huge smile on my face to find his sparkling blue eyes full of mischief. "You're trouble," I joke.

"Me?" he laughs. "I guess we're a good pair then." He takes a step closer to me and my breathing picks up its pace. "You're all wet," he smirks.

"I wonder who's fault that is?" I reply sarcastically.

He chuckles and reaches for me, letting his hand slide gently down my arm until he entwines our fingers together. He gives me a light tug, "Come on, let's go find something to watch." I nod, unable to respond and follow him out to the living room. He sits on the couch and pulls me down next to him. "So what do you like besides chick flicks?" he asks as he reaches for the remote.

I purse my lips like I'm deep in thought and struggling to come up with an answer when I hear him groan as if he's in pain. I can't hold back my smile when I finally reply with a shrug, "I'll watch almost anything."

"Really?" he asks surprised. I nod and his grin grows so wide. "I knew I liked you!"

I laugh, "You need a movie to tell you that?"

He shakes his head and smirks, "No, but it helps." He flips through Hulu and we agree on an action movie. He pushes play and tosses the remote on the coffee table before releasing my hand. He wraps his arm around me and pulls me into his chest before I have a chance to feel the loss of his touch. I immediately relax into him with a content sigh. His hand begins mindlessly playing with my hair as the opening credits begin, causing me to fight to keep my eyes open.

"Sam," he gently jostles me awake.

"Hmm," I murmur groggily.

He chuckles, his breath warm on my cheek. "Do you do this often?" I lift my heavy head and blink up at him blankly. "Fall asleep on your dates? I don't think it's looking too good for a second date when you slept through so much of our first one," he teases me.

It takes me a moment to register his words, but when I do I push myself up from his solid chest. I look at the television rolling the credits from the movie that I don't remember at all. "I'm so sorry," I rasp. "I'm like the worst date ever, but you were so comfortable. Then you were playing with my hair and I'm so tired," I ramble.

He chuckles again and smirks, "I definitely didn't mind, believe me. You're cute when you snore."

"I don't snore!" I yell defensively.

His eyes twinkle as he answers, "You didn't, but you still could." I roll my eyes at him when he adds, "Besides, you can make it up to me by going out with me again Thursday."

I smile sleepily up at him and agree without overthinking, "Okay. What are you doing tomorrow?" I ask curiously.

He grins, "Thursday isn't fast enough for you?" I roll my eyes and he laughs softly. "I have to go by my parents tomorrow. I also promised them I would go to the restaurant with them tomorrow night for a while," he informs me.

I nod my head and open my mouth to say something when he lets his fingers run gently down the side of my face and along my jawline. My breath catches in my throat and my heart begins hammering in my chest as I stare at him. "I should go and let you get some sleep," he whispers as he traces my bottom lip with his thumb.

I subtly shake my head and lean slightly towards him. He acknowledges my consent by closing the distance in seconds, firmly pressing his mouth to mine. I gasp for a breath the second his soft lips cover mine sending a jolt through my whole body. I instinctively reach up to wrap my hands around his neck and pull him closer. He takes that as an invitation and nudges my mouth apart with his lips. I willingly open, welcoming his intrusion as his tongue meets mine. He tastes of spaghetti and something sweet I can't get enough of. His fingers tangle in my hair and he gently tilts my head to meld our mouths together pushing the kiss deeper. I groan into his mouth, loving every velvety stroke of his tongue and wanting more. I don't remember ever being kissed like this before. I never want to stop. I cling a little tighter to him, losing myself in this kiss.

I don't register the sound of the front door opening until I hear Cory giggle, "I guess your date went well tonight."

I rip my mouth away from Brady and jump away from him to the other end of the couch like his parents just walked in the room. I'd laugh at my behavior, but I'm too breathless to do anything except stare at Brady in awe and try to catch my breath. "Hey Cory. How was work?" Brady mumbles slightly breathless while his eyes remain on me.

Cory hangs her coat up on one of the hooks behind the front door. "It was fine, but I know neither of you really care right now, so I won't bore you with any details," she grins. "Goodnight. I'll be in my room!" she calls over her shoulder.

"I should go," he tells me regretfully after we hear her bedroom door close. I nod my head in agreement. It's overwhelming how much I want to tell him to stay and kiss me again, but I know that's not a good idea when I don't know where I want this to go yet. He reaches out and pulls me back to him. Then he tips his head towards me, his lips meeting mine in a soft kiss, in his own way giving us a chance to slow down our momentum together. He pulls back with a groan, "Damn."

"Thank you for dinner," I tell him appreciatively. I smirk adding, "And I'll just say for everything else since I don't even know what movie you watched while you were my personal pillow."

He chuckles, "Anytime Sam, anytime."

He stands and I reach my hand out for him to help me up. He pulls me up and keeps hold of my hand as we walk to the door. "I guess I'll see you Thursday," I tell him.

"Yes you will. I even promise we'll leave the apartment next time," he grins. I giggle and he tilts his head down giving me a chaste kiss. "Good night Sam."

"Good night Brady." He releases my hand before he walks out the door. I shut the door behind him with a content sigh.

"I didn't think he would ever leave," Cory jokes, startling me as she steps back into the room. She grins, "You two looked pretty cozy."

I blush and smile back at her. "I like him," I admit. The reality of my words forces the air out of my lungs. I'm here to find my father, not a new boyfriend I remind myself. I feel myself beginning to panic. My heart rate speeds up and I struggle to catch my breath.

Cory's head tilts to the side assessing me. I feel her intense stare and attempt to calm my anxiety. "He really is a good guy Sam," she emphasizes trying to give me a sense of comfort.

I force myself to slow down my breathing as I take in her words. Maybe starting up something with him will be okay. I immediately push away any doubts attempting to surface and enjoy the moment while I can still feel him and taste him on my lips. I smile to myself as my hand automatically touches my slightly swollen lips. I know better than anyone how time can disappear before you have a chance to appreciate it. I remind myself, "Enjoy the moment and hope you have many, many more."

Chapter 8

I cradle a cup of coffee in my hands as I notice a note Cory left for me by the coffee pot with a huge smiley face, "Good morning Roomie! Hope you're still smiling this morning like you were last night! ~ Cory." What's strange to me is that I am smiling. I don't remember the last time I woke up smiling. Everything has felt mechanical or forced for so long. I'm already starting to feel more like myself again and I've been here less than a week. I don't know if it's my new environment, or my new friends, or Brady and the thought of what could be, but I do know it's better than the stagnant life I've been living at home.

I pull out my phone and text Cory, "Just curious...do you ever text?"

The dancing bubbles appear and I wait for her reply. It's a silly face emoji followed by, "Of course I do! I just like old-fashioned notes too. They're more personal!"

I laugh and reply, "Lol. Thanks for the note!"

I walk back to my room with my coffee and sit down on the edge of my bed. I place my phone and coffee on the nightstand and slowly open the drawer like something might jump out at me. The stack of letters from my birth mother sits glaring up at me. I feel a little braver today. I'm not sure if Brady has anything to do with it, but either way I'm ready to push myself a little more. I take a deep breath, preparing myself to read another letter.

I pull out the third one since I already read the first two and the last one. I scoot back so I can lean against my pillow and pull my knees up towards my chest. I slowly open the letter with shaky hands.

June 12 – Your 1ˢᵗ Birthday
To My Beautiful Baby Girl,
Happy 1ˢᵗ Birthday! I can't believe you're already a year old! Time has flown by so quickly. I'm having a cup of coffee before I go out to meet up with some friends and I'm wondering what you're doing today. I'm sure your parents have something wonderful planned to celebrate you today. I still think about you every day, but I believe you're where you belong. I have to believe it or I don't know if I would make it through the day.

I'm curious about so many things that I'm sure happened with you this past year. I realize I gave up the right to know, but that doesn't change how I feel. I want to know what your first food was, how old you were when you got your first tooth, what your first word was, when you started crawling and if you've taken your first step. I wonder what your laugh and your cry sound like. I wonder if you look like me, or your father, or if you have a little of both. I wonder if you're eyes changed from the blue they were on the day you were born to something darker. I wonder if you have my curls or if you ever will.

Whatever you look like and whatever you do, I know in my heart it will be amazing and filled with love. All I want for you is happiness. Have fun!
With Love...
Catherine Schepp

My heart clenches to know she thought of me and was curious about me just like I have always been about her. I guess I have her curls. I reach up and run my fingers through my tangled mass of hair. I wonder what else I have of hers or of his. Will I ever really know? I reach for the next letter craving more.

June 12 – Your 2ⁿᵈ Birthday

To My Beautiful Baby Girl,

Happy 2ⁿᵈ Birthday! Have you started your "terrible two's"? I'm sure you're running your parents ragged, curious about so much. I just hope you don't take after me and get into too much trouble. I was never a very good listener.

I'm getting sick of moving around, so I decided it's time to try something different. I rented an apartment and I'm staying in one place for now with a close friend of mine. I'm even starting a new job today waitressing at a Mexican restaurant. They have the best burritos! I wonder if you have tried any Mexican food before. I'm not sure...you might be a little young for that.

I hope you have a wonderful day.
With Love...
Catherine Schepp

I can't help but feel a wave of disappointment deep in my gut. This letter is so short. I guess I have no right to want more. I should be grateful for what she decided to give me. Then again, I kind of feel bitter too. She should give me more. Don't I deserve it? I groan at my scattered thoughts and pull out the next one, hoping for a different result.

June 12 – Your 3ʳᵈ Birthday
To My Beautiful Baby Girl,

Happy 3ʳᵈ Birthday! I can't even imagine how big you're getting! I keep trying to picture the little girl you may be now. What kinds of things do you like to play with? Do you like to use your imagination when you play or do you like to play following the rules? I wonder if you're a curious child and constantly ask, "Why?" I used to do that and it would drive my mom nuts!

Where do you live? Are you in the city, or do you live on a farm, or maybe something in between. I've been wondering what your parents do for a living. Do they both work or does one of them stay home with you? Either way, I'm sure they cherish all their time with you. I wonder if you're in day care or maybe have a babysitter during the day. Will you start pre-school in the fall? If so, I hope you remember to share! I'm sure your parents are teaching you so much. I just hope you listen to what they have to say.

I'm still living in the same place, but I'm not sure how much longer I'll stay. It's hard to stay on my feet all day at the restaurant. I would like to find a job where I don't have to do that anymore. I think it may be time to move on soon.

With Love...
Catherine Schepp

I wish she would give me more answers than questions. I don't understand why she's asking so many questions she knew at the time may never be answered. I want answers, not more questions, but I'll never be able to tell her what I want. I'll never be able to answer any of her questions either. I just have to accept what she's given me and that I'll never be able to give her anything in return. I grimace in frustration and take a deep breath to try to calm my growing anxiety. "Okay, one more. It has to have something more. Then I'm going to take a shower," I whisper, attempting to make a deal with myself.

June 12 – Your 4ᵗʰ Birthday
To My Beautiful Baby Girl,
Happy 4ᵗʰ Birthday! Did everyone sing Happy Birthday to you? Do you have a favorite song or a favorite nursery rhyme? I don't really know too many nursery

rhymes, but I love music. What kind of cake do you have this year? What kind is your favorite? I love white cake with the pudding inside. And what flavor of ice cream is your favorite? Everyone loves ice cream, so there has to be a favorite. What's your favorite food? Are you a picky eater? Do you have family dinners every night?

I moved again. I have a studio apartment all to myself for the first time in my life. I found a job as a secretary for a consulting firm so I don't have to be on my feet all day. It's actually the exact opposite of waitressing. I sit and type memos, meeting minutes and reports. I file paperwork, answer the phone and coordinate schedules. It may sound boring to you, but I like it. I think it may be just what I need.

I hope you have a wonderful day and enjoy your cake!

With Love...
Catherine Schepp

I let out a frustrated sigh. I hate that I'm feeling more and more unsatisfied with every letter I read. I realize it's not fair, but I can't help it. So far the letter from my 18th birthday gives me the most answers. Maybe she wasn't ready to give me anything before that, even in a letter she thought I might never have the chance to read. I'm not overwhelmed and emotional like last time, but I am confused. She sounds curious, but distant, like she's writing to a stranger. I guess in a way that's exactly what I am to her. I wouldn't really blame her if that were exactly what she's trying to do, but...I ache for more. I want to know where I came from. I can't believe that's all I'm going to get. I don't understand why I'll never have the chance to ask her any questions, not even one. Then again, I don't really know what I'm looking for either. I put the letters back in the stack and shove them into my nightstand drawer before I slam it closed dropping my head into my hands. I can't read anymore. I'm just setting myself up to feel agitated all day if I do.

Maybe it would do me good to get in the shower and go into town. I could go see the shop Cory works at and say, "Hi." She asked me to stop in this week. Then if I'm in town, maybe I'll walk down to Hometown and try to muster up some courage to walk inside this time. Maybe meeting my biological father will give me some of the answers I'm looking for, instead of searching for them in papers and letters that can't answer me back. "I need to do something to move forward," I mumble, attempting to encourage myself to physically move. My phone pings with a text, but when I lift my head and take a glance at my phone, Paul's face lights up the screen. I groan in irritation and add, "I definitely can't move back."

I push myself up and off my bed. I walk over to my closet and pull the door open to find something to wear. I grimace at my temporary storage set up and lack of clothes. Some of my clothes hang from the bar with a couple stacked bins with more clothes, including my underwear and bras, along the bottom. Sooner or later I'm going to have to go home and get some furniture along with more of my things. Then again, if I plan on staying, I have to get a job! I groan having no idea where to even start when it comes to looking for a job.

My phone pings, notifying me of another text. I'm about to ignore it, assuming its Paul, when I have a sudden urge to look. I walk away from my closet and grab my phone off the nightstand. The tension in my body instantly slips away at the sight of Brady's name on my screen. I anxiously open the text, smiling before I even read his message. "Hey Sam. Just wanted to tell you I had a great time last night! Since I'm not looking forward to today, I'm already planning tomorrow with you in my head. Can't wait!"

I take a deep breath, enjoying the flutter of my heart as I read his words. I open my eyes and reply with a smiley face emoji. I have no idea what we're doing tomorrow, so what else would I say?

"Can I stop by tonight if I don't get home too late?" Brady texts.

I squeal out loud in excitement. "Sure, I'll be here," I reply casually when inside my body is in excitement overload. My heart pounds and my hands shake while my stomach turns eagerly. My face hurts from smiling so wide causing me to laugh at myself. I barely know him, yet he changes me from feeling anxious and unsettled to giddy and content. "How is that even possible?" I grumble happily.

"Hope to see you later then!" he texts. My whole body warms in anticipation of seeing him even though he won't be here for several hours, if he makes it at all.

I return my phone to my nightstand and wander back to my closet to get ready to go into town. I feel a little more courageous about trying to find my way around after only a few words from Brady and he doesn't even know what he did for me. "I'm in so much trouble with him," I murmur with a smile on my face.

Chapter 9

By the time I get into town, my anxiety is creeping back in. It takes all my inner strength to park my car at the end of Main Street when I drive into downtown Chance so I have to walk past my birth father's store. It's starting to warm up and feel a little more like spring, so I don't mind strolling the few blocks to Cory's shop. I walk at a snail's pace as I approach Hometown. I notice movement inside, but I can't see any faces. Then again it's not like I would recognize anyone if I did. I hear the jingle of bells as the door to the store opens and my breath hitches instinctively. In this moment, I freeze as my heart clenches and I swear, completely stops. I try to focus, first seeing the black sole of a man's shoe as I wait for the rest of him to appear. Time seems to be moving agonizingly slow, but I finally meet the smile of a dark haired and olive skinned guy who's probably still in high school. His grin widens when he sees me staring. "Hi!" he greets me.

"Hi," I squeak and quickly dodge around him and down the street. Whoever he was, he probably thought I was crazy. I roll my eyes at my behavior and mumble, "I'm being ridiculous. I'll go inside after I see Cory. He's probably not even there anyway," I reason aloud. I look up just as I'm approaching Cory's shop, thankful I'm the only one walking on this side of the street. I don't need the whole town thinking I'm crazy for talking to myself.

The sign above the door says simply, "Chance Beauty Salon." I walk up the three cement steps to a small platform and pull open the glass door framed in a thick black oak and step inside. A girl, about my age, with silvery blue hair and matching eyes, greets me with a friendly smile from behind a large curved white desk. "Hi! Do you have an appointment?" she asks sweetly.

I shake my head, "No, I'm just here to see Cory."

At the sound of her name, I hear Cory's squeal from across the room, immediately drawing my attention to her. "Sam! I'm so glad you're here!" she shrieks. Say Hi to Becca, then come over here while I finish up!"

I turn back to the girl at the desk uncertainly. "Are you Becca?"

She nods and stands, laughing. "Yeah, Hi. You must be the new roommate?"

I nod and blush, feeling slightly out of place, "Yeah, I'm Samantha." The girl in front of me is beautiful. I'm surprised at how petite she is when she stands, but I think it makes her look even more glamorous, so much beauty in such a small package. Her skin is flawless and her smile is contagious. "You're really pretty," I blurt out awkwardly.

She blushes, but then grins widely. "Thank you. So are you. No wonder Brady is already going crazy over you."

My body heats with embarrassment and I stutter, "Wh...What?"

She laughs, "I'm Brady's younger and extremely fabulous sister. Cory told me all about you!"

I feel my blush deepen, "Oh." I didn't know he had a sister and I hate that I didn't even think to ask him. I feel so stupid! "Um..." I stammer not knowing what to say.

"Don't worry, Cory had all good things to say about you," she insists. She glances over at Cory before looking back at me, "Go say Hi. We can talk later!"

I nod and smile down at her, "Thanks. It was nice meeting you Becca."

She waves happily as I stride around the desk and over to Cory. She sets her scissors down on a white wooden cabinet with four drawers down the center and cubbies on both sides for her things and wraps her arms around me, giving me a quick hug. "I'm so glad you're here!" I can't help but grin at her excitement. "Ruby this is my new roommate Samantha. Ruby is a friend of my grandmother's," she explains gesturing to the older woman sitting in her chair.

I smile, "It's nice to meet you."

"You too, my dear. Cory was just telling me all about you," she grins.

Cory picks up her scissors and continues trimming Ruby's gray hair as I take in my surroundings. The chair itself is black with silver hardware to match the smooth silver oval mirror above her station. There are five more chairs down the line, two on one side of her and three on the other. Two stations are empty, but other stylists occupy the three other stations. Cory tilts her head to her right, "This guy right here is Ben. He's great with color!"

"Thank you girl!" he exclaims. "Hi Sammy. You're already famous around here!"

I look over at Ben and smile, "What do you mean by that?"

I can already tell by his playful manner, Ben is a good friend to Cory. He's nearly six feet tall and somewhat lanky. He has light brown skin and dark eyes with short dreadlocks in his hair. He's wearing a bright pink button down shirt that hangs outside his faded blue jeans with a pair of black work boots. "Good news travels fast in a small town and you my dear are good news in more ways than one," he answers cryptically with a broad smile.

Cory laughs and waves her hand at Ben in dismissal, "Ignore him. I was just bragging a little bit about you!"

"That's not all," he mumbles under his breath.

She glares at him before attempting to move on. She points to the woman on the other side of Ben with short, dark hair and the body of a model, "That's Diane, the owner of this place." I wave politely and Cory adds, "Would you believe she's a grandmother?" My mouth drops open in surprise and Cory laughs, "I know, it's crazy!" She points to the woman on the other side of her that reminds me of one of my mom's friends, "And that's Aggie. Sheila has today off and Jodi went to grab all of us lunch," she explains the empty chairs. I nod my head, processing all the information. "Got all that? I'll test you on it later," she teases, helping me relax.

"It's really great though Cory. This is a nice place," I compliment her genuinely. I am surprised there are so many chairs in such a small town though. Maybe some people from the college come here instead of in the city.

"Thank you," she smiles proudly. She looks in the mirror and meets her customer Ruby's eyes, "What do you think?" She slowly spins her around, holding up a black handheld mirror so she can see the back as well.

"I love it. Thank you Cory," she grins happily as she plays with the back of her hair.

Cory nods her head in satisfaction and pulls the black plastic cape off Ruby before helping her stand. "Well then you can pay Becca up front and I'll see you next time.

"Thank you Sweetie," Ruby croons. "I'll leave your tip at your station. Tell your Grandmother I said Hello!"

"Thank you and I will. Bye Ruby," she says and offers her a quick wave. Then she spins on her heel and links her arm through mine, striding straight for the back of the shop. "You're here just in time. I have a short break before my next client," she informs me.

I follow her into a small break room with a mini refrigerator, sink and a couple black, backless stools by the back counter with the same modern theme as the front. Both above and below the counter the cabinets are wood, but painted silver to give a different appearance. "How long do you have?" I ask her.

She shrugs, "I guess about ten minutes. Ruby usually likes to talk so I leave extra time with her, but since you walked in, she gave me a break so I can spend that time with you."

"Are you and Ben good friends?" I ask curiously.

She nods, "Yeah, he's a lot of fun. Plus he's loyal and a great listener."

I nod like I understand, but lately I can't relate. I try to ignore the unwanted pang of jealousy in my chest, but it's hard when I haven't felt like I've had a friend like that since before my parents died. Nobody knew what to say to me, so they eventually stopped texting, or coming around and since we no longer went to school together, I'd just see them when I was out with Paul or Taylor. Now thinking back, although Taylor was my best friend, she was always competitive. I guess I never realized that until I saw her with Paul. I wonder if I ever really had a genuine friend like Cory seems to have. I sigh audibly forgetting momentarily where I am.

"Are you okay?" she asks her eyes full of concern.

I clear my throat and murmur, "I'm fine, thanks."

She assesses me for a moment before she asks. "So did you finish unpacking?"

I shrug, thankful for the change in subject, "Sort of. I still have to go back to Illinois sometime and get my dresser and some more of my clothes along with a few other things."

Her mouth drops open in mock surprise, "How can you go without your wardrobe?" I giggle softly and shrug. Her grin widens and she suggests, "Brady could probably take you. He has a truck, so you could fit any furniture in the back in addition to whatever else you need to pick up."

I ignore her question and narrow my eyes, "Why didn't you tell me you work with his sister? I didn't even know he had a sister!"

Her eyes widen in surprise, "Neither of us told you?" I shake my head. She smiles and shrugs her shoulders, "Oops. What does it matter anyway?"

I'm not sure how to answer her because honestly she's right, so I don't. "She seems nice and she's really pretty. I'd kill to have skin like hers," I confess.

Cory laughs, "I know what you mean! And you're right, she's beautiful," she agrees with my assessment. "She's great too. She's always kind of done her own thing. Lucky for her, she's the kind of girl who can get away with it, especially when you have a big brother like Brady who will stand up for you no matter what." She laughs to herself like she's remembering something, "She's grown up the last couple years though and let's just say she does a good job of driving her parents and her brother a little crazy."

"Is it just Becca and Brady?" I ask curiously.

Cory nods, "Yeah." Her grin grows and she asks, "So when are you going out with Brady again?"

I laugh, "What is it with you and wanting me to go out with Brady so badly?"

She leans back against the wall and crosses her arms in thought. "Honestly, Brady hasn't had a real girlfriend since he broke up with Jackie, even though they didn't date for very long. Don't get me wrong, he's dated lots of girls since then, but either Brady wasn't really interested or Jackie got in the way and Brady let her," she grimaces. "I don't think I've seen him really go after a girl, let alone be truly interested in one like you. Plus he knows he'll see you all the time, so he must be sure about you. I guess you could say he's kind of careful about that kind of thing," she admits with a scrunch of her nose. "It's just obvious he likes you." She shrugs struggling to explain her thoughts. "It's just different," she emphasizes again, "I can tell."

"But you guys just met me..." I begin trying to understand. I may think Brady is gorgeous and incredibly sexy, but we don't know each other, not really.

Cory rolls her eyes at me, "And I obviously like you already. I am living with you." She laughs and then her face turns serious. "He'll be worth it. You just have to give him a chance." I purse my lips in thought, "When are you going out with him again?" she repeats her question with a smirk.

I blush and admit, "Tomorrow, but he also said he might stop by when he gets home tonight if it's not too late."

She grins as Becca steps into the room, "Cory, sorry to interrupt, but your next appointment is here."

Cory groans and jumps off the stool, "Okay, thanks Becca." She turns to me and gives me a quick hug, "Thanks for coming by and stop thinking so much!" We both laugh although her advice is easier said than done. I follow her out of the break room and wave goodbye to everyone as I head for the door. Their goodbye shouts are cutoff as the door closes behind me.

I take a deep breath and turn to walk back towards my car and the store I promised myself I'd walk into this time. With each step closer to Hometown, I ignore the anxiety clawing at me from inside my brain and instead try to focus on Brady and analyzing why I feel such a strong pull towards him. I've met a lot of good-looking guys in my life, but he's the first one to ever take my breath away with just his smile. Once I add in the rest of him, my whole body vibrates and my heart pounds with something I can't even explain to myself. He makes me laugh after only knowing me for a few days and it's been a long time since anyone has been able to do that. He seems to genuinely care about what I have to say; I can see it in his eyes. I want to talk to him, to tell him things I haven't been able to talk about to anyone since I lost my mom and dad. Is Cory right? Is Brady worth it? What am I so afraid of?

I sigh and look up a second too late as I crash into someone on the sidewalk, causing her to drop everything in her hands. "Watch where you're going!" she screeches.

"I'm so, so sorry," I stammer. I gasp in surprise as I bend over and help Jackie pick up the boxes I knocked to the ground.

She's wearing dark blue skinny jeans and tall brown fur lined boots with a matching brown faux fur lined winter coat. She quickly grabs her things and finally pauses to look at me. "You," she accuses her voice full of venom, "You were the one with Brady the other night at the Pit Stop." I nod my head slowly, already wary of her intentions. Her eyes narrow slightly and the corners of her lips turn up into a sneer as she introduces herself, "I'm his girl Jackie."

I bite the inside of my cheek to stop myself from saying anything to her I might regret and wait for her to continue. She huffs in annoyance with my silence. "Brady is mine. You may have had him for a night or two, but you might as well go back to where you came from. I'm his priority and I always will be, just like I was the other night," she taunts. She glares at me one last time before she steps around me and stomps down the block. I watch as she stops at a black BMW X5 and tosses the boxes in the back before getting behind the wheel and driving away. Only then do I release the breath I didn't know I was holding.

I turn back around and nearly storm into "Hometown", irritated with Jackie's declaration. How dare she try to tell me what to do! Does Brady even know she claims him like that? Doesn't that bother him? Why does she hold so much power over him? I don't get it!

I'm standing in the middle of an aisle filled with picture frames and decorative signs when I comprehend where I am and look around. The reality of here hits me, completely dissipating my anger. I walk slowly to the end of the aisle and look from one end of the store to the other. In my quick perusal I spot jewelry, vases, dishes, toys, hardware, cleaning supplies, pillows, wrapping paper, cards, hair accessories, storage, lamps, seasonal items, electronics, decorations and gifts. "Wow," I mumble to myself feeling completely overwhelmed.

"Can I help you find something?" I spin on my heel and come face to face with a guy about the same age as me. He's good looking with his dark wavy hair and green eyes. My eyes widen and I open my mouth to answer him, but nothing comes out. I can't stop staring at him. His hair is so much like mine. Is he my brother? His eyebrows draw together in concern and he asks, "Are you okay?"

I shake my head slowly and finally rasp, "I'm fine. I just remembered something I forgot to do. I have to go. I'll come back another time."

He nods his head appearing confused, but doesn't call me on it, "Okay. Have a good day." He steps back, giving me room to pass by him. I hesitate for another moment before I rush out of the store and don't stop until I'm sitting behind the wheel of my car.

Chapter 10

It's nearly midnight and I'm still sitting on the couch in black yoga pants and a teal fitted sweatshirt with my legs crossed, debating if I should follow Cory's lead and just go to bed. Brady said he might stop by, he never said he definitely would. I grit my teeth, annoyed with myself for hoping Cory was right and I am different to him. I don't really know if that's the right thing for me to hope for after my run-in with Jackie, but I can't help it. Maybe if he answered some of my questions, I could get over this anxiety I'm having about him one way or another.

I should really just stop thinking about him and start focusing on what I'm going to do about finding my birth father, the whole reason I'm here in the first place. It could be so easy to find him, but I can't decide if it would really be a good thing for me. Then again, I know I won't be able to move forward until I come face to face with him. Maybe he'll have some answers for me and maybe he won't, but I have to know. It's not just curiosity that's pushing me anymore. I have the strongest need to know as much as I can about my history, almost like I'm being pulled in a certain direction. I could kick myself in the ass for practically running the other way at the store today. I groan and drop my head in my hands. I'm just terrified I'm not going to like the answers.

A soft sound near our front door causes me to lift my head and perk my ears up, wondering if I just imagined the noise. I hear a soft knock and I stand slowly, attempting to stay quiet. I tiptoe to the front door and lean against it to peer through the peephole. My heart skips a beat at the peephole-distorted sight of Brady standing in front of my door and nervously running his fingers through his already messy brown hair. I fall back on my heels and my hand automatically goes to my chest as I try to calm the overwhelming sense of relief encompassing me just knowing he's here. I reach for the cool metal of the knob and turn, slowly pulling the door open. He immediately stops fidgeting at the sound and movement. He greets me with a half-smile, showing off his dimple, "Hi."

I grin back at him, "It's pretty late."

"I could go," he tells me, twisting towards his apartment.

I reach out to grab his forearm to stop him, "No!" His smile grows and I add, "You can come in for a little while."

He steps through the door and whispers, "I was going to text you, but I didn't want your phone to wake you if you were sleeping." He smirks and admits, "Or give you a chance to tell me not to come."

I grin as heat rushes to my cheeks. "Don't ever worry about waking me. I turn my phone on do not disturb at night," I inform him. "Do you want something to drink?"

He shakes his head, "No thank you. I just wanted to see you," he admits.

My stomach flips and my whole body heats with his words. I walk back to the couch and sit down in the corner. He drops down right next to me and wraps his arm around my waist, giving me a slight tug. "Will you use me as your pillow again? I had a shitty day," he informs me.

I let him pull me into the crook of his arm and attempt to hide my smile. "Well, I'm not happy you had a bad day, but I could get used to this," I joke.

He chuckles and murmurs almost inaudibly, "Me too."

I relax into him feeling content. "Why did you have such a bad day?" I ask softly.

He sighs and I enjoy the heat of his breath on the top of my head. "I don't think I have any right to complain, but my parents are pushing me to take over the majority of responsibilities at the restaurant after I graduate. It's not that I don't want to, but I'm not sure I want to either. I don't know what I want to do or even if I really want to live here for the rest of my life. My sister can do anything she wants, but not me," he claims somewhat bitterly. "I guess I would just love to have that luxury instead of all the pressure they're putting on me. I want a chance to be good at something I'm truly craving to do, not just what I'm obligated to do."

I nod in understanding, although I did have the same freedom as Becca before my parents died. Now I feel like my time is limited. I can't live on what they left me forever. I have to figure something out. "I get it. I'm sorry," I mumble. "I met Becca today," I add as an afterthought.

He pulls back to look me in the eyes, his own filled with curiosity. "You met my sister? How? Where?"

I giggle, "I stopped in at the shop to see Cory." His eyes register understanding, but I continue anyway, "She was working at the desk."

"I forgot she was working there part-time. Lately she's been into fashion and she's been taking a few classes for it on-line."

"Lately?" I question.

He shrugs, ignoring my question and buries his face in my hair. He takes a deep breath and mumbles, "You smell so good."

My body heats with his compliment and his touch. I struggle to steady my own breath. "Brady," I whisper his name shakily.

He lifts his head and assesses me. His eyes narrow and he asks, "Are you okay?" I hesitate to answer. He continues, "I'm sorry I'm complaining about my stupid shit."

I shake my head, "No, don't be. I like that you want to talk to me," I admit. I blush and look down at my hands, fidgeting in my lap.

He lifts his hand and gently slides his fingers down the line of my jaw to my chin. He tilts my face up to meet his eyes, searching my face for answers. "Sam?" he prompts.

I release a large breath and look up at him. "I don't understand what you do to me," I murmur quietly.

"What?" he questions.

I shake my head, needing to go in a different direction for now. Everything feels so intense when he's around. I tell him nervously, "I ran into someone else today too." His eyes narrow as he stares closely at my expression. "Your friend Jackie," I inform him unsuccessfully keeping the bitterness out of my voice.

His body instantly tenses and he moves slightly away from me so he can look at me better. "What did she say to you?" he asks tightly.

I wince at the tone of his voice, "I'm sorry. I shouldn't have said anything."

"Yes, you should have," he declares. "What happened Sam? What did she say to you?" he questions with forced gentleness.

I shake my head, "It doesn't matter." He clamps his mouth shut and his jaw clenches, but I don't know if he's mad at me or at the situation or at her. "I just need to know what's going on with you two," I explain urgently.

"Nothing is going on between me and Jackie," he insists, "and it hasn't been for years. What did she say to you?" he repeats.

I continue as if I didn't hear his declaration, "I'm sorry if I'm being too pushy Brady, but I have to ask about her again. I just can't put myself in that kind of position, not after..." I trail off realizing my slip.

His blue eyes widen in surprise and snap up to meet mine, "After what Sam?"

I pinch my lips tightly together and take a deep breath in, slowly releasing it. I feel an odd comfort with him sitting next to me. I try to rationalize with myself, telling myself he doesn't know any of my friends. It won't hurt to be honest, but I can't look at him when I speak. "It's not really a big deal, but my last boyfriend cheated on me with one of my closest friends." He gasps but I keep going, "I didn't want to be with him anymore, but I guess I was staying with him because I was comfortable with him. After my parents died, I needed that familiarity. If I were honest with myself sooner, maybe it would've never happened and saved me all the embarrassment. I just wish it didn't happen when we were together. I feel like it's my fault it did," I tell him with a shrug.

"It definitely wasn't your fault your ex cheated on you," he insists.

I don't acknowledge his affirmation and instead continue my thoughts. "I guess I believe if I'm dating someone, they should be my priority and I should be theirs. I realize we've only known each other a few days and we're not really dating, but..." I trail off, blushing at my admission.

"Aren't we?" he smirks.

"I haven't even been here a week," I remind him again.

He sighs and reaches for my hands, entwining our fingers together. "Look Sam, I don't know what it is, but I'm completely drawn to you. I can't get you out of my head," he confesses. He smirks and begins, "Well actually that's not true." My eyebrows scrunch together in confusion as I wait for him to explain. "I do know a lot of reasons why I'm already so consumed by you. You're absolutely gorgeous," he declares with a sexy smile, his deep dimple on display. "You're funny and you're not afraid to speak your mind. You have a strength and determination that already amazes me. I want to be close to you even seconds after I have to walk away. I want to know everything about you and spend my free time experiencing things with you. You already make me feel comfortable talking to you about shit I don't talk about. In fact you make me want to talk to you about everything."

My stomach churns with both anxiety and hope as his words sink in. Maybe this will work. I take a deep breath and question what I know I need to ask, feeling both optimism and dread before I utter the words. "Does that mean you want to talk to me about whatever's going on between you and Jackie?" I ask nervously, my voice barely audible. "What you told me just wasn't enough," I admit.

He sighs and relents, "Yeah, I will." He closes his eyes tightly and drops my right hand, rubbing his eyes like he's trying to rub away a memory. "Like I already told you, I dated her briefly years ago. I broke it off with her when I graduated high school, but she didn't want to break up. I guess she believed she was just giving me time. After a few months, she found out I'd been dating and slept with a couple girls and I guess you could say, she lost her shit. She flipped out on me and turned into someone completely different practically overnight. She blamed her change of personality on me, even to her parents," he winces.

"What do you mean different?" I ask softly. I gently squeeze the hand I'm still holding, trying to encourage him to keep going.

He focuses his attention on our joined hands and keeps talking as he plays with my fingers. "When we were dating, we never slept together. I thought she was too young and she wanted more from me than I was willing to give her. After she found out I moved on, she decided she was going to prove to me she was ready for a 'mature' relationship. I guess you could say she went a little wild. She started sleeping around, drinking to get wasted and even trying different drugs. She dated one of my friends to try to make me jealous," he shakes his head like he wants to forget about it. "Anyway, one night after some other shit happened I saw her at a party on frat row and she was fucked up on something, hanging on a couple assholes with their hands all over her. I knew then if I let anything happen to her I would never be able to forgive myself."

"It's not your fault," I tell him. "Those were her choices, not yours," I insist.

He nods his head, but I don't think he really believes me. "I pulled her away from those guys and let her sleep it off at my place so she wouldn't get in trouble. Believe it or not, it got worse and one night was bad and I wasn't there for her or," he trails off shaking his head. "Anyway, I promised her I would be there for her if she ever needed me for anything, but she needed to stop doing what she was doing. She agreed as long as I made her my priority," he finishes.

"She's a priority over your own family?" I question.

He grimaces and shakes his head. "She would never expect that from me," he insists.

"But she expects you to choose her over another girl every time," I declare.

~ 111 ~

He sighs, probably knowing I'm right. "I guess it's never mattered to me until now," he whispers. "What did she say to you Sam?" he pleads for an answer.

I sigh in resignation, knowing I should just tell him because he has every right to know what she tries to do to him behind his back, no matter what happens with us. "She told me to stay away from you. She said you were hers and I would never get more than a night or two with you. She said she would always come first just like she did the other night at the Pit Stop," I admit over the lump in my throat. I stare at our hands, my stomach churning with nerves.

"Sam," he encourages, attempting to get me to meet his gaze.

"You've known her your whole life and you've only known me for a few days," I state. "I get it Brady," I admit. I shrug, "But I can't even think about starting anything with you if I know another girl, let alone your ex, would be a priority over me. I don't work like that, especially after what happened with Paul and Taylor."

He nods in understanding, "Paul's your dipshit ex?"

I nod my head slowly, still not meeting his eyes. I mumble, "Yeah." I hesitate and add, "You don't have to feel bad about it Brady. It's okay."

"Sam?" he takes his free hand and gently nudges my chin up until I meet his eyes. "I understand what you're saying and it only makes me want to know you more." I offer him a sad smile and try to look away, but he holds me there. "I already know you're not just another girl to me. I would be fucking thrilled if you'd let me make *you* my priority," he tells me honestly.

"Wh...what?" I stammer surprised.

The corners of his mouth turn up slightly showing off that damn dimple and he adds, "If you'll let me. I can't be the only one who feels this crazy connection and no, it's not just because you're hot," he chuckles making me blush. "I think we could be really good together," he encourages.

My heart flutters with hope, yet I can't help but think he's too good to be true. He has to be. Everything is happening so fast. "I don't know if we're a good idea," I admit quietly.

"Let me prove to you that we're the best idea," he grins like a little kid, making me giggle. "We're spending the day together tomorrow," he declares confidently.

I raise my eyebrows in question and smirk, "We are huh?"

He nods and grins broadly, "You already said yes and I know you would never go back on your word." I laugh and he continues, "I want to show you how much fun we can have together and how you're quickly becoming much more than my priority quite easily."

My heart thumps with his words, but I don't want to hope. I feel such a strong pull towards him that I question whether or not it can actually be real, or maybe it's just hormones. "I should get some sleep then," I mumble as both my agreement and my escape.

He tilts his head to the side, assessing me, before he finally nods reluctantly, "Okay. I'll let you get some sleep, but I'll be here tomorrow at noon." He leans down towards me and my breath hitches in anticipation of his kiss. Just before his lips meet mine, he turns slightly and kisses my cheek, millimeters away from the corner of my mouth. He lingers for a few extra moments and my breathing picks up its pace. He pulls away slowly, leaving tingles in the wake of his kiss. I hold back my groan and look up at him. He sighs, "Goodnight Samantha."

"Night Brady," I barely rasp out the words.

He stands and I watch him as he walks to the door. "Lock up after I'm gone," he reminds me. I wince, realizing I would've forgotten. I have a strange sense of both annoyance and thankfulness with his reminder. It sounded like something my dad would say, but in a way I'm glad he cared enough to even say it. I stand and walk over to the door. He whispers, "Be ready Sam," just before slipping out.

I feel the soft grin on my face as I turn the lock and the deadbolt. These smiles seem to appear more and more with Brady around. "What am I getting myself into," I murmur and trudge back to my room, suddenly completely exhausted.

Chapter 11

June 12th (your 5th Birthday)
To My Beautiful Baby Girl,
Happy Birthday to you!! I can't believe you're turning 5 today. I wonder if you're celebrating in a dress or in something like shorts and a t-shirt. Then again, is it warm where you are today or is it abnormally cold like it is here? Depending where you are, I guess it could be either. Are you having a party? Do you have friends celebrating with you or maybe it's just your family? I'm picturing you playing party games like pin the tail on the donkey and musical chairs. Whatever you're doing today, I hope you're having fun!

I just realized you'll be starting Kindergarten this coming fall. I hope you like school and listen to your teachers. I was never a very good student, but your father was. He was my opposite in so many ways. I hope you take after him when it comes to your education. I did miss a lot of school though, so that might have been part of my problem. Hopefully you'll meet some friends that you'll have for a lifetime in school. My best friend and I went to Kindergarten together so many years ago, so I know it can happen.

I'm still living in the same place since the last time I wrote to you. I met someone here. We've actually been dating for nearly a year now. He's wonderful. He supports me in my interests and doesn't have a problem with all of my issues. I've never been very good at relationships. In fact he's honestly the first real boyfriend I've ever had; so let's hope I don't ruin it. I've only ever had fleeting relationships. I guess I realized it's time for me to slow my life down and take a chance. I'm trying anyway. Maybe one day you'll be able to meet him. I'm getting ahead of

myself. I hope I'm able to meet you one day. In the meantime, I hope you have a wonderful birthday.
    I love you!
    With Love...
    Catherine Schepp

I clutch the letter tightly to my chest, thankful for the new information she gifted to me. This is the longest letter she wrote since I was first born. Maybe the man she was dating was good for her. Maybe he was the one that was able to bring out more to the surface for me. I don't know if that's true, but I feel grateful to this stranger anyway.

I wish she included a picture so I'd know what she looked like. I remember one of the letters said she has curls, but I want so much more information. I'm thrilled to know something about me actually came from someone. It may come from someone who hasn't been a part of my life since the day I was born, but I've always felt so out of place when I'd hear other people say things like, "I get that from my mom," or "Just like my dad." Maybe they were talking about looks, like their hair, their eyes, or their height, or maybe it was a strength or talent like a subject at school or a sport. I love my Mom and Dad so much, but my looks, strengths and talents were always very different from what they knew. Of course that didn't make them any less my parents or make our love any less. I remember how they'd always praise everything about me, especially my unique qualities. Mom would say, "That's one of the reasons you're so special, Sam." I wouldn't trade their love and support for anything in the world, but it didn't stop me from questioning where I fit in.

I glance down at the letter, wondering what my birth mom meant when she mentioned her issues. Were her problems similar to other girls who are in their twenties? Or is there something different about her? Or maybe she's referring to her cystic fibrosis. My curiosity gets the best of me and I pull out my laptop. I type "Cystic Fibrosis" in the Google search bar and click on one of the websites at the top of the list.

At first I skim through the information in front of me, noticing a few key words such as inherited, genetic disease, life threatening, damages lungs and digestive system, and no cure. Then I close my eyes, take a deep breath and attempt to slow my thoughts before I go into a full-blown panic. If I had the gene, would I already know? I close my eyes and then open slowly open them, forcing myself to slow down. I begin reading the website more thoroughly. I feel the tension begin to release from my shoulders as I read, finding most people are diagnosed for cystic fibrosis by the age of 2, but in rare cases can be diagnosed as adults. Unfortunately, that doesn't completely relieve my anxiety. "I need to be tested," I murmur. My parents may have already had me tested, but I can't even ask them. I guess I can go back in my medical records, but what if I'm one of those rare cases? "Mom, I really wish you were here to help me right now," I rasp into my empty room.

I continue to search different websites to find out as much as I can, including information about some of the symptoms, treatments and even studies on patients with the disorder. My brain starts running rapid, imagining I have every symptom on the list. I shake my head, knowing I shouldn't get ahead of myself. I pull up my old pediatrician's phone number and whisper a silent thank you that I didn't delete it from my phone as I press send. I've been to my Ob/Gyn since my parents died, but that's it. I never switched to a new general practitioner after I turned 18. I kept putting it off and then I never made any effort to make the change after my parents died. It just hasn't been a priority.

A woman with a soft voice answers, "Good morning. West End Pediatrics, How can I help you?"

I take a deep breath to calm my nerves before I quickly blurt out, "Hi, my name is Samantha Voss and I was a patient of Dr. Mills before I turned 18. I need to find out if I ever had a particular genetic test and what the results were. Is there any way I can find out?"

"Is your information still current in our files?" a woman asks.

"My cell phone number is the same as the last time I was in and my address is the same, but I'm not staying there right now," I reply.

"Okay, did you or a parent sign the HIPAA form for information to be released over the phone?" she questions.

"I believe I signed it last time I was there," I answer, not really sure, but I hope I did. I remember signing something when I turned 18 and had been planning to switch to my parents' general practitioner.

"Okay, why don't you tell me what you're looking for and then I'll search for your file and see what we can do," she tells me.

"I'm trying to find out if I was ever tested for cystic fibrosis and if so when and what were the results?" I inquire.

"Okay. Give me some time to pull your file and someone here at the office will return your call to the number on file Samantha," she informs me. "

"Thank you," I squeak.

I hang up the phone and continue searching for more information, hungry for everything I can find as I impatiently wait for my phone to ring. I don't understand how there can't be a cure in today's society. There's a cure to nearly everything, but not this. I find an article about a girl who was 20 years old, who died from a common cold due to complications from her cystic fibrosis. She was the same age as me. I feel the panic growing in my chest as my brain skips over all the stories of people who live relatively healthy normal lives. Instead, I'm drawn to the tragedy. It's just like the heartbreak of losing my parents too young. I can't help but question any good.

My phone rings and my eyes snap to the screen to see the pediatrician's number. I quickly pull the phone to my ear as I hit answer. "Hello?" I squeak.

"Yes, this is Dr. Mills office calling for Samantha Voss," she states formally.

"This is Samantha," I reply shakily.

"Yes, did you just call the office for some information?" she questions.

"Yes, I was trying to find out if I ever had the genetic test for cystic fibrosis. My birth mother had the disease," I confirm.

"Okay, we found that you have all the proper paperwork, so we are able to release this information to you over the phone. You did have the genetics testing done as a child. The results show that you do not have cystic fibrosis. The results also show you are a carrier of the cystic fibrosis gene."

"So what does that mean?" I ask for clarification.

"It means you don't have the disease, but you could pass it on to any children you may have in the future if your significant other was a carrier," she answers, "But that doesn't guarantee your children will have it or even be a carrier. You need a carrier gene from each parent to have the disease," she further explains.

"Even though my mom had it, I don't have it?" I verify.

"Fortunately she didn't pass anything on to you. Again, your father would've had to have been a carrier and both of them would've had to pass the gene on to you," she confirms, probably sensing my anxiety.

I breathe a sigh of relief, feeling as if a weight has been lifted from my shoulders, but at the same time, still bitter my birth mom had to endure it throughout her short lifetime. Then again, I'll have to make sure to be aware of this again if I ever want kids of my own. "Thank you," I rasp.

"You're welcome. Also, since you're over 18 I have to ask, have you found a new general practitioner yet?" she questions.

"No, but I will," I reply. I want to decide where I'm going to live before I figure all that out. In the meantime I'm sure it won't hurt to keep Dr. Mills listed as my doctor. It's not like I have a job right now anyway. In fact I don't even know if I have insurance. "Shit," I mumble under my breath at the realization.

The woman continues, thankfully not hearing my muttered curse. "You're due for a physical, so as soon as you find a doctor. Let us know so we can release your paperwork to them," she reminds me.

"Okay, thank you and have a good day," I tell her, feeling a little bit lighter from her answers already. At the same time I have even more questions, but I'll think about that later.

"Thank you Samantha. You too and if you have any more questions, please let us know. Goodbye," she says.

"Bye," I say just before I click to end the call.

I drop my phone on my nightstand and collapse back on my bed feeling the tension release from my body. I feel like my parents are watching over me right now. I'm so thankful I don't have to go through being tested. I can't imagine having to wait for an answer longer than the hour I suffered through just now. It makes me wonder how my birth mom dealt with knowing she was sick nearly every day of her life. My heart clenches just thinking about her pain.

My phone beeps, alerting me of a text. I glance at the screen and a smile tugs at my lips at the sight of Brady's name on my screen. "Dress warm!"

"Where are we going?" I ask.

The bubbles dance across the screen as I wait for his message. "You'll find out when we get there!"

I grimace at his answer and click an annoyed emoji to send him in response. I don't know if I can handle any more surprises today.

"Cute, but that look will be even cuter and probably work better when I get to see it on you in person." I blush at his text even though he can't see me. The bubbles dance on the screen and he continues, "I'll knock in an hour."

I glance at the clock in surprise. After reading her letter, I became so wrapped up in finding out more information about cystic fibrosis that I didn't realize it was almost lunchtime already. I have to get ready and I have no idea what I'm even going to wear. "Ok. I'll see you soon," I text with a smiley emoji.

I jump up, my whole body tingling with excitement in anticipation of seeing Brady again. I know I just saw him last night, but it feels like so much longer, especially since he was barely here and then gone again.

Chapter 12

I assess myself in the mirror for what feels like the hundredth time with a grimace. I hate this kind of weather. "What the hell are we doing?" I grumble at my reflection. It's about 50 degrees outside and a little cloudy, which for me means it's the kind of weather where I get the chills easily. I want to look good, but warm. I think I've changed my outfit ten times. I'm wearing dark blue skinny jeans, frayed slightly on my right thigh and just below my ass on the left. Then I'm wearing a long-sleeved ivory fitted t-shirt with lace along the hem and neckline and a camel brown-cropped sweater that ties in the front, but I leave it hanging for now. I grimace at my outfit and glance at my phone, wondering if I have time to change again. I groan when a knock at the door gives me my answer.

I rush to the front door and swing it open. I hold back my gasp at the site of Brady smiling down at me. He's in faded jeans with dark brown work boots, a plain navy blue shirt and an olive green bomber jacket. He's wearing a blue baseball hat backwards, his dark brown hair sticking out adorably from underneath. "Wow, you look beautiful," he rasps, making me blush.

"Thank you," I whisper, hoping he means it, but the way his eyes rake over me tell me his words are true, making me blush a deeper shade of crimson.

He points to my feet, "Don't wear anything that you don't want ruined." I raise my eyebrows in question and he continues, "Boots would be best if you have them, but not the dressy ones you girls always wear."

"You girls?" I question, letting my attitude show. He chuckles and shrugs without commenting. I roll my eyes and ask, "Where are we going?" I'm completely clueless as to what our plans might be.

He smirks and his eyes sparkle with mischief, "You'll find out when we get there."

"Really?" I ask, surprised he's still not giving me anything. He laughs and I pinch my lips tightly together and irritably grumble, "Fine."

"It's not that big of a deal, but it's just easier to show you than to tell you," he explains. I offer him a smile, appreciating the small detail. It's not that I mind surprises, but I can't seem to get over my nerves!

"Okay, but will rain boots work? I don't really have anything else. I have hiking boots at home, but..." I trail off.

He nods, "That will work."

I slip on my knee-high rain boots with a leopard design and reach for my coat, hoping it will be warm enough. He takes it from me and helps me slip my arms inside. He gently runs his hands down my arms and then steps away. I turn around and smile shyly up at him as my heart hammers erratically inside my chest, "Thank you."

He grins in response, "Ready?" I nod and he pulls my door open and gestures for me to go first. I press the button for the elevator as he steps up next to me.

"Shit, I forgot my purse!" I exclaim and spin around.

He laughs, "Those words just don't sound right coming out of your sweet mouth." I blush again as he reaches for my hand and pulls me back towards him, "You have your phone and your keys?" I nod my head. "You don't need anything else," he informs me. "I'll take care of you." A lump forms in my throat and goose bumps cover my arms, his words thoroughly warming me. I take a deep breath and open my mouth to argue anyway. He shakes his head and interrupts me before I even begin, "Please?" I attempt to swallow down the lump in my throat to answer him, but right now it's useless. Instead I take another deep breath and nod my head conceding. He grins broadly and clasps my hand even tighter as we step into the elevator.

I quietly savor the warmth of his hand in mine as we ride the elevator down. I breathe slowly, attempting to calm my heartbeat pounding harder by the second. I can't tell what it is, but something about this date feels different. Maybe it's his simple touch, or maybe it's just because we're going out and Cory and Cody aren't with us. I don't know, but whatever it is, it's making me nervous. He gently pulls me along to the small parking lot behind our building and walks up to the passenger side of an old silver Dodge Ram pick-up. "Not really what I thought you'd be driving," I mumble.

He chuckles and admits, "I like it and it's the opposite of what my parents wanted me to drive." He pulls the passenger door open and lets go of my hand, placing both of his hands on my waist, quickly lifting me into the truck. I squeal at his unexpected touch. He smirks as he slowly releases me, "Thought I'd help you out."

I feel my face heat and I murmur, "Um, I can handle it."

"I'm sure you can," he grins and shuts the door. I watch as he jogs around the front of his truck and slides in behind the wheel. He cocks his head to the side, assessing me. "Are you okay?" he asks his voice full of concern. I nod my head and offer him a stiff smile to try to reassure him. He stares into my eyes for what feels like hours and only moments at the same time, but in reality, maybe a minute passes. He eventually turns towards the road in front of him.

He starts the truck and quickly checks his phone at the high alert, but instantly drops it back in the console. I turn to stare out the window as he pulls out of the lot. I watch the town passing by in a blur, wondering what the hell I'm doing. I didn't come here for this. Brady is a distraction I don't need right now. I don't get the chance to think too long, when only a few minutes later, he pulls into a half-full gravel parking lot. Behind it sits a sprawling white building with a black roof and a huge porch that spans the length of the building. "Wow," I mumble. "What is this place?"

"This is my parents' restaurant. We're just stopping for a minute to grab something," he explains with a shrug.

I shakily reach for the door handle, but just as I push the door open he's standing in front of me lifting me out of the truck. I fight a smile as he sets me on my feet and I mumble, "Thanks." I tense as we start walking towards the front door. "Are your parents here?" I ask, surprised my voice isn't trembling like my insides.

He instantly laces his fingers with mine and stops, turning to face me. "If my parents are here, they won't have time to even say hello. There's no reason to be nervous."

"I'm not nervous," I snap too quickly.

He chuckles, "We're going to go through the main dining room and just into the front of the kitchen. I have something there I have to grab and then we'll leave right away. I promise." I nod and gulp over the lump in my throat, gripping his hand tighter. I'm really not comfortable meeting his parents. "I figured I could get in and out fast if you're with me, but would you rather wait for me in my truck?" he asks thoughtfully.

I sigh in resignation, greatly appreciating his offer, but I shake my head. "No, I'll come with you." A huge smile covers his face with my answer, telling me I said the right thing. "Just don't leave me," I add pleading.

He chuckles, "You got it." He leans down and unexpectedly kisses me on the corner of my mouth causing my heart to skip a beat. He tugs on my hand, "Let's go."

I trail along, trying to take everything in as I go. As we approach the wooden steps to the front door, I notice the porch is covered with handmade benches and rocking chairs. Just before we reach the door, it's pushed open from the other side. A tall, thin man with salt and pepper hair, a strong jaw and soft brown eyes smiles at us, "Mr. Williams, it's good to see you, Sir."

"Brady please, Lou," Brady grins and shakes his hand. "We're just grabbing something from the kitchen and we'll be gone," he explains.

He holds the door open for us and I smile politely as we pass, "Thank you."

Brady holds my hand tighter and his pace quickens as soon as we take our first steps inside. The front entrance is covered in white tiles with a large green and black intricate design about every ten feet. I attempt to take in more of the décor, but he barely gives me the chance to observe the thick wooden tables and bar inside before we reach the swinging door of the kitchen. I quickly notice the sliver countertops, high-end stainless steel appliances and white tile floors, with a few staff scurrying around. "Thanks for the help Marco," Brady calls to an older man wearing a white chef's hat and apron.

The man waves with the spatula he's holding, never taking his eyes off the food he's cooking in front of him. "Enjoy!"

Brady slings his free hand through the strap of a black insulated bag, still clutching my hand with his other and grins down at me, "Let's go."

He pushes the other side of the kitchen door and halts with a soft groan before running into an older woman about three inches taller than me. She has dark blonde hair pulled up into a bun on top of her head and hazel eyes focused on Brady. "Brady, I'm so glad you're here. We need your help," she says, sounding slightly frazzled.

"Not today Mom," he replies and my eyes widen in surprise. I can tell she's older than us, but she doesn't look old enough to be Brady's mom. She frowns at him and opens her mouth to argue, but he stops her before she begins. "I have plans today. This is Samantha," he offers, smiling apologetically down at me.

Her frown deepens as her eyes drift to our joined hands, but he pulls me closer in response. "Brady," she begins.

He sighs, "I'll see you later Mom."

She lets out a harsh exhale before turning towards me. She offers me a fake smile, as she quickly looks me over, scrutinizing me. "It's nice to meet you Samantha," she says as the weight of her disapproving eyes holds me in place.

"You too, Mrs. Williams," I reply anxiously, barely getting the words out.

"Let's go," he encourages me again. I jump at the chance, focusing only on getting out the door.

When we reach his truck he lets go of my hand and walks around to the driver's side. I climb in and pull the door shut. I sag against the door feeling defeated as he puts the bag from the kitchen behind my seat. He turns towards me with a sigh, "I'm sorry about that Sam."

I shake my head, "You have nothing to apologize for."

He grimaces, "That's bullshit and you know it." My eyes snap over to him in surprise. "Please let me explain," he begs. I nod my head, but continue to cling to the door. I feel uncomfortable around him for the first time since we met. He groans in frustration and takes his hat off, quickly running his hand through his hair before putting it back on his head. "This is going to make me look like an asshole," he grumbles.

I raise my eyebrows and push him to tell me anyway, "Well?"

He sets his jaw and a look of determination consumes his eyes just before he speaks. "My parents have been pushing me in a certain direction my whole life and I guess I've done what I can to fight it, but at the same time get along with them. Well, mostly," he concedes with a grimace.

"What do you mean?" I question.

"After Jackie, I decided I was going to focus on figuring out what I want and I don't mean in a woman. I mean I wanted to focus on college and what I want to do with my life, whatever that is," he adds sarcastically. "I still haven't completely figured it out. I couldn't deal with the drama of a relationship and figure myself out at the same time. At least I didn't want to," he admits. "I began to only go out with girls who wanted a casual relationship," he winces.

"Oh," I murmur, feeling defeated. I quickly look away from him, feeling like a weight was suddenly crushing my chest.

"Not oh Sam," Brady says as he reaches for my hand and clasps it between both of us. "I haven't dated anyone who really matters in a long time and my parents know that. My mom thought you were just another girl and she hates that side of me. Honestly, I don't blame her." He sighs, "I wanted to tell her differently, but I wasn't sure," he pauses, staring intently at me. "Look, I know it's early for the whole meet the parents thing, but the thing is, I want more than a casual relationship with you."

My insides feel like a hurricane is plowing its way through my body as I rasp a reply, "We barely know each other Brady." I want so badly for his words to be true, but at the same time how can they be and what do they even mean?

"You may be right, but you have to stop saying that," he begs. "Every day I know a little more about you and isn't that what we're trying to do? Get to know each other better?" he questions, but I don't answer. He sighs, "I do know that I never talk about myself with girls I date and after nearly a week with you I want to tell you everything. I sure as hell want to know everything about you! When you're not with me I already miss you and when I'm with you..." he stammers uncomfortably. "You make me smile, Sam."

"You just want my body," I tell him sarcastically, attempting to loosen the hold I feel like he already has on me.

He chuckles and admits, "Well that's a given." I blush, even though I brought his comment on myself. He pauses before he pleads with me, "But you have to know it's so much more than that." He gives my hand a squeeze, "Please tell me I'm not alone here and you feel this intensity like I do?" he implores anxiously.

My breath stops along with my heart as I stare into his eyes, hoping they bleed the truth. I shake my head trying to urge myself to tell him what I'm thinking. His head falls and his body sags in defeat causing me to realize what he thinks my actions mean. "Brady, no, no, that's not...I mean I do feel it, but that's crazy right?"

His head tilts up and he meets my eyes as his grin grows, showing off his dimple. Suddenly his soft, full lips are on mine before I can react and I gasp into his mouth. His hand weaves into my hair, holding my head in place as his tongue pushes in to meet mine. I lean towards him and gently let my hand slide up his chest and curve around his neck, pulling him closer. His kiss goes deeper and I whimper into his mouth just before he groans and pulls away, leaving me breathless. "Sorry, I couldn't help myself," he rasps.

"You better not be sorry for kissing me like that!" I exclaim on a harsh exhale.

He chuckles, "Definitely not. But I do think I'd like a little bit more privacy instead of making out with you in the parking lot of my parents' restaurant.

I blush, "Oh." He just laughs harder and kisses me chastely before leaning back and starting his truck.

I rest back against the seat, no longer clinging to the door. I may not know what I'm doing, but for some reason, I want to do it with Brady by my side, especially if he wants to be there with me.

Chapter 13

Brady parks next to an old red and white barn. I climb out of the truck as I take in my surroundings. We're encircled by trees just beginning to sprout their spring leaves and grassy fields, but I have no idea what's in them. "Wow, I know you said your parents' restaurant was on the edge of town, but I guess I thought it wouldn't be so country." I shrug at my explanation as he chuckles. "I like it though," I admit.

He grins at my simple confession and then begins telling me a little more. "We have about fifteen acres of property behind the restaurant. This barn is pretty close to the center of the property. The house I grew up in is at the end opposite the restaurant." He gestures behind the barn. "I always loved coming out to the barn when I lived here. I felt like I was in another world when I was out here. We never really used it for much of anything, but," he shrugs, "I was very attached to everything out here. When I was a kid and I would get in trouble or if I was mad at my parents or something, I would 'run away' to this barn."

I grin imagining him as a little boy, "Did you run away often?"

He smirks and shrugs in answer. "As I got older, this just became my place to think. My parents and even my sister would know to just leave me be if I was out here."

"It's so peaceful," I reflect, looking around me. "Do you use the fields to farm food for the restaurant?" I ask curiously.

He laughs, "Yeah, we're more like fake farmers. We have some land and a barn, but I know nothing about farming." He admits, "I really love that idea though."

I smile up at him and begin asking another question, "Do..." My stomach grumbles loudly, cutting me off.

He laughs, "I'm not very good at this dating thing. I can't even remember to feed my girl!" My whole body instantly heats with both embarrassment and hesitant excitement at his words. Am I really his girl already? What's crazy is I think I want to be. I don't want him to be just a distraction from finding my birth father. I shouldn't feel this way, but I can't fight it. I sigh and look shyly at the ground.

He turns back to his truck and reaches in, pulling out the insulated bag and a blanket. He walks back over to me and reaches for my hand, "Come on, it will be a little warmer in the barn. We can eat, then maybe take a walk."

"Okay," I agree and follow him towards the barn.

He releases my hand to push the oversized door back. To the right sits furniture and boxes pushed together. To the left sits empty sectioned stalls for animals. "When I saw the barn I imagined at least hay or something," I giggle.

He chuckles as he lays the blanket off to the side by the stalls, just out of the way of the open door. "Yeah, I guess it was an actual farm years ago. I think it was my great grandfather's or something, but he had to sell everything off, including a lot of the land to keep what we still have now." He sits down and unzips his coat. He leans back on his hands, sticking his legs out in front of him and crossing them at the ankles. "Or something like that," he finishes, changing the subject. "Let's eat."

I sit down next to him, curling my legs up beside me and leaning on my right hand. He pulls out two white plastic plates, forks, napkins and two cokes. He holds one out to me, "I hope this is okay?"

I nod as I take if from him. "Thank you, I'm impressed. It looks like you remembered everything."

He laughs and admits, "Only because I had help."

I chuckle, "Well at least you're honest."

"I hope that gives me some points," he teases.

"A lot from me," I answer him truthfully. He grins broadly, causing my heart to flip and the butterflies to begin churning in my stomach. I clear my throat and readjust, attempting to peak into the bag to shake away my nerves. "Any actual food in there?"

He laughs and begins pulling containers out of the bag, "We have grilled chicken with roasted peppers and mozzarella on French bread, turkey club on a croissant, Caesar salad, homemade coleslaw, fruit salad and some fresh brownies, mmm." He licks his lips, making me want to kiss him, but I take a deep breath and focus on the food instead.

"The chicken sounds delicious," I answer shyly.

"Aw that's the one I wanted," he frowns.

"You can have it then. I'm not picky," I stammer.

His lips twitch in amusement, "Well thank you, but since I didn't know what you'd want, there's two of everything, so we're good." I glare at him as he puts a sandwich on my plate along with a little of each salad, but that just makes him burst out laughing. "I was right, that look is much cuter in person," he smirks.

I roll my eyes and pick up the sandwich, taking a small bite. The sweet and savory flavors seem to burst on my tongue. "Oh my God this is so good," I rave as I savor my first bite and quickly shovel more into my mouth. "What kind of dressing is on here?" I ask curiously.

Brady laughs, "Slow down or I'm really going to feel like shit for waiting too long to feed you." I blush and glare up at him. "I'm just kidding Sam, but I do feel bad. Next time tell me when you're hungry."

"Okay," I agree. "But seriously what is this?" I repeat.

He shrugs, "It's a homemade dressing. I think it's one of our family recipes," he answers like it's no big deal.

After a few bites of the salads, Brady peers at me from under his long eyelashes, pushing his food around on his plate. "So...can I ask why you moved here?" My stomach drops and I set my fork down slowly releasing my breath. "If you're not ready to tell me yet, that's okay. I just want you to know you can talk to me. And I really do want to know," he admits.

I nod my head in understanding as so many explanations run through my head. Brady covers my hand with his waiting patiently, but expecting nothing. I soak in the simple comforting warmth of his touch as I take another deep breath before I turn my head, seeking out his gaze. "I already told you about my parents, but what I didn't tell you is that they adopted me when I was a baby." His eyes widen in surprise and I quickly continue before I lose the nerve. "It's okay, I've always known and I love my parents more than anything. My mom and dad always supported me in finding my birth parents if I wanted. I had started really thinking about it the summer I graduated from high school, but it was my last summer at home before college," I shrug. "Anyway," I gulp, "after they died, I just wasn't ready...until now." I slowly inhale another deep breath and release it. "I'm sorry, this is hard to talk about," I confess quietly.

"You don't have to tell me anything you don't want to, but I would really like to know," he tells me in encouragement.

I look down at our joined hands as he starts to trace a simple pattern on my hand and wrist. I watch the mindless movements and just start talking not even knowing what I'm about to say. "I guess I was kind of living in a gray area since I lost my mom and dad. I've been surviving and just doing what was expected of me to make it through the day. Ironically, Paul cheating on me was probably a good thing," I admit with a grimace. "It's what pushed me over the edge and kind of made me completely determined to force a change. I want to be me again," I declare sitting up a little straighter. "I guess I decided that finding out about my family history is something I need to do to help me get there."

"Did you find them?" he asks cautiously, placing his free hand on my knee in support.

I cringe, not really knowing how to answer that question. "Yes and no. My birth mother died not too long ago," my voice cracks at the end, giving away my emotions.

"I'm so sorry Sam," Brady tells me as he gently gathers me into his arms. I duck my head and willingly fall into him, burying my face in his chest. I inhale his masculine scent, mixed with light cologne, reveling in the safety of his embrace. He rubs the back of my head and his other hand finds its way under my coat to my back. "You never got to meet her," he states, knowing it's the truth.

I shake my head, "No, but she left me letters."

"What?" he asks, pulling away to look into my eyes.

I sigh, "She wrote me a letter every year on my birthday until I turned 18. I just got them though, since it was a closed adoption and I didn't search for her right away. I haven't read all of them yet, but she left me information on my birth father in the last one. He lives close to here."

"Really? Have you contacted him?" he asks. I shake my head and he hesitantly asks, "Do you want to?"

I laugh humorlessly and admit, "Yeah, I'm just scared. There's so much more to it. I have so many questions and he has a family and a life that has nothing to do with me."

"What can I do?" he questions. "I want to help you."

I shrug, "I don't really know yet. I guess just being here for me like this is perfect for now," I confess quietly. I don't want to do this alone, I admit to myself.

He pulls me a little tighter and kisses the top of my head sweetly. "Well that's good because right here is exactly where I'll be."

The butterflies take flight in my stomach and climb up my throat. I struggle just to whisper, "Thank you."

"Wait a minute, is he from here in Chance? This is a really small town. I might know him," he says in realization. "Do you know his name?"

I flinch, "Um, I'm not, I mean I do, but I don't, I can't, um...I'm just not ready to deal with it yet Brady," I stammer. "If you know him, it will make everything so real before I have time to process it. I'm not there yet!" I exclaim, feeling like it's suddenly hard to breathe.

"Relax Sam, it's okay. I was just asking. You can tell me when you're ready. In the meantime we can concentrate on figuring each other out," he suggests.

It takes me a minute to register his words, but when I do I breathe a sigh of relief. I just want to forget about all of it for now. "I like that idea," I murmur as my whole body relaxes into his. I grasp the lifeline he's throwing me and grin up at him. The intense, yet soft look in his eyes sends a jolt through my heart. I wrap my hand around the back of his neck and pull him to me, pressing my lips to his without giving him a chance to say another word. I gently nip his bottom lip and push my tongue in to find his the moment his lips part. His tongue greedily meets mine and I moan into his mouth, leaning further into him. I slide my fingers up into his hair, shoving his hat off in the process, making him chuckle lightly. He attempts to slow our kiss, but I'm not ready to stop. I push my body closer to him and he groans as he gently pulls back.

"Sam," he rasps, "Wait," he pleads out of breath.

I sigh and fall away from him in defeat. My whole body feels like it's on fire with embarrassment. "I'm sorry," I mumble.

He chuckles, "Please don't be. I really fucking enjoyed that," he gasps.

I tilt my head slightly and look at him from under the protective veil of my hair hanging down in front of me. "Then why'd you stop me?" I whisper.

He bites his bottom lip, his blue eyes darkening every second. "You're driving me crazy!" he groans. "I'm going to take this farther than we're ready for if we keep going like that," he admits making me feel sexy and I love it.

I tuck my hair behind my ear so I can see him better. I smirk and ask playfully, "Why is that such a bad thing?"

He groans again, his head falling back until he's staring at the ceiling before dropping it back down to look at me. "Like I just said, you're killing me!" I try to fight my smile, but in seconds I'm grinning at him like a fool. "I know what I want Sam. I guess it could be just insane chemistry, but I don't believe that and I don't think you do either. I want to prove I'm right," he smirks. I roll my eyes in response and he laughs. "Seriously though Sam, for the first time I want whatever this is to be more. Once I start touching you, I'm afraid I won't be able to stop and something is telling me I *need* to do this right with you."

My heart beats erratically in my chest and my body grows warm. "This is crazy. It hasn't even been a week," I remind him again trying to be a voice of reason.

Although I can admit to myself that my heart is telling me he's right. At least I want him to be.

"I am a little crazy," he grins playfully, "but you moved in a week ago tomorrow." He softly presses his lips to mine and pulls away before I have a chance to move closer. "Eat some more of your lunch, you barely ate anything," he encourages me.

"That's a weak attempt to change the subject," I joke.

He laughs and readjusts his legs, "Eat, then we'll go for a walk."

I giggle and shake my head as I take another bite of the coleslaw, fighting back another appreciative groan.

Chapter 14

We step outside the barn onto the soft moist dirt. It's not mud, but I don't think it would take much rain or water to make it that way, I think to myself as my rain boots sink slightly into the ground. No more snow covers the ground and I hope it stays that way. The fields around us appear to be a combination of brown and green grasses with dirt roads leading from the barn in three different directions. Straight ahead is the road we drove in on, but Brady nods his head to the right, "Let's go this way."

"Okay," I agree taking a step towards him. He reaches for my hand and laces our fingers together, shooting heat up my arm and into the rest of my body, causing me to pause slightly. He smiles softly and gives my hand a gentle tug. I stutter step into him and reach for his forearm for support.

He chuckles and apologizes with false remorse, "Sorry."

I roll my eyes and take a deep breath of the fresh air. "It smells like spring," I grin.

He smirks, "What's spring smell like?"

I shake my head, "I don't know. I guess it smells like everything is new or starting over again. The air smells clean and I can smell the start of the trees blooming." I smile to myself. I love the idea of starting over, just like I'm trying to do now.

Brady cocks his head slightly, looking at me thoughtfully with a soft smile. My heart stutters in my chest and I gulp down the growing lump in my throat. I tear my gaze away from his eyes that appear slightly brighter than the blue sky behind him. How can someone be so beautiful? I laugh softly at my thoughts. I wonder what he would think of me calling him beautiful? "What's so funny?" he asks curiously.

I smirk, "Nothing." His eyes narrow like he's trying to read me, so I change the subject. "So where are we going?"

He shrugs, "There's a small stream on the edge of this end of the property. After all the snow melts or right after a good rain is when it's at its widest."

"Are you and your sister close?" I ask.

"I guess. We played together growing up, but I'll be honest, she probably thought I was a pain in the ass. I was always teasing her," he admits, laughing softly. "I would do anything for her though."

"As you should," I declare.

"So who are you close to Samantha?" he asks casually, as he glances at me out of the corners of his eyes.

I laugh humorlessly, thinking how I probably would've answered that so differently not that long ago. Although, I feel like I have a more honest answer now than I would have before. "Well I guess my cousins. I'm actually really close to one of my cousins who's just a year older than me. I was always really close to my mom too. I would talk to her about everything," I smile as I fondly remember our girl talks in my room or hers.

Brady gives my hand a soft squeeze, "It sounds like your mom was pretty amazing."

"She was," I admit proudly. Brady stops and turns towards me. He slowly brings his hand towards my cheek and gently wipes away a tear I didn't know escaped. "Sorry," I murmur and begin turning away from him.

He stops me, reaching for my arm and grasping me behind my elbow, spinning me towards him. "Don't be sorry. That's one of the things I like about you. I can see how much you love your family, but I also see how strong you are to be here at all," he confesses, warming my heart. I gulp and quickly look away.

Brady's phone buzzes with a text, pulling his attention away from me. He drops his hand and reaches for it. I watch as he glances as the screen and clears the message without responding. Another pops up while it's still in his hand and he grips his phone tighter, quickly clearing the message again. When his phone buzzes for a third time I tell him, "I don't expect you to ignore your phone when you're with me. I'm not that girl," I insist. "If you need to answer them, it's okay."

He shakes his head, "It's not important." His phone buzzes again and he turns it off without even looking, quickly stuffing it in his coat pocket. He grasps my hand and gives me a tight smile, "Come on, I want to show you something."

My body feels tight as I walk along silently beside him on the dirt road. I can't help but wonder if it was Jackie texting him. If it was I guess I can be thankful he ignored her, but...then why do I feel so anxious? "Brady," I start.

He turns to look at me and his blue eyes instantly begin pleading, "Sam, don't. Don't doubt this. Let's just have fun today. Nothing else is important."

"Was that Jackie?" I ask simply.

He flinches, but answers honestly, "Yeah, but I'm not answering her. It's not important. You are," he insists.

I sigh and stop walking again. I close my eyes when I respond, "Go ahead and answer her. You guys are friends. She'll probably just blow up your phone." I don't want to be the controlling, jealous girlfriend. Then again, I'm not his girlfriend. I hold in my groan and open my eyes, focusing on him. "I don't want to change who you are Brady," I tell him.

He reaches with his free hand to gently stroke my cheek. I can't help but lean into his touch as he searches my face for answers. Eventually he tips his head towards me and lightly brushes his lips against mine. He pushes into me a little more, his lips feeling so soft and full as he moves over me, keeping our kiss sweet and sensual. I whimper against his mouth and he pulls back with a dimpled grin before pressing his lips to mine one more time. "I could do that all day," he mumbles, before straightening up, still holding my gaze. "I'll text her back so she'll hopefully leave me alone," he informs me.

He pulls his phone out and turns to stand next to me. He holds his phone out in front of both of us so I can see what he writes. "I'm out with my girlfriend. Can't help. Find someone else." He turns his phone off and puts it back in his pocket.

"Girlfriend?" I question shocked, but hopeful.

"Hell yes! If you haven't already figured it out, I'm staking my claim right now while I have the chance. I don't want you seeing anyone else," he declares.

I giggle, "I wasn't planning on it. In fact I wasn't planning on any of this."

"Me?" he questions. He smirks, "Ah, but you can't resist me right?"

I roll my eyes, "Why don't we test that theory?"

He chuckles and throws his arm over my shoulders. He turns right and guides me down a dirt path, "Well I've got the perfect place to do that."

I laugh, "I should probably be nervous hearing that. You are taking me to an isolated place in the middle of a field."

He chuckles, "Actually, it's even better, it's in the woods." My eyes widen and he amends, "Well sort of. The stream is just beyond the tree line at the edge of this field, but don't worry. I wouldn't let anything happen to you."

"I can take care of myself," I insist.

He smirks, "I'm sure you can." My feet start to feel like they're sticking in the ground a little, making them harder to pick up. After walking in silence for a few minutes my whole body finally begins to relax again. He breaks the silence asking, "Are you okay?"

I nod and smile up at him, "I'm good."

Brady stops and states, "I can hear it, listen."

I close my eyes to better hear the soft sounds of water flowing gently over rocks. I smile to myself as I lean back slightly into Brady. He pulls me a little closer and takes a deep breath before kissing me on the top of my head like my dad used to do. I sag into his chest a little deeper, enjoying the feeling more than I should so soon, but I don't care. After a moment, I straighten up and open my eyes. "I want to see it," I tell him.

He puts both hands on my shoulders and leads me out of the field to the narrow tree line. I immediately spot the stream through the trees. We walk past the trees and I stare down at the small stream, which appears to only be about five or six feet wide. "Here it is," he announces. He wraps both arms around my waist and pulls me into his chest.

"It's smaller than I thought it would be," I tell him as I lean back against him.

"That's not something a guy ever wants to hear," he mumbles. My body tenses slightly and I feel myself blush. He clears his throat and nods to the stream in front of us. "It's actually a little wider about half a mile down, but my sister and I stayed around this area mostly. I used to catch a lot of frogs around here. Then I'd bring them home and give them to my mom," he chuckles. "I learned pretty quick she didn't like that very much." I laugh and he pulls me tighter. I hear laughter in his voice when he continues, "So I thought I'd try that on Becca. Of course she reacted the opposite of how I wanted her to. She was excited and decided I could help her build a frog farm out here." He chuckles, "The only problem was the frogs didn't like it too much and every single one would be gone when we came back."

"It sounds like Becca was a pretty good sister. You try to torture her and end up helping her instead," I smile at the thought.

He laughs, his breath warming my cheek, "Yeah, but I got her to dig up worms and go fishing with me too, so it all worked out." The rumble of his voice sends chills down my spine, "Are you cold?" he asks.

I nod, "Yeah, maybe a little."

"Then I have one more thing to show you before we head back." He kisses my cheek just below my ear warming my face and clogging my throat with butterflies. Then he lets his left hand drop to his side as he gives me a gentle tug towards the trees. "Come on," he encourages, sounding like an excited little kid.

"Where are we going?" I ask, feeling giddy from his eagerness.

"Just over here," he informs me as we walk quickly along the trees. He stops suddenly and I glance up at him in confusion. He grins broadly as his blue eyes glimmer with excitement, causing my heart to flip flop down to my stomach and bounce right back up again. I have to stop myself from leaning in and licking his deep dimple. "Look up," he demands.

I mentally shake myself out of my Brady-induced stupor and look up into the trees. My eyes widen in surprise at the sight of a small tree house built up above, supported between two trees. "Wow! I always wanted one of those," I confess. He grins proudly. I request, "Can we please go in?"

He nods, "Of course." He holds his arm out, gesturing for me to go up the ladder hanging down in the middle, "It's safe. I promise."

"I'll take your word for it," I mumble as I step on the bottom wrung. I tease, "No checking out my ass."

He chuckles, "No promises."

I climb up to the top and through the small hatch. I sit down on a red woven rug partially covering the wood floor and scoot out of the way so he can come up as well. I laugh as his broad shoulders come into view and he twists slightly before pulling himself up. "It looks like you might need to cut a bigger door," I laugh. "Is this really going to hold both of us?"

He nods, "Yeah, my mom and dad used to come up here with us sometimes. If it can hold my whole family, it can definitely hold the two of us."

I feel his eyes on me as I look around the small cozy space. I spot a small wooden bookshelf with a few old books and toys, a couple wooden chairs and a long wooden bench. I reach for a brown-haired doll with a yellow and white dress covered in medical tape, making me laugh. "What is this?"

He laughs, "That's Becca's old doll. I used to torture it to piss her off, but she'd just tape it back together."

I turn, noticing a toy box in the corner behind me and ask, "What's in there?"

"Blankets and a couple games," he informs me.

"Games?" I ask as I scoot back to raise the lid. I spot a couple decks of cards, an Uno deck, then underneath I find Clue, Sorry, Star Wars Monopoly and Battleship. "These are awesome!" I declare. "I used to love these games. I haven't played any of them since I was a kid." I turn to look at Brady and his appreciative smile makes me blush. I turn back towards the toy box adding, "Although I admit I've never played the Star Wars version of Monopoly."

"You've seen Star Wars though right?" he questions. I purse my lips, but don't answer. "You're kidding?" he asks in shock.

"Hmm?" I question, playing dumb.

He groans, "You've never seen the Star Wars movies?" I shrug and he clutches his chest as if in pain. "Star Wars films are classics," he states.

"I saw one, but I don't know which one," I confess. "I was never really into it."

His eyebrows shoot up in surprise. "You're going to watch all of them with me," he informs me.

"I am?" I question.

He nods, "Yeah, I'll admit when I was younger I was obsessed with them. Becca and I both were."

"My boyfriend is a Star Wars geek?" I tease, testing out the word.

Something passes through his eyes with my words. "Watch it," he warns as he swiftly reaches across me, gripping my waist tightly. I squeal as he squeezes. "I already know you're ticklish," he reminds me playfully and squeezes again. I hold my breath and attempt to squirm away, but he quickly pins me to the floor with his hips, holding both of my hands in one of his. "I think I already told you, I'll win this kind of argument every time," he reminds me breathlessly. I exhale and try to catch my own breath as my heartbeat picks up and pounds erratically inside my chest. He stares intently into my eyes, his blue eyes beginning to bleed a darker blue. He states softly, "You said boyfriend."

I attempt to gulp down the growing lump in my throat. Eventually I give up and rasp around it, "I was just testing it out." He chuckles and I smirk, "I don't think it's going to work for me."

His eyes flash and he presses his mouth firmly to mine, pushing his tongue in to play with mine. He turns his head pushing the kiss deeper. I moan into his mouth and try to get closer, but he still has me pinned. He pulls back and I whimper at the loss of his lips. He grumbles, "Are you sure about that?" I attempt to reach his mouth again, but he holds me still and I glare at him in frustration. "I've never wanted anyone so much, just say your mine," he pleads.

My breath catches in my throat and I cautiously admit, "Crazy chemistry or something more I don't know, but I want you too." I try to push for him, but he doesn't budge, his eyes pushing for more. I add hoarsely, "I'm yours Brady."

He groans as he releases my hands and weaves those fingers into my hair, his other fingers digging into my hip. He kisses me again, my whole body igniting from the touch of his lips. My now free hands push his hat off his head again so I can run my fingers through his soft strands. Then I let my hands run down his thick neck and over his broad shoulders, down his hard muscled arms and back up again. His hand at my hip slips underneath my coat and shirt until it finds my tender heated skin. I attempt to do the same and his hand shoots out to stop me. "Too much," he groans as he rips his mouth away.

"Brady," I groan in frustration. "I'm not a virgin," I inform him.

He looks away from me, but not before I see his eyes flash as a strange look passes over his face. "Not here and not now," he insists as he turns back to me. "Besides the fact it's too cold and you'll freeze, it's too soon. I told you I want to do this right with you and I mean it."

I flush feeling overwhelmed and embarrassed. I mumble my apology as I attempt to push him away, "Sorry."

"Don't fucking apologize!" he grits out. He takes a deep breath, "You're driving me crazy. I just need to slow down." I don't say anything and he sweetly begs, "Please. You're not like anyone I've ever met and I want to treat you that way."

I gasp at his words, seeing the sincerity in his eyes. I take a deep breath and barely nod my head. "Okay," I consent softly.

He brushes his thumb over my bottom lip and murmurs, "You're so beautiful." He kisses the corner of my mouth and drops his head into the crook of my neck, taking a deep breath of his own.

I run my fingers through his hair again and I suggest, "Well, how about we go back to your place and you can explain the first Star Wars movie while you force me to watch it."

He chuckles and lifts his head, "Cody will be there."

I shrug and push my bottom lip out in a pout. "Maybe that's a good thing with your stupid rules."

He laughs and nips at my bottom lip before he kisses me sweetly. "Maybe you're right."

Chapter 15

I notice the similarities in our apartments right away. Theirs has the same layout as ours, except everything is flipped. The living room is on my left when I walk in while the small kitchen is on my right. The kitchen looks nearly the same with white appliances, a blue-gray Formica countertop and whitewashed cabinets. The small table with a curved booth that I like so much is built-in to the corner of the kitchen just like ours. Even the tile floors look the same. The short hallway leads to the bathroom at the end with Cody's room on the right and Brady's on the left, backing up to my room. I grimace as my thoughts bring me back to my first night here, when Cory joked about not bringing girls back here so I wouldn't have to hear it. I don't think I could handle it if I ever heard Brady in here with anyone. I involuntarily shudder at the thought. "Are you cold?" he asks, his voice laced with concern.

I take a deep breath and swallow the lump in my throat before I answer without looking at him, "I'm okay."

I feel him staring at me as we both stand quietly while I pretend to be enamored with looking around at the hallway's white walls, adorned with a lone movie poster next to the thermostat from one of the Fast and Furious movies. The poster has Vin Diesel and Paul Walker along with their cars and some girl in a yellow bikini top and blue jean daisy dukes. Brady gestures to the poster apologetically, "Cody's."

I smirk and nod my head, "Sure."

He chuckles and pushes his bedroom door further open. By the looks of his room he's telling the truth about the poster, unless he just didn't want it in his room. Of course he has the white walls like everywhere else in this building, but he has a Field of Dreams movie poster and a poster of what appears to be every MLB team logo. "Do you have a favorite team?" I ask him, pointing to the poster.

He shakes his head, "I guess I like the Brewers, but I tend to like watching certain players more than anything. Then sometimes there's a team that's incredible to watch playing together. I just like watching anything baseball," he admits timidly, with a shrug.

I smile at his response and continue to take in everything in his room. His bed is right to my left as I walk in the door. It's like mine with just the box spring and mattress, but with a black and white pinstriped comforter and slate gray pillows. A small mahogany nightstand sits next to the bed with nothing but a lamp, a small speaker and a few charging cords. A matching dresser sits against the wall to the left that backs up to my room with the closet on the wall to the right. A dark wood desk with drawers down the right side lies across the room under a window covered with the same plastic white blinds. I walk across the room and glance outside at his view. I chuckle at a similar view of the black rooftop of the smaller red brick building next door as well as the garden and walkway down below. His desk appears to have some kind of order with cups filled with pens, pencils and other desk supplies, a large pile of books and a separate pile of folders and notebooks. His laptop rests on top with the ends of a couple charge cords banded together through a hole in the back. He has a tall black bookshelf lined with books on the bottom two shelves while the top three shelves have a few pictures and some baseball paraphernalia.

I turn towards the doorway to ask him a question, but as soon as I meet his eyes, the words exit my thoughts. With my mouth agape, I stare at him leaning against his doorframe watching me with a small smile. He took his jacket off. His arms are crossed over his chest causing his biceps to bulge and my throat to go dry. My eyes drift up to his strong jaw showing just a hint of his dimple. I try to calm my erratically beating heart as I meet his gaze, his blue eyes appearing even brighter with his navy shirt. "So do I pass inspection?" he smirks.

"What?" I ask confused. I give my head a slight shake to pull out of the obvious fog I'm in as I blatantly ogle him.

He grins and gestures to our surroundings, "My apartment, my room? Do you approve?" he jokes.

I smile and tease, "I don't know. What will happen if I open your closet? Will piles of dirty clothes fall out?"

He chuckles, "Not today."

I laugh along with him and walk up to his bookshelf to look at his pictures. One is of a baseball team in red and white uniforms. I pick it up to see if I can find him. "Is this from high school?" I question.

He steps up behind me softly pressing his front to my back. The heat from his body and his musky scent surround me. I struggle to maintain my steady breathing, longing to soak him in. He rests his left hand on my hip and uses his right to point to himself in the back row of the picture, "There I am. That was the last game of my senior year."

"You were still pretty cute back in high school," I murmur.

He chuckles, "I'm just cute?" I feel my face turning pink as I set the picture down. I stay quiet and let him explain the different pictures instead of asking questions. I don't think I can get the words out right now anyway. He points to a picture of him with two of his teammates. "That's Cody and me with our friend Max."

I turn my head slightly to try to catch his eyes and maybe read what he's thinking. I recognize Cody, but what bothers me is his tone of voice as he mentions Max. It sounds like pain, but I can't be sure. His eyes roam his bookshelves, skipping over another picture of the three of them in the stands of a Brewers game, before moving swiftly on to a picture of him with both Cody and Cory, looking very young. Whatever I saw quickly disappears as he clears his throat and informs me, "We were probably 12 in this one." I let it go for now, but my brain is already working overtime trying to figure out why.

The last picture is a relatively recent one of him and his sister Becca. "You two look close here?"

He grins admiringly at the picture, his shoulders visibly relaxing as he replies, "Mostly." I laugh and he twists me around to face him. He reaches up and gently runs his finger over my lower lip, "You have a really great laugh."

I blush, but hold his gaze steady, "Thank you." I don't think I've ever blushed as much as I do around him.

He tips his head down as his hand slides along my jaw and cups the back of my neck, pulling me in close. All the air leaves my lungs at the touch of his velvety lips. I push up onto my tiptoes to get a little closer to him. I take a deep breath, inhaling nothing but his scent as he pushes into me, moving over my lips in a slow, sensual rhythm. He parts my lips with his tongue, but just as the tips of our tongues meet and I can really taste him, a loud greeting startles us and breaks us apart, "Hi Sam! You got so bored on your date with Brady, you came back to see me," Cody bellows with an enormous grin covering his face.

I drop back on my heels pulling further away from Brady's lips and turn my head to look at Cody standing in the doorway. I blush and giggle self-consciously, "Hi Cody."

Brady groans, "What do you want Cody?"

Cody chuckles and ignores him. He looks at me and asks, "What are you guys up to the rest of the night?"

I shrug and fight a smile when I reply, "I guess we're watching some stupid movie I need explained to me."

Brady smirks and raises his eyebrows as if to ask, "Really?"

"What movie?" Cody asks.

Brady answers for me, "She's never seen Star Wars."

Cody gasps dramatically, "What? That's just wrong!"

I roll my eyes and ask, "Want to watch with us?"

Cody grins wide, "Watch a movie with you? Like a date? Absolutely!"

Brady turns his head slightly towards the doorway, catching Cody's eyes and comments, "No hitting on my girlfriend asshole." The butterflies go crazy in my stomach hearing Brady call me his girlfriend to Cody. I don't remember having this feeling with Paul, or anyone else for that matter.

Cody's mouth drops slightly open before his lips turn up in a slow smile, "Well all right then. I'm still going to watch with you," he adds. "I need a break before I go out later."

Brady kisses my lips one more time before reluctantly releasing me completely. He asks, "Would you like some popcorn and something to drink?"

I nod my head and smile up at him, "Sure, a water or something would be great. Thank you."

He turns and purposely bumps into Cody as I follow him out of his room. "Hey," Cody warns, but quickly turns to me without waiting for a response.   He throws his arm around my shoulders and guides me to the black leather coach, "Come sit with me while Brady gets us snacks."

"I never said I was getting you anything," Brady calls from the kitchen.

Cody ignores him and pulls me down on the couch next to him. He casually asks, "What did you guys do today?"

I shrug and answer vaguely, "Hung out, ate, talked."

His eyes widen and he informs me, "You're already sounding like Brady. Do you have any real answers?"

I laugh, "He just packed up some food and showed me around his family's property. We had fun," I answer honestly. His eyes widen further and I feel the need to elaborate. I uncomfortably ramble, "We picked up food at the restaurant and then he showed me the fields, the old barn, the creek and the old tree house you guys used to play in."

Cody appears momentarily stunned before he questions, "He brought you to the tree house?" He turns to Brady as he enters the room, "You've never brought a girl that we're not related to, to our tree house!"

Brady shrugs as he sits down on my other side. "Never wanted to," he mumbles. My heart bounces up to my throat at Cody's obvious surprise. Does that mean today really meant something to Brady? I glance at Brady out of the corners of my eyes and watch as he sets a large bowl of popcorn and three bottles of water down on the coffee table in front of him. He leans back and gently tugs me so I fall into his side and away from Cody. He reaches for the remote and moves through a few different screens before he clicks on Star Wars: Episode One.

I relax and lean back into him, trying to turn my focus on the TV. As soon as it starts I ask, "Wait, this can't be the first one can it?"

They both groan at my question. A knock at the door, stops them from answering as Cody yells, "Come in!"

The door swings open and Cory walks in with black leggings and a long dark green V-neck sweater. "Hi guys!" she greets us as she walks over and flops down in the black leather recliner next to the couch with an exaggerated groan. "Star Wars?" she moans. "It's always either Star Wars or baseball movies over here I swear! Don't you guys ever watch any other movies?" Neither of them bothers answering her. She turns her head towards the three of us on the couch and her grin grows when her eyes fall on Brady and me. "I guess you two had fun today?" she asks giddily.

I blush and nod with a small smile, "We did."

"Definitely," Brady agrees and leans down to kiss the corner of my mouth. I feel my face turn a deeper shade of red as both Cory and I smile a little wider.

"He threatened me," Cody whines, making all of us laugh. He looks pointedly at Cory, "And showed her the tree house."

Cory's eyes widen and her smile grows. I feel myself blush again, but I'm honestly not quite sure why. Brady tugs me impossibly closer and grumbles, "Can we just watch the movie?"

Cody and Cory laugh as we all turn our focus to the huge flat screen in front of us. I declare, "I think this TV is like three times the size of ours."

"Damn straight," Cody agrees.

"That's why we watch movies and sports here," Brady informs me.

"No chick flicks on this screen," Cody warns.

"But I had my heart set on it," I whine, holding back my smile. Brady laughs into my neck, giving me chills up and down my spine. I take a deep breath, attempting to calm my hormones and settle even further back into him. I don't even care what we're watching. I just want to enjoy the warmth of Brady's arms.

Chapter 16

June 12th (your 6th Birthday)
To My Beautiful Baby Girl,
Happy Birthday to you!! You're six today. I'm having a hard time with the fact that it has been six years already. I really wish I knew what you looked like and what you're like. I want to know if you're at all like me or maybe you're more like him. I don't know if I'll ever have any more kids. I would have so much to worry about if I did. I don't think I can handle that. In fact I probably shouldn't have had you, but it's too late for that now. It's not like I planned it, but you came anyway. I'm assuming you're with a good family. They told me your new parents couldn't have kids, but really wanted them. I assumed that meant they would love you. I may not have been ready for you, but I did love you.

I'm still dating the same man and living in the same town, except I moved in with him now. It's a definite record for me. I'm not sure if we'll last though. I've pushed him away before, but tonight he looked as if I shoved him off a cliff. We went out to a party earlier and since it's your birthday, I drank to you like I do every year on your birthday. He started asking questions I never answered before, but I decided it was time. I finally told him about you. I don't know where he is now or if he'll come home tonight, but I seem to always find myself in the same place because of you. I'm sitting here waiting, hoping and celebrating you alone again. Cheers.
Catherine Schepp
P.S. I'm so sorry...

I finish the letter and drop it into my lap with my mouth hanging open. I feel queasy and I'm struggling to breathe. My heart feels as if it's weighing down my whole chest from unexpectedly getting punched in the stomach. I'm honestly not quite sure what to do with this letter. It may be short, but it feels bitter and filled with resentment. I almost wish I never read this one at all.

I stand robotically from the couch at the sound of a knock on the door, quickly shuffling my feet. I pull the door open without checking to see whom it is. I find a sexy smiling Brady leaning against the doorjamb. At the sight of me his face instantly falls and he stands tall. He steps in front of me, his blue eyes filled with concern. "What's wrong? Are you alright?" he questions frantically. He reaches for my face and tenderly wipes away the tears I didn't realize had fallen.

I sigh in defeat and whimper, "I'm fine."

He steps into my apartment and envelopes me in his arms, "I call bullshit," he whispers. I release a quiet sob into his chest as he walks me backwards and closes the door behind him. He lifts me, just barely raising my feet off the ground and backs me up to the couch. He turns and lowers himself into the corner and swiftly pulls me into his lap. I attempt to hold back another sob as I try to stifle the continuous stab of pain. I don't even know why I'm crying. I guess I always knew she didn't want me or she would've never given me up in the first place. It doesn't make being rejected hurt any less.

"What is this?" Brady questions as he tries to pry the letter I didn't realize I was still holding out of my hand. "What's wrong?"

I shake my head and fist the letter to my chest. "Its...It's just...It's just a letter...one of the letters from my birth mom," I stammer.

His eyes soften and he cups my cheek with his hand. "Talk to me," he simply encourages me. "Please," he begs. "I don't like seeing you like this," he admits.

I meet his gentle gaze with a sigh, "I guess until this one, her letters have mostly asked questions about what I might look like or what kind of things I was interested in or what my family might be like. It's almost like she was wondering on paper who I might be. She would also tell me a little bit about her, but..." I trail off and attempt to gulp down the burning lump in my throat. His brow draws together apprehensively as he runs his hand gently up and down my spine. He slides his other hand along my jaw, then softly over my neck before continuing down my arm until he holds my hand in his. He remains quiet, patiently waiting as I build up my courage to talk about the letter I'm still clutching in my free hand.

I take another deep breath before something in his eyes pushes me to continue, "I guess in this one I hear her underlying resentment that I exist." His jaw twitches and his hand stalls momentarily as it flexes against my back. I shrug, "I always knew I was a mistake or she would've never given me up for adoption. She didn't come right out and say it, but close enough. I guess she had told her boyfriend about me and I don't think he took it very well. I could practically smell the alcohol coming off the letter with each word she wrote. Then even though her words were so hurtful, I don't feel like I really have a right to be upset about it because she's not even alive to defend herself." I laugh humorlessly, "Is that messed up?"

He shakes his head, "No Sam. That just proves what a good heart you have."

"I don't know where the hell I got it from," I grumble sarcastically.

He chuckles lightly, "And the fact that you can even joke about it shows me what a good person you are. The way you talk about your parents, you probably got it from them."

A soft smile covers my face at the thought of my mom and dad causing me to feel a little less stressed about this letter. "I think you might be right," I murmur loving that they gave me something wonderful.

I exhale slowly, attempting to breathe out some of the tension in my body before letting myself fall into his chest. He lets go of my hand and wraps both arms around me. "You should get used to that," he teases, "I'm always right."

I try to pinch his stomach, but his abdominals are so tight I can barely get any skin. He still pretends to flinch for my sake. "That's not fair," I complain. I hold him a little tighter and listen to the soothing beat of his heart. "Thank you," I mumble.

He pulls back slightly to see my face and I tilt my head up to meet his gaze. "What are you thanking me for?"

I shrug, "I just...I always wonder what I got from my birth parents and what I got from my mom and dad. I like having a piece of my mom and dad that's not just one of my memories, but a part of me, a part of who I am. Does that make sense?"

He smiles reassuringly, "Yeah, it makes perfect sense." He tilts his head to the side and proposes hesitantly, "You know if you want someone to be here with you when you read the letters, I'd like to be that person." My eyes widen and he talks a little faster to get everything out before I speak. "You don't need to show me any of the letters or read anything to me, or even tell me anything. I just want to be here in case you want someone to talk to or just to hold you in support if you want." He sighs and adds, "I want you to know you don't have to be alone in this, or anything else."

Goosebumps instantly cover my whole body as butterflies take over my insides with his offer. I open my mouth and barely squeak out, "Thank you." I don't feel like those simple words do justice to what I'm feeling, but they're all I have. I don't think he realizes what his offer means to me and I can't help but feel overwhelmed. My whole body aches from the inside out.

He reaches up and brushes a fallen tear off my cheek. He holds my gaze as he asks, "Are you alright?"

I nod and squeeze him a little tighter as I enjoy the warmth of his embrace. "I'm doing a little better," I admit. "I think I want to read one more today," I inform him.

"Are you sure?" he asks surprised.

I nod and push back from him, "Yeah. After that I need a little more. I can't start the day thinking about it like this," I admit feeling abandoned. "I need to read the next year."

"Do you want me to stay?" he asks.

"Please," I beg not wanting to be alone. He nods and leans back against the couch. I straighten out the half crumpled letter in my hand and reach for the rest of the stack. I.fold up the letter I just read and put it back in its envelope. I place it back in the pile in the right order and pull out the next one. I drop the stack next to me and open the envelope, pulling out the next letter. I lean back under the crook of Brady's arm and curl my legs up next to me. I feel safe here with him and that scares the crap out of me, but not having his comfort is even more terrifying. I turn my head up to look at him with a small smile trying to understand the strange soothing effect he has on me. I whisper, "Thank you." He leans down and gently presses his lips to mine in reply. I grin appreciatively and settle back under his arm. I open up the letter and begin to read.

June 12th (your 7th Birthday)
To My Beautiful Baby Girl,

Happy Birthday!! I hope you're having a wonderful time celebrating turning 7! I wonder if you're having a party with your friends from school or maybe with your family or even both.

I looked back at the letter from last year and I need to start by saying I'm sorry. I know it's no excuse, but I was in a bad place. I tell myself that it's not like my six year old daughter would have read that letter since you won't see a single one of these until you're at the very least an adult. Well, I guess that's if you ever read them at all. I will leave them for you, but I realize you may never come looking for me. I guess I wouldn't blame you if that were the case. I just want you to know that I have always thought of you and wanted what was best for you. I admit sometimes it hasn't been easy, but I know you're better off with a family that can really take care of you and be there for you. I couldn't do that when I had you. I honestly wonder if I could even do it now. Looking at the letter I wrote last year on your birthday just reinforces that I made the right decision. I was going to throw the letter away, but I guess I thought you should see how hard giving you away really was for me. You may not have been planned or expected, but whether you believe it or not, I loved you from the very beginning. I believe I wouldn't have been able to give you a chance at a better life if I didn't.

I do want you to know that I worked everything out with my boyfriend. He proposed to me a few months ago. It looks like I'll be getting married this year.

Please forgive me. I really do love you and hope you're happier than ever!

With Love...
Catherine Schepp

I read the last line three times before I drop my hands to my lap with a sigh. "Are you okay?" Brady asks as he tucks a lock of my hair behind my ear. I nod my head, not quite ready to speak over the lump in my throat. He gently caresses my cheek from my ear then down my jawline, "Are you sure?"

I take a deep breath, attempting to steady my anxiety and nod again. "I'm okay," I whisper hoarsely without looking at him.

He slides his hand underneath my chin and tilts it up towards him until I meet his eyes. His eyebrows are raised in doubt, "Please talk to me."

I bite my bottom lip and slowly pull it from my teeth before answering. "I'm okay, I promise. She apologized for her other letter."

"If it's something she had to apologize for, why would she let you read it?" he questions, his eyes full of concern.

I shrug, trying to make sense of her words. "I think she wanted me to know that she struggles with her decision to give me up. She wanted me to know that even though I wasn't planned, she loved me and always wanted the best for me. She wanted me to know that she wishes things could've been different, but she still doesn't believe she was the best thing for me and that letter was kind of like proof to her."

"Do you want to tell me what you know about her?" he asks.

I shrug, but start talking about her anyway. "I guess in each letter I learn a little bit, but I have more questions than answers."

"And those are questions you'll never be able to ask her," he utters the exact words that cross my mind, drawing me in closer to him. "But you might be able to get some answers from your dad," he adds. My breath catches and my heart begins pounding in my throat in awe of him. He listens and he really understands what I'm thinking. How does he do that?

I cuddle even closer to him and tell him more about her. "She met my dad at one of those weekend concert things and they spent that whole weekend together. They thought they'd never see each other again. I guess when she found out she was pregnant she started looking for him to tell him. When she found him, he was engaged to someone else and his girlfriend or fiancée was a few months pregnant. I guess I have a brother or sister out there somewhere that's only a few months younger than me," I confess. "I might even have more siblings than that since they were just starting their family at the time."

He studies me closely as his thumb continues to caress my cheek. "I can't even imagine what that feels like." I twist my body in his arms to look into his eyes. His hand reflexively reaches for my cheek. He tenderly slides his fingers down my cheek and around to the back of my neck, holding me firmly. He stares intently into my eyes and whispers, "I can't imagine ever knowingly or willingly giving up the treasure of you."

My heart skips a beat and tears roll quickly over my cheeks. I bury my face in his chest as reality hits me. His words in a way are one of my biggest fears. My dad gave me up. He chose his other child over me. I realize that's irrational when he was engaged to their mom and barely knew mine. But how do I live with that? Will I be able to forgive him for that when I meet him? My breath stutters when I realize my brain just told me when, not if. I wrap my arms around Brady's middle, needing to feel his warmth. He wraps both arms around me and pulls me tightly to his chest. I close my eyes and take a deep breath, enjoying the smell of the combination of his soap and light cologne. "Will you just hang out with me here for the rest of today?" I rasp.

"Of course Sam," he murmurs softly, "I'm happy to."

I feel my body finally begin to relax and whisper, "Thank you."

Chapter 17

I lay on my bed staring up at the white ceiling, debating if I should read another letter from my birth mom or not. I could skip a day since I read two yesterday, but one of them was pretty bad and I don't want to read another letter like that while I'm sitting alone in my room. Hopefully I don't have to read another one like that at all, but what if I do? If I'm by myself, I might really lose it this time, but do I really want someone to be there with me if I do break down? What if it's nothing? I sigh, annoyed with myself. I can't exactly ask Brady to come sit with me for a few minutes while I read a letter. Besides he's going to think all I do is cry if I keep this up and what fun is that?

I sigh happily at the thought of him, recalling last night. We spent it with takeout and a movie. Cuddling with him and the way he kissed me breathless until my whole body was on fire, drives me insane. I could make-out with him like that for days if he'd let me. His lips were so full, both firm and tender in his touch. I groan just thinking about him. I shake myself, trying to clear the fog from my head.

It's probably for the best I don't see him right now with my state of mind. My head seems to be all over the place. Brady has to help out his parents at the restaurant again today. He said he had only committed to a couple days over his vacation, but I guess today is one of those days. I try to convince myself that it's fine. I haven't known him that long and I really shouldn't feel this strong of a pull towards him already, anyway. This is good for me. I'll read the next letter from her. I have other things to do anyway, I insist, trying to convince myself it's true. I pull out the next letter and drop it on the bed next to me with trembling hands. "I'm pathetic," I mumble as I let my head fall into my hands.

A knock at the door gives me a reprieve and I jump at the chance to answer it. I throw the door open and my mouth drops open in surprise. Brady stands in the doorway looking hot as hell and slightly nervous. His hands are stuffed into a pair of black dress pants. He has on a white dress shirt with the sleeves rolled up to just below his elbows. His hair is damp like he just got out of the shower, but styled back a little neater than I've been seeing on him. He looks incredible. "Morning," he grins, showing me his dimple, causing my heart to flutter and my stomach to flip.

"Hi," I squeak. "What are you doing here?" I blurt out.

He laughs, "Right to the point." My face instantly heats with embarrassment, but he continues before I have a chance to defend myself. "I'm headed over to the restaurant, but I wanted to come see you first." My lips twitch up as he takes a step towards me, continuing to explain. "You said you wanted to read a letter every day and since you had such a hard time with one of the letters yesterday, I didn't want you to be alone." My heart lurches with his admission. He shrugs, "If you already read it, no big deal, I just wanted to be here for you if you needed me." I can't speak. I can't believe he did this. I know it's not hard to stop by when we live next door to each other, but I still can't believe it. "I can go if you want me to," he offers as he pulls his hand out of his pocket and points towards the door with his thumb.

I shake my head and close the space between us, wrapping my arms tightly around his hard middle. He chuckles lightly as his arms encircle me. "Thank you," I whisper.

"I guess it's okay I stopped by then?" he teases me.

I pull back and roll my eyes at him with a huge smile on my face. "Definitely!" I grab his hand and guide him with me to my room. I release his hand and climb up on my bed. I crisscross my legs and pick up the letter, holding it in my lap. I continue staring at the letter as he sits down next to me. I blush and admit, "I've been staring at this letter or my ceiling for nearly an hour trying to decide what to do. After reading the first letter yesterday, I feel like my courage has been stripped away when it comes to this."

I feel him shaking his head, "You have so much more courage than you believe. You wouldn't be here if you didn't." I know he's right, but I'm having trouble trusting it. "Without courage, you probably wouldn't have gone looking for your birth family in the first place," he reminds me.

I sigh, "You're right, but every time I even think about it, it feels like I'm opening myself up for pain or failure or rejection." I grimace and finally lift my head and look into his eyes, finding security in his gaze. "It's hard to explain, but..." I gulp down the lump forming in my throat. "Just thank you for coming by. It really means a lot to me," I insist sincerely.

He leans down and kisses my lips so softly without taking his eyes off me. He gently caresses my cheek as he pulls away. "I'm glad I can help," he murmurs.

I suppress a groan and pick up the letter in my lap, quickly unfolding it before I lean into him for support.

June 12th (your 8th Birthday)
To My Beautiful Baby Girl,
Happy Birthday!! I hope you're enjoying your birthday today. It's the middle of the week, so you're probably at school. Did you bring cupcakes or maybe something else for your classmates? My school always

allowed that, but I had a friend at a neighboring school and she could never bring birthday treats to school. I never understood that. Do you like school? I bet you're really smart. What's your favorite subject? And no, recess is not a subject. Recess was always my answer to that question.

I'm a married woman now. I never thought I would be, but I'm happy. It was a very small ceremony. It was perfect for us. I want you to know, I wish you could have been there, although I know that would never be possible. I realize I gave up all my rights to have you with me on important days like that.

I hope you have a wonderful birthday. Maybe you're planning on celebrating this weekend? No matter what you do I hope you have fun!

With Love...
Catherine Schepp

I breathe a sigh of relief and my whole body sags against Brady momentarily. "Are you okay?" he asks quietly.

I nod my head, "Yeah. It was fine really. Nothing crazy." He gives me a gentle squeeze. I want to tell him he can read it if he wants, but I don't know if I'm ready to share that part with him yet. The thought makes my stomach turn with guilt. How can I use him for support and not share them with him? "You...you can read it if you want," I force out the words.

He tilts his head to the side and sighs softly. "If you want to share the letters with me, I would love to see that part of you. In the meantime, I would love to hear about the pieces you want to share with me."

My eyes widen in surprise, wondering if he can read my mind, yet I can't help but feel defensive. "I'm not hiding anything," I declare.

He tucks a stray lock of hair behind my ear. "I don't think you are, but I don't have a lot of time today. Plus, I want you to be able to talk to me when you're ready."

I drop my gaze to my hands. I hope he doesn't regret stopping here this morning. "Brady," I murmur. The buzz of his cell phone disrupts us. He glances at the screen and clicks it off, but it rings again almost immediately. He groans in frustration as he glances at the screen again. "You can pick it up. It's okay," I encourage him.

He looks up at me, "I'll call back, but I better get going." His phone buzzes again, but he ignores it. He slides his hand under my chin and subtly lifts it as he leans towards me, gently pressing his lips to mine. His tongue shoots out to lick my bottom lip before he pushes his way in to search for my tongue. He tilts his head to the side, fusing our mouths perfectly together, pushing the kiss deeper. My hands slide around his neck and my fingers tangle into his hair. I lean back, trying to pull him closer. He groans and holds himself in place. I drop my hands in frustration. He mumbles against my lips, "I'm so sorry Sam, but I really have to go." He kisses me one more time before he pulls away. "Believe me, I'd much rather stay here. Are you sure you're okay?"

I nod and push myself up off my bed, "Yeah, I'm good."

I follow him out of my room and back towards the front door. "I'll text you later." He turns towards the door and pulls it open. "What are you doing today anyway?"

I shrug, "I'm not sure. I think I might go run some errands in town. We need some groceries and a few other things." His phone buzzes again and he groans in annoyance. He tilts his head down and firmly presses his lips to mine. I drop back with a smile, "You better go before they send out a search party."

He chuckles, "You have no idea. I'll see you later. Have fun."

"Bye Brady," I wave. "Thank you," I call after him as he walks straight for the stairs. I close the door with a content sigh. "I can't believe he did that," I murmur, smiling to myself. I don't remember anyone except for my family ever doing something like that for me. It's not like he went out of his way to get here, but still...he came for me. Paul or Taylor would've just texted to ask how it went, if they remembered at all. I never realized how much my relationships with both of them were mostly about them. I grimace with my understanding. It wasn't always like that with Taylor, but I guess things began to change with us the moment Paul and I started dating. I can't believe I didn't see it until now.

My phone buzzes with a text. I glance at the screen and grin at the message from my cousin. "WTF? You moved without telling me?"

I laugh, "Didn't know you were my keeper."

"Can't believe you forgot about me," he texts back. I shake my head, imagining the fake pout on his face.

"Hey, Ry, I'm moving to WI. Thought you should know," I text ignoring his comment.

"I'm coming to see you!" he exclaims.

"Did your Dad put you up to this?" I ask, wondering if Uncle Tim is sending him up here to check on me.

"I can't come visit my favorite cousin without being told to do so?" he questions. Even though I know he's teasing me, I have a sudden flash of guilt. I should've told him. I start typing back, but another message comes through from him before I get too far. "No, but he was the one who told me you moved. It should've been you," I read, followed by a couple emoji's that I'm not sure what they're supposed to mean.

"Don't use emoji's anymore – you don't know how to use them, like most things," I tease.

"I know how to use everything important. Got a couch for me?" he asks.

"I'll have to check with my roommate, but if not, you can have my floor," I smirk, even though he can't see me.

"How honorable of you. I'm still on break so I'll see you soon. Leaving now. I'll call when I'm close," he adds.

I know I won't hear from him again until he shows up at my door. "Ok," I acknowledge anyway.

I smile to myself. I like the direction this day is going. Brady stops by for me and Ryan is on his way to visit. Maybe it's a sign it's a good day to go find my dad. I turn back towards my room to grab my wallet and keys before I change my mind. In a matter of minutes I'm in my car and I have my dad's address punched into my GPS. I start my car and back out of my parking spot, easily pulling out into the empty street.

In less than ten minutes, I pull into a neighborhood with beautiful homes. It's easy to tell everyone here takes care of his or her property. I grew up in a great neighborhood, but this neighborhood is definitely a little more upscale than where I'm from. It reminds me of something I've seen in a few movies.

I pull up across the street from my father's large white Victorian home. There's a long blacktop driveway and a huge front yard with large trees scattered for shade. The grass appears greener than it should be this early in the spring. The front porch extends the length of the house with four tall white pillars, two on each side of the black front door. The shutters and roof are the same black as the door with a huge set of double windows on each side of the front door and three sets of the same windows across the second floor. A 6-foot tall white fence goes from the back of the house and wraps around what I assume is their back yard.

As I stare at the house, I feel like I'm watching the scene in front of me as an outsider. I guess that's what I am though, an outsider. I wonder what my life would have been like if I had never been adopted. Is this where I would have grown up? Would I have lived with my mom or dad or both? Would I have been the outsider even then?

I sigh and turn my focus to the front door, trying to get the courage to get out of my car. But what happens when I knock? What would I say? What if his wife answers? Or what if one of his kids opens the door? How many kids does he have? Do they know about me? I groan in frustration and close my eyes, dropping my head onto my steering wheel with a thump. "What am I going to do?" I whine. "I have no idea how I'm supposed to do this!" I complain.

I open my eyes and turn my head towards the house, but leave it resting on the steering wheel when I notice the front door open. I hold my breath as a beautiful woman with blonde hair steps onto the front porch followed by a smaller boy with the same hair who appears about 12 or 13 from here. I watch as the two of them walk to a black Escalade and climb in. I can't take my eyes off of them as they quickly pull out of the driveway like they might be running late for something. When they disappear down the block, I finally release the breath I didn't know I was holding. I take a couple deep breaths to calm my anxiety before I admit to myself that I'm just not ready for this. I glance at the house one more time before I pull away. I turn my car towards the grocery store, trying to forget about what I'm leaving behind. Instead I start making a mental grocery list. I'm definitely going to need more food than I thought now that Ryan is coming to visit.

Chapter 18

"Can you ask my sister to call me when she gets home," Cody requests as he walks out the door.

"I'll tell her as soon as she walks in. I promise. She said she had to stay late for a few appointments tonight," I inform him. "I'll see you later Cody."

I move to close the door behind him, but a hand comes up to stop me. "I drive all this way just to see you and instead of a hug I get a door in my face?" Ryan teases, grinning down at me.

I squeal and jump up to throw my arms around my cousin. He tosses his duffle bag just inside the door and picks me up, squeezing me tightly with a playful groan.

He sets me back on my feet and out of the corner of my eye I notice Cody still standing in front of his apartment. I happily introduce them, "Cody this is Ryan. Cody lives next door and he's also my roommate's twin brother," I briefly explain to Ryan.

Ryan turns towards him and holds his hand out with a grin, "Nice to meet you man. Hope you're watching out for my girl."

Cody nods slowly, assessing Ryan, "You too." He shakes Ryan's hand, both looking as if they're putting a lot of muscle into the handshake. "Drove all this way just to see Sam?" Cody questions repeating Ryan's words.

Ryan nods and drops Cody's hand. He immediately throws his arm around my shoulder and pulls me close. "Yeah, I'm going to stay with her for a few days, so I'm sure I'll see you around," he announces like a proud father.

I laugh and wave to Cody as I spin out from under Ryan's arm and into my apartment with Ryan on my heels. "I'm so glad you're here," I express genuinely.

He shuts the door behind him and shrugs off his navy coat before dropping it on his duffle bag. He walks over to the couch, immediately flopping down on it with an exaggerated sigh. "So what's going on Sam?"

"Isn't it obvious? I moved. I have a new roommate, a new apartment and a few new friends," I reply sarcastically.

He chuckles, "Already at it." I shrug and he explains even though we both know he doesn't need to. "Distractions," he shakes his head, smiling dismissively. "Have you found him? Your birth father?"

"We're going to jump right into it huh?" I question lightly. He just stares at me waiting for my answer. I sigh and trudge over to the couch. I shove his feet onto the floor and they drop to the ground with a thump. I slowly sit down at the opposite end from him. He sits up and scoots back. He looks at me, patiently waiting for me to tell him something about what's going on. "Sort of," I mumble.

His eyebrows rise in question, "What do you mean by sort of?"

I wince, not really knowing if I'm ready to talk about this yet. I begin fidgeting with my fingers and stare mindlessly at the repetitive movements. I take a deep breath and hold it momentarily before I release it, along with my explanation. "I know where he lives, where he works and I know he has a family. I don't know what he looks like though because I've been too much of a chicken shit to go knock on his door or look him up on social media for that matter." I mumble under my breath, "Then again, I've been avoiding social media for a lot of reasons."

He sighs and scoots closer to me, gently wrapping his arm around me. "You know it doesn't matter what happens with him. You always have me, along with the

~ 176 ~

rest of our pain in the ass family. No one will replace your mom and dad. I miss them every day too."

I sigh and look up at him, my heart clenching tightly in my chest. I didn't realize how relieved I would feel seeing him. Then to hear those words from someone who knows my parents and me so well is overwhelming. "I miss them so much, but I'm not looking for someone to replace them. I promise. I know that's impossible. I just want to know more about where I came from. Honestly I don't really know what I want from him, but I know I want something," I admit hoarsely.

He bites his lip and suddenly a knowing look crosses over his face. "You're afraid he'll want nothing to do with you."

I wince hearing the truth and confess, "Maybe." I quickly add, "I'm also afraid his family knows nothing about me, or they won't want me to come looking for him. It's just a lot of pressure coming from so many different directions."

He nods, "I know Sam."

He opens his mouth to say something else when the front door swings open and Cory walks in. "I'm starving! Do you wanna' order some pizza?" she yells as she shoves the door closed behind her. She freezes the moment she sees Ryan, grinning at her from the couch. "Um, Hi," she blurts shyly.

"Pizza sounds great! Especially if I'm eating with you," he flirts.

I groan and roll my eyes, "Ryan."

He looks over at me innocently, "What?"

I shake my head in annoyance and look back at my roommate with her mouth hanging slightly open. My mouth turns up into a smile as I try to imagine what she's seeing. Ryan is a good-looking guy and has never had trouble finding a beautiful girl who's interested, but contrary to popular belief due to rumors from his ex, he's more of a relationship kind of guy. He's six feet tall with broad shoulders. He spends a lot of time at the gym or running to stay fit and even I have to admit it shows. He has short, dark blonde hair, but it hangs slightly down in the front, and gray eyes currently ogling Cory.

"Cory this is my cousin Ryan I told you about. Are you sure it's okay if he stays here for a couple days? He can always sleep on my floor," I offer again. I just moved in and the last thing I want is for her to be uncomfortable in her own apartment.

She visibly shakes herself out of her stupor and steps towards him. "Of course he can stay! As long as he wants," she grins. "It's nice to meet you Ryan," she holds her hand out to shake.

He takes it, but lifts it to his lips and kisses the back of her hand. I roll my eyes at his antics. He rasps, "It's really good to meet you too, Cory."

Two sets of eyes turn to me and I realize I groaned out loud. "Sorry, Ryan can be annoying," I joke, pasting on an overly sweet smile.

They both laugh and Cory asks, "So pizza is okay?"

"Yeah, and your brother asked for you to call as soon as you're home. He even came over looking for you," I inform her.

"Thanks," she replies. "I'll call him first. He'll probably want pizza too."

She walks down the short hallway to her room, already on the phone when Ryan turns towards me with wide eyes. "You didn't tell me your roommate was hot!" he accuses.

"Ryan," I warn.

He looks at me innocently, "What?"

I pinch my lips shut. Ryan really is a good guy. I know he wouldn't do anything that would put me in a bad situation. Plus I just don't have it in in me to argue with him about hitting on my roommate, especially when she might be just as interested if the look she just had on her face is any way to judge. I finally tell him, "Just be careful. She's my roommate," I remind him.

He grins in response just as Cory comes back into the room. I fight my own smile, noticing she changed into a pair of black leggings and a long, pale blue fitted sweater. "You look good," I compliment her. That's definitely not what she normally changes into after she gets home from a long day at work. "Are you going out tonight?" I ask with a smirk.

"No, I just wanted to be comfortable," she says as she sits on the armchair near Ryan. "Cody and Brady are coming over for pizza. I asked Cody to go pick it up so we don't have to wait for the delivery guy."

"Brady is done with work already?" I question. "I thought he was working late."

She shrugs, "Cody said he's on his way home now." I nod feeling my stomach twist in anticipation of seeing him. "So Ryan, do you live in Illinois too?"

"Yeah, but I'm not at home. I'm a junior at Northwestern," he informs her.

I tune them out and let my mind drift to Brady. It's crazy to me that I'm this excited to see him when we just spent the day together yesterday, but I am. I didn't think he would be getting back until late, but I guess something changed with his schedule. Either way, I don't mind, I giggle to myself. Ryan pokes me, "What's so funny?"

I shake my head, grinning, "Nothing."

The front door flies open and Cody walks in carrying two pizza boxes and a bag of something else sitting on top with Brady right behind him. "We're here," Cody announces playfully. "Dinner is served."

Cody drops into the armchair opposite his sister and I scoot closer to Ryan to make room for Brady. Brady walks into the kitchen without even saying Hi. He returns quickly with plates and an armful of drinks. He places everything on the coffee table, grabs a beer for himself, pops the top and sits down next to me. I watch as he tips the beer back and his Adam's apple bobs up and down as he gulps down half the bottle. "Rough day?" I question at the same time trying to tell my stomach to stop churning, but something just doesn't feel right.

He nods stiffly and finally turns his head towards me and looks straight into my eyes. "You could say that," he grumbles, grinding his jaw.

My heart drops into my stomach with his critical look. I don't know what to say. I don't know what's wrong, but I don't know if I should ask in front of everyone either. I feel like I'm going to be sick. "Um, Brady, this is Ryan. Brady lives next door with Cody," I explain to Ryan nervously.

"Nice to meet you," Ryan nods stiffly, without offering his hand. He obviously feels the same tension that I'm feeling and he doesn't even know him. Brady assesses Ryan and barely grunts in acknowledgement, pissing me off, but I'm still not sure if I should say anything in front of everyone.

I don't know if I can eat anything anymore, but I grab a slice of pizza anyway and put it on a paper plate. I cross my legs under me and put the plate on my lap before I begin picking at it. Ryan pokes me in my side and I feel Brady tense on my other side. I look up at Ryan and he mouths, "You okay?" I nod, fighting back the emotion clogged in my throat. He glances over at Brady and back to me again. "You like him," he mouths and wiggles his eyebrows. My eyes widen and I feel my face redden. Ryan laughs and everyone looks over at him.

"Something funny?" Brady asks accusingly.

"Yup," he grins. He throws his arm around me and pulls me towards him, "So, are you sure you're okay with me going to get a drink with your roommate? Since you can't exactly take me out to a bar yet," he teases.

I don't remember him asking, but he could've when I tuned them out before. "Of course. I'll have you for the next couple days, so it's fine. You guys have fun," I tell him.

"What the fuck?" Brady exclaims.

I turn towards him with confusion obvious on my face. "What the fuck is your problem?" Ryan asks Brady, increasing the tension in the room even more.

"My problem?" Brady asks sounding completely exasperated.

"Yes! What is wrong Brady?" I blurt, feeling flustered. I don't know what's going on with him, but he needs to relax.

He glares at Ryan and asks sounding perturbed, "You just get here and you're going out with her roommate?"

"Why not?" I ask in confusion. "It's no big deal."

Brady stands and turns to me, looking at me as if I've lost my mind. Then Ryan and Cory both burst out laughing, while Cody's eyes go back and forth between all of us like we're the entertainment. "Are you kidding me?" Brady asks annoyed with all of them.

Ryan catches his breath and stands clasping Brady on the shoulder. "You like my girl," he says, grinning broadly at Brady. Brady glares harder, his face reddening as he crosses his arms over his chest. Ryan laughs again as Cory's laughter becomes almost out of control. "Calm down, Fido," Ryan taunts. "I really want to mess with you for a while, but I'd rather be talking to Cory, so instead I'll go with honesty. Sam is my cousin, so that's just gross," he grimaces. "And just so you know, she doesn't do well with the whole jealous asshole thing."

Cody bursts out laughing as Brady's head falls down in defeat. "Wait, you thought..." I begin pointing between Ryan and myself. My eyes widen and I scrunch my nose up in disgust at the thought. "Is that why you're being such an ass?"

Brady cringes and meets my eyes, his own full of regret. "I'm sorry. Cody texted and said you were in some guys arms and he was staying with you for a couple days. I flipped," he admits regrettably.

My stomach churns and for the first time with Brady, it's not in a good way. "You couldn't ask me?" I shriek, fighting the hurt pushing on me. "We just agreed we were exclusive," I state. "I wouldn't do that to you," I inform him. "That's not who I am!"

He sits down next to me and reaches for my hands, but I pull them into my lap. "I'm sorry Sam," he says again, sounding desperate.

"How about we go over to your place and eat over there?" Cory asks, giving a pleading look to her brother. "I think these two need some time to talk."

"Do we have to?" Cody pouts. Cory glares at her brother and he immediately concedes, "Fine!"

"Are you coming Ryan?" Cory turns to ask him.

Ryan looks at me and although he's checking to make sure it's okay with me, he's also begging for it to be. "It's fine Ry. Go, have fun! We'll catch up later," I tell him. I stand and give him another quick hug and whisper in his ear, "Thank you for coming. I've missed you."

"Anytime," he insists. I release him and the three of them walk out the door with one of the pizzas and the only box of chicken wings. Cory turns with a sad wave as she closes the door.

I sigh and drop back onto the couch next to Brady. He turns towards me and I feel his eyes on me, but I'm not ready to look at him yet. He sighs, "I'm so sorry Sam. I really like you," he emphasizes. "I know it's not okay, but when Cody said…"

"Why don't you ask me instead of taking someone's word for it next time," I snap.

"He's my best friend. He was watching out for me," he explains, "And what he said was true." He winces, "Everything feels so intense when it comes to me and you. I obviously took it wrong with who he is to you, but I didn't like it."

"That's the problem! We just started seeing each other and you already doubt me," I argue. "How will we ever work if we don't have trust?" I question.

He grinds his jaw, "I don't doubt you Sam, but I don't know anyone in your life other than Cory and Cody. So I only know what you tell me. I realize that's not fair and I'm the one who fucked up. I should've just asked, but I didn't and I can't change that now. All I can do is tell you how sorry I am and insist it will never happen again. I do trust you," he declares.

I huff a laugh of disbelief. I feel torn because I believe trust and communication are so important. My parents showed me that. But at the same time I feel such a strong unexplainable pull towards him. "I didn't come here for a relationship Brady. It's probably the last thing I need right now," I tell him instead.

"A relationship is probably not something I need right now either, but with you I know it's exactly what I want, even if I suck at the whole boyfriend thing at the moment." I hide my smile, trying not to let him pull me back in too quickly. I don't like the kind of power he has over my emotions. "Please give me another chance. I'm sorry I was being a stupid asshole. It won't happen again," he insists.

I smirk, "You sure about that?"

He shakes his head, "I'm sure I'll make mistakes, but I promise to talk to you next time. I was going to this time too. I was just waiting for a chance to talk to you tonight instead of in front of everyone. After Cody called I made up some excuse why I had to leave the restaurant. My mom was pissed, but I didn't care," he shrugs. "I was going to talk to you, but when we walked in and I saw you on the couch with him, I couldn't do anything. I couldn't relax either, though. I was trying to wait until I could talk to you, so I guess I was an ass instead."

"You guess?" I ask sarcastically.

He grimaces, "No, I was definitely an ass." He sighs and attempts to reach for my hands again, but this time I let him, causing his body to physically relax. "I'm really sorry. I should've never assumed. I should've talked to you and I will next time, just give me another chance," he begs. "Please?"

I admit I already knew the answer to that question before we even started this conversation, but I don't ever want to give any guy a reason to think it's okay to act like a jerk. I nod my head slowly, "Just please don't assume the worst of me. I think that's what hurts the most about this. I realize we're still trying to get to know each other, but..." I shrug not really knowing if I should tell him how much I already feel for him and how easily he could break me. "Just please talk to me next time."

"I can do that," he sighs with relief.

"Ryan's right, I don't do well with jealousy. I'd rather not bother if there's no honesty or trust," I inform him.

"I won't make that mistake again," he insists. He leans towards me and lets his forehead softly fall to mine.

He reaches up with both hands sliding them behind my neck. "I will make it up to you," he whispers hoarsely. He leans forward and pecks me lightly on the lips.

"Would you..." I pause hesitantly.

"What?" he prompts.

"Would you just stay here with me tonight?" I ask nervously.

"Of course," he responds immediately.

"No, I mean, would you sleep with me in my room and hold me tonight? Nothing more," I add. "It's just Ryan is going out and I don't want to be alone tonight," I confess.

He smiles adoringly at me and slides his thumbs forward to caress my cheeks. "I'd be happy to and I promise I'll be a perfect gentleman."

"Well, you don't have to be perfect," I giggle, feeling my face redden.

He chuckles, "Whatever you want Sam."

Chapter 19

I slowly wake up from a deep sleep, needing to escape the heat. I try to stretch, feeling completely refreshed. I know it's because I haven't slept as peacefully as I did last night in a really long time. My acknowledgement causes me to instantly recognize the warmth of Brady's hand splayed on my hip and his body heat radiating so close to mine. I smile to myself and take a deep breath, releasing it slowly as I open my eyes. I glance over my right shoulder and shutter as my heartbeat picks up speed. Brady's eyes are closed, making his features appear softer, while he's relaxed in sleep. His dark brown hair shoots out in nearly every direction. I glance down at his chest and grimace at the black t-shirt he's wearing, wishing I could use this time to ogle his hard chest and abs. I wonder what he looks like underneath. What heterosexual girl wouldn't? The hand that's not holding me rests above his head on the pillow. I could stare at him all day, but I need to go to the bathroom.

I cautiously turn my body to try to slip out from underneath his hand. I pick up his hand and gently place it on the bed before I move to escape. My feet hit the plush carpet as he rasps, "Morning," sending shivers down my spine.

I jump slightly and turn back towards him, my face instantly heating with embarrassment. "Hi," I grin shyly down at him.

He scoots towards me and wraps his arm around my waist, pulling me back on the bed. "Where are you going?" he grumbles.

"To the bathroom," I inform him, suddenly anxious. "I'll be right back." He groans, but releases me and rolls back over on my bed.

I stand and rush down the hall to the bathroom. After I use the bathroom, I wash my hands and my face. Then I take the time to quickly brush my teeth and my hair. I'm not one to put on make-up before anyone sees me, but I at least want to feel clean next to him.

I open the door and step out of the bathroom to find Brady leaning against the wall in the hallway. He lifts his head and takes a step towards me when I come out. "You took too long," he complains sleepily. He tilts his head down and kisses me on the cheek. He lifts his head and smirks, "You brushed your teeth." I shrug and smile nonchalantly back at him. He points to the bathroom, "I'll only be a minute."

I nod and walk across the hall to my room. I stand inside the doorway and look around, not really sure what to do with myself. I glance down at my blue and white plaid pajama shorts and matching blue t-shirt. I left my bra on last night since Brady slept here. Although we haven't done anything more than kiss, I want more every time I'm with him. Without a bra on, it would be almost too easy, but I don't think I could handle being rejected by him again, no matter what his reasons.

He steps back into my room and closes the door behind him with one hand as he encircles my waist with the other, pulling my back to his front. He tucks my hair behind my ear and pushes his face into the crook of my neck, taking a deep breath. He kisses my neck with a soft groan and repeats, "Good morning."

I just smile and lean into him, enjoying the feel of being in his arms. "Did you sleep okay?" I ask hoarsely.

"Mmm-hmm," he rumbles. He turns me towards him and fuses his mouth to mine without warning. I gasp into his mouth and slide my hands up his chest, over his shoulders and up into his hair, holding on tight. He pushes his tongue into my mouth and kisses me almost desperately. I cling to him as he walks me backwards until the backs of my legs buckle against my bed, making me fall back and away from his soft lips.

"You brushed your teeth," I accuse him, narrowing my eyes. "I didn't hear you leave the apartment."

He grins playfully, "You're right, I didn't. I used your toothbrush. I hope that's okay."

I scrunch up my nose, not really sure what I think of that and he starts laughing. "How did you even know which one was mine?" I ask suspiciously.

"Well, I already knew which one was Cory's since I've used the bathroom here once or twice," he jokes, "and your toothbrush was wet since you just brushed," he reminds me. "If you're going to let me kiss you like I just did, you shouldn't be bothered by me using your toothbrush," he chuckles as he crawls over me, caging me in. I grimace and he laughs harder. He collapses next to me and swiftly pulls me towards him in the same move. He kisses me lightly and gives me a small tug, aligning my body with his, so I'm half on him and half on the bed.

I pull back from his mouth and drop my head lightly onto his chest. "Thank you for staying with me last night," I tell him as I brush imaginary lint from his t-shirt.

He slides his hand up my side until he finds my chin. Then he tilts it up tenderly and waits for me to meet his eyes. "You don't have to thank me for that," he insists. "Believe me, it was my pleasure to be here with you." "I'm sorry I was such an ass about your cousin," he confesses.

My eyes widen at the reminder of my cousin. "Ryan!" I screech. I push Brady away and jump off my bed. "I forgot he was here!" I admit frantically. "Did you hear them come in last night?" I ask anxiously.

He shakes his head, "No, but I'm sure you have nothing to worry about. Cory knows her way around here," he teases me.

I cock my head to the side and put my hands on my hips trying to glare at him, but the corners of my mouth turn up without my consent. He just laughs and I huff, covering my smirk as I stride for my door. "I'm just going to check the living room," I inform him. "I didn't even give him any blankets or pillows or anything," I flinch, knowing my mom wouldn't be happy about that.

"Do you want me to go?" he asks sincerely as he pushes off my bed and stands in front of me.

I look up at him and the butterflies go to work on my insides. I gulp down the lump in my throat and shake my head, "Please stay. I reluctantly turn and open my door again to step into the hallway. I take my first step towards the living room when Cory's bedroom door opens. I turn towards her, but find Ryan pulling a dark blue t-shirt over his head instead. He pulls the door shut behind him without looking up. I cross my arms over my chest and glare, "Good morning Ryan."

He freezes for barely a moment before he moves, dropping his shirt into place. "Morning Sam," he grins and takes a step towards the kitchen. He calls over his shoulder, "Relax, I didn't fuck anything up for you if that's what you're thinking."

I follow behind him and question, "Then why were you in my roommate's bedroom without a shirt on?"

"Where are your coffee cups?" he asks, ignoring my question, as he steps up to the full pot of coffee.

I pull out two coffee cups covered in colorful graffiti and hand them both to him. I watch as he fills them up. He walks to the refrigerator and pulls out sweet cream, adding that to one before putting it back in the refrigerator. "There's enough for you and Brady too if you're thirsty," he smirks.

My face flushes and I attempt to ignore his comment, feeling somewhat like a hypocrite until I remind myself that he doesn't live here. "We didn't do anything but sleep. What did you do Ryan?" I ask.

He raises his eyebrows and questions, "Really?"

I shrug, "Mostly."

He laughs before he finally notices my serious expression. Then he sighs and places both cups back down on the counter. "I like her Sam. We're both adults and she knows I'm leaving after the weekend. We had fun last night. I will call her after I go back to Northwestern, but we didn't make each other any promises. She pushed me and I couldn't say no to her. I know why you're here Sam. I'm not trying to screw you over. You know me," he reminds me, his expression fierce.

My heart sinks into my stomach. He's right. I do know him. I know he wouldn't do anything with her if he wasn't truly interested. Friends have always been off limits, especially a roommate. I have so much to still figure out here. "Of course it had to be Cory," I grumble making him laugh.

He picks up both coffee cups and kisses my cheek as he passes, walking back towards Cory's room. "We got home kinda' late last night and she's off today," he informs me. "We'll see you in a little while and we'll all hang out."

I groan conceding and wave to his retreating form as he opens the door without dropping either of the cups. I take a step towards my room when Brady's broad shoulders fill the kitchen doorway. "You were taking too long again and I smell coffee," he grins.

My heart flutters at the sight of him and I smile softly. "I was just talking to Ryan," I tell him.

"Where is he?" he asks.

I grimace and gesture to Cory's room.

He laughs humorlessly, but then his eyes widen and his mouth drops open. "You're kidding right?"

My eyes widen. I didn't even think how he would react. He always says Cory's like a sister to him and I just told him my cousin is in her bedroom. "Um, he's a good guy. He really likes her. He wouldn't be in there if he didn't. I know he has to go back to school, but..." I ramble nervously.

He steps towards me and grips my shoulders, "Stop! I just can't hear anything about Cory. It's just too weird for me. Good guy or not."

I look at him skeptically before drawing out my reply, "O-kay."

"Do you want to read another letter this morning?" he asks, obviously trying to change the subject.

"Sure," I answer.

"I'll grab us coffee and you get the next letter and get comfortable. I'll be right there," he informs me.

I nod and tell him, "I like cream in mine," before I walk back to my room. I do as he says and sit on my bed with my knees pulled up to my chest, placing a letter in my lap while I wait for him.

He strides into my room and smiles at me over the rim of his coffee cup. He kicks the door shut with his foot and takes two steps to my nightstand, placing both cups down gently. Then he leans down, softly kissing my lips before he climbs over me and sits back against the wall. He reaches for me and pulls me into him before I have a chance to react. He encloses me in his arms but rests both of his hands on my thighs, warming up my whole body inside and out. My breath picks up as he gives my legs a gentle pat in encouragement. "I'm ready if you are," he says even though I know I'll be the only one actually reading the letter.

I take a deep breath, open the letter and begin reading.

June 12th (your 9th Birthday)
To My Beautiful Baby Girl,
Happy Birthday!! I hope you have fun this year. It's beautiful outside today. I hope it is where you are too. It's the kind of weather that's perfect for playing games outside. Do you like to play outside? Or maybe you like to ride bikes with your friends? I used to play all kinds of games with kids from around my neighborhood like SPUD, foursquare, Mother May I, Red Rover and every kind of tag imaginable. I think freeze tag or TV tag were my favorites. Then at night I could stay up with all the older kids and we would play Manhunt or Ghosts in the Graveyard. Do you know any of those games? I always wonder if kids still play the same games that I used to. I'm sure they'd still be fun. That doesn't really change.

Anyway, for me everything is mostly the same as last year. I'm still happily married and I'm still wondering who you're becoming. Happy Birthday.
With Love...
Catherine Schepp

I fold the letter back up and lean into Brady. He wraps his arms around me without saying a word. It feels surreal being perfectly happy and content in his arms. It's almost like I'm living someone else's life, but I know better than to take anything for granted. I could lose everything in an instant and I don't want to waste anymore time.

I twist towards him and slide my hand to the back of his head, pulling him down to my lips. I push my tongue into his mouth, needing to taste him and he groans in response. I keep moving until I'm straddling him without ever once breaking our kiss. I feel his hard length, my whole body heating instantly. He groans louder with our contact and mumbles, "Fuck." He tilts his head, perfectly aligning our mouths pushing the kiss deeper. Our tongues dance, licking and seeking the taste of one another. He pulls me closer like he can't get enough. For me that's true, I want more. "Samantha," he rasps in warning as I grind against him.

"Please Brady," I beg, hoping he understands what I'm asking and praying he doesn't push me away again.

His lips tear from mine and begin kissing me along my jaw, then slowly down my neck where he licks and kisses a sweet spot sending chills down my spine as I gasp for breath. He chuckles at my reaction while his hands trail up and down my back underneath my shirt. His hands lightly swirl over my skin as he recaptures my mouth. His hands slip up my sides and his thumbs run along the sides of my breasts causing me to whimper. He slides down and back up over my belly, dragging his hands over my nipples instantly hardening them before gently cupping both breasts. He removes his hands from my breasts at the same time tearing his mouth from mine. Before I have a chance to argue he grips me by the waist and flips me over on my back. He leans down towards me, closing the space between us. I stop him by tugging at his shirt and breathlessly request, "Take this off."

He reaches with one hand and pulls his shirt over his head. I struggle not to drool at the man in front of me with his well-defined arms, chest and stomach that actually forms a six-pack. The only visible hair lies beneath his belly button and disappears underneath his gray sweat pants. I reach out to touch him and slide my fingers along his tight, smooth skin. He drops down to my side covering my mouth with his and rests one hand on the soft skin of my stomach. He slowly slides his hand up to cup my breast, running his hand over my nipple through my bra. "Can I take this off?" he rasps over my lips as he gently tugs at my bra strap.

I nod my head feeling lightheaded. I push myself up and use both hands to tug off my shirt before unclipping my bra in the front. I look up when Brady gasps and smirk at him, "This one is front hook."

He grins playfully, showing his dimple, "I can see that." His face grows serious as he stares at me. My body heats with embarrassment, but he quickly puts me at ease with his adoring expression. He blurts, "You are so fucking beautiful, Samantha."

I breathe a sigh of relief as his mouth crashes back to mine, but it's only a moment before he begins moving his kisses down my body. I whimper in anticipation as his lips find my neck. Then he kisses a trail down, stalling between my breasts. His hand slides underneath my breast, cupping gently as his lips glide up the side towards my nipple. He licks around the tip before covering my whole breast with his mouth, licking and then gently sucking. I moan involuntarily as his other hand slips down my stomach and allows his fingers to drift back and forth at my waistband. I arch towards him craving more.

A loud knock at the door startles me. Brady quickly moves to cover me with his body to keep me from sight. "Don't come in!" I screech.

My response is Cory's giggling along with Ryan's disgusted groan. "Believe me I don't want to!" Ryan complains. "But you're coming out. I have class on Tuesday so I have to leave tomorrow. I came here to see you Sam," he reminds me.

I groan and Brady chuckles into my neck. I smack him lightly on the arm, making him laugh harder. "Don't laugh at me."

He lifts his head and grins, "Believe me I'm not. I'm laughing because this is my luck," he explains. "I'm finally touching you and I don't want to stop."

I lift my head and kiss him hard, letting him know I don't want to stop either. A harder knock on the door interrupts us this time. "Come on out Sam, or I'll be forced to come in and get you. You will be responsible for scarring me for life," Ryan complains.

I groan in annoyance as Brady leans back and pulls my shirt on over my head. "I can dress myself," I tease.

He shrugs, "I don't care if he is your cousin, I'm not taking a chance that he walks in here and sees my girl."

A lump forms in my throat and I try to gulp it down. I reach under my shirt and clasp my bra before I look up. Brady stands and pulls his shirt into place. I smile up at him and he bends down, caging me in and gently presses his lips to mine. "We'll finish this later?" I ask.

"If you'll let me," he grumbles and kisses me hard again.

Ryan begins playing a drum beat on the other side of the door. I groan in annoyance. "We're coming!"

Brady stands and then reaches down for my hands. I grip him tightly and he pulls me up into his chest and spins me towards the door in one swift move. I pull it open to Ryan with his hands raised and a smile on his face. "We?" he asks. I roll my eyes in response and walk past him and out into the living room. "Yeah right you were just sleeping," he chuckles from behind me.

I grit my teeth and ignore his comment. Brady's not far behind me and hands me the coffee cup I left in my room as I spin around. "I'm going to go jump in the shower," he informs me.

"Okay," I nod.

He turns towards Ryan with his hand outstretched, "And I owe you an apology. I'm sorry for last night."

Ryan takes his hand and nods in understanding, "I get it. And so you know, I'm taking Sam to lunch," Ryan announces. "We'll meet up with you guys after?"

Brady smiles and nods in agreement. Then he tips his head down towards me and softly presses his lips to mine. He pulls back with a smile. Then he turns towards Ryan and Cory and waves casually, "I'll see you guys in a little while." I watch him walk out the door, feeling content.

"I think it's time we talk about the birds and the bees, Sam," Ryan jokes.

I roll my eyes and burst out laughing.

Chapter 20

Ryan slides into the booth across from me at "The Pit" and begins drumming his fingers lightly on the table. My stomach churns anxiously while I wait for him to ask the inevitable question. He finally peers up at me and ends the silence, "So…" he begins thoughtfully, "What's up with Brady?"

I flinch even knowing it was coming. I take a deep breath and try to answer truthfully. "I don't know. I met him the day I moved in. My roommate Cory has known him forever and he lives with her twin brother who is also his best friend."

He nods, "Yeah, she told me that much. She also said he was a good guy, but I need to hear it from you, especially after he made such a great impression on me," he adds sarcastically.

I know Ryan has always been protective of me, kind of like an older brother, but since my mom and dad died, I think he attempts to step into the role even more. I don't really blame him, especially since I haven't been myself in so long. I shrug, "I don't know Ry. I really like him, even though I probably shouldn't," I mumble. "It's nothing like it was with Paul."

"I sure as hell hope not!" he grumbles. He sighs and asks, "Are you sure it's not a rebound Sam? You and Paul didn't break up that long ago and you have so much going on," he reminds me.

I nod and ignore his commentary. I open my mouth and attempt to describe what I'm feeling, "I don't even know how to explain it. Of course I'm extremely attracted to him," I tell him and fight my smirk at his automatic cringe, "but I know you don't want to hear about that. It's like I feel this really strong weird connection to him and it just feels...natural to be with him. I'm calm and happy. I guess you could even say I feel like I can be myself with him, like really myself," I emphasize.

He stares intently at me, like he's trying to read my mind before he nods slowly, "I can tell."

My eyebrows scrunch together in confusion and I ask, "What do you mean?"

He sighs and softens his tone, "For the first time since..." he hesitates, but I know what he means, so I nod for him to continue. "It just seems like you're *you* again or at least becoming you again. You shut down after everything. You've been quiet. Barely anything makes you react one way or another, you just *do*, but now you're smiling, laughing, joking around and talking again. Besides last night when he was an ass," he teases, making me wince. He smiles tenderly and admits, "It's really good to see you smile and laugh again, Sam. I'll even admit right now, but never again so you better listen carefully, I love when you give me shit right back." He sighs, "If he's the one doing all that in just a little over a week, I can't wait to see what the fuck happens in a month!" he jokes.

I huff out a laugh, "Have I really been that bad?"

He raises his eyebrows and asks, "Seriously?" I giggle and he grins back at me, "See?" causing me to grin wider. "So you guys are exclusive?" he teases.

I blush and nod, "Yeah, I know it's fast." I look at him trying to read the truth in his eyes, "Am I crazy?"

"Yup!" he exclaims and I burst out laughing. His face turns serious and he questions, "I need you to hear me for a minute though Sam." I nod and wait for him to speak. "You're going through a lot of shit right now. It seems you're just now dealing with your parents' accident." My eyes widen and he stares right back, "Don't tell me that's not true! I know you better than anyone." I cringe and sit back in my seat knowing he's right. "Then there's the whole mess of Paul and Taylor, moving to somewhere new, not knowing what you want to do, searching for your birth parents, your mom already gone and not knowing what will happen with the rest of it," he blurts out.

"Wow, when you put it like that," I murmur and trail off.

"Yeah, it's a lot," he emphasizes. "Just make sure what you're feeling is real and you're not feeling this intense connection like you said because he's here for you while you're dealing with so much shit. You don't need a distraction, even though you love them," he smirks. "That will hurt you even more later on than if you dealt with everything by depending on friends and family." I eye him skeptically. "I just need to know you're sure about him before you dive in head first," he explains.

I bite my lip before releasing it and inform him, "I get what you're saying Ryan and even why you would think that. Everything's intense with him, but it also never felt more real."

He nods his head slowly while processing my words. "Okay, I'll take your word for it," he grins, relenting. "He just better not fuck you over like that asshole Paul or I will come for him. You can tell him that," he declares.

I nod in agreement, at the same time fighting the pang in my chest at the thought of losing Brady that way. I was with Paul for a really long time and not once did I feel a pain like this even when he did cheat on me. I need to be careful, but if I'm going to try to live like I've promised myself, I also need to give myself a real chance with Brady. I just have to figure out how to do that.

"What's holding you back from telling him who you are?" Ryan asks and I look at him in confusion. He clarifies, "Your birth father."

I nod my head, acknowledging his quick subject change. I shrug and simply admit, "I'm scared." He gives me a look, telling me I'm stating the obvious and I add, "Okay, I don't know if I can handle it if he doesn't want to meet me. After losing my mom and dad..." I trail off as the familiar ache in my chest overwhelms me.

He sighs and reaches across the table, covering both of my hands with one of his large ones to stop them from fidgeting. "You already have a family Samantha," he reminds me. I look up at him, feeling the tears begin to well in my eyes. "We will always be your family, even your mom and dad still watch over you. I know Uncle Tom would never pass up the opportunity of haunting us," he jokes, making me laugh at the memory of my dad telling us he would haunt us some day. I let the tears spill over and quickly wipe them away. "You don't need anything from him really. It's his loss if he's too much of a dumb shit to see you," he continues. "You know we love you," he murmurs.

"Thank you," I whisper, "I needed that." I offer him a small smile, "I love you too, Ry."

He nods and finishes the last of his coke through his straw. "Do you want me to go with you to meet him?" he asks as he looks around the restaurant.

I shake my head, "No. I think it's something I have to do on my own. I just have to get the courage to do it."

"Maybe Brady can go with you," he suggests. "He seems to leave you feeling all Zen," he chuckles, focusing back on me. He drops his hand in his lap just as the tap of heels stops at our table.

We both look up and I grimace at the sight of
Jackie standing in front of us. I raise my eyebrow and ask,
"Can I help you?"

She glares at me and turns her attention on Ryan,
slowly looking him up and down. He crosses his arms
over his chest and raises his eyebrows in question while
he waits for her to stop ogling him. He grins
mischievously, "Like what you see?"

She ignores him and glances back to me, "I'm just
headed to catch up with our mutual friend." She sneers,
"Thought I'd stop and see who, I mean what you're doing
before I go."

I roll my eyes and don't bother responding. Brady
knows where I am. "Have fun," I tell her sarcastically as I
wave her away.

She grimaces and looks back to Ryan, "You should
find better friends."

"I'm good," he replies, grinning. She spins on her
heal and walks out the door without looking back. "She
seems fun," he says, his voice thick with sarcasm.

I laugh, "Nice." He waits for an explanation. I
shrug, "Brady dated her in high school. I guess she never
got over him."

"So she's a clinger, got it," he leans back against the
booth.

"I thought you were interested in Cory?" I ask
sweetly.

He chuckles, "Not telling you shit, but you can tell
me a little more about your roommate if you'd like."

I laugh, "I knew you were going to get there."

"Did you expect any less of me?" he asks.

I shake my head, "Ready to go meet them?"

He groans, "So I get nothing?"

I laugh, "We'll see." Then I add, "It's your turn to
pay."

He tosses a few bills on the table, grumbling to himself. We both stand and he follows me outside to his black Nissan Maxima. We climb in and pull our doors shut. I buckle my seat belt, before I turn to him just as he starts his car. "Thank you for coming Ryan," I tell him sincerely. I didn't realize how much I really needed to see family.

He gives me a stiff nod and pinches his lips tightly together. I reach across and awkwardly hug him with my seat belt on, making him laugh. "Of course, Sam. Like I said before, we're family. We're all here for you." He pauses and leans back, buckling his own seat belt. He puts the car in drive and tries to lighten the conversation again with a shrug, "Everyone knows you like me best."

I laugh, "Whatever you say, Ryan."

A few minutes later we walk through my front door. Ryan calls to Cory, "We're back."

She steps out of her bedroom with a huge smile on her face, probably for Ryan. "Hi! How was lunch?" she asks.

"Good," Ryan answers. "Now I'm all yours until I have to leave, well mostly," he grins mischievously. She giggles in response. I look away and pull my phone out to text Brady.

Yelling in the hallway brings all of our eyes to the closed door. "What the hell is going on? That sounds like Cody," Cory contemplates.

She walks to the front door and starts to open it slowly, but suddenly switches gears throwing it forcefully open. She crosses her arms over her chest and glares down the hall. "You're not welcome here!" Cody grits through his teeth.

"Brady," a girl calls. I wince thinking I know whom the voice belongs to, but my feet move to the door to verify.

"What do you want Jackie?" Brady asks in exasperation as he steps into his doorway. "You know it's better if you don't come here. Is something wrong?"

She shakes her head and focuses on him. "I know he doesn't like me," she says gesturing to Cody, "but it's really important and you weren't answering your phone."

He sighs and runs his hand through his dark hair, "What is it Jackie?" He looks up and notices the three of us standing in the hallway by our door. He smiles and gives me a small wave.

I grin back at him and Jackie mumbles sarcastically, "Oh great, she's here."

Brady turns and glares down at her, "Watch it Jackie. You and I have been friends for a long time, but Sam's my girlfriend. If you want to stay friends, be nice to her," he warns.

Her eyes widen in surprise. "Brady," she whines. He crosses his arms over his chest, daring her to test him. I watch her gulp, take a deep breath and swiftly pull herself together, standing a little taller. "Your *girlfriend* is already cheating on you," she grits out.

I raise my eyebrows and lean back against the wall. I cross my arms over my chest and wait to hear what she has to say. I watch as Brady's lips twitch in amusement at my reaction. "Is that so?" he asks.

She shakes her head, her voice thick with sympathy, "Brady, I'm sorry, but this isn't a joke. I saw her and that guy at 'The Pit'. He was holding her hand and I heard them say I love you." Brady cringes and she puts her hand on his arm, "I'm so sorry."

All of us except for Brady and Jackie burst out laughing. I cover my mouth trying to smother it, but it doesn't matter. I can't hide. She notices and glares over at me. Brady sighs in sympathy and begins, "Jackie..."

She interrupts him, "I have proof." She pulls out her phone and holds it out to him.

He shakes his head as he gently pushes the phone away. "He's her cousin," he informs her.

Her mouth drops open and she flushes instantly. "Wh...what? That's not possible," she stammers.

"We have proof," Ryan grins. "Besides, I have my eye on another girl and she's not in my family," he smirks. He tilts his head and winks at Cory, who giggles in response.

Jackie appears to choke on her words as she murmurs, "I'm sorry. I was just trying to protect you, like you always do for me."

Cody huffs a laugh and sarcastically mumbles, "Yeah, right."

Brady grits his teeth and informs her softly, "I don't need you to protect me. I need you to be my friend and back off Sam."

"But, you barely know her," she argues. She looks up at him with pleading eyes, but it only takes a moment for her shoulders to drop in defeat.

"If you can do that, we're good," he adds, ignoring her comment. "If not, well...I don't really want that to happen," he ends not finishing the thought.

"I really am sorry Brady. I'll back off, but I have this strange feeling about her," she grimaces. "I just don't believe she's right for you," she whines. "I don't want her to hurt you," she adds quietly and spins on her heel.

Ryan laughs and she turns her glare on him. He grins and waves, "Bye! It was very entertaining meeting you!"

While she waits for the elevator, Brady comes to my side and rests his hands on my arms. "I'm sorry."

I shake my head, "It's not your fault."

"You okay?" he asks.

I grin, "You stood up for me. I'm great." He slides his hands up my arms and neck until he cradles my face in his hands. He leans his head down slowly and gently kisses my lips just as the elevator doors close.

A huge burst of laughter breaks free from Cody, "That was fantastic! Let's go out and celebrate!"

"We could go to The Dog by campus," Cory suggests.

"That's a great idea. I'll call an Uber for all of us in about two hours so Cory has time to get ready," Cody declares, teasing his sister at the same time. He pulls up the app on his phone, "Done," he murmurs.

Brady ignores them and smirks at me, "You can get in there." He gives me another quick kiss before striding back towards his apartment.

"Is it a bar?" I question.

Cody turns towards me with his mouth agape, "You've never been?" I hesitantly shake my head no, making him laugh. "It's a restaurant and bar with a really fucking good burger!"

Cory rolls her eyes, "They have a lot of food. Everything is pretty good. I'm sure you'll find something you like."

I shrug and glance up at Brady disappearing into his apartment. I quietly mumble, "I'm afraid I already have."

Chapter 21

I sit quietly in the tall booth taking in my surroundings while everyone drinks their beers and discusses what they want to order. The cherry wood tables have booth seats covered in a burgundy vinyl. Oak wood floors lie underneath my feet, but shades of brown tiles with hints of red cover the front section where we first walked in. Across the room behind a wall of windows, we have a view of rooms with large silver vats where it appears they brew their own beer. I glance up to the second floor and notice right above those sits both silver and copper vats, along with a little more seating. On the other side of the bar sits a long tabletop shuffleboard and three or four pool tables with a couple TV's playing a baseball game.

A poke in my side brings my focus back to everyone at the table. "I said, what are you having?" questions Ryan, talking slowly.

I feel my face heat with embarrassment, realizing he's been trying to get my attention for a while. "Sorry," I apologize. "I was just looking around. It seems like a pretty cool place."

Ryan nods in agreement, "Yeah, who would've guessed," he jokes.

"I've always liked this place," Brady says, pulling my attention across the table to him, "but I haven't been here in a while," he admits.

A tall and lean guy wearing the signature black t-shirt with the black dog restaurant logo steps up to our table. He has short black hair, a black armband tattoo around his right bicep and a small red W on the inside of the opposite wrist. He glances quickly around the table until his sparkling green eyes land on me. "Hi, I'm Kyle. I'm taking over for Jodi for the rest of the night. What can I get for you?" he asks with a flirtatious smile still staring at me.

"Um...I'm not sure...I didn't look at the menu yet..." I stammer as heat rushes to my cheeks.

"I'll have a cheeseburger medium with fries," Brady interrupts, drawing the waiter's attention. His jaw is clenched and his eyes narrow on our waiter, almost daring him to say something.

Ryan chuckles as Kyle smirks, appearing to shake it off. He slowly works his way around the table taking orders before his focus returns to me. "I guess I'll have a cheeseburger medium-well with fries. Thank you," I add appreciatively. He flashes me a broad smile before he turns towards the kitchen.

"He definitely wouldn't mind your phone number," Cory giggles. I roll my eyes in response.

"Not gonna' happen," Brady mumbles.

I smirk, "What was that?"

He chuckles, "Nothing."

"Better be careful man or you might end up with more in your food than you were hoping for," Cody chuckles, causing Brady to flinch.

"Do you want to share my beer with me Sam?" Cory asks.

"No thanks. I don't want to get caught," I admit.

"The waiter sure isn't going to tell on you," Ryan jokes. "You can always have some of mine too. I'll just order another one," he grins.

I shake my head, "No thanks. I'll make sure everyone makes it home okay."

"Another reason to love having you around," Cody teases, making me laugh.

I give him a grateful smile for putting me at ease. I admit I'm too chicken to even attempt drinking anything while we're out. It's just not worth the risk to me. Taylor used to give me a hard time about it. I should have known then she wasn't really a good friend. It's not that I don't drink, but I'm not comfortable drinking while we're out. Anyone could be in here. I'm not one to break the rules, although I don't mind having a couple drinks when I'm at a friend's house and no one is driving. Then again, maybe being afraid to take chances is why my life remained stationary for so long after my parents died. I was too afraid to break away from what I knew. I kept going through the motions and following the rules. Now that I'm finally here, am I going to be able to get the courage to take a chance at finding my dad? I know I need to for me, but I'm scared. Then there's Brady. I wonder if I should really take this chance with him? I don't know if I'm going to stay or what I want to do with my life, which makes everything even harder.

Ryan lightly nudges my leg and I lift my eyes to his. "You okay?" he asks, his eyes full of concern.

I nod, "Yeah." I sigh and quietly admit, "I'm just thinking about why I'm here." I don't bother telling him the whole reason. Besides, I definitely don't want to announce it to the rest of the table.

Ryan nods slowly and purses his lips, trying to read me. He finally asks quietly, "Have you gotten any further on finding him?"

I shake my head, "Not really." I don't add that I haven't tried. Out of the corner of my eye, I notice Brady watching me closely. I turn my head towards him and attempt to change the subject. "You have to go back to classes tomorrow?" I ask him.

He sighs, "Yeah, but I'm almost done. I figure if I keep reminding myself of that, I'll be able to get through this semester quickly."

"I wish I was at that point," Ryan comments, "but I guess soon enough. At least I'm smart enough to plan a schedule with no Mondays," he grins in satisfaction.

Cory laughs, "Must be nice." He smiles at her and she asks, "What time do you have to leave tomorrow?"

"I'll probably head back after lunch," he grimaces staring at her. My stomach suddenly growls loudly, interrupting their moment. Ryan chuckles, "Hungry? We didn't eat that long ago!" He smirks, "Then again you always could eat a lot. Still don't know where you put it all."

I roll my eyes, but award a thankful smile to our waiter as he sets my plate down in front of me only moments later. "That was fast! Thank you!" I exclaim and ignore the laughter as I grab a French fry and stuff it into my mouth.

"Can we have another round of beers?" Cody requests.

"No problem," Kyle says with a nod before he turns and walks towards the end of the bar closest to us.

As soon as his back is turned, I take a huge bite of my burger and groan in satisfaction, "Mmm." I look up to find Brady's wide eyes staring at me. "I'm sorry. This is so good!"

His mouth falls slightly open and he licks his lips. He straightens in his seat and snaps his mouth closed, quickly clearing his throat. "Good," he grumbles before lifting his own burger and stuffing it in his mouth, almost aggressively.

A hush falls over the table as all of us practically inhale our food. The waiter returns with another round of beers and a coke for me even though I never asked for it. I sit back in my seat with an audible sigh, reaching for one more fry before I grab my napkin. I wipe my mouth and hands to get rid of the salt and grease. "Great idea guys. That was really good," I praise no one in particular as I toss my dirty napkin on my nearly empty plate.

Brady asks, "Do you want to play pool?" I shrug, unsure if I'm ready to get up. "I could show you how to play," he offers, misunderstanding my willingness to play. I fight to hold back my smirk as Ryan covers his mouth with his hand to hide his laughter, probably remembering the same things as me. We used to play together when we were younger and eventually we won nearly all the time.

"Okay," I agree slowly. "Are we playing partners?"

Brady nods, "Sure, that's always more fun."

"Do you mind if I play with my cousin since he's going home tomorrow?" I ask innocently. Ryan's knee bounces next to me letting me know he's struggling to hold back any reaction.

"Ok, who wants to partner with me first game?" Brady asks looking between Cody and Cory?"

Cody's eyes narrow on me as he makes the decision for them. "I'm out. I see someone I need to talk to." He stands and strides purposefully towards the bar and two scantily dressed brunettes leaning against it.

Cory shrugs and Brady nods in agreement, "Okay." Cory and Ryan stand and walk together towards the tables. "So are you any good?" he asks.

"Definitely," I grin, my face tingling from my comment. Brady laughs and places his hand possessively on my waist as the waiter approaches. "We're going over to the pool tables. Should we pay now or can we start a tab?"

"How about I close out your dinner and I'll start a tab at the bar for the rest of the night?" he suggests. His eyes wander down to Brady's hand on my waist and he noticeably grimaces before he meets my eyes.

I smile softly, "Thank you." He pulls out our bill from one of his pockets and hands it to me.

Brady takes it out of my hands and immediately gives it back to him with his credit card. "You can use this for the bar tab too. Thanks," he says simply. He slides his hand to the small of my back sending chills up and down my spine. I take a deep breath to calm the butterflies as he guides me towards the pool tables where Cory and Ryan are already racking up the balls.

Just before we reach them, Brady spins me around and possessively presses his lips to mine. He moves his mouth smoothly over mine. Then he pulls away just as quickly as he started, leaving me breathless. "What was that?" I rasp.

He shrugs, "Just making sure to let all the assholes drooling over you know they don't stand a chance."

I laugh, "Are you sure about that?"

He chuckles, "While you're mine I am."

He kisses me on the nose and swiftly steps around me, missing my flinch at his words. I don't know if he meant to say it that way or not, but his truth hurt. My chest clenches painfully. Does he really think I'm only a temporary girlfriend? Why did he get my hopes up with everything he said before? Does he think I'm going to leave? Or does he not see this as seriously as I do? Am I the only one that feels the strong connection between us? Maybe he just sees the physical. Maybe he's not in it for the long term. No longer sure what he wants, I suddenly feel defeated. I take a deep calming breath and look at the floor as I step over to Ryan. He holds a pool cue up to me and taps it on the floor. I reach for it, but he doesn't let go. I glare up at him irritably. "Is this for me?" I ask snidely.

He raises his eyebrows and asks, "Did I miss something?"

I shake my head, feeling more irritated with myself than anything. I hate how he can read me so well. "No, nothing. I'm fine," I snap.

His eyes flare trying to call me out on my lie without voicing it. I hold my hand out for the pool cue instead. He releases it with a reluctant sigh. "If you say so," he mumbles.

"I'm just getting my head ready to kick their asses," I joke, forcing a smile.

He shrugs, "Alright. Works for me." He murmurs, "For now." I roll my eyes, but he's not getting much more from me tonight.

Chapter 22

June 12th (your 10th Birthday)
To My Beautiful Baby Girl,
Happy Birthday!! I can't believe you're 10 this year! Double digits are a big deal! How are you celebrating this year? Another party? Maybe going somewhere cool with a bunch of friends, or a slumber party? Do you have sleepovers? I was never allowed to have any, but I was invited to a few. I remember painting each other's nails, watching movies, eating a lot of junk food and playing games like truth or dare. I always chose dare. I figured what did I have to lose? Then of course, as we got older, we would talk about boys, but I'll tell you about that another time.

My husband and I just adopted a puppy from the animal shelter. They found her on the street and are guessing she's only about 6-8 months old. I can't believe someone would abandon this poor thing. She's black with white all around her nose and four white paws, almost like she's wearing mittens. She's absolutely adorable. They aren't sure how big she'll be though since she's definitely a mixed breed, but that's okay.

I didn't abandon you, you know. I wanted what was best for you. I definitely wasn't what was best. I hope you understand that. If you don't believe it now, maybe you will some day. No matter what, it's my truth. I hope you have a wonderful birthday!
With Love...
Catherine Schepp

A lump forms in my throat as I realize that's what I'm afraid of, being abandoned. She may not think she abandoned me, but sometimes it feels that way to me anyway. I wouldn't change anything though if it meant never having my mom and dad. Tears form in my eyes at the thought of them. I know they never intentionally left me, but they're gone just the same. Taylor abandoned our friendship and Paul...I can only admit he's a selfish asshole, but it's the same thing. Then there's my birth father... He already left me once. If I find him, what will stop him from doing the same? Maybe that's why I'm holding back from finding him. He doesn't know me. I sigh as my mind drifts to Brady. He's been saying all the right things, but last night he said, "While you're mine..." Does that mean he's going to leave me too? I feel like I'm already in too deep with him. Maybe I should stop this now before he has a chance to completely obliterate me because I know he has the power to do it.

A knock on my bedroom door pulls me from my depressing thoughts. "Come in," I call from my bed.

Brady peeks his head around the door and smiles, "Good morning."

I jump from surprise and quickly pull a pillow in front of my body, hugging it to my chest. I've been lazy this morning, so I'm still wearing my pajamas. I have on a cobalt blue tank top with white lace at the top, but no bra. On the bottom I have white pajama pants with a lacy design lightly patterned along the sides. I run my hand through my hair hoping I don't look as bad as I feel at the moment. "What are you doing here?" I ask anxiously.

"Um, I'm sorry, I'm..." he stammers. He huffs, "Damn you're beautiful."

My whole body instantly heats from his compliment. "Thank you," I murmur as I feel the burn of his eyes roaming up and down my body.

He clears his throat and explains, "Cory let me in." I nod, still clinging to the pillow in front of me. "I have to leave for class and since I didn't hear from you yet, I wanted to come by and see if you wanted me here to read the letter from your mom," he offers.

My heart takes off sprinting right for him. He took time to come deal with my shit, again. He's amazing. I smile appreciatively up at him, "Thank you Brady. I actually just finished reading it though."

He nods in acceptance. "You okay?" he asks. I nod my head slowly. He approaches me cautiously and sits down on the edge of the bed near my feet. "Is something going on Sam?"

I shake my head, "No, I'm good. I just wasn't expecting you," I explain telling part of the truth. He eyes me skeptically and I sigh, and drop my head in defeat. "That's not true. I have to ask you something."

His expression turns cautious and he sighs, "Okay."

I take a deep breath and begin fidgeting with the edge of the pillowcase in my hand. I nervously look up at him from under my lashes and ask, "Are you really in this?"

"What?" he asks with wide eyes.

I groan and attempt to rephrase, starting over. "Last night you said, 'while you're mine'. Does that mean that this thing between us is only temporary for you?" I try to swallow over the lump in my throat dropping my head and focusing on the way my hands move over the pillowcase. "If it is Brady, I don't know if I can do this with you," I murmur painfully.

"Shit," he mumbles and pulls my hands into his lap with both of his. Then he holds both of them with one of his and uses his other hand to gently slide his fingers along my jawline until they're underneath my chin. He gently nudges my head upward until I meet his warm gaze. "When I told you I wanted us to try to find out what's between us, I meant a lot of things, but not a single one of my thoughts has you only being a temporary part

~ 215 ~

of my life. I'm not promising you forever Sam and I hope that's not what you're asking because it's too soon for that, but I want us to work." He pauses and I watch as his Adam's apple bobs up and down. "I don't know what will happen with us, but I want this with you to be anything but temporary," he insists.

I release the breath I didn't know I was holding and nod my head slowly, "Okay."

He places a soft kiss to my lips, making my insides quiver. He pulls back and searches my face for answers. "What brought this on?" he asks. "Besides my stupid comment."

I grimace and instead of answering I hand him the letter from my mom, "Here."

"You want me to read this?" he asks, his eyebrows nearly hitting his hairline in surprise. I nod slowly and he gives my hand a squeeze in encouragement. Then he looks down at the paper in his lap and begins to read. I watch his face, knowing the moment he realizes my insecurity as his eyes go soft. He lifts his face to mine and holds my gaze. "I'm not going to abandon you Samantha," he declares.

I throw myself into his arms and he catches me with a chuckle, falling backwards onto the mattress. I wrap my arms around him and hold him tightly. He runs his hands lightly up and down my back in a comforting motion. I open my mouth and blurt out my fears before I hold back from him again. "She's right. I do feel like she abandoned me sometimes. Not all the time, but I do. I also think it was for the best because I love my parents, but they abandoned me too."

"Samantha..." he begins softly.

I shake my head, "I know they didn't want to leave me Brady, but God obviously had other plans and sometimes I feel like they abandoned me anyway, even though I know that's stupid." I sigh and add, "Then of course there's Taylor and my ex. They both willingly left me." I shrug, "Sometimes I think there's something wrong with me."

"There is definitely not a damn thing wrong with you Sam. There's so much right. I don't want to stay away from you, even for a minute," he insists.

"Ok," I chuckle humorlessly.

"I'm serious Sam, you're beautiful, smart..." he starts

I shake my head, slightly embarrassed, "I'm not fishing for compliments Brady."

He laughs, "I know, but that doesn't mean you don't deserve them."

I smirk and try to give him as much honesty as possible. "I have a lot of issues Brady. If you want to run, now's your chance."

He chuckles and reinforces, "I'm not going anywhere."

I grin, feeling overwhelmed with a sense of relief. "Good, because I don't want you to," I admit.

He tilts his head towards mine and seals our mouths together in a warm and heated kiss. He pushes into me a little further, meshing our mouths perfectly together. I push my tongue through a slight opening between his lips until my tongue tangles with his. I groan into his mouth, tasting him and fighting to get closer. I run my hands up and down his back and he pulls away from me with a groan. "Fuck, I really don't want to go," he complains making me giggle.

"I need to see Ryan before he leaves anyway," I tell him.

He gives me a chaste kiss and sits up, "I have to get to class too. Will you have dinner with me tonight?"

I nod and smile, "How about I make you something here this time?"

He grins back at me, "Sounds like a plan." He stands and leans towards me. He gives me another chaste kiss, making my lips tingle. I stand to follow him out and he stops me with a gentle hand on my waist. "I know he's your cousin and all, but would you please get dressed before you go out there?" Brady pleads, making me blush. "Besides, knowing my luck Cody will be out there too," he jokes.

I pull a raspberry pink fitted sweatshirt on over my head with a V-neck and Brady's eyes are drawn to my chest before he awkwardly turns around mumbling, "Not much better."

I laugh, "Too bad."

I step into the living room and Ryan calls, "Good morning Sam! You slept late. Were you tired from kicking your boyfriend's ass at pool last night?" he smirks.

"Nope," I grin popping the p. "That was easy," I smirk, waving him off.

Brady chuckles and shakes his head. "I'm going to class before you two have a chance to give me any more shit." He kisses the corner of my mouth and murmurs, "Bye, Sam." He pulls the door open. "It was nice meeting you, Ryan. Hope we'll see you again," he says, waving to my cousin.

"Oh you will," Ryan replies. "It better be on good terms," he threatens.

"No worries here," Brady smiles and waves as he walks out the door. "Bye!"

I grimace, but Brady misses my reaction. Unfortunately Ryan doesn't. "What's that about?" he asks.

"I don't know what you're talking about," I feign ignorance.

He crosses his arms across his chest and glares at me, "Sam?"

"Where's Cory?" I ask attempting to maintain my façade.

"She went to talk to her brother and then go get us some lunch so I could have a little while to talk to you before I had to leave," he explains.

I sigh and flop down on the couch next to him. "Nothing's going on. I'm just being a little dramatic."

"What's new?" he smirks.

I roll my eyes. Then I admit with a sigh, "I'm just a little nervous about how much I already like Brady. What if it doesn't work out? I don't know if I'll do well with someone else leaving me," I confess.

He gives me a sad look of understanding and sighs, "Sam, you can't go into a relationship thinking that way."

I nod reluctantly, "I know, but I wasn't planning on getting into a relationship at all right now."

"If you like him, go for it. I'll be here if anything happens and I need to come kick his ass," he smirks.

"You aren't coming back to see my roommate anytime soon?" I ask with raised eyebrows. Ryan blushes uncharacteristically and cocks his head to the side.

He grins and shrugs, "If she'll let me."

I laugh and remind him again, "She's my roommate Ryan. Be careful!"

He smiles, "I always am."

I chuckle. He reaches for me, messing up my hair like I'm a little kid, making me screech. "Ryan!" I yell.

He jumps up laughing. "Don't you love having me around?"

I put my hands on my waist and fight a smile as I ask him sweetly, "Do you need help packing, Ry?"

He throws his head back and laughs. He steps towards me with his eyes sparkling, "It's really fucking good to have you back, Sam." I don't respond. I don't have to. We both understand what he's saying. He turns around to gather his things to stuff in his duffle. I take a deep calming breath, knowing I only have about five minutes before he's done.

Chapter 23

June 12th (your 11th Birthday)
To My Beautiful Baby Girl,
Happy Birthday!! I believe you will be starting Middle School very soon. Those were definitely not my favorite years! They weren't horrible, but bad hair, acne, braces and hormones are just the beginning. Did you get your period yet? I got mine at 11. Hopefully you won't have yours for a few years yet, but you never know. I didn't know what it was when I got it. We hadn't reached that lesson yet in school and my mom and I never really talked about those kinds of things. Honestly, we never talked about much at all. I'm sure you're mom is much better at it. I hope you have some good friends and all the kids are nice to you. Unfortunately, I found out that kids can be really mean, especially girls! It all started in Middle School for me. I guess it's your chance to find out who your real friends are though, when you see who sticks by your side through the good and the bad.

My husband and I had a good year this year. He got a promotion at his job and I'm still enjoying my office work. Our dog is our only child and it will probably always stay that way for us for so many reasons. It took her a little while to trust us and get comfortable in our home, but she's finally there. She's about thirty pounds and since they think she's almost two I don't think she'll get any bigger. She loves to cuddle with me. Do you have any pets? I hope you get the chance to have a pet sometime in your life. They may be hard work, but their unconditional love is something I can't even explain. You may not believe this, but I have that for you too. I may not know you, but I do love you.

Enjoy your birthday!

With Love...
Catherine Schepp

"Are you okay?" Brady asks quietly as I fold up the letter.

I lean forward and slip the letter onto the coffee table in front of me. Then I turn to glance up at him with a small smile, "I feel like you're constantly asking me that."

The corners of his lips turn up just enough to deepen his dimple, "Well, I can't read your mind yet, so..."

I giggle, "I'm good." I lean back and relax against him on my living room couch. It's comforting being in his arms, which makes it even easier for me to talk to him. "It was pretty much generalizing Middle School, puberty and their dog," I inform him. "It's strange," I tell him thoughtfully.

"What is?" he questions.

I shrug as I try to gather my thoughts. "She always says Happy Birthday, so I know she was thinking of me on my birthday. It may be small, but it's not to me," I confess. "Then with each letter it's like she's remembering things she went through when she was my age. Well, the age I was when she wrote the letter anyway. Then she attempts to connect it by trying to figure out the person I might be at that time in my life, but she also gives me a small taste of what's going on in her life at the time as well," I explain. "Her letters bring back memories of growing up with my mom and dad, but at the same time they bring a lot of questions of 'what if'. What if she kept me? What if he kept me? What if they shared me? Then in all those scenarios I imagine so many different directions my life could have taken by using the smallest amount of information she gave me about either of them. It's almost like my life's possibilities were endless and all

~ 222 ~

of the 'what if's' take on a life of their own in my head, but every scenario is also constantly changing. I can't help but question everything. It's overwhelming," I admit, sounding tired.

He runs his hand lightly up and down my arm, helping to relax me and I revel in the quiet. After a few minutes he tells me, "I know I can't really understand how you're feeling or what you're going through, but I do get what you're saying. I think I would do the same thing if I was in your shoes."

"Thank you," I murmur, appreciating his acknowledgment.

He twists his body and tilts his head so he can look into my eyes. He runs his thumb softly down my cheek, his eyes sparkling. "What are you thanking me for?" he asks incredulously with the corners of his mouth twitching up.

I shrug and smirk back at him, "Lots of things." He laughs. "But mostly for listening to me and being here for all of this. I just met you and yet I already feel so close to you. You do things like come to see me just so I don't have to be alone when I read her letters and that really means a lot to me. You're supporting me so much just by being here and holding me in your arms. It's hard for me to explain, but honestly this whole situation is really overwhelming and just having you here with me means so much. Then you go and try to relate to what I'm going through," I laugh at how surreal this whole situation feels. "Just, thank you, Brady," I whisper, trying to choke down the emotion rising in my throat. Sometimes I question why he's not running from me with all my drama, but I don't want to admit that to him, afraid that's exactly what he'll do.

He uses his thumbs to wipe the tears I didn't know had fallen and I smile up at him. "I'm happy to be here for you, Sam. Honestly, I'm honored you're letting me be a part of all of this." I glance up at him with doubt clearly in my eyes. He laughs, "I mean it. This is really personal and you're letting me go through it with you. Watching you and being a part of this, no matter what happens, shows me so much about you. I see your strength, courage, resiliency, determination and so much more. It's beautiful. You're beautiful inside and out," he murmurs. "I should really be the one thanking you for letting me be a part of it."

As I stare into his sparkling blue eyes, my heart begins pounding so hard I feel like it might burst right out of my chest. My whole body heats and my hands feel clammy. I take a deep breath to try to slow down my breathing but it's no use. I drop my head to his chest for support and wrap my arms tightly around him, needing to be closer to him without looking at him. I nearly breathe a sigh of relief when he encircles me with his strong arms and pulls me into his lap.

I want to wrap myself around him. I feel like my whole body is vibrating with need for him. I want so much more from him right now, but I know he can't give it to me because he has to leave for class. I take a deep breath, inhaling his scent of soap and light, musky cologne, wishing I didn't need to let go. I need to change the subject before I don't let him leave. "Um," I rasp. I pause and clear my throat before I try again. "So did you finish everything you needed to last night?" I ask hoarsely. I slip off his lap and turn towards him so I can distance myself just enough to get my body under control. I reach for his hand resting behind my back and pull it between us, easily entwining our fingers together and clasping tightly for support.

"Yeah," he answers on his exhale. "I'm sorry I had to cancel our plans last night. This professor is really tough. I'll fall behind quick if I let the work slide now," he concedes. "Did you and Cory have fun hanging out?" he questions.

I nod my head, "Yeah."

"What did you two do?" he asks.

"Not much," I admit. "We had macaroni and cheese and then ice cream for dessert. We talked a lot and then Cody came by and we all watched a movie."

"That's where he disappeared to. I should've known," he chuckles. "What movie did you guys watch?"

I shrug, "I don't know. I fell asleep." He laughs hard and I grin up at him. "It was probably for the best you had so much to do anyway. Cory seemed kind of down after Ryan left. I guess she really likes him. She needed some girl time and I was happy to oblige, even with Cody," I smile. "I guess I haven't really had that in a while. Of course Taylor and I haven't been talking and after my parents died I wasn't much fun to hang out with," I admit with a grimace. "Besides, I probably would've been way too distracted if you were here more than the few minutes you were," I joke.

He chuckles, "Distracted huh?" He reaches up and tucks a loose strand of hair behind my ear. "I know what you mean," he mumbles, making me smile.

He glances at his phone to check the time and I ask, "You have to go?"

He nods, "Unfortunately." He grimaces and informs me, "I have to stop at the restaurant after I'm done with classes today. I'm not sure how long I'll be there."

"That's okay," I tell him, even though I really want to see him. I don't want to be one of those needy or clingy girlfriends.

"No, it's not," he states, making me smile. "Hopefully it won't be too late though and I'll stop by when I'm done if that's okay."

I nod, "Of course."

"Either way though, do you want to have dinner with me tomorrow night? Something simple, so I can study if I need to."

"Okay, that sounds good," I admit, smiling up at him.

"Good," he grins, "It's a date." He leans down and firmly presses his mouth to mine, sending chills down my spine. His full lips feel soft and smooth as they move tenderly over my mouth. I lean towards him to push the kiss deeper, but he quickly pulls back with a regretful groan. "I'm really sorry, but I have to go. I have to get to campus," he reminds me again. He lets go of my hand and cradles my face in both of his before he presses a light chaste kiss to my lips and my stomach flips over in response. My eyes flutter open as he stands and backs away.

I sigh and stand reluctantly, following him to the front door. "Okay, if you have to go, just leave," I say feigning annoyance.

He chuckles and kisses me one more time on the nose. "You're cute when you don't get your way."

"Cute?" I question. His only answer is to flash his dimple with his broad smile, nearly causing me to melt into a puddle at his feet. I give myself a slight shake and ask with a smirk, "So I'm the only one who wanted you to stay huh?"

He laughs, but doesn't respond to my taunt. "What are you going to do today anyway?" he asks instead.

I shrug, "I'm not exactly sure, but I do have some things I have to do in town. I'll probably try to get that done sooner rather than later." I leave my answer as general as possible, not ready to give him any details.

He nods and reaches for the door handle, "Okay, have fun with that. Text me when you have a few minutes. I'll be in one of my economics classes. I'll savor the distraction, especially from you," he grins. "Bye Sam."

He pulls the door open and I lift my hand in a small wave, "Bye Brady." I watch him saunter away. Then I slowly push the door shut behind him and collapse against it, already emotionally exhausted just thinking about what I'm about to do.

The errands I have to do are even more personal than I voiced to Brady, but ironically I was afraid I'd lose the courage to do anything if I said it out loud, or he'd try to skip class to go with me. Either is not an option for me. I think this is something I need to do alone. After reading so many letters from my birth mom, I still have so many questions. Between Ryan's visit, everything that's happening with Brady and my new friends, I don't feel quite so alone anymore. I believe it might be time to gather my courage and at least introduce myself to my birth father. Hopefully he's where I think he is. After I let him know I'm here, I guess I'll leave things up to him. I'm not naïve. I realize it will be a shock for him to see me, no matter what his state of mind. Then after his initial shock wears off, I can't help but wonder what he'll think or do next. If anything, I at least want a little more background and medical information than what was in the paperwork the Department of Children and Families provided me.

I push myself up off the floor and stride for my room. I need to find something to wear. "What the hell do you wear to meet your father for the first time?" I sigh to myself. Hopefully I have something in the clothes I brought up here. If I plan on staying, even for a while, I'll need to make a trip back home to get more of my things very soon. I don't have room for too much more, but I have to make space for at least some of my things I left home while I figure everything out.

Chapter 24

I'm sitting in the driver's seat of my Volvo clinging tightly to the steering wheel even though my car is parked and the keys are already in my coat pocket. I can't seem to do anything but stare at the pale yellow, sprawling Victorian house in front of me. Just when I think I've built up the nerve to approach the house, the same blonde woman with the same boy from the other day, walks out the front door and climbs into a BMW this time before backing out of the driveway, taking my courage with them. I don't know why I didn't question who else would be here. When I drove through town, I noticed the same guy working the register from when I was at the store last time, so I drove here instead without thinking. I assume it was his wife and son who just left, but what if it wasn't and they're still inside. Plus, I know he has at least one "kid" about the same age as me. I'm barely ready to meet him. I'm definitely not ready to meet anyone else in the family, especially if they don't even know about me. That would be a disaster!

I sigh and drop my head against the steering wheel in frustration. "What should I do?" I mumble. I close my eyes and think of my mom and dad, feeling their warmth all around me. I take a deep breath and then another as I feel myself slowly coming to a decision for better or worse. "I'm here. If I don't walk up there now, I may never come back," I tell myself. If anyone except him answers the door, I'll say I have the wrong house or something.

I push myself away from the steering wheel and clench my fists trying to steel my nerves, but it doesn't help. I grip the door handle with shaky hands and push it open, feeling like I might throw up. I step out of my car onto trembling legs and slam the door shut with sudden determination. I briskly stride up the red brick walkway before I change my mind again. I lift my head slowly as I approach the front door. I force myself to knock on the large black door instead of ringing the doorbell and quickly pull my quivering hands back to my sides. My heart pounds erratically inside my chest as I hear heavy approaching footsteps. The door swings open and I freeze at the sight of an older man about 5'10" with dark brown hair, graying at his temples. He's barefoot and wearing dark blue jeans and a long sleeved black t-shirt with the sleeves pushed up to his elbows. I look up and gasp at the sight of his caramel eyes that look just like mine.

"Can I help you?" his deep voice questions. I open my mouth to respond, but nothing comes out. I realize I'm not breathing and I attempt to force air into my lungs as tears spring to my eyes. His eyes widen, "Oh my God! Are you okay? Do you need help? Should I call an ambulance?" he rambles, mistaking my panic for pain.

I frantically shake my head and force out the words, "No!" I yell. "No. I'm sorry. I'm fine." His eyebrows draw together in confusion at my words and I take a deep breath and ask, "Are you Lincoln Scott?"

He nods his head hesitantly, "Yes. Who's asking?"

I take another deep breath and make myself explain. "I'm your daughter," I blurt out awkwardly, without preamble.

His mouth drops slightly open and his eyes widen in shock, "Excuse me?"

I swallow over the lump in my throat and try again, my voice trembling. "My name is Samantha and I'll be 20 in June. You and Catherine Schepp put me up for adoption when I was born nearly twenty years ago." I watch as the blood slowly drains from his face. "So, I guess, Mr. Scott, that makes you my father," I whisper hoarsely.

He slowly assesses me from head to toe and back up again. I imagine what he's seeing as he looks me over with my high black leather boots, black leggings and my long cream sweater hanging down to about halfway between my hips and knees. I'm wearing a crystal pendant hanging from a long black leather string, small silver hoop earrings and a bunch of silver bangles on my right wrist. I put on minimal make-up with just a little bit of pink lip-gloss and I let my wavy dark brown hair hang loosely down my back. His eyes eventually come back to meet my matching ones. I have no idea what he's thinking, but I do notice one thing in his eyes, acceptance. "Um..." he glances back into his house and then back at me again. "Do you...um...want to come in?" he barely chokes out the words.

I nod stiffly and stutter, "Th...Thank you." I take a step into his house and find myself in a large open foyer with a large oak staircase off to the left and a door leading to a small office just in front of the stairs. He gestures to my right and I walk into a large living room with ivory chairs decorated with wood trim and a matching couch. In front of the couch lies a large gray shag carpet just in front of a huge gray stone fireplace. The mantel is bare, but above the fireplace rests a huge flat screen TV. I stop and glance at the man dressed in jeans and can't help but think he seems out of place in this room. Maybe his wife decorated it.

I sit down awkwardly on the edge of the couch, not sure what to do or say now that I'm here. "You have her hair," he murmurs.

"What?" I ask.

"You have her hair," he shrugs. "Well, it's my color, but you have the same loose curls she did," he elaborates.

~ 231 ~

I smile, feeling a burn in my chest. "I have your eyes," I state, looking up at him.

He grins, "Yes, you do. My daughter has them too, but hers have a little more gold."

"You have a daughter?" I ask.

He flinches and looks away from me nodding. "Yeah, she's only a couple months younger than you," he informs me. I look down at my lap, feeling incredibly uncomfortable. "I didn't know at first," he says as his voice catches in his throat. "She," he hesitates, "your mom...when she found me she was already about six months along. It was also right after my wife and I found out we were pregnant. We had already been planning our wedding and..." he sighs softly. "At the time, I couldn't afford two babies and my wife and I were just starting out together. We weren't even married yet," he rambles his explanation.

My heart clenches painfully. I don't want to hear why I wasn't worth keeping. I get that it wasn't about me, but that doesn't stop my heart from understanding it. I close my eyes and remind myself how my mom and dad always told me how much they loved me and how much they wanted me. I'd always hear how grateful they were that my parents had given me up for adoption because I was their greatest gift. I know they meant every word they said and I love them more than anything, so this can't hurt me. My whole body tingles with anxiety anyway. My stupid heart wants to know why he gave me away. It doesn't matter what my brain tells me. I look over at him, my shoulders so tense my neck is beginning to ache. I force myself to breathe slowly and calm my rising anxiety. I gulp over the lump in my throat as I take in his eyes, full of both wonder and regret. "I've had a good life," I blurt, hoping he sees the truth in my eyes. "I couldn't have asked for better parents."

He sighs and his lips curl slightly up in a soft smile. "Good, good, that's good," he murmurs staring at me. I begin rubbing my arms uncomfortably, waiting for him to break the silence. After a few more soundless minutes, he sighs, "I'm sorry, I can't stop looking at you. This is just so strange to see you. You look so much like her, yet..." he shakes his head, obviously struggling to wrap his head around this situation.

"What did she look like?" I ask softly. "Do you have a picture of her?"

He shakes his head, "I honestly don't know if I do, but..." he rubs his hand over his face and through his hair before dropping it to his side. He places his elbows on his knees and clasps his hands in front of him. He looks down at his hands, fidgeting with them as if he's attempting to pull a memory from a long time ago. He looks up at me and begins telling me some of what he remembers. "She was beautiful. She was probably about your height and same build. You have her hair, like I said, but hers was a soft deep red with those curls. She was full of life and had a beautiful smile. She didn't seem to have a care in the world. She just wanted to enjoy the moment, enjoy life...so that's what we did."

I take a deep breath and look away, letting my breath out slowly. "She died in October," I inform him, my voice cracking.

I notice his flinch out of the corner of my eye. "I knew she wasn't doing well. She contacted me recently to tell me she didn't think she had long. She said she left the letters we talked about with the Department of Children and Families. Did you get them?" he asks. I nod my head in response. He pauses, momentarily lost in thought before looking back at me. "So, from your question, I assume you weren't able to meet her," he states. I wince and nod my head slowly. "I'm sorry," he responds sincerely.

I gulp over the lump in my throat and croak, "Thank you."

He rubs his knees, looking slightly uncomfortable, before asking, "Do your parents know you're here?"

I shake my head and reply with a hoarse whisper, "My mom and dad died in an accident about a year and a half ago."

His eyes widen in shock and he gasps, "I'm so sorry!"

I offer him a tight smile and force myself to say, "Thanks."

I watch as he fidgets uncomfortably and my wariness begins to grow. He shakes his head, "I'm going to admit that I have no idea what to do here. I don't know what I'm supposed to say or do," he sighs.

I shake my head and confess with a small smile, "Neither do I." He smiles back a little more genuine and I feel myself begin to relax, but only a little. "Can I ask about you and your family?" I ask hesitantly.

He nods and relaxes back against the chair. "My wife Ginny is my world. I met her shortly after your mom and we fell in love fast. I proposed after only 3 months. I knew she was it for me. We started planning the wedding, she got pregnant with our little girl and then your mom found me." My heart skips a beat at the fond look on his face when he mentions his daughter. I never had that chance with him. My mother was just a fling. I hate myself for the queasy feeling in the pit of my stomach, but I can't help it.

I remain silent as he continues, "We couldn't care for both of you at the time, although Ginny was willing to, but we were struggling to keep our own heads above water. We got married in her parents' backyard a month later. We lived in a small apartment when our daughter was first born, but I got a great management job right out of college. Then my dad passed away and left me a big chunk of money. That's when Ginny and I opened Hometown, the home store in town. We've been doing pretty well ever since. We had our son a couple years later and we bought this house just before he was born. He just turned 13," he informs me.

I nod and turn my head as I fight the tears trying to force their way out. "Do they know about me?" I ask weakly.

He sighs in defeat. I turn back to him just as he looks away shaking his head. He closes his eyes and takes a deep breath before opening them and returning his gaze back to me. "No," he confesses. "I didn't want to tell them something they didn't need to know. I had no idea if you would ever come looking for either of us," he says as explanation. I get it. I wouldn't expect him to. "But my Ginny knows. If we had more at the time...she would have been a wonderful step-mother to you," he insists.

I nod, not able to speak over the gravel in my throat, but even if I could, what would I say to that? I take a deep breath and stand on my shaky legs. He stands with me and his eyebrows rise in question. "I...I should go," I stammer, suddenly eager to leave.

He reaches out towards me, but doesn't move from where he's standing. "Wait!" he calls sounding desperate. "Do you want my number? Or can I have yours? Can I see you again?" he stammers.

I breathe a sigh of relief at the rapid fire of his questions. He wants to talk to me more. He wants to see me again. I reach up and push a tear off my cheek and answer with an exaggerated nod. "Yeah," I rasp.

He smiles broadly, appearing relieved. "I'll tell my family," he informs me. I nod my head quickly, needing to escape. We exchange phone numbers and I tuck my cell phone in my coat pocket as he walks me to the front door. "Samantha?" he calls as I step outside. I turn to face him and he grins down at me. "Thank you," he rasps.

I'm not exactly sure what he's thanking me for, but I don't have any strength left in me at the moment to ask. Instead I force myself to smile back at him the best I can, hoping it doesn't appear feral. My whole body prickles, overwhelmed with emotion. I wave and walk quickly to my car, trying not to break out in a run. I feel myself beginning to crumble. I need to get out of here before I break.

I make it to my car and buckle my seat belt. I pull away holding my breath. I drive two blocks before the tears begin flowing freely. I'm barely able to comprehend what I'm feeling or thinking. I blink the tears away, attempting to keep my vision clear to see the road. I whisper up to my mom and dad, "I love you," at the same time focus on getting myself safely back to my apartment.

I quickly park my car in front of my new building, but I don't move from behind the wheel as I pick up my cell phone and glance at the new entry, "Lincoln Scott". In another life, it would have said "Dad". I grimace at my thoughts. I take another deep breath and feel an overwhelming urge to at least hear a comforting voice on the other end, but the name my fingers go to without even thinking is Brady. How do I already feel this way about him? I sigh and text him instead, knowing he should be in his last class of the day by now. "Been a long day...looking forward to seeing you later! Stop by no matter what time you're done. I'll be up."

Chapter 25

I begin fidgeting, quickly losing interest in the old Saturday night live episode on TV. With Cory asleep, I can't stop myself from glancing impatiently at the door every thirty seconds. "I'm pathetic," I grumble to myself. I attempt to force my focus back to the TV, but I really want to talk to Brady.

A few minutes after 11:30 I hear a quiet knock on my front door. I instantly spring up from the couch and peer through the peephole at a distorted view of Brady's head. I throw the door open, grinning brightly at the sight of Brady still holding his hand up from knocking. His hair is a mess like he's been running his hand through it and he smiles down at me, flashing his dimple, "That was fast."

I blush and smile back at him as I reach for his hand. "I've been waiting," I reply emphatically.

He chuckles, "I'm flattered."

I roll my eyes and give his hand a gentle tug, pulling him inside. I shut the door behind him and walk to the couch with him in tow. I turn, but before I can sit down he cradles my face in his hands and his lips crash down on mine. He moves his mouth slowly, tasting and caressing my lips like they're his treasure. My heart speeds up and I push into him wanting to drive our kiss deeper, but he holds me in place. I sigh feeling the sensuality of his kiss all the way to my toes.

Just when I think my legs will give out, he pulls away still cradling my face as we both catch our breath. "I've been waiting to do that all day," he mumbles, his blue eyes sparkling. I feel the heat in my cheeks as I smile up at him. I always seem to be smiling when he's around. He chuckles and presses his lips to mine hard, but briefly this time before he lets me go. I flop down on the couch, not able to stand without his support. He sits down right next to me, turned slightly so he's facing me. He puts his arm over the back of the couch with his hand landing gently on the back of my neck. He smirks, "Waiting huh?"

I roll my eyes again, "Don't go getting an ego. I just wanted to talk."

"If you don't want to see me, I could go home and change and get in bed to call you," he teases.

"So, being in your bed is better than seeing me?" I challenge.

"If you're in it," he mumbles. I raise my eyebrows in surprise. "I'm sorry, I shouldn't have said that," he stammers.

I chuckle, "I don't take any offense to that, believe me."

He sighs and relaxes back against the couch. He keeps his hand on the back of my neck and begins rubbing small circles with his thumb as he studies me. "What did you want to talk about? You okay?" he asks.

I nod my head, "Yeah. I just had a little bit of a crazy day." His eyebrows draw together in confusion and I rush to explain. "Well, yes it was crazy, but more emotional than anything," I stammer. "The things I said I had to do in town weren't really regular things. I went to meet my father today," I blurt out before I lose the nerve.

Brady's eyes go wide, his hand tensing on my neck. He asks, "You did what?"

"I went to my father's house today to meet him," I repeat, reminding myself it really happened, at the same time telling Brady.

"Wait, you went to his house?" he asks in shock. "Why would you go to his house? You have no idea who the guy really is! Something could've happened to you!" he rasps.

I roll my eyes and respond sarcastically, "Thanks Dad."

He drops his hand from my neck and crosses his arms over his broad chest. He glares at me, "Sam, did you even tell anyone where you were going?" he asks. I slowly shake my head. He groans my name, "Sam. I would've gone with you."

I feel the weight of his words on me as I realize what could've happened. I didn't even think about it. "I'm sorry," I apologize, suddenly feeling guilty. "You're right. I should've at least told someone, but I'm obviously fine. I just needed to do this by myself and I thought I'd chicken out if I told you. I was going to go to try to see him at his job, but he wasn't working. Plus, that probably would have been weird if he wasn't the only one there or if he was busy."

He sighs in defeat and thankfully drops it. My parents wouldn't have let that one go. He pulls me into his lap and wraps his arms around me. I lean my head on his shoulder and just enjoy the comfort of being in his arms. After a few moments of silence, he asks cautiously, "So how'd it go?"

I shrug, "Okay, I guess. He didn't kick me out," I attempt to joke. I feel him shake his head and he squeezes my side making me squeal. I push his hand away from my side and wrap my arms around his waist. I give him a gentle squeeze and relax further into his warmth. "He answered the door. As soon as I told him who I was he invited me in. He was obviously surprised to see me, but like my mom had said, he wasn't surprised I existed at least." I take a deep breath and push myself to keep going. I need to get it all out. "Luckily he was the only one home. I don't think I could've handled it if he wasn't. I probably would've made up a stupid story that made no sense and ran out of there." He chuckles and slides his hands down my back where he continues his circles, only bigger, going all the way up and down my back.

"His wife knows about me, but his kids don't. He has a daughter only a couple months younger than me and a 13-year-old son. It's strange to think I have a brother and sister I've never met. I've never had a sibling," I reflect.

"It's not all it's cracked up to be," he says, but I hear the laughter in his voice.

My stomach churns just thinking about what it would be like to be them and hear this kind of news from my dad. "I hope they don't hate me," I mumble.

Brady sighs, "They're lucky to have you. If they don't believe that, it's all on them, not on you. You can't worry about something you can't control," he reminds me. "Besides, a lot of brothers and sisters don't get along. It wouldn't be anything new."

"Yeah," I concede pensively. "Cody and Cory get along most of the time though."

"They definitely don't always and when we were kids, Cody used to torture Cory any chance he could get," he informs me.

I chuckle, "I could see that. You and Becca get along," I add.

"Yeah, but definitely not always. We have always been good at pissing each other off," he admits. "I'd do anything for her though."

I smile thoughtfully, "That's what I'm talking about."

Brady gently kisses the top of my head, "You may not have the same kind of relationship that you would if you grew up together, but if you spend time with them, you could still have something great." His hand freezes on my back and I feel his body briefly tense before he forces himself to relax. His hand begins moving on my back again and he clears his throat. He tenderly asks, "Do you think you're going to meet them?"

I pause for a moment, thinking over our conversation. "I think so. He asked for my number and gave me his. Then he asked when he could see me again," I inform him.

"That's good," he encourages me.

I nod into his chest, "Yeah. He also said he was going to tell his family. I think I just need to process everything for a couple days and if I hear from him, great, but if not, I'll text him or something to meet me for coffee. Maybe," I add, making him chuckle.

"What was he like?" he questions.

"I guess he had the same color hair as me and I have his eyes. He actually said I have my mom's hair, but his color. He said I look a lot like her. It's hard for me to understand that," I admit.

"What do you mean?" he prompts.

I shrug, "I've never looked like anyone before. My parents both had blonde hair, blue eyes and fair skin. People would always tell me I looked nothing like them. Of course, they didn't know I was adopted, but I didn't like hearing it," I confess. His hold on me tightens and I continue, "I used to try to find something, anything that looked like either of them." I chuckle humorlessly, "Sometimes it would be the stupidest thing, like a toe," I laugh to myself. "They were great parents. I guess I just wanted to be like them," I admit.

"There's nothing wrong with that Sam," Brady insists.

"What twenty-year-old admits she wants to be like her parents?" I question, my face scrunched up in distaste.

He laughs along with me before reminding me, "A twenty-year-old who lost a hell of a lot! I personally think you're pretty incredible," he praises.

I lift my head off his shoulder and smirk up at him, "I figured."

He grins, "You did huh?"

"Yeah, all that touching and kissing you do with me kind of gives it away," I tease, ready to change the subject.

He chuckles, "Like this?" He tilts his head down and presses his lips to mine, but pulls away much too quickly.

"Exactly like that," I pout. He laughs louder and I twist towards him pressing my fingers over his mouth, "Shhh. Cory's sleeping."

His body shakes slightly as he suppresses his laughter. He moves one hand down to my waist so I don't fall and wraps his other hand around my wrist near his mouth. He presses his lips to my fingers and then pulls them away, enveloping my hand in his. "She'll leave us alone either way," he tells me. "What else did he say?" he asks.

I shrug, "I don't know. Can we talk about something else?" I question.

He nods, "Sure."

"I'm just exhausted from all of this. I guess I was holding everything in waiting to tell you about it and now I don't even want to think about it anymore," I admit. Although, there's no way I'm not going to think about it at all.

"Did you tell Cory?" he asks. I shake my head. "Did you call someone? Like your cousin?" he questions.

I shake my head, "No, why?" He looks at me with wide eyes making me feel the need to explain further. "I waited to talk to you about it. I guess it was something I wanted to share with you first," I admit suddenly feeling shy. I bury myself back in his chest with a sudden fear he'll think this is too much.

He doesn't move for a moment and then suddenly he does. He swiftly grips my face with both hands and tilts my head up so I can't hide from him. He stares at me in awe, melting my anxiety. He's so close that his warm minty breath mixes with mine. Just when I think he's about to say something, his mouth crashes down on mine, taking my breath away. He pushes his tongue into my mouth. When I gasp, my tongue immediately finds its way to his. His kiss is frantic, yet firm and possessive, completely consuming me. I slide my hands up around his neck and turn so I'm straddling him without breaking our kiss. I pull myself closer to him and he groans in response as he slips his hands into my hair, melding our mouths even more perfectly together.

Brady's cell phone rings and I try to pull away so he can answer it, but he grips me tighter, holding me to him as he continues his assault on my mouth. When the ringing stops, his hands loosen and he slides them down my neck and continues down my sides. I gasp as he gently passes over the sides of my breasts, continuing down my belly and gripping my hips. I can feel his hard length underneath me so I try to push my hips closer, but he holds me still. I groan in frustration and he chuckles breaking our kiss. "Why are you laughing? It seems I'm getting to you..." I taunt.

"You definitely are," he smirks. His lips go to my jaw, gently kissing a line up to my ear before working their way slowly down my neck. I let out a shaky moan. Then his phone starts ringing again. He groans in annoyance, but tries to keep going. This time when the ringing stops, it starts right back up again. "Fuck," he grumbles and drops his head against my shoulder.

"Maybe you should get that. It is after midnight and whoever it is...they're pretty insistent," I tell him.

He groans and pushes back, but keeps one hand on my hip as he pulls his phone out of his pocket. His jaw tightens when he looks at the screen. He presses it and brings it to his ear. "Hello," he answers sounding annoyed. He pauses, but I can't hear the other side of the conversation as he talks. "Yeah, I did. I have classes in the morning. I have to get some studying done and get some sleep, so I left. It was slow and everything was done that needed to be. Mel is fine closing up and you know it." His jaw twitches as he listens, then he continues, "Fine Mom. I'll take care of it later this week." He pauses before answering, "I have plans tomorrow after class." After her response he replies, "Okay, love you too. Goodnight Mom." He hangs up the phone and slips it back into his pocket. He drops his head onto the back of the couch, looking defeated.

"You okay?" I ask tentatively.

He shrugs, "Yeah, it's fine. It's just something with the banquet room. I swear they double-check every little thing I do. It's like they have no faith in me at all," he grimaces. "I would actually probably like working there if they didn't try to micromanage everything I do. I know what I'm doing...well mostly."

"Why do you say mostly?" I ask curiously.

"Well, every once in a while something comes up with the banquet room that I'm not prepared for. The bar and restaurant side aren't a problem, but I guess I'm not exactly a party planner. It sucks coordinating everything with all the outside vendors or whoever is hosting the party or even working with a bride and groom for a wedding. Honestly, I'll probably have to hire someone to do all that shit if I end up taking over," he admits.

"That sounds like it would be fun," I encourage him.

He raises his eyebrows in surprise, "Really?" I nod my head and he jokes, "You want the job it's yours."

I laugh and kiss him on the corner of his mouth before relaxing against him. "Will you stay here with me tonight?" I ask into his neck. "After today, I don't want to be alone," I admit.

He stands up, taking me with him and I instinctually wrap my legs around his waist and my hands around his neck. "I'd love to," he grins as his hands grip my ass to hold onto me and carry me to my room. He walks into my room and closes the door behind him. He loosens my hands and legs and then he tosses me on my bed, making me giggle as I bounce lightly. He immediately slips his shoes off, followed by his shirt, causing my mouth to go dry at the sight of his toned abs. He kicks off his jeans and his rock hard thighs stick out from his black boxer briefs and I bite my tongue to hold back my groan. His thick length still covered, but obviously huge, causes my stomach to flip. I lick my lips as he lowers himself onto the bed and under my comforter. "Are you coming?" he asks playfully, showing off his dimple.

I move towards him and lick his dimple just before I kiss it, making him laugh. I shrug as I climb under the covers with him, "Sorry I couldn't resist."

"Don't apologize for that. You can kiss me or lick me anywhere or anytime you want," he grins. My face heats and my heart nearly pounds out of my chest in excitement. I take a deep breath and curl into his side.

"What time do you have to leave in the morning?" I ask changing the subject.

"Actually, I have to be out of here by 7 tomorrow morning. I have an 8 o'clock class and finding parking sucks," he complains. I have my alarm set for 6:30," he informs me. "Do you still want me to stay?" he asks.

I nod my head and smile, "Please?" He settles in further and pulls me even closer to him. He wraps me in his arms with me facing him and makes sure I'm covered up. "I guess I should let you get some sleep then," I offer.

He tilts my chin up to meet his gaze. "Yeah, but in a few minutes. I want to go to sleep with the taste of your lips embedded in my mouth." I smile and he leans in only rewarding me with a chaste kiss. My lips turn into a pout when he pulls away laughing, "That's a good look for you." He kisses me again before adding, "Besides, I want to have enough energy to enjoy every bit of our date tomorrow night. Want to go into Madison?"

"Sure," I smile.

"Good," he murmurs right before his lips find mine in an all-consuming kiss, setting my whole body on fire. Brady makes sure I go to sleep with my whole body tingling and tasting nothing but him. If he didn't have class so early, I would definitely try to push my luck with him!

Chapter 26

June 12th (your 12th Birthday)
To My Beautiful Baby Girl,
Happy Birthday!! It's your Golden Birthday this
year, at least that's what they say when the day and your
age match. I don't know who "they" are, but I've always
thought that was kind of an odd tradition. What are you
even supposed to do for a Golden Birthday? I don't get it.
Anyway, do you have any birthday traditions? Something
you do every year? Birthday cake and singing Happy
Birthday of some kind are really my only birthday
traditions. I guess birthday gifts too, but I missed a couple
years between when I moved out of my parents' house to
when I met my husband.

Do you have any other holiday traditions? I'm
assuming a Christian family raised you as I requested,
although I'm not sure what religion. I'm Catholic, but not a
very good one, so I figured as long as we celebrate the same
religious holidays like Christmas and Easter, I'd be happy
with that. For Christmas we do what I consider the basics.
We go out to a Christmas tree farm and pick out a live
Christmas tree. I don't like the plastic Christmas trees, I
want to be able to smell Christmas and the smell of pine is
part of that for me. I also love decorating for the holidays
while listening to repetitive Christmas music. My favorite
tradition is definitely the Christmas cookies, although I've
never been very good at making them. I sure have fun
trying and then buying some when that doesn't work out as
I planned. As for Easter, I celebrate with my husband's
family with a big meal. None of my Easter traditions
carried over with us. I couldn't even really tell you what
they were. We stopped hunting for eggs when I was seven.

Do you have a favorite holiday? My favorite holiday to celebrate is Halloween. I love being able to dress up as something or someone else and have a good time. I wonder if you enjoy Halloween as much as I do...

Everything here is the same as last year, just as I like it. I never would've guessed since I couldn't wait to get away from home, but I love the consistency of staying in one place and working the same job. I love knowing what I'm walking into every day. I don't know if I'd feel the same without my husband, but I hope I don't ever have to find out. I've lost enough already in my life. My grandparents died when I was young, my cousin died when I was just 13 and in a way I lost my parents when they didn't like most of my decisions. Most importantly, I lost you. I realize I gave you up, but it was so you could have a better life than what I could offer you. I hope you understand that. I still feel like I lost you even if it was the right thing to do. I hope you never have to endure a serious loss, but if you do, just know that I'll be thinking of you and praying for the best for you from wherever I may be. Try to remember to keep moving forward. I know you'll find someone out there who can give you what you need. I love you.

Enjoy your birthday!
With Love...
Catherine Schepp

I sniffle and attempt to wipe the tears from my eyes before they reach Brady's shirt where I'm lying in the crook of his arm, trying to hide my face from him. "Sam?" he questions, attempting to twist to see my face. "Sam, are you okay?" he asks, reaching across and running his free hand down the side of my damp cheek. He sits up and swiftly pulls me with him before I have a chance to react. He spins me to see my face and his body instantly sags with concern as he takes in my appearance.

"You're not," he states the obvious. "What did she say?" he asks. When I don't answer, he pleads, "Please, talk to me."

"I'm fine," I murmur trying to look away, but he doesn't let me. "Don't you have to get to class?" I ask slightly exasperated. He should leave before I lose it.

He sighs, "Class can wait. Talk to me." He searches my eyes for answers, begging me with his clear blue eyes to talk to him. I just can't say no to those eyes.

I concede and quietly request, "Can you just hold me for a minute? I'll talk," I gulp over the lump in my throat. "I just need a moment," I admit. He gently cradles my face in his hands and gives me a look that sends my heart into overdrive. He slowly leans in and kisses my lips so tenderly I almost wonder if it's real. He slides back down on my bed and I slip back into the crook of his arm, but this time his hand holds me firmly to his side. His other hand slides softly down my neck and arm until he finds my hand, then he covers it with his own. He gives my hand a quick squeeze before he loosens his grip, but begins with the mindless circles on both my lower back and my hand, helping to relax me.

I close my eyes and soak in his touch. I open my mouth and rasp, "This has to be getting a little old for you. You might not believe this, but I'm usually not this...emotional," I stammer for lack of a better word.

He sighs, "Sam."

I shake my head and begin explaining, "She said she hopes I don't ever have to endure serious loss." I take a deep breath and try to shove the lump down my throat as I swallow. "She obviously didn't know, but..." my voice falls off and I just stop talking, not able to say any more yet, but it's not like he really needs me to. I clutch his hand holding mine tightly to his chest, attempting to dull the pain.

"Oh Sam," he breathes, tightening his hold on me.

I realize I haven't felt this kind of comfort since before my parents died and try to cuddle even closer to him. I don't understand how he already has such a strong hold on me, but he does. Just seeing him or hearing his voice calms me. Then there's the way he looks at me, holds me and kisses me...I can't even explain it. Maybe I should grab onto it like Catherine suggests. I'm trying. I know I don't want to go back to what everything was like before him. I cringe remembering the feeling of living in darkness and clinging to the repetition of my every day life so I didn't have to come out of my bubble. I wasn't naïve enough to think I was really living, but I did what I needed so I could survive. I admit I was just getting by, living almost robotically, but it worked. Maybe I'm finally ready for that to change.

I hold on to Brady and try to force myself to relax. I take another deep breath and tell him more about the letter. "She also asked about my holiday traditions," I inform him. "We had a lot of family traditions. My parents loved holidays. Any holidays really," I shrug with a small smile on my face, which is quickly replaced with a frown. "When my parents died, every tradition I tried to do left me feeling empty," I confess. "This past year if it wasn't for my Uncle Tim and his family, especially Ryan, I probably wouldn't have even celebrated anything. It hurt too much," I admit, feeling another twinge of sadness in my chest.

"Maybe we can come up with a few new traditions to do together," he suggests after a few minutes of silence.

I push myself up onto my elbows and stare at him in shock. "You're already planning for the holidays?" I ask.

He shrugs and questions, "What holiday is next? Easter?" My eyebrows furrow and I nod my head, trying to figure out where he's going with this. He continues, "Well, would you want to do something with me for Easter? Make our own tradition?"

"I...I...I don't know Brady. What about your family?" I ask, feeling somewhat anxious yet hopeful at the same time.

He shakes his head, "I'm not suggesting forever here Sam, if you don't want to, it's okay. I just thought we could find something we could do that could be your own. Something you do that won't hurt so much, but you'll still be celebrating. Then when you're ready you can bring back some of the traditions that are too hard for you to do now." My heart seizes with the sweetness of his suggestion and I fall back into my spot on his arm.

"My parents will be at the restaurant for Easter, like usual. I wasn't planning on being there this year anyway. There's always a big Easter brunch at the restaurant with an egg hunt for the little kids and the Easter Bunny. Then they clean up and repeat everything for a dinner crowd. I guess it was one of those holidays that never really mattered much to my family. Also they used to remind me when you own a restaurant, you take care of everyone else first and we could always celebrate another time," he grimaces bitterly. "That's one of the things I didn't really like about that place, but I don't have a right to complain." He shrugs and slowly exhales brushing it off like it was no big deal when it obviously was a big deal to him. "Sometimes I ended up spending holidays with Cody and Cory and their family. Those were probably my favorite holidays," he confesses quietly.

"Brady," I look up at him with empathy, not knowing quite what to say. He has his parents, but I can't imagine not being able to spend holidays with my family or if I do, having to spend it with all of us working. I wince thinking I understand what that's like now, but when I was growing up...I can't even begin to comprehend it. I loved spending the holidays with my family. It didn't matter what holiday it was as long as we were together.

He interrupts my thoughts, "We don't have to do anything special, but either way I would love to spend Easter with you if you're going to stick around here that weekend."

I shake my head and smile softly to myself. "I think that's a great idea," I tell him softly. I'm not sure what Uncle Tim will say about me being here, but if he knows I won't be by myself he might stop harassing me. "Thank you."

The corners of his lips turn up just enough that I can see the start of his dimple. He tilts his head down and leans in close, lightly kissing my lips. He pulls back, keeping his head close and questions, "Are you alright?"

I nod my head, feeling relaxed and content and answer him on my exhale, "Yeah. You need to get going or you're going to be late for class," I remind him giving him a playful shove.

He chuckles lightly, but doesn't move an inch. He focuses on my eyes and asks again, "Are you sure you're okay?"

"I'm beginning to hate that question," I grumble.

He chuckles, "Get used to it."

I giggle and push back from him, but he quickly pulls me forward. I fall back to his chest just as his mouth lands on mine for a searing kiss. He moves his right hand to tangle in my hair and hold me in place. I slip my tongue between his lips to search out his tongue. He tilts his head further to push our kiss deeper, as our tongues continue to dance, taste and explore. He pulls away on a groan, as we both struggle to catch our breath. "Damn," he mumbles. I glance at him with my eyebrows raised in question. He chuckles and shakes his head. He leans down and gives me a chaste kiss before stepping away. "You're right, I gotta' go. I still have to shower before I leave. I'm definitely going to be late, but so damn worth it," he grins.

I chuckle as he jumps up and grabs his shoes off the floor. "I'll see you tonight Sam," he calls as he walks out my bedroom door, pulling it closed behind him.

I lay in bed with a small smile still on my face after I watch him go. This letter really got to me, but I think it's more about missing my mom and dad than anything. Maybe Brady is right and we could come up with some new traditions. Maybe that will help me enjoy one or two holidays again. I gulp over the lump in my throat. I know my parents would want that for me, so I could at least try.

I wonder what kinds of traditions Lincoln has with his family. My nerves settle back into my stomach at my first thought of him. I don't even know if he'll ever really want me to meet his family. It feels surreal to even think about it. They are all strangers to me, including him. How do I change that? Does he even want that to change? Just because he told me he wants to see me again and he was going to tell his family about me, that doesn't mean he wants me to be a part of his life. I shake my head and grimace. I don't even know if that's what I want. What do I want out of all of this? I just needed to know more and I still do, but what kind of more? I slowly take a deep breath and close my eyes as I slowly release it. I guess we both have to figure out what more means to us.

I shake my head in an attempt to push thoughts of my parents and my birth family to the side and focus on today instead. I have no idea what I'm going to wear tonight on my date with Brady. I stand and walk to my closet, pulling the doors open. After a few minutes I groan in frustration and mumble, "I have to go back to Illinois this weekend to get more of my things." But I still have to figure out something fantastic for tonight. "Maybe a skirt..." I contemplate aloud.

Chapter 27

Brady

I run my hand through my hair and pat the top to tame it down. I roll up the sleeves of my light blue button down shirt to stop just below my elbows. I want to dress up a little for Sam, but I'm still wearing dark blue jeans and dark brown work boots. I don't want to look like I'm trying too hard and I still need to feel like me. Although if I'm honest, I've never wanted to impress a girl like I want to impress Sam. To say I'm trying is an understatement. It's a little warmer tonight so at least I don't need a jacket. I could always warm up with her, I groan at the visual in my head.

I grab my phone and wallet, quickly stuffing them in my pocket before I walk out of my room. A loud catcall whistle comes from Cody, mocking me as soon as I step into the living room. "Going somewhere fancy?" he smirks.

I grind my jaw and give him a humorless laugh, "In jeans? I don't think so."

He raises his eyebrows, "Really?"

I shrug and add, "You should add something besides t-shirts to your wardrobe and maybe you'll get a second date with Olive."

He huffs a laugh and smirks at me, "I already have one of those. She just works a lot of hours." I nod placating him and he quickly changes the subject. "Where are you taking Sam tonight anyway?"

I shrug, "I don't exactly know. We're going into Madison. She said she's never really spent any time there. I thought I'd drive around campus to show her around. Then maybe we'll go down to State Street since it's unusually warm out. I thought I'd figure dinner out when we get there."

"You really thought this through, huh?" he smirks.

I glare at him, "I just want to show her a little more about where I've spent the past few years."

He nods his head in understanding and jokes, "Don't take her out to the bars there. Either you'll get her arrested for being underage or you'll get arrested for hitting some guy for trying to pick her up." I chuckle in response. "Have fun and treat her right...use lubrication," he grins mischievously.

I shake my head and flip him off, "Later Cody!" I grab my keys and walk out the door, listening to Cody's laughter follow right behind me.

I take a deep breath to try to calm my nerves as I knock on her front door. I stuff my hands in my pockets to keep myself from fidgeting and roll back on my heels as the door opens. I look up, instantly feeling as if the wind gets knocked out of me at the sight of Samantha. Her hair lies in soft waves around her shoulders. She's wearing a silky, jade green, V-neck, loose fitting top with wide sleeves, along with a matching pendant hanging right between her breasts, drawing my attention there. I force my eyes to move, but have to bite my tongue when I notice her black leggings showing every curve, with her tall black boots, completing her sexy as hell look. I take a deep breath and exhale, "Wow." She grins, causing my heartbeat to pound harder against my ribcage. "You look absolutely incredible," I tell her honestly.

She blushes beautifully, "Thank you."

I step into her, reaching to slip my right hand around her neck, keeping my thumb on her pulse as I tip my head down and gently press my lips to her soft full ones. "Mmmm..." I groan softly, enjoying the vibration between us, before pulling slightly away to look down at her. "I just had to do that," I mumble. Her giggle in response makes me smile. I want to make her laugh and smile like that all the time.

"Had to?" she asks with a smirk.

I grin broadly and change the subject quickly. How crazy she makes me is not the best topic of conversation if we ever want to leave. "Ready?" I question hoarsely.

"Yeah," she murmurs breathlessly. Her caramel eyes holding me captive, making it even harder to step away from her instead of pushing her backwards until she falls on the couch. I remind myself again, I need to do this the right way with her. She deserves it after all the shit she's been through and I don't want to mess this up. I press my lips to hers, briefly and step completely away, attempting to exhale all of my tension. She reaches for her coat and slides her phone and a small wallet into one of the pockets before zipping it closed.

"I don't know if you really need that. It's actually kind of warm outside for March," I inform her.

She grins, "I get cold easy and warm for March isn't the same as warm." I laugh and help her slide on her coat. I put my hand on the small of her back, just wanting to touch her any way I can and guide her out the door, pulling it closed behind me.

We stand waiting quietly for the elevator, my body practically vibrating just being near her. When the doors open, she walks to the back of the elevator and leans against the wall. I stand next to her, waiting impatiently while the doors rattle close. The moment they do, I push off the wall and press my whole body into hers, diving in for a heated kiss. I lick her bottom lip and push my tongue inside to find hers enjoying her minty taste. I feel the jolt as we stop on the first floor. I pull back regretfully and press my lips to hers one more time before the doors begin screeching open and I have to pull completely away. I grin widely at the stunned look on her face. I shrug, "I couldn't help myself."

She pushes off the wall of the elevator and laughs as she exits. "That seems to happen a lot with you," she teases me.

I admit, "When you're around." I enjoy watching her pale skin redden as we reach my truck. I open the passenger door and quickly place my hands on her waist, lifting her up and set her down inside the cab of my truck before she has a chance to move. She opens her mouth to probably tell me she didn't need my help, but I grin and shut the door before she has the chance. I jog around to the other side and hop in, giving her one more perusal up and down while sitting in my truck before I turn the key with a broad smile on my face, feeling incredibly lucky.

I drop my phone into the center console before I put my truck in gear and back out. I begin driving through town and towards Madison when she asks with slight exasperation in her voice, "What are you smiling about?"

I laugh, not realizing I was still smiling. "You," I admit, glancing quickly at her pink cheeks before focusing back on the road. "I really like having you here beside me."

She sighs, sounding content and reaches towards the console, turning up the volume of the radio. "Do you mind if I turn it up?" she asks as Thomas Rhett's "Craving You" blasts through the speakers.

I laugh and shake my head, "Go ahead." I don't think there could be a more fitting song on right now. I listen as she sings every word to the song. When the next song begins, I turn it slightly down and smirk, "I can't believe I didn't know you like country."

She laughs and the sound sends another shock to my erratic heartbeat. "All I did was turn up the volume," she reminds me. I don't respond because we both know we're sitting in my truck and I was most likely the last one listening to anything in here. I just usually don't announce it because Cody likes to give me shit, although I know he listens to it too. She shrugs and ignores my non-answer. She concedes, "I like almost anything I can sing along with or dance to."

I turn the radio back up and listen to her sing nearly every word to every song on the short drive. She looks out the window at the passing trees and buildings quickly becoming closer and closer together. We both temporarily get lost in thought, but she easily pulls me back with her soft voice. "So where are we going?" she asks curiously.

"Madison," I grin mischievously. I can see her roll her eyes out of the corner of my eye. I laugh and tell her what I'm thinking. "I thought I'd show you around campus a little bit. Show you where I've been spending a lot of my time the last few years. Then I thought we could go down to State Street to walk around. We can see if some stores are open and also find something to eat if that's okay with you?" I propose.

"That sounds perfect. Are you going to show me where you used to play baseball?" she asks in anticipation.

My heart flips at the excitement in her voice. It's almost overwhelming knowing she really listens to me. She can tell how important baseball was to me and seems genuinely interested. I love that she wants to know more about me, even the parts of me that are only memories. I swallow the growing lump in my throat and casually clear it before I answer, "I uh, I actually played for University of Wisconsin-La Crosse my first year of college and then transferred over here my sophomore year. Believe it or not, Madison doesn't have a baseball program."

"What?" she asks, shock obvious in her expression and voice. "How do they not have a baseball program? And why didn't you tell me about La Crosse?"

"It wasn't that I didn't want to tell you about La Crosse, it's just a really long story. I'll tell you about it later," I promise, not wanting to start our date talking about something so painful. Thinking about Max always hurts and I can't talk about my freshman year at La Crosse without talking about him. "As for Madison, I guess they got rid of their baseball team in 1991. I'm not really sure why. I'd love to see it come back, but I don't know if it will ever happen."

"Wow, I can't even believe a school as big as Madison would get rid of baseball," she admits and thankfully lets the conversation about La Crosse go for now. Hopefully when it comes up again I'll be a little bit more prepared to handle it.

"Both football and basketball have a ton of fans though and it's a blast to go to those games. You'll have to come with me to a couple games next year," I tell her.

"That sounds like fun," she admits.

My hand twitches, wanting her close to me. I reach across my truck and pull her hand out of her lap, swiftly entwining my fingers with hers. The warm, soft feel of her hand in mine gives me a sort of comfort I haven't felt in a long time, especially when I think about Max. I give her a quick glance and smile down at her, gently squeezing her hand. She grins back at me, knocking the air out of my lungs in the process. I focus back on the road in front of me and take a deep breath to get myself under control.

"So, what would your friends say about you going to a Wisconsin game?" I tease her, attempting to lighten my mood.

She bursts out laughing and her whole face lights up, giving me the desired effect as I drive around Camp Randall Stadium. I relax back into my seat and start a quick driving tour of campus before we head over to State Street.

Chapter 28

Samantha

"State Street was so cool!" I praise, as we walk into my apartment. "I love how you can walk down the middle of the street."

"There is some traffic," he laughs, "You know...buses, police cars and bikes. You can still get run over," he teases me.

I shrug, "Yeah, but not like normal." I hang up my coat and pull my phone and wallet out of my pocket. He raises his eyebrows in amusement, barely containing his laughter. I set everything down on the coffee table as I attempt to describe my fascination. "You know what I mean," I insist. He chuckles and I continue, "To me that compares to being able to walk down Michigan Ave in Chicago. Have you ever been?" I ask.

He grins widely at me and shakes his head, "No."

"It has the shopping, restaurants and bars, but with tons of traffic," I complain. "I loved all the cute little shops too! Although it was getting a little crazy when we left."

He nods and steps towards me with a huge smile, showing off his dimple. "Yeah, that starts to happen later when the bars fill up." He takes another step closer to me and my breath hitches. I try to keep talking not sure where Cory is and tell him, "The Capital was really beautiful, especially at night."

"Nothing compared to you," he responds flippantly and I burst out laughing. His eyebrows draw together in confusion and he asks, "What?"

"That was too perfect and too cheesy to be anything but a line," I giggle.

He shakes his head and tilts it to the side still staring at me, "I guess you're right about it being cheesy, but it was definitely true, so I don't think it qualifies as a line." My heartbeat picks up as he takes another step closer to me, his warm breath brushing my lips. "I could do this with you every day. I love seeing you smile like that," he tells me with awe. "The way your whole face lights up," he sighs and barely brushes my lips with his, "it's incredible."

He brushes my lips again and I gently push him away, blushing. "Wait," I insist and take a step back. "Cory?" I call, walking down the hall towards her room. "Cory?" I yell again.

"In here," Brady calls from the kitchen. I turn around and walk back towards the kitchen. Brady stands in the doorway holding out a piece of paper for me, "She wrote you a note."

I take the note from him and quickly look it over. I murmur, "She went out with some friends."

"So we're alone?" he questions, grinning at me.

"I guess...I..." I stammer as he steps towards me. "Do you find that strange?"

"That she went out with friends?" he asks sounding perplexed. "No."

I shake my head, "No, I mean that she writes notes all the time instead of texting. What if I didn't go into the kitchen tonight?" I ponder.

He chuckles softly and steps towards me. He grips my shoulders and turns me around before nudging me back towards the living room. "She says it's more personal that way. She's always been that way, probably because Cody is the opposite. He's always on some kind of computer or electronic. Although he hates texting because he claims his fingers are too big." We stop at the couch and he wraps his arm around my waist, swiftly tugging me down with him and into his lap. I twist my body to look at him and he grimaces. "Honestly, I don't care about what either of them are doing or how they communicate. I have you here in my arms and I want to focus on that," he declares hoarsely, sending chills down my spine. "Is that okay with you?" he rasps.

My insides prickle starting in my stomach, moving through my chest and stall in the form of a lump in my throat. I attempt to swallow it down as I stare into his darkening blue eyes. I don't think my voice will work, so instead of trying to talk I finally nod my head in agreement. Leaving one hand around my waist he uses the other to caress my cheek as he lowers his head down to mine. It feels as if he's barely moving as I anticipate the soft touch of his lips. His warm breath heats my whole body as it feathers across my jawline searching for my mouth. I breathe a sigh of satisfaction when we connect. He kisses me slowly, savoring the intimate touch. I lean into him to push the kiss deeper. He licks my lower lip causing my mouth to automatically open for him. Our tongues collide in a playful dance, licking and searching for more. I readjust myself and slip my leg over him so I'm straddling him, completely facing him. I push myself closer to him both with our kiss and with my body, making him groan. He tears his lips from mine and mumbles my name in warning, "Sam."

"I want more Brady," I tell him breathlessly. He pulls back a little further to look into my eyes. "I've been through a lot and if I've learned anything from all of it, I know I need to take full advantage of the time I have with someone I care about."

He gulps and his eyes seem to want to tell me so much as he tenderly searches for his answers. After a moment, he grins showing me his dimple. I lean forward and lick it, followed by a kiss. "You care about me," he states. I suddenly realize what I just said, causing my heart to flip-flop in my chest. I attempt to laugh to lighten my comment, but he leans in and kisses my neck, giving me chills starting at the point where his lips touch my sensitive skin. He chuckles and does it again, chasing my goose bumps with his lips. "I care about you too Sam. More than I thought I could for anyone, let alone after only two weeks."

"Almost two weeks," I murmur as I internally breathe a sigh of relief.

He laughs, warming my whole body through with the sound. "Almost two weeks," he concedes.

"Let's go to my room," I suggest.

I wrap my arms around his neck and hold on as he stands instead of answering. I wrap my legs around him and he puts one hand underneath my butt to hold me up. "I like this," he grins, tapping my ass lightly twice.

I laugh and bury my face in his neck, inhaling the light scent of his cologne. "You smell good," I mumble.

He pushes my bedroom door open and kicks it closed behind him. He lowers me to my bed, coming with me. He releases me and cages me in with his arms. He slowly looks me up and down appreciatively. He murmurs, "How did I get so lucky?" I feel a heated blush rush to my cheeks, making him grin in response before closing the distance between us.

He holds himself up, hovering over me as he presses his lips to mine. I close my eyes and savor the taste of his kiss. He lowers his weight off to my left side, never pulling away from our kiss. His right hand slides up my leg, pulling me a little closer, before sliding underneath the hem of my shirt. My breath hitches as his hand brushes my bare skin along my side. His fingers lightly trail up, along the side of my breast and back down before swirling over my belly. Then his hand slides up the center of my chest, taking my shirt with it until he lands between my breasts. His hand runs lightly over my breast, cupping it gently while he rolls his thumb over my nipple, which instantly hardens through my bra. My breathing becomes erratic as he does the same with the other side.

I tug at his shirt, not able to speak. He leans back and swiftly pulls his shirt over his head with one hand. My eyes widen at the sight of his defined muscles in his arms, shoulders, chest and stomach. I reach up and lightly run my fingers over his abs. He pulls me from my perusal, "Sam?" I look up and meet his heated gaze. "Can I take this off?" he asks with the hem of my shirt fisted in his hand. I nod and give him a shy smile. My shirt is off before I can really lift my arms and I fall back to the bed. I move my hand towards the front clasp of my bra, but he gently pushes my hands away, "Let me," he requests.

He unhooks my bra and pushes the material away with the palm of his hand. He leans down and kisses the side of my breast as his thumb rolls over my bare nipple. Then his tongue shoots out and swirls around it before sucking it into his mouth, before repeating the treatment on the other side. I cling to him harder with each touch, lick and kiss. Finally I can't take anymore and push up to kiss him hard, devouring his lips. I groan into his mouth and allow him to break our kiss. "Damn," he mumbles breathlessly.

"I need more Brady," I plead pulling him towards me with one hand and tracing the line on his hip angled down under the waistband of his jeans with the other. I flip the button open and tug at the zipper. I let my hand slide onto the waistband of his Black Calvin Klein's.

He leans in and kisses me firmly before rasping, "Are you sure Sam?"

"Do you have something?" I ask in answer.

I watch his Adam's apple bob up and down as he swallows before answering, "Yeah." He pulls his wallet out of his back pocket, unfolds it and grabs a condom before tossing his wallet on my nightstand. He cradles my face in his hands and kisses me with such tenderness, moving his mouth in perfect rhythm with mine. One hand slides down my side and around my back to caress my ass. He continues moving his hand lower until he reaches the back of my knee and gently bends my leg, so my knee raises off the bed. He then moves his hand around to the inside of my leg and slides his hand up my thigh. My hands slide over his stomach and grip onto his waist as his fingers lightly trail over my heated core making me whimper. His hands slide up to my waistband and I reflexively lift up as he tugs gently, taking my black leggings and panties with them. His breath rushes out in a whoosh as his eyes roam my body causing me to feel suddenly self-conscious. I move to cover myself, but he stops me with his words. "You are absolutely gorgeous and so fucking sexy Samantha," he rasps. I look into his eyes and immediately know he believes it.

He kicks his jeans off and stands in his boxer briefs in front of me while I take a moment to appreciate his body with all the hard lines of his muscles. The only spattering of hair is a thin line from his belly button that disappears underneath his waistband. I look up to find his eyes as he begins to crawl over me. "You're kind of incredibly gorgeous too," I say, feeling myself blush with the admission, which only makes me laugh at myself. I wouldn't be here if I wasn't attracted to him. He quirks his eyebrow in question and I ask, "What?"

"What's so funny?"

I shake my head, "Nothing. I'm just happy to be here with you. It's all happening so fast, but it feels right. This feels right," I insist.

He grins and I lean up to kiss his dimple before finding his lips and pulling him down with me. Our mouths move in perfect rhythm as our tongues quickly find one another, tasting, licking and sucking. I moan and let my hands wander over his back and down his firm butt cheeks, before moving back up and down his shoulders as he slides his hand down over my stomach and between my legs. I can't help but be thankful I've kept up with my Brazilian wax as he runs his finger right through my center. He groans into my mouth as he pushes one finger inside making me gasp. He slides his finger out, adding another before he pushes them both in, curling them just right. "Fuck," he moans as he breaks our kiss.

"Brady," I whimper. "I want you," I insist, feeling as if I might burst at any second just from his touch. "Please," I beg.

He removes his hand and kicks off his briefs before reaching for the condom. He tears it open and tosses the wrapper back on the nightstand. I look at his impressive thick length for the first time as he rolls it on. I swallow down the lump in my throat, my nerves showing their face again. He lowers himself until he's barely hovering over my body. He searches my eyes as he caresses my cheek, "Are you sure Samantha? I don't want to do this until you're ready."

I slowly release my breath and feel my whole body relax underneath him. "I'm sure Brady. I want to be with you," I insist with a small smile.

He presses his lips to mine and pulls away just enough to look into my eyes as he slowly enters me, the intrusion awkward at first, but welcome. He suddenly thrusts all the way in, making me gasp and stops at the hilt. He kisses me tenderly without moving his body and I feel my own body adjust and relax around him. He tears his mouth away and asks, "Are you okay?"

"Yeah," I croak. "I'm good," I smile up at him. He stares into my eyes, searching for the truth before he starts moving slowly, filling me up. He kisses me again as he begins to move faster. I feel like I'm on fire, while my heartbeat and breathing rapidly speed up. I drop my head back breaking our kiss and he catches my eyes, holding my gaze. "You feel so good. I don't think I can last this time, but I want you to come," he rasps. He reaches between us and touches me with his thumb making me whimper. I pull him closer, forcing him to pull his hand away.

I start to feel dizzy and my whole body begins tingling, starting with throbbing where we're connected. I don't think I can respond, so I cling to him tighter. He runs his hand over my breast and gently pinches my hard nipple. My eyes close involuntarily as my body arches into him, pushing him deeper and making me gasp. "Brady," I whimper as my swollen insides begin to pulse around him. He pushes in again and again, riding out my climax. His whole body suddenly tenses over me, his loud groan vibrating our bodies. He pushes in and out again and again, slowly coming down. He exhales harshly as his head drops to my shoulder. He places a soft kiss there and stays, trying to catch his breath. I turn and kiss the side of his damp neck, tasting salt. "You're salty," I inform him.

He laughs and lifts his head to look down at me. "Are you alright?" he asks. I nod my head in response, smiling up at him. He sighs and leans down, pressing his lips to mine. "You're amazing Samantha." He brushes my hair out of my face and shakes his head in awe. "You're so beautiful," he says with admiration. He smiles down at me, making my whole body tingle, starting from the inside and working its way out to every inch of my body. He presses his lips to mine again before pulling away. "I better get us cleaned up."

He slowly pulls out and quickly removes the condom, tying a knot on the end and throwing it in my garbage can. He pulls his boxer brief's on and opens my door. I wince, hoping Cory doesn't come home early. I don't care if they've known each other forever, I don't want her to see him walking around in his underwear. Any girl would want to jump him in his current state. I reach for his undershirt and notice it's actually a white Hurley t-shirt and not an undershirt at all, making me laugh. I quickly pull it over my head, stopping halfway to inhale his scent. I slip my comforter over my legs just as he steps back into my room and pulls the door shut behind him crawling into bed beside me. "May I?" he asks as he holds up a washcloth. I nod slowly as my heartbeat goes out of control in my chest. I've never been taken care of like this. He gently rubs between my legs and tosses the washcloth onto the clothes I wore on our date tonight.

"Thank you," I whisper.

He gathers me into his arms with a chuckle. "I like my shirt on you," he grins.

"Me too," I admit smiling happily.

Chapter 29

Brady

My chest feels tight just watching her sleep. Her curls are fanned around her head in disarray and I couldn't imagine a sight more beautiful. I take a deep breath and gently trace a line down her neck, grinning when I reach my t-shirt hanging off her shoulder. I have to admit seeing her in my shirt took my breath away. I felt like I should bang my chest or something, which is fucking ridiculous. She's amazing though and last night was incredible. I close my eyes and gulp down the growing lump in my throat just thinking about being buried deep inside her. My chest felt like it was about to explode. I've never felt like that before when I'm with someone. I already knew I was crazy about her, but I didn't realize how crazy until last night.

I honestly thought I was pushing her too fast. I was afraid I was going to screw it up by going too far, but she knew what she wanted. I can't help but wonder if it has anything to do with losing her parents. I'm surprised her asshole ex doesn't seem to have more of an effect on how she looks at relationships, but she doesn't seem to care about what happened with him at all. I guess I'm thankful she doesn't give his betrayal too much weight, or I'd be fucked. Now that I realize how much I want her and want her in my life, I'd lose my mind if she pushed me away.

My phone buzzes with a text and I quickly reach for it, hoping I don't wake her. I glance at the screen and grimace at a text from Jackie, "I need your help! Please! SOS." I sigh and drop my phone in my lap and my head to my chest. If anything screws this up with her, it will be

Jackie and I really can't let that happen. I don't understand how she doesn't get that I'm done, that I've been done for years, but then again, with how much I'm always there for her, Cody's probably right, I wince. I probably got myself into this mess.

Samantha stirs under my arm with a sexy moan and my hand instantly goes to her hair, "Good morning beautiful," I whisper as her stunning caramel eyes flutter open to look up at me.

She smiles and stretches, raising her arms above her head and arching her back up off the bed making my mouth water. "Good morning," she murmurs in a sexy morning voice. I bite my lower lip attempting to maintain my control. "When do you have to leave?" she asks glancing around her room like she's looking for something.

I glance at my phone and grimace, "Soon."

"What time is it? I don't know where I left my phone," she informs me.

I chuckle, "Almost 10 and I think you left it in the kitchen."

She rolls towards me and wraps her arms around my waist before placing a soft kiss on my abs, burning my skin under her lips. "I wish you didn't have to go," she declares causing my heart to skip a beat.

"Me too, but I have about a month and a half until I'm done. I can't fuck it up now," I remind her for her sake as much as mine. My phone vibrates, indicating a text, immediately followed by another one. I don't bother reaching for it, almost positive I know who they're from.

Sam looks up at me with raised eyebrows, "You can check your phone."

I nod my head, "I know."

It goes off again and she sighs and pushes up. I reach for her hand and catch her wrist, stopping her. She informs me, "I just have to go to the bathroom. I'll be right back."

I pull her back to me and kiss her firmly on the lips before I let her go, "Okay, you can go now," I smirk.

She laughs and replies sarcastically, "Gee, thanks." She takes a step towards her bedroom door when my phone vibrates again. She twists back towards me with a forced smile. "Why don't you check your phone when I'm gone," she suggests.

I sigh as she pulls the door closed behind her and flip my phone over, already knowing what I'll find. "Please Brady, I'm desperate!" Then, "911." Followed by, "I don't have anyone else I can ask for help with this. PLEASE!"

I grit my teeth and clench my fist, then quickly type out a response. "What?"

"Are you going to class? I need you to come get me," she replies.

"Sounds simple enough, why can't anyone else do it?" I ask, already dreading her answer.

"I'm on Frat Row. The girlfriend of the guy I was with last night is pounding on his door while I'm hiding in his bathroom. I don't remember what happened. She sounds pissed. I'm scared," she rambles.

"Fuck," I mumble and run my hand through my hair in annoyance. Her parents will flip if they know she went to another party there. "I'll figure it out and text you back in a few." I stand and pull my jeans on, mumbling, "Why does she do this shit?"

"Who does what shit?" Sam asks as she walks back into her room.

I wince, but answer honestly, "Jackie. She doesn't deal with things very well. I guess you could say she goes a little crazy when she doesn't like something. She's stuck in a bad situation by campus and needs help getting out."

I notice her flinch at the same time she nods in understanding. I sigh and step towards her. "Sam if you don't want me to help her, I won't. I can help her find someone else to get her out of this mess, but I'd be leery leaving anyone in her spot," I tell her. I'm not letting Jackie mess this up with us, no matter how worried I am.

She cringes slightly before schooling her features. She shakes her head, "I can't ask you to do that Brady. I'm not asking you to be someone else for me." She pauses, "Besides, what kind of person would stop you from helping someone who needs it?"

I look over her face and into her eyes, searching for the whole meaning behind her words. Eventually I give up and sigh in frustration, "I can help her quick before class starts since I have to be there anyway. I won't lie to you. Most of the time she can find someone else. I just think it will be easier for me this time," I tell her, not quite sure if I believe the bullshit coming out of my mouth, but I'm not sure what else to do besides be honest with her.

She pinches her lips tightly together and nods her head, "Okay."

I step towards her and pull her into my arms. I breathe a sigh of relief when she doesn't push back in any way. I cradle her face in my hands and tilt her chin up to look at me. I softly press my lips to hers. Then I tilt my head, turning our kiss deeper, almost like I'm desperately trying to reassure her with my mouth. She drops back on her heels, breaking our kiss and letting my hands fall away. "I had a lot of fun on our date last night," she says smiling up at me, but this time it doesn't quite reach her eyes. A dull ache begins to grow in my chest, at the same time a lump forms in my throat. I suddenly feel anxious like something will happen if I let her out of my sight, but that's ridiculous.

"I always have fun with you Sam," I tell her honestly, feeling an overwhelming sense of emotion in my chest. "Do you want to read one of your letters before I go?"

She shakes her head, "No, that's okay. I don't want you to be late for class or whatever else you have to do."

The ache grows and I plead with her, "Sam, I told you I'd be here for you and I meant that. Let's read a letter," I tell her, hoping she'll say yes.

She shakes her head again, but it feels like she just punched me in the gut instead of not taking me up on my simple offer. "No, I don't think I want to read one right now. I think I'll shower and grab something to eat first," she tells me. I grind my teeth, trying to figure out what doesn't feel right about this. I open my mouth to argue, but she's done with our conversation and turns away from me. She opens her bedroom door and walks out. "Come on Brady. You better go," she insists.

I sigh, feeling defeated and grab my shirt off the floor. I put it on without buttoning it, knowing I have to stop at my place to grab a clean shirt anyway.

I follow her out to the living room, but reach for her hand and spin her around before she opens the front door. "Sam, stop. Please," I beg. She reluctantly turns around and I declare, "I'm not leaving like this. You're too important to me."

"I'm fine. We're good," she tells me flatly.

I groan and run my free hand through my hair in frustration. "There's *nothing* going on with me and Jackie. I just can't leave her stranded like that," I grimace trying to explain. She looks up at me with sadness in her eyes. I close my eyes momentarily, feeling as if my heart is breaking. I sigh, "To put it simply, a long time ago, I lost someone I really cared about because I wasn't there for them when they needed me. I can't have any more regrets like that," I tell her, my voice cracking.

She looks into my eyes and I think I see a look of understanding pass through them. I hope that's not just wishful thinking on my part. She steps closer to me and offers me a soft smile, "It's okay Brady, I understand. Go help Jackie now so you're not late for class. We're good," she insists. She stands on her tiptoes and leans in to give me a chaste kiss. I wrap my arm around her and hold her to me licking her lower lip and pushing my way in to explore the moment her lips part. I want to still be able to taste her when I have to leave.

I finally break away, both of our chests heaving for breath. "I have to work tonight, but I'll come by after?" I ask.

She nods, "You can stop by. I'll answer if I'm up."

I kiss her briefly again before reluctantly letting her go with a sigh. "Okay, I'll text you when I'm back from campus."

"Bye Brady," she replies with a tentative smile. I hate the feeling in my gut. The one telling me that her goodbye sounds a lot more like a long goodbye than I'll see you later, but I don't believe she would just leave.

I hesitantly step out the door and she closes it softly behind me. I walk towards my apartment and step through the door, trying to go over everything that happened this morning to see if I did something wrong. I wander to my room, slip off my button down and grab a blue long sleeved Brewers t-shirt and slip it over my head. I mindlessly grab my backpack, already filled with everything I need for classes today before walking back towards the living room.

"What the fuck did you do?" Cody asks, tearing me out of my thoughts. He's standing directly in front of me, blocking my path.

"Huh?" I ask looking up at him.

He crosses his arms over his chest and glares at me. "I asked how your date was when you just walked in here, half dressed, and you keep walking like a zombie towards your room. I'm guessing something happened because you're too much in your head."

I sigh in frustration and run my hand through my hair, "I don't know Cody. Everything went great last night. We really had a lot of fun in Madison. I showed her around campus a little bit and then we went down to State Street. We had dinner and she wanted to go into a few stores, so we did. She didn't stop smiling all night Cody. She was so happy. I stayed at her place..."

"Obviously," he interrupts.

I ignore his comment and continue, "Then this morning my phone kept buzzing and she told me to check it."

"Fucking Jackie," he mumbles irritably.

I grit my teeth, "I thought it was best to be honest with her. I didn't have time to tell her the whole story. I need to tell her the whole story, but I have to get to class and..." I grimace.

"You didn't," he says with dread clear in his voice. I look over at him feeling helpless and he drops his head back and stares at the ceiling. He focuses back on me and grits out, "Brady, I told you if you want this to work, you can't take off to be superman for your ex."

"That's not what it's about and you know it!" I yell. I flinch at my own reaction and sigh in defeat, "I can't leave her stranded. It's been a while, but she really fucked up this time. She's hiding in some guy's bathroom on fraternity row that I don't think she even knows while his girlfriend is doing who knows what on the other side of the door and she says she doesn't remember what happened! Her parents would kill her," I exaggerate.

"Let them! She needs something to wake her the fuck up," he insists.

"Something must've happened," I contemplate. "She won't call them. You know she won't. She was probably drunk or something. If I let her figure it out and something happens to her..." I trail off.

"Or high," he mumbles. I shrug, not knowing the truth. He nods stiffly, his jaw twitching in anger. "And what about Sam? She's okay with all of this?" he asks.

I sigh and run a hand through my hair, "She said she is." I shake my head, feeling lost, "But something doesn't feel right."

He steps towards me and clasps me hard on the shoulder. "If it doesn't feel right Brady, it's probably not."

I wince, knowing he's right. I just have to figure out how to make it right. I can start by telling her about Max. If she's awake I'll tell her tonight. If not I'll have to wait until tomorrow. This is something I have to tell her when we're together. I can't do it any other way.

Chapter 30

Samantha

I should know better. I can't get any more involved than I already am. I laugh humorlessly and grumble to myself, "I don't know if it's possible to be less involved!" I have to take a step back. He's already hurting me and I've known him for two weeks! I don't think he's trying to, but...I just can't be second anything to another girl when it comes to the guy I'm with, not ever again. I can't be blindsided like last time. It hurt with Paul, but I realize now I didn't love him anymore, if I ever did at all. Everything changed so much and so fast after my parents died. I turned into a different person. If something like that happened again with Brady, I know I would be devastated. I can feel it. I can't ignore the warning signs. His ex calls him a lot. He said they're still friends, but he hasn't had a serious girlfriend since her, doesn't that say something?

I groan in annoyance and collapse onto my bed. I shove my nose in his t-shirt that I'm still wearing and inhale his scent. Last night everything was perfect. We had so much fun in Madison. I honestly don't remember the last time I had that much fun. Then being with him, I blush at the memories flashing through my mind. I wanted him so much. I've never wanted anyone so bad and I wasn't letting him back down. I grimace at the sudden pang in my chest, knowing he's on his way to help her after what we just shared. Maybe I should've let him stop us. I close my eyes as a tear rolls down my face. I shake my head in annoyance. I refuse to have any regrets. I didn't want to waste my time with him. I wanted him and everything about it was amazing. I can't ruin it with what happened this morning. I just have no idea what to do now.

I sigh and sit up, putting my feet on the floor. I open the drawer to my nightstand and pull out the next letter, knowing I need to think about something else. I smirk at the irony. Brady was only supposed to be a distraction from thinking about my birth parents. Now I'm in deep with him and I'm using my need to find out more about my birth parents as the distraction. "How do I get myself into these messes?" I mumble, gently tugging on my hair. I grimace and lean back against my wall, propping my knees up towards my chest and unfold the letter.

June 12th (your 13th Birthday)
To My Beautiful Baby Girl,
Happy Birthday!! Wow, you're officially a teenager. Do you feel any different? I remember being so excited for this birthday, but I was very sick the week I turned 13, so I definitely didn't feel any different. Did you get your period yet? I might have asked you that already, but that's when I felt like everything changed. I started worrying about my body, shaving and pimples. Hopefully you have beautiful skin and I have no doubt about how beautiful you are. Show your confidence and be yourself no matter what. Nothing else really matters. You can't listen to the "mean" girls. They're just jealous of something you have that they don't. Being 13 can be hard, but it can also be amazing. I believe it's your choice. I always believed in making every minute count and having no regrets.
My husband and I went on a vacation to Florida a few months ago. It was still cold here, so it was a great time to go. I love the warm weather and palm trees in the middle of winter. We went to the beach, swam in the ocean and sat listening to the sound of the waves. It was so

relaxing. I'd love to be able to go to the islands some day. That's somewhere I've never been. I wonder what types of places you've been to or what kinds of vacations you've taken. Everyone needs some kind of vacation or at least a break, even teenage girls. I hope you savor every minute of them, whether you're relaxing or exploring...they're memories that can last forever. I hope you have a wonderful birthday and start your teenage years off right!
With Love...
Catherine Schepp

I fold up the letter and hug my knees to my chest, thinking about the vacations we did take. I believe my favorite one was when I was 9 and we went to Walt Disney World in Florida for the first time. There was so much to see and do while we were there. It was incredible! I think my favorite part of that vacation though were the days we stayed at the resort for the day. My mom and dad went swimming with me. We ate at some fun places, even one where we met Mickey, Minnie, Pluto, Goofy and Donald, which was cool, even for a 9-year-old girl. I remember looking around in the resort shop. My parents let me pick something out to remember the trip. We even explored the resort looking for hidden Mickey's and enjoying everything they offered. I wouldn't change a moment of it because it was a perfect week with my family.

I close my eyes and give myself another hug. I miss my parents every day, but it's slowly becoming easier. I hate that it is, but at the same time I need it to be. I sigh, wishing Brady was here to hold me and flinch at my errant thoughts. I told myself not to think about him, but even memories of my parents lead me to Brady. Maybe because I feel better when he's around...most of the time.

I push off my bed and slip the letter back in its place in my nightstand. Catherine's words of how she believes you should make every minute count float through my mind. It's strange how I'm trying to live the same, but I didn't always think like that and sometimes I have trouble living it. It's my circumstances that brought me here. I lost both of my parents. I waited too long to find my birth mother and now she's gone too. Paul and I didn't last. Taylor and I didn't last. I'm afraid my time with Brady will be fleeting as well, but I'm also scared to try if he's already tied up. Would our time together be worth it? Then there's my birth father. I haven't heard from him. I wonder if he told his family? I thought I would've heard from him by now...why haven't I?

I physically shake myself to stop all my unanswered questions and quickly stride out of my room to grab something to eat. As soon as I enter the kitchen, Cory glances up at me with tired eyes from the corner table with a cup of coffee in her hands. "Good morning. You look exhausted," I tell her. "Are you okay?"

"Morning," she groans. "I'm fine. Just a little hung over. I'm not really much of a drinker," she admits with a grimace. I chuckle as I pour my own cup of coffee and sit down across from her. "I just couldn't sit here all night when I had off today. You were out with Brady and Cody was working on something and said he couldn't stop." She sighs, "If I would've sat here, I might've drank a bottle of wine by myself and done something stupid like drunk dial a hot guy at Northwestern and tell him how pathetic I am." I burst out laughing and she yells, "Shhh, too loud." I keep grinning when the corners of her lips twitch up and she admits, "So instead, I went out and got drunk at a bar with some friends and then came home and drunk dialed a hot guy from Northwestern."

I cover my mouth laughing, "Did you talk to him?"

"Apparently," she laughs humorlessly. "He sent me a text this morning asking me how I feel and to call him when I'm up." She purses her lips, "I'm afraid to call. I don't really remember what he said, or what I said for that matter."

I stifle another laugh and insist, "Call him. If he didn't want you to he wouldn't ask." She looks at me skeptically, so I continue, "He may tease you, but I guarantee he wants to hear from you."

She sighs and leans heavily on her arms draped across the table in front of her. "I'll call in a little while," she relents. "So how was your date last night?" she smirks. "I heard Brady leave this morning," she admits.

I grimace and tell her, "We had a lot of fun last night."

Her eyes narrow and she asks, "Really? Because that's not what your face just told me."

I chuckle and mumble, "I can never hide anything."

"And..." she prompts.

I heave a sigh and concede, "We really did have a lot of fun last night. It's just this morning his phone was going off every two seconds."

She groans, "Jackie."

I wince, "Yeah. She was stranded somewhere or something like that and couldn't call anyone else for help." Cory rolls her eyes. "Yeah, that's how I felt, but I didn't think it was my place to tell Brady not to go," I shrug.

"Why not?" she asks perplexed.

"A lot of reasons, but most of all because I'm not going to be the kind of girl to make him someone he's not," I inform her.

She cocks her head to the side, assessing me. She finally whispers, "You're really good for him."

I shake my head and admit, "That's the thing Cory, I don't know if I am. I have enough going on. I can't have a boyfriend that makes me feel like his ex is more important than me whether that's his intention or not."

She sits up a little taller and insists, "That's definitely not true."

I shrug, "That's not what he shows me when he rushes out to help her." I pinch my lips shut, briefly wondering how much I can say to her when I know she's close to Brady. I shake my head and inform her, "I haven't done anything or decided anything Cory. I really like Brady. Honestly, I probably like him a lot more than I should. I'm just having a hard time understanding their relationship, especially since Brady and I are so new. It's hard to tell what he really wants, which makes it tough to figure out what's best for me, no matter what I want."

She sighs, "Believe it or not Sam, I get it. I hate their relationship myself and Brady knows it. Even Cody tells him he should stop helping her."

"Then why does he?" I ask.

"He didn't tell you?" she asks surprised.

"He told me a little, but..." I shrug as I trail off.

My phone rings and I glance down at the screen, a picture of Ryan flashes, making me grin. I press answer and cheerily greet him, "Hi Ryan!"

"You're chipper this morning," he replies, making me laugh. "How's your roommate feeling?" he questions without preamble.

I laugh and tilt my head to the side, assessing her. She stares at me wide eyed and leans as far across the table as she can, probably hoping to hear my conversation. "Why?" I ask sweetly.

I hear his exaggerated sigh through the phone before he informs me, "She called me last night. She was funny as hell, but I'm thinking she might not be doing the best today."

I grin, "Yeah, she seems a little hung over, but still funny."

"Okay, good. So how are you doing?" he asks, changing the subject.

"I'm actually thinking of driving home this weekend," I tell him.

"What?" both Cory and Ryan say at the same time.

"Is Brady going with you?" Ryan asks innocently.

I sigh and answer both of them, "I didn't mention anything to Brady. I'm not moving back home. I just think I want to get out of here for a couple days. Plus I have to pick up more of my stuff if I'm going to be here a while anyway. I'm running out of clean clothes and I don't want to do laundry," I joke, trying to lighten the mood.

Cory's eyebrows are drawn together in concern while Ryan asks, "How about I come up and meet you there? I'll skip my Friday classes and we can hang out again this weekend. You could even bring your roommate with you if you want," he suggests saucily.

My eyes snap to Cory and I laugh, "That's so sweet of you!"

"That's just the kind of guy I am," he teases.

"Okay, I'll talk to her and let you know, but either way I'll see you soon," I tell him.

"Alright. Later," he says and immediately disconnects.

I set my phone down and fight my grin as Cory anxiously sits waiting to hear what I have to say. "That was my cousin, Ryan." She rolls her eyes and waits. I sigh and tell her what I'm thinking. "I really have to get out of here for a couple days. I've been waiting for a phone call and I can't sit here and wait anymore."

"From Brady? She questions.

I shake my head, "No, but maybe it would be good for me to be away for the weekend. Then he can do what he needs to do and figure out what he really wants."

"I think you should say something to him," she tells me.

"Yeah, I know, but he's sort of another reason I have to get out of here for a couple days. I can't think straight when he's right next door and I have to get my head straight about us." She nods sadly in understanding, but I turn my head away at the sympathetic look in her eyes. I take a deep breath and put the focus back on her. "Ryan is going to meet me at my house for the weekend," I inform her. Her eyes widen and I smirk, adding, "He said my roommate should come, but I don't know..." I tease her.

She grins and leans back in her seat appearing relieved. "Really?"

I nod, "Yeah. Do you want to come? When do you have to work again?"

She groans, "Saturday, but then I have Sunday off." She pauses, "I sound like shit. It's obviously my fault, but they don't have to know that. I could just call in sick and ask them to change all my appointments for Saturday to another time."

I smile and tell her, "It's up to you, but it would be nice to have someone with me for the boring drive."

She grins, suddenly looking much better, "Okay. When are we leaving?"

I chuckle, "Tomorrow morning like 10ish? We could get there and grab some lunch on the way to my house."

"That sounds good," she grins. "I'm going to shower and pack my bag!" she declares.

I watch her leave and send a quick text to Ryan to let him know Cory is coming when my phone beeps with a text from Brady. "I don't know if you read the letter yet, but I wanted you to know I'm here if you want to talk." My heart flutters at his thoughtfulness when another text comes through, "We really need to talk later. Can't wait to see you." I leave my phone on the table without responding and walk towards my room. I'm just not ready to talk to him yet.

Chapter 31

Brady

I slip my phone into my coat pocket and hope Sam will call me back. I've never worried about a girl calling me before and I fucking hate it. It was so much easier when I didn't care, but definitely not better I admit to myself as I think about the way she looked in my arms last night. Everything was perfect until I had to deal with Jackie. Maybe my friends are right and I should just sever ties with her completely, but that's really hard to do in a small town when we all grew up together. But after seeing how she fucked up again last night, I worry about what Jackie would do if she needed help and I wasn't around. I run my hand through my hair in frustration. I really need to figure this shit out fast.

Walking into the frat house earlier, I was lucky to find I knew a couple of the guys who lived there. I told them the situation and thankfully they helped me get Jackie out of there without any bloodshed. One of them made up a nearly unbelievable story about sending her to this bathroom because his was a shithole. The guy's girlfriend had her doubts, it would be crazy if she didn't, but she's not my problem. Then again, Jackie shouldn't be either.

I left for class, while Jackie went and hung out at the student union to wait for me to drive her home. I try to recall any information from the classes I just sat through as I quickly bypass the nearly empty Terrace, scattered with its iron, orange and yellow, sunburst chairs. It's too cold to be out here with the wind whipping off the lake. I walk into the main lobby where

Jackie told me she would be waiting. I immediately spot her sitting in a chair with her back to me, near three long curved windows. I step around in front of her and tap her on the shoulder. "Ready?"

She looks up at me and sighs, "Can you at least let me explain? Please Brady?" she begs.

I glance down at her and notice her red puffy eyes. The red could be from whatever she did last night, but the puffiness is most likely from crying. I sigh in resignation and drop my backpack on the floor before I flop down on the chair next to her. "Okay, what's going on with you Jackie? What was last night all about?" I ask, trying to cover up my irritation so we can get this over with and go home.

Unfortunately, I don't think she buys it. "That's not fair Brady. I'm really having a hard time. Between you abandoning me..." she begins.

"I didn't abandon you Jackie. I just can't be there for you all the time. We're not together! And it's not fair to Sam," I insist.

She flinches and continues as if I didn't say a word, "and now my Dad and even my Mom!" she complains. I look at her in confusion and she continues to ramble, "Everything blew up in my face! I'm so pissed at them Brady and then you wouldn't even return a stupid text!"

I put my hand up, trying to stop her rant, "Wait a minute Jackie. What happened with your parents? Is everything okay?"

She shakes her head as more tears roll down her cheeks. "No," she croaks, "everything is not okay! They lied to me Brady and they wouldn't listen to what I had to say. It was too much! I just couldn't handle it and I couldn't get in touch with you. You know I can't go out with my friends when I'm like this. I couldn't deal with their catty comments, but I went anyway." She winces and admits, "I stopped at your place before I called them. I needed to see you, but you wouldn't answer your phone," she whines. "Cody said you were out with Samantha," she scrunches her nose up in disgust when she says Sam's name and I fight to hold back my reaction. I don't need to piss her off any more than she already is at the moment. "I knew the frat was having a party and I wanted to get wasted, so I went with my friends," she shrugs like it's no big deal. "I needed to forget about everything. I drank a lot and I guess I took something, but I don't know what it was," she confesses looking defeated, but not remorseful. "I guess the girls left without me."

"Jackie," I whisper in disappointment, "they aren't your friends." She doesn't respond and I stare out the windows a moment, not quite sure what to say. "I'm assuming you slept with that asshole. Did you use protection?" I ask her stiffly.

She closes her eyes and for the first time appears embarrassed about her behavior. "I don't know. I was just trying to forget about you," she says accusingly.

I shake my head and glare at her, "Don't you fucking put any of this shit on me. We haven't been together for years Jackie. You shouldn't even be calling me to help you out of this mess you made!"

She winces, "You've always helped me until *she* came along."

"Jackie," I warn.

"Brady, you did! And you never complained, not once," she emphasizes. "You just tried to get me to change, to be better and I wanted to do that for you," she declares. "Then she's here for two weeks and now you don't care what I do."

"That's not true," I grind my jaw, trying to control my growing anger. "Besides, you have to want to do it for you!" I grit out.

She shakes her head, almost like she's confused and insists, "I just don't get it Brady. You haven't really dated anyone since me. I always thought you would eventually come back to me!" She snaps her mouth shut as her face instantly reddens.

"Jackie," I say in sympathy.

She shakes her head, "Don't...I don't want to hear it! Especially from you."

"I'm sorry, but even you know I have to say something," I insist. I kneel down in front of her so she can see me better and she pinches her lips shut, appearing to look through me. "Jackie, you can't do this shit anymore. You have to take care of yourself. Something could happen to you and you can't depend on me to pick you up every time. It's not fair to me or you."

"Or Samantha," she grumbles sarcastically.

I ignore her comment and keep going, "I don't know what happened with your family, but you have to be the one to figure it out, not me. There is no you and me and there never will be again. Yeah, I've had extremely casual relationships since you and I broke up, but I was focused on school. Besides I never met anyone that was worth more for me...until now. I'm sorry, but I'm crazy about Sam and I really want it to work with her," she flinches when I say her name. I sigh, "I care about you Jackie and I don't want anything to happen to you, but I can't lose her because of you. I want to help you, but this can't keep happening. It just can't," I emphasize. I sigh and force out the words I now realize she needs to hear. "I'm sorry, but even if there was no Sam, there would be no us," I tell her, gesturing between us. She turns her head away from me, refusing to look at me. "I just don't feel that way about you. I'm sorry."

I feel sick with guilt, almost like rocks are rolling around in my gut as I watch the tears roll down her face while she stares out the window. But I don't feel that way about her. I never have. We live in a small town and there aren't a lot of options. I always thought we were more a relationship of convenience. Cody told me, but I didn't believe she felt like that for me. I could've stopped this a long time ago if I would've just believed him.

A couple sits down in the chairs just behind us. I reach for her hands and pull her up, "Come on. Let's get out of here." I pick up my backpack and slip it onto my shoulder as she curls into my chest trying to hide her tears. I instinctively put a protective arm around her and walk her out.

We walk in silence to my truck and I stop at the passenger door to let her in. She wipes her cheeks and turns to face me. "Thank you for coming to get me Brady. I'm sorry. I'm really not trying to hurt you," she insists.

"I know," I tell her, wanting to believe the best.

"I'll always be here for you if you need me too you know," she informs me. I pinch my lips shut and nod my head slowly, knowing she's the last one I'd go to if I needed something, especially now. She moves like she's going to climb in my truck, but twists at the last second and kisses me quickly on my lips. I assume it's a goodbye kiss and keep my mouth shut, letting her have her closure.

I walk around to the other side of my truck and throw my backpack behind my seat. I check my phone and grimace when I still don't see any messages from Sam. I sigh and start my truck, ready for the day to be over, but I still have to go to the restaurant. We drive home in silence. I drop Jackie off at her house and wish her good luck with whatever she's dealing with and head to the restaurant hoping I can escape early. I need to see Sam.

I try calling Sam as I walk into the restaurant, but grit my teeth when I hear the sweet sound of her voice on her recording. I clear my throat and quickly decide what to say, "Hey Sam, I thought I'd try calling instead of texting. I'm walking into the restaurant right now. I'll try to cut out early and I'll be by to see you. Hopefully you'll still be up. I really want to talk to you Sam," I sigh. "Okay, see you soon."

The night absolutely drags by at the restaurant with a fake smile plastered on my face. It's been busy now that everyone is back from spring break and trying to find an easy way to get out of town for the night, even if it's just for dinner or drinks.

I finally step into my truck for the short drive back to my apartment a little after midnight and check my phone before I pull out of the parking lot. My heart leaps at the sight of a missed text from Sam. I quickly pull it open, but a sour taste immediately forms in my mouth at her message. "I'm sorry, but I'm exhausted and going to sleep. I'll talk to you tomorrow. Night!"

I grumble, "Fuck," and hit my steering wheel in irritation. I swiftly start my truck and head home. My phone buzzes on the short drive and I anxiously wait to check it until I'm parked behind our building.

I pull my phone out and grimace at Cody's name. I open it as I climb out of my truck, my whole body feeling like I'm about to fall over. "Check Instagram," he states. I sigh and try to pull it up as I take the slow elevator, too tired to trudge up the stairs. As soon as I step off the elevator, my account opens, but I quickly glance at Sam's door before moving to unlock mine. I huff a laugh, surprised I already think of it as Sam's before Cory's. I look down at my phone as I push the door open and freeze at the sight, "What the fuck?"

"Exactly," Cody mumbles from the middle of our couch.

I look up at him wide-eyed before focusing back on my phone, hoping it's not what I think. Unfortunately, I'm not so lucky. A friend of Jackie's posted three pictures of Jackie and me from today. In one I have her hands in mine when I'm pulling her up from the chair. In another my arm is around her and she has her face in my chest. I know it's because she's crying, but it just looks intimate. The last picture is when she kissed me. "I didn't fucking kiss her! She kissed me!" I begin defending myself.

"Does it matter when it looks like you're making out?" he asks and my panic immediately begins to escalate. "Did you read the captions?" I shake my head and he replies, "They're all the same."

"Look who's finally back together! We all knew it would happen! #JackieandBrady4Ever." I read the caption three times before I delete it from my feed. I feel like I'm back in high school with this petty bullshit.

I grip my phone so tight, I think I might break it and close Instagram. I pull up Jackie's phone number and hit send, not giving a damn what time it is. "Hello," she answers hoarsely after only one ring. "Are you calling to check up on me?" she asks, sounding hopeful.

I take a deep breath to try to calm my anger, but it doesn't really help. My voice comes out harsh when I answer, "No!" I take another deep breath and grit out, "Did you set me up?"

"What?" she asks, sounding surprised.

"Instagram Jackie," I declare. "Did you set me up?" I ask pointedly annunciating every word

"What's on it?" she asks, innocently.

"Tracy put up a couple pictures of you and me at the student union today," I inform her.

She remains quiet for a moment before she responds, "Oh. I didn't see her there while I was waiting for you." Seconds later she complains, "I look terrible!"

"That's what you care about?" I ask, exasperated. "Did you read her caption? Besides these pictures look bad Jackie. Tell her to take the fucking pictures down," I demand.

I hear the annoyance in her reply, "Who cares what anyone thinks if it's not true?"

"I do! If Sam sees this..." I begin.

"Oh, so it's about her again," she states in annoyance.

"Don't Jackie! You've pulled enough bullshit to last me a fucking lifetime. I can't believe you would do this to me after all I do for you," I rant.

"I didn't do this Brady! I just talked to her for a few minutes. I told her I was waiting for you, but I wouldn't do that to you," she declares.

I grind my jaw, trying to control my anger, "You just said you didn't see her while you were waiting for me!" She gasps realizing her slip. "Get all of it taken down, now!" I demand icily.

She huffs in annoyance, "Fine." She disconnects the call and I throw my phone on the couch and run both hands through my hair irritably.

"You better hope like hell she didn't see that because it looks really fucking bad," Cody informs me.

I sigh and drop my arms, slipping my coat off and tossing it on the couch. "I know," I groan in frustration.

"I didn't know you were popular enough to have your own paparazzi," he smirks. I glare at him as I drop down on the couch. He sighs, "Don't let her fool you. She may not have told Tracy to do it, but you know she could've just hinted at doing something like that and Tracy would've been all over it. All Jackie had to do was say she was waiting for you and she would jump at the chance to fuck with you and Jackie knows that too," he reminds me.

"Yeah," I groan, feeling defeated. I'm not ready to lose Sam, especially not over something so fucking stupid. I'll just have to hope she didn't see it, but either way I need to tell her what happened. If I don't I guarantee this will come back to bite me in the ass. "Thanks Cody," I mumble. He nods sympathetically, only making me feel worse. How did I mess this up so much in just a couple weeks? I close my eyes and picture Sam smiling up at me and hoping like hell she'll do it again.

Chapter 32

June 12th (your 14th Birthday)
To My Beautiful Baby Girl,
Happy Birthday!! I wonder what you're doing for your birthday today? When I was 14, it was more about hanging out with my friends than anything. I had stopped having parties a long time ago. What are your friends like? Do you have a lot of close friends you hang out with or just a few? Or maybe one best friend and a lot of other friends? I hope you have the kind of friends you can tell anything to and they'll keep your secrets. It's good to have at least one person you can trust with absolutely anything. It doesn't matter who they are, as long as they're loyal to you and you do the same for them.

I believe you're going to be starting high school soon. High school was better for me than middle school, but still not the best time in my life. Then again, maybe it was. I found a group of friends who loved the same kind of music as me. We loved to go to concerts or just hang out listening to music and maybe dancing. We would skip school and party together. I probably shouldn't tell you that, but I hope you didn't ever follow my example. It's not like you could, but I don't think that's something that's in your DNA. I didn't listen to my parents much once I was in high school. I did what I wanted, when I wanted. I didn't really care about much of anything except enjoying life, so that's what I did. Then again, I guess that's how I ended up with a daughter I haven't seen since the day she was born. I hope you're more responsible than me.

Anyway, we're going to try going camping with some friends for the Fourth of July. I'm not sure how I'll do, but it should be fun. Have you ever been camping? Have you ever done any of the things that go along with camping like fishing or starting a campfire? The closest things to camping that I've done are roast marshmallows for Smores and tell stories around the campfire, so this should be interesting. My husband says I'll be fine, but...Anyway, I hope you have a wonderful birthday and good luck with high school!

    With Love...
    Catherine Schepp

    I sigh and fold the letter before slipping it back in its place in my nightstand, wishing Brady had been here for support. I know it's my fault he isn't here, but I was hoping he'd show up before class this morning even after I avoided him all day yesterday. I've known him for two weeks and I'm already losing my mind.

    I groan and push myself up off my bed. I slowly wander out towards the kitchen to grab a cup of coffee and find something to eat. I'm having trouble processing what I just read with so many other things on my mind. I wish I could stop thinking about Brady. Then there's the fact I still haven't heard a word from Lincoln. Is that what I should call him? I grimace and mumble, "It doesn't matter." I have to actually talk to him to call him anything. I don't know what to do. Maybe I should just forget about it, but I know I can't do that yet. I need to know more about my family history, if nothing else.

    I pour my coffee and sit down at the table, tightly gripping my phone and praying for it to ring. I glance up as Cory walks in with a huge smile on her face. "Good morning!" she practically sings, bringing a soft smile to my face.

    "You're chipper this morning," I inform her. She just grins and grabs a blueberry muffin from out of the cabinet before sitting down across from me. "I just want to finish this and maybe eat some breakfast. Then I'll take a quick shower," I tell her. "I should be ready to leave in about an hour."

She nods, "Okay, sounds good." She takes a bite of her muffin before she hesitantly asks, "Did you talk to Brady?"

I sigh and relent, "I'll text him now."

"Good," she murmurs and continues to eat her breakfast.

I pull up his name and begin typing before I change my mind. "Good morning! I'm going to meet my cousin back at my house in IL for the weekend. I need to pick up a few things to bring back with me."

"I'll come with you," he offers instantly.

"Cory is coming with me," I respond.

"Can I come too?" he asks.

I sigh and respond with a question, "Aren't you in class right now?"

"Yeah. Almost done with this one. Then I have one more. I'm done at noon today," he informs me. I don't reply and he asks, "So can I please come with you?" I hesitate and he begs, "Please?"

I know I need to talk to him. I can't help thinking I'm being a little childish by avoiding the whole thing. I give in and type a simple, "Ok."

"Awesome! See you soon," he texts back.

I feel as if a weight has been lifted off my shoulders with my decision and I smile to myself. "I texted Brady," I murmur. "He wants to come with us," I say as I look up at Cory. She's sitting with her eyes wide and her mouth hanging open in shock, staring at her phone. "What is it?" I ask curiously and glance over at her screen reflexively.

"Nothing!" she yells, turning off her phone. She quickly flips it over on the table and stares at it with both fear and disgust as if it were poisonous. Unfortunately, it's too late. I saw what she was looking at.

"Is that picture from yesterday?" I rasp, my stomach suddenly churning with anxiety. I've done really well at avoiding social media since I left Chicago and the first glimpse I see is something I definitely wish I didn't. Well, that's not true. I don't ever want to be the ignorant fool again. I guess I mean I wish what I just saw wasn't real.

She shakes her head in denial, but her eyes full of sympathy tell me everything I need to know. "I'm sure it's not what it looks like," she insists, her own doubt evident in her voice. "I know Brady and it can't be," she declares.

"It looks like he was kissing Jackie," I tell her, my voice cracking at the end. My overactive imagination wouldn't make that up.

She winces, "Yeah, but..." she huffs in irritation, not able to explain it either. "It has to be old or something," she says desperately searching for an answer. We both know that's exactly what he was wearing yesterday when he went to help Jackie. Besides the fact, I'm sure he didn't look like that four years ago when he was actually dating her. I may not have known him then, but I'm not stupid.

"I'm going to finish getting ready," I inform her robotically, attempting to ignore the sudden stabbing pain clawing at me from the inside out. I stand up, leaving my coffee cup on the table and not bothering to grab anything to eat. I take a deep breath and walk with fake confidence toward my room. I feel like I'm losing my mind, while my heart is getting smashed into oblivion. I stride into my room forcing myself to move and do what I need to do to get ready to get the fuck out of here. I frantically look around my room, trying to focus on one thing at a time. I spot my clothes for today and grab them. I walk numbly towards the bathroom when Cory's voice pulls me out of my haze. Realizing she's on the phone, I freeze. I don't mean to eavesdrop, but I can't help it.

"I don't care Brady! It looks like you were making out with her! Gross!" she makes a noise as if she's gagging. "Then the picture of you with your arm around her just looks like it confirms it! What the fuck were you thinking?" she whisper yells. My stomach churns and a lump forms in my throat as I unwillingly question what the other picture looks like. I didn't see anything else. There's a pause before she continues, "I don't think we're going to be waiting for you anymore. I know I wouldn't," she grumbles. "Can't you just stay away from Jackie? She doesn't care about you or what you want! She just cares about herself. You have to realize that by now, especially now!" she emphasizes. I fight the tears welling up in my eyes in the silence, my whole body taut like I'm waiting for a final blow. "Who cares if she fucks up? Let her!" Another pause, "Well Cody can be smart sometimes. He's right. You really messed up Brady. It doesn't matter what you were trying to do," she explains, exasperated. "When was the last time you were in a real relationship? You don't have a clue what you're doing!" she exclaims. "Sam should feel like she's important, like she's not only more important than your ex-girlfriend, but the most important thing in your world." She sighs, sounding defeated, "No one wants to feel like your second choice, Brady. I think that's exactly what you just did to Sam and so much more." She pauses, "I don't know..."

I force myself to take the last few steps down the hall not wanting to hear anymore. He's obviously sorry for whatever he did or didn't do, but is that enough for me? Do I even want to know what really happened? I fist my hand and hold it to my chest, trying to control the pain. I take a deep breath as I let the tears roll quietly down my cheeks. It didn't hurt like this when I walked in on Paul and Taylor. How is that even possible? I wince and admit to myself it's because it felt different with Brady. I felt like he could see the real me. I felt like he listened to me because he wanted to hear what I had to say. I felt like I could tell him anything. I swallow over the lump in my throat again as the letter from my birth mom comes to my mind at that thought. I already felt like he was my best friend and we could share anything and everything with each other. I guess I was wrong. I flinch at the thought because this is the first time I really started feeling like myself again. "I wanted so much more with him," I confess softly.

I turn on the water and the bathroom fan to add to the noise and drown out my inevitable anguish. I pull off my black and white pajama bottoms and tank top. I slowly step into the shower. I barely feel the still cool water hit my body. I lower myself to the floor of the bathtub. I pull my legs up to my chest and wrap my arms around them. I lower my head underneath the spray of the shower and release my sobs as quietly as possible as the pain overwhelms me. "I feel so stupid," I whimper to myself.

I try to rid myself of the pain, but if I know anything about pain, I know it doesn't just go away no matter how much I want it to. I do know how to act like it's not there. I'm actually really good at that. I slowly stand and stick my face in the shower, letting the water wash my tears away. I swallow hard and force myself to control my breathing as I turn around and start washing my hair. "I can do this," I remind myself. I think about how strong my mom always was and how I've come so far since I lost them. I'm not going to bury myself in the grief, I'm going to stand tall and keep moving forward. He's just a guy, I insist, trying to convince myself, even though I feel like he's so much more. I'm not going to let Brady or anyone stop me from being me again. I'm ready to show everyone just how strong I can be.

Chapter 33

Brady

I hand in my test and run out the door of my advanced economics classroom. I hear someone call my name, but I stuff my hands in my pockets and put my head down, pretending like I didn't hear anything. I try to weave through the crowd of people coming or going from class. I'm stopped when someone reaches for my shoulder. I spin around, feeling defensive, only to find my friend Owen towering over me with his blonde hair hanging down in his eyes. "Whoa," his eyes widen and he holds his hands up as if resigning a fight I doubt I could ever win.

I heave a sigh in frustration at my behavior and explain, "Sorry O, I'm a little on edge. What's up?"

"The test wasn't that bad," he comments, fishing for information.

I grimace knowing it wasn't my best. I hope I at least pass. I probably would've skipped the class all together if it wasn't for the fact I knew we had a test today. "Nah, but my head is somewhere else," I respond.

He grins knowingly, "Ah." I don't explain any further and he eventually continues, "A bunch of us are going out tonight. You around this weekend?"

I hold back my flinch at his innocent question and reply honestly. "I'm actually hoping to go down to Chicago this weekend with my girl."

He nods, "Alright, text me if things change." He slaps me on the back and breaks off in the opposite direction as we walk out the front door of the brick building we both spend too much time in. "Later!"

I wave, thankful he doesn't ask me any other questions. I stride to my truck as quickly as possible, needing to get out of here and get to Sam. I pull out my phone as soon as I sit in my truck, checking my messages. My hands start sweating as soon as I notice a message from Sam. I open it, hoping for the best. "Cory and I are leaving. It seems you're already too busy for me," I read and I swear I feel my heart wretch inside my chest.

"Fuck," I grumble and slam my hand on the steering wheel in irritation. I quickly type back, pleading with her. I don't give a shit how pathetic I sound. I'm the one who fucked up. "Please talk to me. It's not what you think."

I hold my breath as the dancing dots appear and wait for her message. "I don't play games Brady."

I flinch and reply, "I don't either. Just please talk to me."

"I'm leaving now and I'm driving. Figure your shit out and we'll talk when I get back," she tells me.

"I do have everything figured out," I insist and hope she doesn't take it the wrong way. I wait for a response, but nothing comes.

I give up and drop my phone in the console. I start my truck and turn quickly towards home. I need to pack a bag and go after her. I need to tell her what happened and I need to tell her about Max. I'm not losing her now. Not when I just found her. I press the voice prompt on my Bluetooth, "Call Cody."

"Hey asshole," he says as his way of greeting.

I clear my throat and try not to comment on it. I don't want to hear another lecture from him. "Are you home?" I ask.

"Yeah, but Sam and Cory just left," he informs me.

I sigh in resignation, "Yeah, I know. Can you get Sam's address for me from Cory?"

"Why don't you ask her yourself?" he challenges, probably knowing the answer.

I grit my teeth and answer honestly, "Because she probably wouldn't give it to me."

"Then why should I give it to you?" he asks curiously.

"Because I fucked up and I want to fix it," I tell him because it's not only what he wants to hear, but it's also the truth.

"Yeah you did," he grumbles. "I'll hold back on I told you so for now and see what I can do," he relents.

I breathe a huge sigh of relief, hoping he can come through for me. I'm not waiting until she gets back to talk to her. I need to straighten this mess out now. "Want to go with me to Chicago?" I ask him trying to feel hopeful.

"I think I'll hang out here and enjoy having the apartment all to myself for the weekend. I'm not big on listening to you grovel," he says, obviously trying to keep the laughter out of his voice. "Although, I'd love to see a video or at least a few pictures."

"Fuck you," I throw out, making him chuckle. I sigh and inform him, "I have to stop out at the restaurant. I think I'm on the schedule for Sunday and I'm not about to rush back. The only way that's happening is if I go see my mom."

"Good luck," he says.

"I'm going either way," I grumble and Cody laughs as he disconnects the call.

I go over what I should say to my mom as I drive to the restaurant, but as soon as I pull in I forget everything that was in my head when I walk into the back office and meet my dad's eyes. "Brady," he barely greets me before focusing back on the papers in front of him. "You're here early," he tells me.

"I'm not here to work," I inform him. "I was hoping to talk to Mom."

He stops what he's doing and looks up at me. "Well, Mom is meeting with the alcohol distributor. She should be done in a few minutes, but in the mean time you're stuck with me." His eyes narrow and he assesses me slowly before meeting my eyes again. "What's going on Brady?" he asks, his voice full of concern.

I groan quietly and flop down into the cherry armchair adorned with black leather adhered to the seat and the back of the chair with gold buttons. I run my hand through my hair before resting my elbows on my knees. I clasp my hands in front of me and focus back on my Dad. "I need to take off this weekend," I tell him simply. I don't know why I'm so nervous to tell him about Sam.

"Is everything alright with you?" he asks, sitting up a little straighter.

I nod, "Yeah, I'm fine. I just...I need to go after Sam. She's from Chicago, or around there somewhere," I stammer.

He looks at me with confusion, "Who's Sam?"

I sigh and start again, "Sam is the girl I had the chef make up the picnic for. She's the girl I showed our property to. She's the girl I want to know everything about and she's the girl I want to know everything about me. She's the girl I want to be a part of my life and I want to be a part of hers," I ramble, as my father's smile grows.

"I saw her in here with you. She's a very pretty girl," he informs me.

"Dad, she's not just pretty, she's gorgeous and she's beautiful inside too. But I...I really messed up," I finally admit feeling the lump forming in my throat again. He raises his eyebrows and waits for me to continue. I begin fidgeting with my hands, cracking my knuckles gently as I admit, "Jackie needed help again, so I went. One of her friends posted a few pictures of the two of us on campus that even I admit looked really bad, but I didn't do anything," I insist, needing someone to believe me before I go to Sam. "I know I shouldn't have gone at all, but..." I trail off.

My Dad sighs, "Old habits die hard."

"Yeah," I admit hoarsely.

He nods his head and asks, "Does Jackie know there is no you and her?"

I nod my head feeling somewhat disconnected from my body, "If she didn't before she sure as hell does now."

"Does she know about Sam?" he asks. I nod my head, trying to figure out where he's going with this. "Then if Jackie is really a true friend, she'll stop asking you to bail her out, but even if she doesn't if this Sam really means something to you like she seems to, then you have to stop helping either way. She's not your responsibility."

"I know," I croak.

He smiles sadly at me and says, "You know, when I met your mom, I knew she was the one for me immediately. Of course, she didn't believe me, but I didn't let her give up on us. I had just broken up with this girl Phyllis and she thought she was my rebound, but that's the furthest thing from the truth. Phyllis and I treated each other like a placeholder until we found what we were really looking for, but we both knew the score. Your mom and I had just been out on a date when she saw me talking to Phyllis. I waved when she glared at me thinking the jealousy was good for her." He shakes his head, "Damn was I stupid and so damn lucky your Mom forgave me." He pauses, watching me for a moment, "If this Sam girl is the one for you, go after her and fix it."

I breathe a sigh of relief, "That's what I'm trying to do. Thanks Dad." I stand, suddenly feeling over-anxious to get to Sam. I freeze and my brow furrows as I ask hesitantly, "What about Mom?"

"What about me?" she asks as she steps into the office. She steps into me, giving me a gentle hug, "Hi Brady. What about me?" she repeats.

I grimace, "I can't work this weekend. I have to go to Chicago."

"For what?" she asks, her eyes already disapproving.

"Sam," I state. Her mouth drops slightly open and she stares at me in shock. "It's short for Samantha," I add awkwardly, feeling as if I need to say something else.

"Is it the same girl you had in here recently or a different one again?" she asks, unsuccessfully trying to hide her displeasure.

"The same one Mom. There is no other girl for me. Just Sam," I confess.

She meets my eyes and I watch as her face transforms into a hopeful smile. "Really?"

I nod, "If I can get her back."

"What did you do Brady?" she gasps.

I sigh and plead for help with my eyes towards my Dad. I can't explain the whole thing again. It took a lot out of me the first time and I have to save my energy for when I find Sam. He sighs, "Sweetheart, he really needs to get going. I'll tell you everything he told me, but I think we should let him go."

Hearing my Dad say that feels surreal. My mom nods her head and gives me another hug, "Okay." She smiles up at me showing her matching dimples, "Good luck," she whispers.

I take a step towards the door and tell them, "Thank you."

My dad gives me a small wave in response while my mom reminds me, "Don't forget to bring her a gift!" My dad laughs and reaches for her waist.

I turn saying, "Okay, thanks! Bye!" I slip out before I see something I don't want to. I jog to my truck feeling as if I just had an out of body experience. I haven't talked to my dad like that in years. For the last five years everything always seems to be about the restaurant. I think that was the first time my mom looked happy when I mentioned a girl too. I cringe just thinking about what my mom must have thought of me.

I back out of the parking lot and turn towards my apartment, hoping Cody had luck with getting her address. As I was sitting in that office talking, I realized all the shit I just admitted to my dad was true. I'm already falling for Sam and I can't lose her now. I have to go after her and tell her everything before she decides she doesn't want to give me that chance. I'm not letting Jackie and my past ruin this for me. Sam's too important.

Chapter 34

Samantha

I walk with Cory into Polly's Paninis and sit down at a round, natural wooden table with four mismatched wooden chairs in every color of the rainbow, off to the side. "This place is adorable!" Cory gushes.

I shrug, "Yeah, it's been here for as long as I can remember. The food is good too. They just serve breakfast and lunch, but they're almost always busy when they're open."

A young, dark-haired waitress immediately ambles up to our table with a bright smile. "Good afternoon! Would you ladies like something to drink while you look over the menu?" she asks sweetly.

"Uh, sure. Can I have a Diet Coke?" Cory asks.

The waitress nods and looks over at me, "Can I have the same? But," I say quickly before she walks away, "We're waiting for one more, so we'll wait to order lunch until he gets here if that's okay?" I ask.

"Of course. I'll be right back with your drinks," she informs us. She's back almost instantly and we take a sip of our Diet Cokes while we wait for Ryan.

I glance around at the old-fashioned pictures, signs and even curtains hanging in the windows. The tables and chairs are all worn and mismatched going from round to square to rectangle in various colors just like the chairs. The wait staff all wear jeans and either a plaid or paisley shirt of some kind, in any color, and a pale blue apron with the restaurant's name and logo imprinted on it. "I haven't really looked around and taken everything in like this in a while," I admit to Cory.

She laughs, "That's because you're from here and now you're back visiting. Everything seems new and different or brings back some kind of memory for you when before it was just the same boring old thing you saw all the time."

I nod in agreement, completely understanding what she means. My memories of this place are the first thing I thought of as I looked around. I have a lot of those here. "You're so right," I whisper in appreciation. I'm grateful I'm finally enjoying remembrances of my parents without crying. "My mom and I would eat here sometimes if we were having a girls' day out or if we didn't want to make anything and sometimes we'd come as a family too," I tell Cory as she smiles over at me. I used to come here with my friends a lot too, especially Taylor. She loved this place! Then there's Paul...

"Sam?" a low voice questions from over my shoulder. I tense and turn slowly around to find Paul staring at me with wide eyes. "You're home," he states. "You look fantastic," he tells me with a nervous smile.

I shake my head lightly to pull myself out of my momentary fog. I finally find my voice and tell him, "Thank you. I'm not staying though. I'm just here for the weekend. I needed to pick up more of my things."

He winces and nods slowly, "Yeah, of course. I guess I'm only here for the weekend too." I stare at him unwilling to make him even the slightest bit comfortable. He clears his throat and asks, "How are you doing?"

"I'm good," I state simply.

He sighs, "Look Sam, I think we should talk while you're here. I miss you. I heard..." he begins.

He's interrupted when a bouncy Taylor sidles up next to him and kisses him on the cheek. He flexes his jaw as she greets him exuberantly, "You're here! I got us a table back there." She turns towards us and feigns surprise, as if she had no idea who he was talking to. I can't help but notice Cory roll her eyes and I smother my giggle with my hand. "Samantha, I see you're back already. Things didn't work out so well for you...again?" she asks smirking.

I take a deep breath trying to control my anger. I refuse to be anything like her. Instead, I paste on a fake smile and inform her in an overly sweet voice, "I'm just here to pick up some more of my things."

"Hi, I'm Cory, Sam's roommate," Cory interrupts when I don't bother introducing them.

"Hey Cory, I'm Paul," Paul introduces himself, smiling down at Cory.

"Oh," she says knowingly. "I've heard about you," she informs him. His smile falls off his face and his brow creases with worry, as it should. She turns to Taylor and smiles wide, "Then you must be that slut Taylor."

Taylor's mouth drops open in shock. She glares at Cory and yells, "How dare you!"

Cory nods and looks up at her apologetically, "I'm sorry, would bitch be more appropriate?" I huff a laugh and cover my mouth with my napkin. Taylor grunts in anger and I notice Paul fighting his own smile. Cory shrugs nonchalantly, "What else would you call someone who poses as your best friend and tries to steal your boyfriend?"

"Tries?" she questions. "Oh, I did steal him," she declares as if that makes it better.

Paul grimaces and insists, "Um, we're not together, not at all and even you know that night was a drunken mistake."

She glares at him and pushes her shoulders back, feigning confidence. She turns her back on us as she tells Paul, "I'm over there when you're done."

He doesn't reply, he just keeps watching me as I try to contain my laughter. "How were you ever friends with her?" Cory asks in exasperation and we both burst out laughing.

"I can't believe you did that!" I giggle.

"Someone had to," she grumbles, making me laugh again.

"Sam?" Paul questions as our laughter fades. He shifts awkwardly on his feet and asks, "Can I please talk to you while you're home? I understand why you've been avoiding me. Hell, I deserve it, but I just want to talk. I can come to you or we could go out somewhere if you'd rather be around other people. I just want to talk...Please," he pleads.

I sigh and relent, "Okay Paul. I guess I can give you that. I'm a big girl though," I say sarcastically. "I can handle being in the same room alone with you. You can just come by my house," I inform him. "Just text me before to check if it's okay. I promise I'll answer you this time," I tell him.

He smiles wide and his whole body relaxes with evident relief. "Thank you," he whispers appreciatively. He takes a step towards me and I instinctively lean away from him making him wince. He steps back and forces another smile. "I'll see you later then." He nods at Cory, "It was nice meeting you."

She smiles politely, "Wish I could say the same." He turns and walks away. She tilts her head to the side as she watches him go. She finally looks over at me with a smirk, "It's too bad he's such an asshole. He's actually really cute!" I laugh at her assessment, while at the same time I'm thinking he's not as cute as Brady.

"Who's really cute?" Ryan asks as he wraps his arm around me in a quick hug as his way of greeting me. He does the same with Cory before he sits in the chair next to her, scooting it a little closer so he's able to rest his arm on the back of her chair. "Do I need to be worried?" he asks jokingly, even though I know he's very serious.

Cory laughs, "Definitely not!"

I tilt my head towards Paul and Taylor and inform him, "Paul and Taylor are here."

The waitress steps up to our table and asks kindly, "Do you guys know what you'd like to order?"

Ryan begins speaking before either of us have a chance. "Yeah, can we order a special, a chicken club Panini and a turkey club Panini with one of each side? And can we take our order to go?" Ryan asks. "We've had a change of plans."

"No problem," she replies smiling as she turns back towards the kitchen.

"You guys can pick which one you want or we can share," Ryan offers as explanation for ordering for us.

"We don't have to do that. They don't bother me," I declare knowing his real reasons. "Besides, Cory did a nice job of making Taylor want to stay away from us," I smirk.

He looks at her and raises his eyebrows in surprise. "Really?" he grins.

She waves him off and mumbles, "I'll tell you about it later."

He nods and they both focus back on me, assessing me and searching for the truth. Ryan finally nods and smiles softly, "Alright then, but I don't think I can look at that asshole for too long without walking over and beating the shit out of him. I know I can't hit a girl, but I can hit him." I raise my eyebrows in surprise and he shrugs, staring at me momentarily so I understand he'll be there to watch out for me or whatever else I may need him for. My chest gets tight, appreciating the gesture.

Then he adds, "And is there someone else you need protecting from?"

I grimace and Cory groans in irritation. She blushes when Ryan looks over at her. She blurts out, "Sorry. I'm just pissed at him right now. I think maybe more than Sam."

"Nah, she's just really good at hiding her feelings when she wants to," he tells her. Cory looks at me curiously while I shake my head and wave my hand in dismissal. We both know he's right, but I'm not about to admit it.

Ryan turns to Cory and grins widely at her, "Did you miss me?"

She rolls her eyes and smirks, "Nah, it feels like I just saw you."

He laughs heartily and leans down surprising her with a chaste kiss. I chuckle as her face slowly reddens when he rasps, "How about now?"

Her breathing sounds erratic and I hear her gulp before she answers, "Well, maybe I missed you a little bit."

He chuckles and kisses her lightly again. "I'm man enough to admit I missed you and I'm really happy Sam brought you with her." She smiles and he kisses her again before he leans back in his chair appearing completely satisfied with himself.

"How have classes been this week?" she asks. I take this opportunity to take myself out of their conversation so they can catch up.

I turn my head and stare out the window and into the busy streets. I watch as all the people rush to lunch, work, home or wherever else they might be headed. Most of them are still bundled up in their winter coats, but a few are trying to brave the cold weather in long sleeved shirts or sweatshirts. I guess they assume since it will be

April 1st this weekend it should be warmer. Too bad the weather doesn't seem to be cooperating with that theory.

I glance at my phone, hoping for something from my birth father, but the only message is another missed text from Brady instead of the one I'm really waiting for. I hesitate only for a moment before I open it. "I just want to talk Sam. Please?" he begs.

I sigh, wondering what I should do. I told Paul I would talk to him, the least I could do is talk to Brady. Then again, I'm only asking for a couple days away from him. What will I do with the time though? Will I just push him further away? Should I let him explain now? I don't know if I'll like what he has to tell me, I grimace.

"Are you okay?" Ryan asks. I look over to find him and Cory both looking at me with concern etched in their features.

I grind my jaw and respond, "I'm fine. I'm just thinking."

Both of their faces turn to sympathy. I open my mouth as I search for what to say, but I spot the waitress coming towards our table carrying two bags of food. I breathe a sigh of relief and stand saying a quick "Thank you," as she approaches. "Can I meet you two back at the house?" I ask. Ryan nods and I glance over to Cory who appears ready to argue with me. "It's a short drive, but that way you two have time to talk before you're stuck with me," I rationalize quickly. "I'll see you both in a few minutes," I ramble.

I turn and rush towards the exit before either of them have a chance to say any more. I feel Paul's eyes following me through the restaurant, but I keep my eyes focused in front of me as I walk confidently out the door. I reach my car and set the food on the floor of the passenger side before I climb in behind the wheel. I start the car and exhale slowly beginning to relax just from being out of there. I slowly back out and turn the car towards my house. I gasp as I pull away, realizing I never paid for my part of lunch. "Oops," I mumble. I'll have to pay them back for that!

Chapter 35

June 12ᵗʰ (your 15ᵗʰ Birthday)
To My Beautiful Baby Girl,
Happy Birthday!! What kind of plans do you have for your birthday this year? Are you doing something with friends, family or both? Or maybe even a boyfriend...Do you have a boyfriend? By the time I was 15, I had a new boyfriend nearly every month. I really liked boys, I still do! In fact, some people might say I was always a little bit boy crazy. If you do have a boyfriend, be careful! Boys can be trouble, believe me. I can't help but wonder when your first kiss was or your first date, or even if you've had either one. I hope you pick better boys than me. Until I met my husband, I never seemed to pick the right kind of boys. Then again, I was never looking for much. I guess that's not true though, even some of the good boys I dated just weren't right for me, like your father. He's a good man, we just weren't good for each other. I wonder if you have the same kind of taste in men (I mean boys for you) that I did?

So now that you have some experience with high school, what's it like for you? Do you do any sports or activities? Do you do well in school? What are your favorite subjects or maybe it's just favorite teachers? We had one teacher that everyone had a crush on, including me. He was only a few years out of college so I'm sure you can imagine. Of course we had plenty of our own boys to choose from and I loved dating them! What kind of boys do you like? Do you go on lots of dates like I did? Or are you more of a one-guy kind of girl like I am now? Or maybe you're more of a one-girl kind of girl, that's wonderful too, as long as you're happy.

Anyway, my husband and I have a date tonight. He's going to take me out to dinner for your birthday. We'll

toast to you hoping you have a wonderful day today! He's a
good man who's good for me. I know I'm very lucky. I hope
you find the right man for you some day, but in the
meantime take it slow. Happy Birthday!
    With Love...
    Catherine Schepp

I laugh to myself as I fold up the letter thinking about how she talked mostly about boys when boys are currently my biggest problem, even my birth father for that matter. I think that's the first letter she mentioned him since the one from when I was born. She didn't really say anything substantial, but she did say he was a good man. If he's such a good man, why haven't I heard from him yet? It was hard enough to force myself to go there and now I have to sit and wait to hear from him? *If* I hear from him at all I think and groan in frustration. Waiting and not knowing is absolute torture! My thoughts are quickly interrupted by the ding of the doorbell. I put the letter back in my backpack so I don't forget it here later. I'm grateful I thought to bring the last three letters with me, just in case I wanted to read them while I was here.

I stand and march towards the front of the house calling, "I'm coming!" I'm thankful I was able to put Paul off until today. Last night I felt so overwhelmed emotionally, between being home and flooded with memories of my parents, to the letters and my birth father, to all the bullshit with Brady. It's just a lot to process. Ryan and Cory left about a half hour ago to go out for brunch after I insisted I would be fine alone with Paul. Honestly, I just want to get this over with. I take a deep breath as I cross the living room.

I pull the door open to find Paul with one hand stuffed in his jeans pocket and the other holding a bouquet of long stemmed red roses. He's wearing a long sleeved dark grey Henley, but no coat. I think Brady has the same shirt, but he wears it much better. "Hi Sam," he grins.

I hesitate for a moment as Brady crosses my mind before I pull the door open further to let Paul in. "Hey Paul," I sigh, "Come on in."

He steps towards me and I close the door behind him. He holds out the flowers stiffly, "These are for you."

I give him a fake smile and whisper, "Thank you." I take them and he follows me to the kitchen, watching everything I do. I pull out a vase and quickly fill it with water. I take the tissue off the roses and drop them into the water without clipping the ends. I set the flowers on the table and walk out to the living room. I sit down in the corner of the couch and curl my legs up underneath me and wait.

I watch as Paul fidgets nervously, bouncing slightly from one foot to the other. He finally drops down in the middle of the couch, twisting to look at me. "I need to start by saying I'm sorry. I really messed up. I can honestly say I've never regretted anything more in my life." I shake my head and open my mouth to respond, but he stops me. "Please don't say anything yet. I need to explain first," he insists. I relent and nod my head for him to continue. "I know this is no excuse, but after your parents died, you started pulling away from me. It was like even when we were together you were barely there, barely functioning. I felt like I tried everything to pull you out of it, to help you, but you didn't want my help and that fucking killed me!" His voice cracks and he pauses to clear his throat. "I was so in love with you, but it's almost like you didn't even care." He glances down at his hands and admits painfully, "I was so lonely. We were together, but I was so fucking lonely!"

"I'm sorry," I whisper as I wipe away my tears at seeing his pain, pain that I caused.

He shakes his head, "Don't! You were going through a lot," he concedes. "I'm not putting any of the blame for this on you. I don't want you to think that," he emphasizes. "It's all on me. I just need you to see my side, to see how I felt." He scoots closer and wipes my tears away and I let him. He sighs and shakes his head in disbelief, "I should've told you about Taylor."

My eyebrows draw together in confusion, "What? Do you mean..."

He shakes his head emphatically and interrupts me, "No! No, nothing happened before that night, but she hit on me all the damn time. At first it was annoying, but I didn't want you to believe your friend over me and break up with me, so I didn't say anything. Then when you wouldn't come back to me...I mean I know we were together, but sometimes it didn't feel like I had anyone, even when you were with me." He grimaces and admits, "So I started to enjoy the attention she gave me. That night, I kept texting asking where you were and I drank and drank and drank while I waited for you. I went to my room to use my bathroom and Taylor followed me. At first I told her to leave. She ignored me and took her top off. She told me you texted her saying you weren't coming anymore."

"That was a lie!" I rasp.

"I know that now," he whispers. He gulps and looks away from me, "I was drunk and I was so pissed at you for blowing me off again that when she started kissing me, I just let it happen." He shakes his head in disgust and mumbles, "I should've known she set me up." He sighs, "I know it's no excuse Sam. I know it never should've happened no matter what. I know I fucked up and I've never been more sorry for anything than I am about this."

I sigh and wipe my tears away again. "I'm not about to say it's okay, because honestly it's not, but I get it. You're right. I was pushing you away. I didn't mean to, but I couldn't help it," I admit. "I'm sorry, Paul. Everything was so hard for so long. I didn't know who I was." I huff a laugh, "Honestly I still don't." I reach for a Kleenex and wipe my nose. I take a deep calming breath. "Thank you for telling me everything and I'm sorry I didn't listen sooner. I guess I wasn't ready," I admit with a shrug.

"I understand why you didn't want to listen to anything I had to say for a while. I don't blame you," he concedes. "I have to ask though, do you think you can forgive me?" he asks hopefully.

I release my breath slowly, realizing I need this closure with him. I nod and tell him, "I forgive you Paul. I'm sorry I hurt you too," I tell him sincerely.

Relief encompasses his whole body and he insists, "It's okay. I should've been more understanding about what you were going through. I can't imagine what you were feeling and it was selfish of me to ask so much of you."

I nod my head and swallow over the growing lump in my throat. I really appreciate that he's saying all this to me. I didn't think it would matter to me, but it does. "Thank you," I whisper hoarsely, not quite sure what else to say.

He reaches up and wipes my tears away. "I hate seeing you cry."

I laugh, "It's just a lot to let go of I guess."

He nods like he understands. His hand slips down to the back of my neck and his finger begins rubbing soothing circles on the back of my head. "I don't want to let you go," he confesses. "Sam, I'm still in love with you. I've missed you so much. I want you back," he tells me.

I shake my head, "Paul, I'm sorry, but..."

He interrupts my words with an unexpected kiss, knocking the breath from my lungs. More tears stream down my face, the taste of salt giving me a shock as I belatedly pull away. "I love you Sam," he declares. "We've been through too much to give up without a fight."

I shake my head, "I can't. I just can't," I insist. "That's not what this is. This is our closure."

He shakes his head, "Not for me. We are not over."

"What about Taylor?" I ask. His eyebrows draw together in confusion and I add, "You said you weren't together, but why were you together today then?"

"We were both home and no one else was around. I had nothing to do. She asked if I wanted to catch up and have lunch. I agreed and even reminded her before it wasn't a date," he insists.

I shake my head, "It doesn't matter Paul. I can't go back."

"Then we'll start over. We can take it slow, as slow as you need to go. We can figure this out Sam. I just don't want to do it without you!" he exclaims reaching for my hand.

The doorbell rings, startling me. I pull my hand away and swiftly jump up and out of his reach, feeling panicked. "I'll be right back," I blurt out as I race for the front door. I throw it open, grateful for the unknown distraction.

I gasp at the sight of Brady standing nervously on my doorstep. "Hi Sam," he whispers hoarsely. I stand staring at him momentarily with my mouth hanging open. He's in faded blue jeans, a long sleeved marbled blue t-shirt with the Brewers Logo across the middle of his hard chest and no coat looking hot as hell. "Can I come in?" he prods anxiously.

"He came after me," is the only thought going through my mind. He quickly looks me up and down as he waits for my answer, sending chills down my spine. When his pale blue eyes come back to mine, I shake myself out of my stupor and nod my head. "Yeah, sure," I stammer.

I step back and Brady steps into my house for the first time. "How'd you know where I live?" I ask already knowing the answer.

"Cory, eventually," he shrugs, smiling sadly down at me.

I barely close the door behind him when I feel Paul step up beside me. "Who the hell are you?" he asks accusingly.

I watch Brady's demeanor transform at the sight of Paul. He clenches his jaw, pushes his shoulders back, flexes his fingers and stands a little taller as his eyes narrow on him. Brady has about 2 inches on Paul and his body is definitely more toned. I take a deep breath and shakily answer for him, feeling the tension vibrating between the two of them. "Um, Paul this is Brady, Brady, Paul," I say, my eyes bouncing back and forth between the two of them. I have no idea what either of them is about to do, but I can guess what they're both thinking.

Chapter 36

Brady

My chest feels tight and I want to punch the guy in front of me for so many reasons, but mostly for hurting Sam and then for being here with her. What the fuck is he doing here? He's already acting all territorial with her and he doesn't even know who I am. I glance around her living room hoping they aren't alone and ask, "Where's Cory?"

She opens her mouth to answer when at the same time the asshole asks, "But who is he Sam? Why is he here?"

She closes her eyes and slowly opens them answering me first. "Cory went to brunch with Ryan so Paul and I could talk."

I grind my jaw, pissed she's here alone with him, but she obviously agreed to it. I know what he wants to do with her and it's not talking. At the same time my stomach twists with jealousy. She'll talk to him, but she won't talk to me? What the fuck? I focus on him and answer his question for her through my teeth, "I'm her boyfriend."

She looks at me with her mouth hanging open and amends my statement, making me flinch, "I'm not too sure about that right now. You've been a little busy with someone else." She closes her mouth and glares at me.

Paul laughs humorlessly, "Let me get this straight, you've been dating this guy since you left?" She doesn't answer, but she doesn't have to. "We've only been broken up for a couple months!"

"And you haven't fucked anyone since?" I ask crassly. I huff, "Didn't bother you when you were together!"

"Brady," Sam admonishes.

At the same time, he turns to me with a deadly glare and spits out, "Fuck you!"

"Sounds like an admission to me," I grumble.

He takes a menacing step towards me that I would welcome at this point, but Sam jumps in front of him, "Paul don't," she begs.

"This guy Sam? Really?" he asks in disgust. "It sounds like he already fucked up and you've barely been together. I wouldn't do that," he declares.

I laugh manically, "You already did!"

He jumps towards me again, but lets Sam stop him by wrapping her arms around him and pushing him back. "You should go," she tells him with her arms still around him, supposedly holding him back. I can't decide if I'm happy she's asking him to leave or sick that she's touching him.

"We're not done talking," he tells her.

She shakes her head and replies, "We'll talk later," making my stomach flip uneasily. I don't want her to see him again.

He shakes his head and insists, "He's just a rebound Sam. He's not worth giving up everything we have."

She sighs and pleads with him as a tear rolls down her face, "Paul, please just go."

He wipes her tear away making me turn my head away to swallow my gag. "Fuck," I murmur inaudibly at the pain in my chest.

He sighs and concedes, "Okay, I'll go, but we're not finished. If you need me to come back, call me," he says, holding up his phone, giving me the urge to roll my eyes like she does. "I won't be far."

"I'll be fine," she insists, at the same time appearing lost and fragile. I want to go to her and pull her into my arms.Instead, I watch as he pulls her in for a hug and she lets him, causing my insides to twist into painful knots.

He kisses her on the forehead and whispers, "I love you," just loud enough for me to hear. I bite my tongue so hard, the coppery taste of blood fills my mouth, as I force myself to stay rooted to this spot with my arms crossed over my chest. If I move, I'm afraid I might do something stupid and fuck everything up even more, if that's possible.

He finally releases her and nudges me as he walks by, but I hold my ground, barely moving. He walks out pulling the door shut behind him. I finally release the breath I didn't know I was holding and turn my eyes to her. "What was he doing here?" I ask sounding desperate.

She glares at me, "It's none of your business." She sighs and glances up at me, looking completely defeated, making me want to comfort her any way she'll let me. "What are you doing here? I told you we would talk when I got back."

I sigh and drop my arms down to my sides, "I'm sorry Sam, I couldn't wait that long. I couldn't take the chance that you would already have your mind made up about what happened. I need you to know the truth and I need you to know now."

"I should have a say in that Brady!" she demands.

I wince, "You're right. I'm sorry." I put all my feelings into the look I give her and beg for her to talk to me. "Please, just let me say what I need to say and then if you still want me to leave, I'll drive back to Wisconsin right away. I just couldn't wait, you're way too important to me. I would've been here sooner, but Cory wouldn't tell me where you live until this morning," I admit.

She pinches her lips together adorably while she thinks over my request. I can tell the moment she gives in and my whole body sags with relief. "Okay Brady. Do you want something to drink before we sit?"

"No thanks. I need to talk to you first," I insist. If I put anything in my stomach before I talk to her, I just might throw up in her lap.

"Okay," she murmurs. I watch her walk across the room and sit in the corner of the couch. She curls her feet up under her and she pulls her dark loose curls back from her face, before letting them fall behind her back. Then she wraps her arms protectively around her stomach and stares at her lap, waiting for me. Damn she's beautiful, what the fuck was I thinking? I huff in annoyance with myself. She finally looks up at me and asks, "Are you going to sit down?"

I force myself to move, "Um, yeah, sorry. I just..." I sigh feeling lost. "I don't know where to start," I tell her as I sit down near her on the couch.

"Why don't you start with why you were kissing Jackie," she grimaces.

I flinch, "I wasn't kissing her. She kissed me." Her eyes scrunch together with doubt, making me feel like she punched me in the gut. But I understand. I deserve that. "Listen, I know I fucked up, but not like you think I did."

She laughs humorlessly. "I feel like I just had this conversation. Oh wait, I kind of did," she mumbles sarcastically.

"Sam," I plead, hating that she just compared me to the asshole that just walked out the door. "Please just let me explain. Then I'll give you the apology you deserve. I promise."

She nods and quietly agrees, "Okay."

I exhale slowly, building up my courage to tell her about what happened four years ago, my reason for wanting to always be there for Jackie. "I need to tell you about Max first. Then I can explain what happened with Jackie," I propose nervously.

"You've mentioned him before...wait the picture in your room," she begins.

I nod, "Yeah." I try to gulp down the lump in my throat. "I became friends with Max in high school through baseball. We were actually at competing schools, but I admired his talent. Anyway, he moved during his junior year of high school and we ended up playing together that year and our senior year. I probably saw more of him than I did of Cody for a few years. We both wanted to play baseball in college, so we worked our asses off to try to make that happen. We both got into UW-La Crosse and went to a baseball camp there the summer before our freshmen year. We were lucky the coach noticed both of us. We were roommates in Hutchison Hall together and we both made the baseball team. Since baseball starts in the spring, we didn't have much training our first semester, so we did what everyone else seemed to be doing...meeting girls, going to parties, drinking beer and going to class or studying when we had to." I sigh and run my hand through my hair, knowing the tough part is coming.

"Baseball started and at first it was going great. It was just school, baseball and parties. Then one weekend Jackie came up with one of her friends. She came to our game and afterwards she came out with us. Max thought she was the shit, but she barely gave him the time of day. Anyway, he came home with me a couple times after that to see her and she came to visit more. Whenever I saw her, she was either on something, drunk or all over some guy. When Max was around, her attention turned towards him and I loved that. I even encouraged it with him. I never realized she was doing it to try to make me jealous," I shake my head in disbelief. "One time when she was up he overheard her say something to one of her friends. It wrecked him. He was usually the responsible one, but he got really shitfaced that night and the next and the next. He didn't stop. The following weekend Jackie came up again and tried denying what he overheard about her using him. She got him to go out with her to a party. I was at a different party, honestly hitting on some girl that I don't even remember anymore. I remember getting a phone call from Max, I could barely hear him, but I could tell he was fucked up. I just know he said he was looking for Jackie. I laughed," I grunt in irritation. "I fucking laughed and said good luck because I didn't want to miss curfew for baseball."

I look down at the touch of Sam's comforting hand on my leg, grateful she scooted closer to me. "Are you okay?" she asks, her soft caramel eyes full of concern.

I shake my head and keep going while I'm still able to get the words out. "Jackie called me about an hour later sounding completely frantic, begging me to come get them. She'd pulled that shit before and it was nothing. I thought it was nothing," I ramble desperately. I realize tears are running down my cheeks and I'm at a point of no return. "She told me she was at a party with Max and they needed help. I figured she had Max to help her, so I didn't worry about it. I thought if it was worse than that, we could fix it in the morning, but I was so fucking wrong," I spit out guiltily.

"The next day I woke up to a shitload of missed calls and texts. Max and Jackie were in a car accident and he didn't make it." I struggle to breathe over the pain in my chest, "I guess someone slipped her something at the party. Max caught some asshole trying to take advantage of her and hit him. His friends didn't like that too much and went after Max. He freaked and just wanted to get Jackie out of there as fast as possible. They were afraid to call a cab since they were so wasted and underage. He didn't' want to lose baseball. When they couldn't get me, he took his car and..."

"Brady I'm so sorry," Sam murmurs softly. She leans into me and wraps her arms around me, squeezing me tightly.

I take a deep breath and release it as my arms come around her, savoring her comforting touch. I bury my nose in her hair and inhale deeply, loving the soft scent of vanilla and coconut. "The messages he left me after I fell asleep," I shake my head trying to forget. "He was just trying to protect Jackie. If I would've just gone when she asked, he would still be alive."

"You can't blame yourself for that. They could've found another way," she insists.

I pull back to look down at her, "But that's the point Sam, I can't help but think it's my fault." She opens her mouth to argue and I stop her, "Rationally I know all the other decisions they made that night put them there, but I can't help it. He was one of my best friends and I should've been there. Every time I think about not going to help Jackie when she asks, I think about Max. Then what if something happened to her this time? I don't know if I could ever forgive myself," I confess.

"I understand Brady, but you can't live your life that way," she tells me.

I nod, "I know, but just like I keep telling Cody and Cory, it's easier said than done." I sigh and pull her close to me, even if she's only allowing me to do so in comfort, I'm not missing the opportunity. "I barely finished the semester and transferred to Madison. Baseball wasn't the same after he was gone," I confess. "Plus, I needed to be closer to home."

"Have you ever told anyone about this?" she asks quietly.

I shake my head, "No. There's people who know and there's people who don't, but I've never really talked about it to anyone," I admit.

I feel her sigh through my whole body and I hold her a little tighter. I'm afraid to ask what she's thinking, so I don't. I just hold her close and hope I don't have to let her go. I don't know how long we've been sitting in silence when she finally asks, "Brady?"

"Yeah," I croak.

She sighs and informs me, "I understand why you think you need to help her, but I still don't understand why there's pictures of you two looking like you're a couple right after..." she trails off, wrenching my heart with the realization. We had just been together. Then I go and leave to help Jackie and she sees those pictures.

I groan and loosen my hold on her so I can watch her reaction. "Jackie waited for me at the Student Union until I finished class. When she was apologizing, she admitted to me she thought I would eventually get back together with her. I told her it wasn't going to happen. I said you're that person for me. I also told her even if there was no you, I wouldn't be with her. She was upset about what I said and about what had happened and she was crying. I helped her to my truck while she hid her face in my chest. Then when we got to the truck she caught me off guard when she kissed me. I really wasn't expecting it. She claimed it was to thank me for helping her."

"So, she didn't tell her friend to take the pictures and post them?" Sam asks skeptically.

I shake my head, feeling overwhelmed with sadness and whisper her name, "Sam." I pause, "I honestly don't know how to answer that, but I want to think the best of her after everything."

She grimaces and leans away from me, falling back towards the couch. "Listen Sam, I know I need to apologize, but I need to apologize for not finding someone else to go help her or not telling her to do that in the first place. I need to say I'm sorry for not saying anything when she kissed me because I hoped it was her closure since I just told her I was crazy about you. Maybe that's wishful thinking, but...I didn't kiss her back." I reach up and gently run my fingers through her curls admiringly. "I want you. I want us more than I can express right now, but I understand if you're not ready for that after everything. I'll be whatever you need me to be. If you just want to be friends, I still want to be there for you. I want to help you through finding your birth family and all the other crap you're dealing with...even with your ex," I wince. She fights a smile and my heart clenches with hope. "If you only want to be friends, I'll deal with it even though it's not what I want. Just please don't shut me out," I beg.

"That's not what I want either," she admits, "but I don't know if I trust you, Brady," she tells me honestly making me flinch.

I nod in understanding, "I get that, but I plan on earning your trust back." I take another, slow and controlled breath. "So, I have to ask you three questions..." I tell her, pausing nervously.

"Okay..." she says slowly.

"Do you believe me?" I ask.

She pauses before nodding slowly, "Yeah, I guess I do.

"Do you forgive me for how stupidly I handled her?" I ask my stomach churning with nerves.

She sighs, "I forgive you, but I can't keep doing this over and over again. I understand now, but..." she trails off. "I don't want to do it again, Brady," she whispers painfully.

I wince, even though I wouldn't expect any less from her. "Which brings me to my last question," I pause and try to contain my nerves. "What do you want Samantha?

Chapter 37

Samantha

What do I want? Wow, that's a loaded question. I want things I can't have. I want my parents back. I want to be able to talk to my mom and have her tell me her opinion again. I want things I don't know exactly how to get. I want to feel like myself again. I want to know who I am. I want to know where I belong. I want to know more about where I came from. I want to be accepted in some way by my birth father. I want to know what I want to do with my life. I want to be a part of a family again. I want to have friends I can share everything with. I want to trust Brady more than anything right now because the truth is I want to be with him. I just don't know if that's the right thing for me. I sigh in frustration.

"Sam?" Brady questions anxiously.

I look up into his clear blue eyes, showing a range of emotion. I see fear, pain, concern, admiration and something a lot like love, but it couldn't be. I tear my eyes away from his, but I only make it down to his soft full lips making me want to kiss him. I start to look away, but my eyes linger on his broad shoulders and thick muscled arms, wanting him to wrap them around me and hold me close. I slowly close my eyes and take a deep breath. I exhale and open my eyes to his searching ones. "I'm not exactly sure. I guess I want a lot of things," I concede. I gulp over the lump in my throat and admit, "I do know that I don't want to be friends with you. I don't think I could do that." I watch as he clenches his jaw and his mouth thins. I quickly speak up halting his thoughts. "I want to be with you, but I'm scared you're going to hurt me, especially after everything with Jackie."

He visibly flinches as if I punched him, "I'm so sorry. I don't want to hurt you Sam and I hate that I did." He takes a deep breath and declares, "I will make this right."

I sigh in resignation, "There's nothing you can do except prove yourself to me." I scrunch my nose up in dislike, "I don't like saying it like that, but I don't know what else to say. Seeing the picture of you kissing her Brady...that really hurt," I admit, holding a fist to my aching chest. He reaches for me and I put my hand out to stop him. "No, I need you to understand. It wasn't even like it was when I walked in on Paul and Taylor and I'd been dating Paul for a few years," I inform him. "It was so much worse than that," I emphasize. "I don't know what this is between us, but I'm not ready to give up on it yet," I confess and his whole body sags with relief. "Sometimes this just feels so overwhelming that I don't even understand," I admit, shaking my head in disbelief. "Please, just don't do something like this to me again," I plead, feeling helpless.

"Sam," he sighs, "I will do everything I can to keep you from getting hurt. Seeing you like this is killing me," he grimaces. "But you have to make me a promise too," he requests.

My eyebrows draw together in confusion. "What?" I ask hesitantly.

"Don't run away from me again. If you see something or hear something or whatever, talk to me first. Please," he begs.

I nod in agreement. "Okay. You're right, I'm sorry. Sometimes it's hard to think straight around you," I admit.

The corners of his lips twitch up and he mumbles, "I know what you mean." I chuckle and he asks, "Does that mean I can kiss you now?" I blush and he grins, slipping his hands behind my neck. "I'll take that as a yes," he proclaims right before his lips come crashing down on mine, making me gasp. My hands move up to rest on his chest as his mouth slides over mine slowly, his tongue peeking out to lick my lips. I open my mouth to let him in, wanting to taste him. He pulls back with a satisfied groan, holding my head in his hands. "Damn I missed you," he rasps then kisses me again. "You taste so good," he whispers pressing his lips to mine, tilting my head to delve deeper.

His words bring a rush of guilt, even though I did nothing wrong, but I still need to tell him. It's the right thing to do when I expect him to do the same, especially with how everything turned out today. I gently push on his chest, trying to back away from him, "Brady," I rasp.

He pulls back and looks into my eyes anxiously, "Are you okay?"

I nod and wince slightly, "Yeah, I just need to tell you something else and I need to do it now."

He sits back a little further and lets his hands slide slowly down to my knees, a worried look crossing his face. "Okay..." he says hesitantly.

"It's about Paul..." I begin.

Brady's whole body tenses and his face pales slightly. I watch his Adam's apple bob up and down as he swallows. He takes a deep breath and asks stiffly, "What about him?

"Well as you know he was just here," he nods his head, his jaw clenching. "We ran into him in town yesterday and he wanted to talk. I thought he just wanted his chance to apologize, get closure and move on. Probably because that's what I wanted to happen," I admit. I exhale slowly, not really wanting to continue, but I know I have to.

"Okay," he prods.

I grimace, "Well, that's how it started. He told me what happened and didn't happen, not just that night, but before and even after. I also realized I'd been pushing him away for a while."

"So what, you think it's your fault now that he cheated on you?" he spits out angrily.

I shake my head, "No, that's not what I think, but I did have a part in everything that led to us breaking up. It's not all on him, although cheating is completely unacceptable," I reiterate. He shakes his head slightly as if he doesn't agree I hold any blame. I ignore it and continue. "Then after I told him I forgive him for everything," I gulp and mutter, "He admitted he wanted me back."

"I got that when he told you he loved you," he grits out.

I wince, "You heard that?"

He laughs humorlessly and nods his head. "Yup…" he says slowly popping the p and mumbles, "he made sure of it."

"Well, I told him I couldn't get back together with him. He didn't want to take no for an answer," I inform him.

"What are you trying to tell me Sam?" Brady asks impatiently.

I sigh in defeat and blurt out, "He kissed me."

Brady's jaw drops and eyes widen as his body presses deeper into the couch, reacting as if I punched him. I watch nervously, waiting for a verbal response. He rasps, "Did you kiss him back?"

I shake my head, "No, but I didn't pull away right away. It was because I was shocked though," I tell him as realization washes over me. "Oh!" I exclaim feeling like an idiot, my whole body instantly heats in embarrassment. I should have thought of that sooner.

He closes his eyes and opens them slowly, appearing pained. "Now I know how you felt," he groans, dropping his head in his hands in defeat. "But you had to actually see it," he grimaces.

"I guess I know how it happened with Jackie. I mean how she took you by surprise," I admit. "This is just really hard for me to deal with after Paul. I guess even though it didn't really matter to me much at the time, we were still together. He still betrayed me, no matter how you look at it. I don't want that to happen again, especially not with you," I add quietly.

Brady drops his hands and lifts his head to look up at me. "It won't," he declares confidently. "I wouldn't do that to you." He sits taller and reaches for me, cradling my face in his hands. He looks into my eyes, taking my breath away with the sparkle returning to his blue ones. "I am so crazy about you Samantha," he whispers vehemently. "I want to protect you and take care of you, not hurt you," he informs me, his eyes full of determination. "I don't want to think about Jackie or Paul anymore. I think they've taken up too much of our time already. It's time to focus on us," he tells me. "Okay?" he adds as an afterthought.

I laugh, "Okay."

He grins, "There it is." He kisses me softly on the lips.

"What?" I ask confused.

"Your smile," he says as he presses his lips softly to each corner of my mouth. "I missed your beautiful smile," he confesses making me blush. He licks his lips and leans down, gently kissing mine. I sigh into his mouth in satisfaction. His hands slide down my neck, over my shoulders and down my arms as he continues to kiss me. He braces his hands on the couch on either side of me as he kisses me harder, nudging me to lie back on the couch.

He moves one hand to my waist as he slips under the hemline of my shirt to caress the bare skin of my belly in slow circles, lighting my whole body on fire with his gentle touch. Our tongues dance in perfect rhythm and I groan into his mouth while fighting to pull him closer and push our kiss deeper.

The sound of the front door opening startles both of us. I quickly jump to the opposite corner of the couch like we were just caught by our parents. I heave for breath, not able to take my eyes off Brady doing the same. I can't even look up to confirm who just walked into my house. "We're back," Cory says cheerfully finally grabbing my attention. I turn my head to find her grinning at us. "I see Brady made it here okay!" She makes a show of looking around like she might be looking for something or someone, "And Paul's gone," she announces. She looks back and forth between the two of us smiling broadly before adding, "And it looks like you two have already worked everything out. My job here is done," she announces. She dusts her hands off by smacking them together proudly, making all of us laugh.

"Don't ever make me see something like that again! That was just cruel," Ryan teases with an exaggerated groan.

I roll my eyes and smile, trying not to laugh. Brady scoots over to my corner of the couch and puts his arm around me possessively. "Don't walk in without knocking next time," Brady suggests.

"You weren't supposed to be here! You're on her shit list," Ryan says, gesturing between us.

"He dug himself out," I answer for him.

Brady grins and kisses me on the top of the head. Ryan looks at me intently and asks, "Are you sure about that? I could still kick his ass if you want me to."

I laugh as I feel Brady bury his face in my hair. I curl into his touch answering, "I'm sure, for now."

Brady lifts his head and looks at me with raised eyebrows questioning, "For now?" I laugh in response.

"So," Ryan begins, "What do you guys want to do today? But my number two rule is it has to be something all of us can do together."

"What's your number one rule?" Cory asks.

He turns to her with a smirk and informs her, "It's just for you. No getting naked without me."

"Ew!" I screech as I watch Cory blush instantly. I look away and bury my head in Brady's chest. "Not around me!"

Ryan laughs, "Don't worry about that with me!"

"I meant I don't want to hear it Ryan!" I mumble from the protective barrier of Brady's arms.

"I just walked in on you about to..." he grimaces.

"Don't!" I yell. Brady's body begins bouncing with his laughter and I focus on the feel and sound of that, happy to be in the moment.

Chapter 38

I stretch my arms above my head and collide with a hard, warm chest. Brady's gravelly sleepy voice rolls through me, sending chills down my spine. He leans in from behind my back and presses a kiss to my temple.

I roll over with a smile, "Good morning. How long have you been up?" I ask.

"Not long," he answers casually, "but long enough to watch you sleep and see all the snow we got overnight."

I giggle, "Ha-ha. April Fool's?"

He shakes his head with a smirk, "Nope. It's still snowing. I don't think we should go anywhere today."

"What?" I ask with disbelief. My brow furrows and I attempt to push up off the bed to go look out the window, but his arms clamp tightly around me.

He chuckles, "I need a kiss first." I roll my eyes, but oblige with a chaste kiss. He sighs and lets me go, "I guess that will do for now."

I laugh and push out of bed. I step on the cool floor and shiver. I stretch my arms above my head again and arch my back to try to wake up. I sigh and drop my arms when I hear Brady groan. I look over at him, but his face is buried in my pillow. I take two steps towards the window and open the blinds with a pull of the string on the side. I gasp at the sight in front of me. "It's snowing!" I declare in shock.

Brady chuckles and pushes out of bed, quickly stepping up right behind me. He wraps his arms around my waist and leans down, resting his chin on my shoulder. He looks out my window at the sea of white. "It's crazy, right?"

"I thought you were kidding! Isn't it supposed to be spring?" I question.

He shrugs and kisses me on the neck allowing a sigh to slip from my lips. "It happens every once in a while. It gives us a fantastic excuse to stay here for another day."

I laugh, "Don't you have classes tomorrow?"

"Yeah," he groans. "I could miss them though."

"You have like six weeks left, don't you?" I ask surprised. He is the one that said he wanted to stay focused and finish strong.

"Something like that," he grimaces. "Let's just see how the day goes. I'll drive back later if we can," he suggests. "I like that I get to see where you grew up," he grins. "I want to look around your house and have you tell me stories. It was great going into the city yesterday, but I want to see more of you," he murmurs and places another soft kiss on my neck.

My whole body ignites from his words and his tender touch. I take a deep breath and attempt to control my desire before I speak. I nod in agreement and rasp, "Okay." I glance back over to my bed and scrunch my nose up suddenly feeling awkward. "It's strange to have you here in my room. I mean where I grew up," I explain.

He chuckles and spins me the rest of the way around, keeping his arms around my waist. "Are you okay?" he asks, assessing my eyes for the truth.

I grimace and grumble, "I'm really starting to hate that question." His eyes widen still waiting for an answer. I sigh and reply, "I'm fine." He continues to watch me and I request, "Do you mind if I read a letter?"

"Of course I don't mind," he insists.

I walk him backwards towards my bed before I extract myself from his arms. I walk over to my backpack and pull out the next letter before returning to my bed.

Brady's sitting with his back against the headboard, showing off his bare chest and I have to stop to take another deep breath to slow my heartbeat down. I climb up and position myself between his legs, his arms immediately surrounding me as his head falls to the top of mine. "Thank you," I tell him, not expecting a response. I unfold the letter and begin reading in the comfort of his arms.

June 12th (your 16th Birthday)
To My Beautiful Baby Girl,
Happy Sweet 16th Birthday!! What are you doing for your birthday this year? It's a big year! I think I was at a concert with a group of friends for my 16th birthday. I don't really remember because it wasn't really anything too special. My friends were all having big Sweet 16 Birthday Parties or they were going somewhere special for their birthday. I do know that my goal was to get out of my house for the night. I hope you're doing something fantastic that you love, no matter what it may be. I would've taken you to your first concert, well if I hadn't already. Or let you have a party with all your friends, whatever you wanted. I'm sorry, I guess I'm feeling a little emotional today. I can't believe you're 16 years old! Is there anything you're hoping to get for your birthday this year? What kinds of things do you like to get now that you're older? Maybe you're hoping for clothes, music or movies? Then again it could be an electronic, there's so much technology now. I'm sure you have your own phone already. I wish I could text you to say Happy Birthday. Honestly, I wish I could call you. There's so much I need to tell you, but I can't yet.
I'm still with my husband and he takes very good care of me. I've had a tough year, but he's still sticking by my side. I'm so incredibly grateful for that...for him.

I need to go, but I hope you're doing wonderful. I hope you're happy and healthy. Enjoy your day and I hope you have a great year! Happy Birthday!
With Love...
Catherine Schepp

I fold the letter up and set it gently on my nightstand before leaning back against Brady. "You know I think it gets both easier and harder at the same time to read each letter," I tell him.

"What do you mean?" he asks, giving me a gentle, encouraging squeeze.

I exhale slowly, trying to pull my thoughts together. "I guess I mean a few different things. I can tell she did love me in her own way. I think by giving me up, she just hoped I would have something better than what she could give me. Sometimes I even hear pain in her words because she doesn't know me." I push myself closer to him and feel his arms tighten, helping me admit, "I also know the letters are coming to an end and there will never be another one when I finish. I'll never be able to meet her or really know who she was beyond these letters and what I might hear from someone else someday, but even that's not a guarantee. These letters and the court documents and papers might be all I'll ever have of her and I don't want that," I concede.

"Sam," Brady whispers my name, his voice full of empathy.

"With my Mom and Dad, I have not only my memories, but also this whole house. It's full of everything from our lives, how much they loved me and every moment we shared together, both good and bad. We also have memories from everywhere we've been together. I'm thankful I have that with them, but what about her?" I rasp, choking on the last word.

Brady runs his fingers through my hair, down my arms and back up again, soothing me. "I realize I can never really understand how you're feeling, but I do get what you're saying. You can remember her in your own way though, the same way she loved you," he reminds me. "It doesn't take anything away from your parents to remember her, or think of her," he tells me.

I quickly suck in a breath as butterflies take over my insides with how clearly he sees me. I turn to look him in the eyes and ask, "How did you know to say that?"

He smiles admiringly down at me. His hand slides up and gently caresses my cheek, as he looks deep into my eyes. He informs me, "Because I feel it in your body, see it in your eyes and hear it in your voice every single time you talk about them and then when you talk about her. It's obvious how much you love your mom and dad, but it's also natural to want to know where you come from and to love them for the decisions they made. It's okay to be mad at them for the same reasons. It doesn't mean you wished your life turned out different."

"I don't," I shake my head. "I wouldn't change anything if it meant I couldn't have my Mom and Dad."

"That's what's important. I'm sure your parents knew that when they were here with you and even know it now," he says comforting me.

My nerves settle and I lean towards him slowly, glancing down at his lips as his tongue slips over them, anticipating my move. I softly press my lips to his. I pull back and whisper hoarsely, "Thank you."

I keep my eyes on his and push up to my knees. I grip his shoulders for leverage as I straddle him. He groans as my weight settles in his lap making me giggle. I wrap my arms around his neck and pull myself closer to him. His Adam's apple bobs up and down as he swallows hard. I grin broadly and cover his mouth with mine. I tilt my head and thrust my tongue between his lips, searching for its mate. Our tongues tangle in a playful dance and he groans into my mouth as my hips reflexively grind down on his hard length. He slides his hands to my hips and holds me steady. He pulls back and mumbles, "Door."

I chuckle and mumble over his lips, "It's locked."

He kisses me harder as his hands immediately slide up my back underneath my shirt. He gasps and tears his lips from mine, "You didn't sleep with a bra on?"

I shake my head laughing, "I never do."

He shakes his head and mumbles, "I'm so screwed." He grips the hem of my shirt and pulls it off in one swift movement leaving me bare. His eyes roam my chest reverently as he reaches up, gently cupping a breast in each hand. "You're perfect," he rasps. I swallow over the lump in my throat while my whole body suddenly feels like it's on fire. He leans his head down and kisses my breast, slowly working his way towards my nipple. His tongue juts out slowly, circling my nipple, before he covers it with his mouth and sucks gently making me gasp. He slowly kisses his way to my other breast while his hand occupies the first and gives it the same sensual treatment. "Brady," I rasp gripping his shoulders tightly. He pulls his face from my chest and wraps his arm around my waist as his lips crash into mine almost desperately. He flips me over onto my back falling from my lips as I land. He grins wickedly down at me and buries his face in my neck. He slowly kisses and licks his way down my body. "Brady," I rasp with both nerves and excitement.

He pauses as his fingers slide gently along the hemline of my panties. He looks into my eyes and tells me, "I want to taste you."

"Um, I don't, um..." I stammer.

His grin turns pleased and he asks, "Has anyone ever done this to you before?" I shake my head, my breath coming in rapid bursts. He quickly moves up my body and cradles my face in his hands. He stares into my eyes and insists, "I just want to take care of you. Anytime you want me to stop, just tell me, but I promise I will make you feel good." He holds my gaze until I nod nervously in agreement, making him smile. He moves down my body again and whispers, "Just relax Sam."

I take a deep breath and attempt to do exactly that, but it's nearly impossible as he slides my navy blue bikini underwear down my legs before tossing it somewhere behind him. His thumbs slowly caress the inside of my thighs as he slides my legs open a little further and settles between them. He lightly kisses me right at my core, making me whimper as tingles spread quickly throughout my body. His tongue shoots out and licks me along my seam and again with a little more pressure. He does it firmly a third time before circling my clit and then gently sucking it into his mouth. "Ah," I cry out, gasping for breath. His tongue focuses on circling and sucking on my clit as his thumb moves to my opening and pushes in. I moan, not able to stay quiet, causing him to pick up his speed. I arch into him and shove my fist in my mouth to quiet my moans just as my body begins throbbing. He groans and greedily laps up my juices, lengthening my high. I slowly come down sighing his name, "Brady."

He pushes up and crawls over me grinning. I lean up and lick his dimple, quickly falling back to the bed limp. "You taste so sweet," he whispers as he kisses my neck. He continues to place kisses along my jaw until he finds my lips and dives in for a passionate kiss.

I pull back and whimper, "I want you Brady."

"I want you too, Sam, but I think we should maybe stop with that today. I have a lot of making up to do and I don't want you to have any doubts when I'm inside you again," he tells me.

"Brady," I say ready to argue when something suddenly stops me. I kiss him gently and agree, "Maybe you're right, but I want to touch you right now."

"Sam," he warns as I reach for his thick hard length.

I grin knowing he's like this because of me. I press firmly and rub him slowly up and down, enjoying his strangled groan. "I want to do this Brady. It's my turn to watch you," I insist.

He lies back and I quickly tug his underwear down his thick thighs and calves before I toss it on the floor next to mine. I crawl back up his body and kiss his lips, his neck, then work my way down his chest and defined abs. I hold him in my hand, but I'm unable to wrap my fingers all the way around him. I kiss his thigh and then the other one before I kiss his tip. Then my tongue shoots out and I lick him from the base, all the way up his hard length and around the end. I open wide and relax as I try to take as much of him as I can into my mouth, encouraged by his low grunts. I glance up at him while I take him in and out of my mouth, trying to watch his reaction. His hands tangle in my hair and he holds on tight. I suck him hard, then swirl my tongue around him and then do it again and again. He gasps my name desperately in warning, "Sam!" But that just makes me want to finish him, so I move faster. Suddenly his warm, thick, salty liquid shoots to the back of my throat. I move up and down his shaft, sucking until there's nothing left. "Holy Shit," he gasps.

I chuckle and move up to his side. He grips me and kisses me fiercely. He pulls away and I sigh in satisfaction as I fall into his side. "You didn't have to do that," he tells me, still catching his breath, "but shit you're amazing."

I giggle lightly and blush in response. "I know I didn't," I tell him feeling completely content and happy with what we just did. "I wanted to. I've never wanted to before," I admit quietly.

He leans back to look into my eyes and smiles, obviously liking what he sees. He kisses me on the forehead before falling back to the pillows. "Do you think we should check on Cory and Ryan?"

I wince, hoping they didn't hear us. I nod in agreement, but I'm slow to move out of his arms. "Probably," I whisper. I lay my head on his chest and listen to his heartbeat slow, mine following along with it. After a few quiet minutes, I sigh in resignation and push myself up and out of his embrace. "Let's get dressed and see what they want to do," I suggest.

"Okay," he agrees as he pushes off my bed. He stands in front of me and kisses me again before he reaches for his discarded clothes.

Chapter 39

I run in the door laughing with Cory right on my heels. "Oh my gosh, they're crazy! It's freezing outside!"

"I'm definitely done with snow for at least a year," Cory grumbles as she takes off her coat and gloves and tosses them on the bench next to the front door.

"Well, that probably won't work out for you unless you move somewhere south, but good luck with that," I joke as I pull off my coat and mittens, tossing them on top of hers.

Cory laughs as Brady and Ryan bound into the house. "You guys give up already?" Ryan laughs as he shakes his head like a dog to get rid of the melted snow on his head. He slips off his own coat and hangs it above ours on a hook as Brady does the same.

Cory grins, "Absolutely!"

"I thought you were from Wisconsin?" he teases her.

"I am, but we don't have all the wind you guys do here," she complains.

He laughs, "We're not that far apart!"

She shrugs and I add, "It's too cold for snowball fights."

"I'll remember that when it warms up enough that all the snow melts," Brady smirks.

I roll my eyes trying to hide my grin. "Want some hot chocolate?" I ask.

"Yes, please," Cory pleads desperately, making me laugh.

"I'll help you," Brady volunteers and follows me into the kitchen. As soon as we step into the room, he cages me in against the counter and spins me around. His mouth crashes into mine and he kisses me hard, igniting my whole body. I gasp into his mouth and he slowly gentles the kiss. He cradles my face in his hands and pulls away just enough to rasp, "Okay that's better."

I giggle, "What?"

He grins and I reach up to run my fingers lightly over his dimple making him chuckle. "I needed that and I didn't think I would get any points if I tackled you in the snow and soaked you." He grimaces, "Actually maybe that's exactly what I should've done."

I shove him in his stomach and he groans as he takes a step back, pretending I knocked the air out of him. I laugh and shake my head at his antics. I turn to grab four blue and yellow mugs out of the cabinet along with the chocolate, while Brady grabs the milk for me to heat. He pours the milk into a teapot and turns the stove on high. "I have to admit, I like your hot chocolate better than the little packets from the store," he tells me.

"You know all you have to do is make it with milk and it's creamier no matter what kind it is," I inform him.

"Yeah, but this is real chocolate," he grins like a little kid.

My heart skips a beat and I quickly clear my throat, trying to clear the gravel out of my throat. "Can you maybe help me put some of my things together?" I barely squeak out.

"Of course, but can I maybe look at some of your old pictures or something too? I saw a few things on the walls, but I want to know more of you." Tingles take over my whole body with his comment. I nod my head in agreement, unable to speak. "I can always ask Ryan to tell me a few stories too," he smirks.

I roll my eyes, "I bet he would love that, but with him it might be an actual story. I guess you'll have to figure that out for yourself if you ask him," I grin.

He steps up to me and wraps his arms around my waist. I let my hands fall to his chest as I look up into his sparkling blue eyes. "Or I could find a way to get it out of you," he grins playfully.

"And how would you do that?" I ask coaxing him.

He leans down and pauses when I feel his heated breath on my lips, "I could..." he barely brushes his lips over mine when the teakettle whistles startling both of us. I jump and bump into his forehead making him laugh as he steps away.

I groan, "Ow," and rub my head in exaggeration. "You have a hard head," I tease him with a pout.

He laughs, "You have no idea." Then he steps back into me and kisses me lightly before stepping back. He gently taps my lip, "Put that thing away, it's dangerous."

I giggle and step up to the stove to remove the milk and mix it with the chocolate before pouring it into all the mugs. Brady grabs two and I grab the other two before following him back out to the living room. Brady hands a cup to Cory and I hand one to Ryan, both of them sitting on the couch. I lower myself to the floor and set my cup on the coffee table in front of me. Brady drops down next to me. After setting his hot chocolate down he stretches his long legs out under the table. "You can sit in the chairs, I just don't want to spill," I explain.

He smiles, "And I just want to sit next to you." I blush and smile back at him. He gives me a chaste kiss.

Ryan groans like we're torturing him and I laugh as I look over at him. He smirks, "Anyway, before I forget, my parents want to know if you'll come for Easter."

I glance at Brady before looking back at Ryan, feeling slightly nervous. "Um, I think I'm actually going to stay in Wisconsin this time."

"You know my dad will come and get you if you plan on spending it alone," he reminds me.

I nod, "I know, but I'm not. Brady and I are going to do something," I blurt and glance down at my lap. I smile to myself as Brady's hand slides to my leg and he gives it a gentle squeeze.

"You're spending Easter with his family?" he asks surprised.

Brady shakes his head, "No, my parents will be at our restaurant all day working." Ryan nods in understanding. Brady adds, "Although, if she wants to spend it there, we could do that too." I catch Ryan and Cory's grins as my head snaps up to Brady's. He turns back towards Ryan hoping to change the subject and asks, "So do you have any good stories to share about Sam?"

Ryan laughs, "Do I ever! Which one do I start with?" he asks glancing over at me with a wicked grin.

I groan inwardly and hope he doesn't embarrass me too much. "I could tell you about the time she went to the movies with some friends and a boy she liked. She was so nervous she threw up all over his shoes," he chuckles. "Or I could tell you about the first time she tried to sneak out of the house and set off the alarm. The police were close by and came before she even made it to the sidewalk. They knew her, so they just escorted her back to her parents." Brady's mouth twitches in amusement as I feel my face burning hotter and hotter by the moment. "Or I could tell you about the first time she ran hurdles. She was so nervous her legs got twisted on the second one and she couldn't finish the race. I was impressed you kept doing it and got really good after that," he concedes.

I grimace and say his name in warning, "Ryan."

He grins wider, "Or I could tell them about the time you dropped the Thanksgiving turkey on the kitchen floor and you made me help you fix it so no one would find out. Of course, you didn't eat any that year."

"You did," I accuse.

"I was a 12 year old boy who would eat almost anything on a dare. Plus, I took meat from the inside, not the outside," he defends himself. "Mine didn't touch the floor," he emphasizes. Cory laughs and I roll my eyes.

"Or I could tell you about how her date to the Sadie Hawkins dance stood her up freshman year. She went anyway and he was there with his friends. She dumped a whole bowl of punch on his head, right before she hit him with the bowl in the stomach. Don't know how Paul had the courage to ask her out the next week when most wouldn't mess with her," he teases. "That also got her, her very first detention," he smirks.

"Can you just stop talking Ryan," I ask, sounding annoyed. "I have a lot more on you than you have on me and we both know it. Like when you pushed a lawn mower into our rival school's pool, or when you ruined Christmas for everyone when you announced during the school Christmas play that there was no Santa Claus because you were mad and thought everyone had a right to know. Or when you accidently pushed your homecoming date into the lake while you were getting your pictures taken...in November!"

He groans and throws up his hands in surrender, "Okay, okay, truce!"

Cory and Brady could no longer contain their laughter. I look between them with raised eyebrows and Brady encourages, "Keep going. This is definitely entertaining."

I roll my eyes and ask, "What if I told you Cory has shared a few stories about you?"

His eyes widen and he glances over at Cory no longer laughing. "What?" he asks.

"Okay, okay," she attempts to appease everyone.

My phone buzzes with a text and I reach for it, ready for a distraction. I quickly glance at the screen. My breath hitches and I freeze at the sight of my birth father's name. I gasp, "Oh my gosh."

I feel Brady's eyes on me as he asks, "What's wrong? Is everything okay?"

I try to gulp down the lump in my throat and nod stiffly as I open the text. Brady's hand slides to my back. I focus on the text, using his hand for comfort. "I'm sorry it has taken me so long to reach out to you. My wife is very excited to meet you. It took us a little more time to explain things to our kids. I'll tell you more when we meet. Can you meet for coffee and breakfast tomorrow morning at around 9am at The Pit? It will be just me this time so we can talk before you meet everyone else," he explains.

I look up from my phone, realizing I'm shaking and my heart is pounding like it's trying to burst out of my chest. I look around my living room, not able to focus on anything until I meet Brady's concerned gaze. I take a deep breath to try to steady myself and inform him, "It's my birth father. He says he wants to see me tomorrow morning for breakfast. He said it will just be him this time, but his wife is excited to meet me. He said he told his kids too. I wonder if that means they're not happy about this. I wouldn't blame them. It has to be a shock," I ramble anxiously.

"Sam," Brady interrupts, his eyes questioning if I'm okay.

I close my eyes and nod my head. I take another deep breath and open them, focusing on Brady. "Oh my gosh! He wants to see me," I rasp anxiously.

He grins, "You're going to be fine."

"Do you want me to come with you?" Ryan asks.

I shake my head, "No, that's okay. I think this is something that I need to do by myself." He nods in understanding.

I glance over at Brady again, "Can we make it back tonight sometime? I don't want to have to reschedule," I explain.

He nods, "Yeah, my truck will be fine in this snow. It's only five or six inches. We'll be fine," he insists.

I laugh nervously at his admission and nod my head, "Thanks." My head goes back and forth between Cory and Ryan and I ask, "Is that okay? I'm sorry," I apologize. "My car," I exclaim forgetting I drove here.

"It's fine," Ryan and Cory both reply.

"Cory can stay with me until the roads are better and drive your car up then if you can wait that long," Ryan offers grinning at Cory. She blushes and smiles shyly over at him before glancing back to me with a nod of her head in agreement.

I murmur, "Thank you." I nod my head, struggling to focus on what I need to do. "Pack...I need to go pack some more of my clothes," I murmur. I push myself up off the floor.

"Do you need help?" Brady asks, looking up at me.

I shake my head and tell him, "Not yet. There are some photo albums in the bookcase next to the television. You're welcome to look at them if you want."

He eyes me skeptically before he finally agrees, "Okay." He stands and wraps his arms around me. He presses his face into my hair and takes a deep breath, holding me tightly and I melt into him. He tucks my hair behind my ear and whispers, "You'll be fine. I'm right here if you need me, for anything," he emphasizes.

I nod and hold him a little tighter before letting go and taking a step back. I feel three sets of eyes on me as I turn and walk out of the room. I wander down the hallway to my bedroom feeling like my head is in the clouds. I turn on my iPod, hoping to drown out the noise in my head running over any possible scenario. I open the door to my closet and start pulling things out to toss into one of my duffle bags. Everything about this moment feels surreal as I try to process what's happening. I'm going to spend time with my birth father tomorrow. He's going to answer some of my questions. I sigh and mumble to myself, "I can do this," trying to believe it.

Chapter 40

While I finish packing, Brady looks at a few of my old photo albums, asking questions here and there, each one flooding me with memories. With each picture, I smile or laugh or even groan, but all of it leaves me feeling good. I miss my parents every day, but it's getting a little easier to truly cherish all of our memories. I hate thinking about a future without them, but I guess I'm finally at the acceptance point in grieving. Sometimes I still have an overwhelming sadness inside from missing them and sometimes I may cling to it, but I can smile again when I think about them. I refuse to feel guilty about that because I believe that's what they want for me.

We leave in Brady's truck, quickly realizing the snow won't be an issue. The ride back to Chance remains quiet, with both of us lost in thought. It's not long before we pull up to our apartment building. We trek up the stairs with our arms full and Brady quickly goes back down to unload the rest for me. I begin sorting through the boxes and putting things away into my closet, as well as the dresser and desk I brought back with me. Brady finishes the trips up and down easily. He kicks off his shoes and lay back on my bed with his arms behind his head and his feet crossed at the ankles, watching me. I don't know how long it has been quiet when he finally breaks the silence, "How are you doing?"

I drop the shoes in my hand at the bottom of my closet with an exaggerated sigh. "I'm fine." He raises his eyebrows with doubt and I chuckle humorlessly. "I've been thinking about my parents a lot with being home and then with you looking through my photo books, but all of it just makes me think. I'm sad, but I'm mostly happy thinking about everything we did together."

"I know I can't really understand, but it's okay to not be sad all the time. Your parents wouldn't want that."

I give him a soft smile, "That's funny, that's what I was just thinking." I grimace thinking about going to breakfast with my birth father tomorrow. "I'm also nervous just thinking about tomorrow," I explain. I crawl up on the bed next to him and he sticks his arm out inviting me into his embrace. I curl into his side as his hand wraps around my back and he kisses the top of my head.

"I'm sure it's completely normal to be nervous, how can it not be," he adds.

I nod, "Yeah." My hand trails up his chest, making random swirl designs. I slip my hand down to his waist and under the hem of his shirt doing the same on his bare skin, making him groan. I smile softly and lift my head to look up at him. "Thank you, Brady," I whisper.

"Thank you for what?" he asks.

I push myself up and move one leg to the other side of him, straddling him. I hold myself up with my arms so I can look him in the eyes. "Thank you for being here for me, for helping me through all of this. I'm really grateful it's you. I think you're really good for me," I tell him. I lean down and lightly brush my lips over his. "I want you to know I'm crazy about you too. In fact, it's probably a little insane, but there's a good chance I'm already falling for you," I tell him honestly.

He grins, "Only a good chance?" I blush, making him chuckle. "That's good Sam, really fucking good because I know I'm falling for you," he insists. He lightly kisses my lips and whispers, "As insane as that might be." We both laugh as our lips connect and begin moving in perfect rhythm.

His tongue slips out and I immediately let him in, tilting my head to kiss him harder. I lick and explore the inside of his mouth with my tongue, tasting him. I pull away breathless and insist, "Brady, I want you," I tell him. I keep talking before he can argue, "I know you said you wanted me to be sure before we were together again, but I am sure," I insist.

"Are you sure you're not just trying to make sex a distraction from everything?" he asks me, trying to catch his own breath. "I'm not letting you go this time," he declares.

I nod, "We are not a distraction. It might have started out that way for me," I admit honestly making him wince, "but it very quickly became so much more. I've never been more positive of anything Brady. I don't want you to let me go this time," I affirm with confidence.

He grins broadly at me, showing me his dimple and making my stomach churn. He leans up, wrapping his arm around my waist and flips me over onto my back before I have a chance to react. He pauses, looking into my eyes with so much intensity, I think my heart might pound right through my chest to get to him. He tilts his head and slowly closes the space between us. I gasp as his velvety soft lips touch mine. He kisses me tenderly as his right hand tangles itself into my hair. I feel so much in this one kiss, but I don't know exactly what's different than before. My whole body comes alive and begins tingling, hoping to get closer to him. His tongue slips out and traces my bottom lip. I gasp, letting him in. My tongue searches for his, licking, tasting and sucking gently. I suck a little harder and he pulls away with a groan. He gently presses his body into mine as his eyes roam over my face, "You are incredibly beautiful Samantha," he groans.

I feel myself blush and try to urge him closer, but his mouth moves to my neck, leaving a trail of kisses until he reaches the collar of my shirt. He leans back and gently tugs at the bottom. I sit up and he swiftly pulls it over my head. I reach for him to do the same. He sees my intention and grabs the bottom of his shirt with one hand, easily pulling it over his head. He leans towards me, making me gasp the moment I feel the touch of his heated skin on mine. My fingers slowly explore his hard chest and my lips lean up to follow their trail. He reaches between us and unclips my bra. I drop back to my bed as his hands brush the fabric away. "Brady," I whimper.

His heated gaze finds mine once again as he kisses me with increased urgency. One hand slides back up the side of my breast and his thumb moves over and around my nipple. My hands slide down to his waist as my back arches into his touch. I let my hands move to his muscled back and down to his butt, my body electrified with desire. Our passionate kiss leaves me breathless. I break away and fall back on my bed. "Can I take these off?" he asks.

I nod my head without even looking to verify what he's referring to. I rasp, "Please and yours too." I feel him removing my pants and lift my head to watch him kick his own jeans off. I slip my fingers into the sides of my black lace bikini underwear. I smirk at his responding groan. "I'll do mine if you do yours," I tease him.

He grins and kicks off his gray boxer briefs. I take a deep steadying breath at the sight of his hard body standing there ready for me. I glance at his hard, thick length and gulp down my nerves. "We've done this before," I mumble.

He chuckles, "Yes, we have." I lift my eyes to his smiling face and feel myself blush. He raises his eyebrows, eyes sparkling like the blue waters of the ocean and prompts, "Your turn." I pull my panties down my legs slowly and toss them on the floor before I lay back. His eyes anxiously roam my whole body taking me in. "Fuck," he mumbles. He shakes his head in awe, "Beautiful doesn't even begin to describe you. A new word should be invented to describe you."

I attempt to gulp down all the emotion clogging my throat as he slowly crawls over me to find my mouth. He starts out slowly, our kiss increasing in both speed and intensity. My hands slide up his chest over his shoulders and down his arms, before trailing back up again. At the same time his free hand trails down my side, back up and over my breast where he pauses briefly to tease my nipples with his fingertips, before moving down to my stomach. His fingers continue their exploration over my hipbone, in towards my thigh and up my leg to my core. He circles my clit before he slides his fingers easily between my folds, making me gasp as he pushes inside with one finger and then again with two. "Brady," I gasp, trying to pull his attention. "I want you, not your fingers. I'm ready," I declare breathlessly.

He groans and pushes in one more time before removing them. "Yes, you are," he grumbles. I slip my hand behind his head and pull him toward me, kissing him hard. He moves to get up, but I hold on tighter. "Where are you going?" I ask desperately.

He grins, "Grabbing a condom."

"In the drawer," I inform him. He reaches to the nightstand and pulls open the drawer. He blindly sticks his hand in, quickly pulling out a small box of condoms. He opens it with one hand and pulls out two attached together. He leans back and opens one with his teeth. He pulls out the condom and tosses the extras along with the empty wrapper back towards the nightstand. He rises to his knees and easily rolls it on.

He positions himself over me and begins kissing me again before his hands continue their exploration. He finds my center and adjusts himself so we're perfectly aligned. He breaks our kiss and holds my gaze as he slowly enters me, thrusting hard at the end and filling me completely. He freezes and holds my gaze, pushing my hair out of my eyes, both of us sweaty and breathless. He opens his mouth like he's going to say something, but quickly snaps it shut and presses his mouth firmly to mine in a searing kiss.

He begins moving slowly as my hands find their way to his neck. My body arches to meet his with each thrust. We both break away from our kiss, gasping for breath. He drops his forehead to mine and holds it there, looking into my eyes as our bodies move together in perfect rhythm. I curl my hands around the outside of his shoulders and dig in, desperately holding on to his now slick skin as we quicken our pace. My breathing picks up its pace even more and my whole body feels like it's on fire, burning hotter with each thrust. I fight to hold his passionate gaze, but it's not long before I lose the battle. My eyes flutter close as my body begins to throb around him. "Brady," I gasp desperately.

He grunts in response and thrusts hard once, twice and the third time I feel him reach the top of his climax right after me. He pauses at the hilt and exhales slowly before slowing his thrusts, bringing us both down from our high. He leans in and kisses me hard before he slowly pulls himself out, making me sigh with exhaustion. He falls to the bed beside me and pulls me into his arms sighing my name, "Sam." He kisses me again, this time slow and tender, causing my already erratic heartbeat to surge with happiness. He pulls back and whispers over my lips, "That was fantastic. You are incredible." Then he kisses me again.

I sigh with both satisfaction and anxiety. I feel like I need to say something, but I'm not sure what. I feel whole and incomplete. I feel taken care of, cherished and loved. I gasp at the realization, feeling slightly panicked.

Brady squeezes me gently, "Are you okay? You're shaking."

I nod and try to gulp down the lump in my throat, "I'm fine, I just got a chill." I clear my throat before I try again. "You better get cleaned up," I remind him ignoring the strong feeling in my gut.

He scans my face, his own scrunching up in concern. Eventually he nods and lightly kisses my lips. "I'll be right back," he informs me as he pushes off the bed.

He comes back quickly holding up a warm washcloth and asks, "May I?" I nod and he gently wipes between my legs.

I push up and reach for his shirt and boxer briefs lying on the floor. I toss him his underwear and he quickly pulls them on. I slip his shirt on over my own head with a smile, making him chuckle. "Are you going to stay tonight?" I ask him.

He pulls me into his arms and lightly kisses my lips before he responds. "If you'll let me," he murmurs.

"I'd like that," I whisper.

I roll over and curl up on my side. He pulls the covers over us and presses in behind me. He grabs me around the waist and gives me a small tug, pulling my back to his front. I relax into him, loving the comfort of his arms and trying not to overthink anything. He leans over enough to kiss the corner of my mouth and whisper, "Goodnight Samantha."

I smile, "Goodnight Brady.

I close my eyes and feel myself drifting off to sleep just as I hear a mumbled, "I love you Sam." My eyes fight to open to see if it's real, but I convince myself to relax and go back to sleep. I must be dreaming. I can't overthink it. I'm trying to live in the moment, but I'm not ready for love yet. It couldn't be. Could it?

Chapter 41

I slowly blink awake, feeling hot, smothered and nauseous. I'm curled up facing Brady, our arms wrapped around one another and our legs a tangled mass. I want to enjoy the moment while his eyes are closed, but they flip open as I scramble to get out of his embrace. "I don't feel good," I barely rasp, my voice not yet awake. He helps me untangle from him and I rush to the bathroom and accidentally slam the door behind me. I kneel over the toilet, but I don't get sick. I sit on it to pee and then stand and flush the toilet. I wash my hands and splash cold water on my face before I glance at my pale face in the mirror. I grab a Dixie cup and drink some cool water right out of the sink. I grab my toothbrush and the tube of toothpaste, squeezing a small amount onto my brush. I quickly brush my teeth before I shakily stumble back to my room.

"Are you okay?" Brady asks, his face full of concern as I crawl back in bed.

I flop down on my stomach and mumble, "No."

"Are you sick?" he asks.

"Don't worry, I'm not going to get you sick. I think it's just nerves about today," I admit with a groan.

His hand rubs gently up and down my back. "I don't care if you get me sick. I just want to know you're okay," he insists.

I grimace and push up, eyeing him skeptically. "No one wants to be sick," I grumble.

He chuckles, "No, but that doesn't mean I wouldn't deal with it to help you."

I drop my head back on my pillow and look up at him. "You're too perfect," I mumble, making him laugh. His hair is a beautiful mess. He doesn't look like he just woke up. He honestly looks sexy as hell in my bed in just his briefs. "How do you look so good in the morning?" I question with annoyance clear in my voice.

He chuckles, "You've seen me before in the morning."

"Yeah, but you always look so good," I groan.

He laughs harder and leans down, lightly kissing my lips. "You're gorgeous right now Samantha. You always are," he tells me sincerely as I look at him with doubt. He chuckles and kisses me again.

I pull away and sigh, annoyed with myself. "I'm sorry I'm so grumpy. I'm just nervous. I need to not think about it," I decide. "When do you have to go to class?" I ask changing the subject.

He grimaces, "In a few minutes if I was going to go, but I can skip today. I was going to anyway when we were going to stay at your house. Now..." he trails off.

"You don't have to skip for me," I tell him, at the same time hoping he will. I just want him to make the decision.

"I want to," he insists. "I thought I could drive you to The Pit and hang out close by in case you need me. Then when you're done, call me and I'll pick you up and bring you home," he offers.

I close my eyes and breathe a sigh of relief, feeling as if a huge weight has been lifted off my shoulders just knowing he'll be close by. "Thank you," I whisper, feeling choked up.

He brushes my hair out of my eyes and smiles softly at me. "You're welcome, but I'm happy to do it. I won't be able to stop thinking about it if I go to class, so it's pointless to bother going," he declares. "I'll get the notes from someone."

I kiss him on the corner of his mouth. "Well, I'm thanking you anyway."

He pushes off the bed grinning down at me. "I'll be right back," he announces. "I just have to go across the hall.

I watch him walk out of my room and hold myself a little tighter. I take a couple deep breaths, trying to slow down my heartbeat and calm the butterflies in my stomach. I groan and push out of bed, going for my backpack to pull out the last letter. "Now is as good a time as any," I mumble to myself. I sit on the bed and scoot back to lean against the wall just as Brady walks back in and shuts the door. I hold the letter up and inform him, "I was going to read the last one."

"Okay," he acknowledges. He strides over to the bed and sits against the wall next to me before he grabs me by the waist and pulls me over to rest between his legs, making me giggle. I lean back against him. He rests his hands gently on the sides of my stomach and his cheek on the top of my head. "Don't worry, I won't read anything," he says into my hair, making me smile.

"You can read all of them, I just want to be the one to read them the first time," I tell him, just now realizing that's how I feel.

He presses his lips my temple in appreciation and holds me a little tighter as I unfold the letter and begin to read.

June 12ᵗʰ (your 17ᵗʰ Birthday)
To My Beautiful Baby Girl,
Happy Birthday!! I can't believe you're 17! What are you doing for your birthday this year? I hope you celebrate even though you're getting older. Your life should be celebrated. One more year and you will be an adult. One more year and you'll have the right to come find me. That's scary and exciting. What if you do? What if you

don't? I guess we'll find out soon enough, but whatever you decide it's okay. It's your decision.

Anyway, you don't have much left of high school. What's your social life like? Do you go to the school dances? I wonder if you'll go to Prom or Homecoming or even the Sadie Hawkins dance (that's the one when the girls ask the boys just in case they call it something else at your school). If you do, I wonder what your date or dates will be like or what kind of dress you will wear. Then I think about what it might be like for you since every school seems to do dances differently. We had ours in our school gym, but I know a lot of schools rent out big venues like a wedding. Did you take a limo or drive...Drive...DRIVE! You can drive. Well at least I assume you can. You probably got your license sometime this past year. I can't believe it! Do you have a car? If so, what do you drive?

Have you found anything that you're passionate about? Maybe something you might want to do with your life? I know you're young and you have plenty of time, but life tends to sneak up on you. I never realized how good planning would be until it was too late.

My husband and I are doing well, although we've been going through a lot, not with each other, just in life. I'll tell you more next year. I don't think it's time. I'm not working as much. I've cut my hours to part time and I tried to spend every minute I can with my husband when he's not working. He's a wonderful man. Our goal is to make each other happy and he definitely does that for me.

I have so many questions I realize may never be answered, but I hope you know in your heart that I'm thinking of you wherever you are and whomever you may be. I hope you have a fabulous birthday. Enjoy your day and I hope you have a great year! Happy Birthday!

With Love...

Catherine Schepp

I fold the letter up and curl into Brady. I wrap my arms around his waist and lay my head on his chest, listening to the sound of his heartbeat. He brushes my hair away from my face and tucks it behind me. Then his hand drifts soothingly up and down my back. "I don't know if I'm glad I know what they all say now or if I'm sad that I don't have any more to read," I tell him. I shrug, "I know I can read them over and over again and I probably don't even remember everything they said anyway, but besides the court papers and documents from my adoption, that's it." He holds me and continues to rub his hand up and down my back, comforting me, listening to me and quietly giving me exactly what I need. "Do you want to read it?" I ask him.

He pulls away from me to glance down at me, "Really?"

I shrug, "Yeah."

I hand him the letter and settle back into his arms as he begins to read. "Wait, this letter is for your 17th birthday," he states confused. "I thought you said there was one every year until your 18th?" he questions.

I smile, enjoying the fact that he really listens to me. "Yeah, I read that one already," I admit. "When I first got everything, I read the first two letters and they didn't say enough, so I skipped to the last one. That's the letter that told me about my birth father and the reason I'm here," I confess.

He gives me a gentle squeeze and mumbles, "I'm thankful for that." He wraps my hair mindlessly around his finger as he quietly reads my letter.

It feels so intimate to be able to share something like this with him. I feel an even stronger pull towards him and that terrifies me, but at the same time I'm reminded how short life can be. I don't know how much time I have with him and I don't want to waste a moment of it. Now I just have to convince my heart to completely let go. I want to be with him, but I can feel myself holding back. It's almost like I know I'm going to lose him and if I let myself really love him it will hurt so much worse. I know what that feels like and I dread feeling like that again. I sigh and squeeze him a little bit tighter. I can't think that way.

Brady sets the letter on the nightstand. He twists his torso, his hand sliding in to cup my jaw and tilt my face towards his. "Thank you for letting me read that," he tells me. Then he leans in and tenderly shows me his appreciation as his lips cover mine. He moves gently over my mouth, caressing my lips with his own. Just when I'm about to push the kiss deeper, he pulls back to look into my eyes, then kisses me chastely before settling back. "I understand what you mean better when you say she has more questions than answers, but I guess that lets you know that she never stopped thinking about you after all these years," he tells me. "She kept you close and loved you in her own way, even though she didn't know you."

My heart flips and a lump forms in my throat. "Yeah," I croak, feeling overwhelmed as a tear slips down my cheek.

"Sam," Brady whispers my name as he wipes my tears away with his thumb. "I'm sorry. I didn't mean to make you cry."

I shake my head, "It's not that Brady." I try to pull my thoughts together and explain how I'm feeling. "Everything about this is so overwhelming. Then sharing it with you..." I trail off, trying to calm the butterflies floating around my insides. "It's something that sometimes is hard to wrap my own head around even though it's my life and I understand it. Now I'm sharing it with you and to have you understand or at least try to..." I gulp hard, attempting to swallow the lump in my throat. "It's just a lot."

He tilts my face back again to look into my eyes, "I told you I want to be here for you. I meant for everything."

I nod my head and lightly kiss his lips. "Thank you," I mumble. I reach for my phone, needing another distraction to get my emotions under control. My phone reads 8:15am causing me to panic. "Oh no!" I screech and scramble out of bed and away from Brady. "I have to get ready!"

"It only takes five minutes to get there. You have time," he reminds me. I nod but stride for my closet, still not sure what to wear. "I'll head back to my apartment to shower so I'm not tempted to distract you," he smirks. "I'll be back in a little while to get you," he informs me. I nod my head in acknowledgement and continue scanning through my clothes. He chuckles and steps up behind me, leaning down to kiss me chastely. "Don't stress. You're beautiful in anything...and nothing at all," he smirks playfully. I roll my eyes. He laughs as he strides for the door, "I'll see you in a few."

Chapter 42

"I think I'm going to throw up," I mumble, staring at the blacktop. My eyes count the number of puddles of already melted snow, attempting to keep my mind occupied with anything except what's currently happening.

Brady leans against his truck and pulls me with him, giving my hand an encouraging squeeze. "You're going to be fine Sam. You look beautiful and you're amazing. He's going to love you," he insists.

I glance down at my dark blue skinny jeans and short tan city boots with a gold buckle on the side. I hold my arms away from my body to scan my dark coral, long sleeved, loose-fitting top to make sure I didn't get something on it on the way here. "I should go in," I mumble shakily.

"Are you sure you don't want me to go in with you?" he asks.

I shake my head and inform him, "No, I need to do this alone. I'll text you when to come and get me."

He nods and pulls me into his arms. I take a deep breath in, taking in his scent to calm me. "Okay," he relents. I shakily start to step away, but he pulls me back, my lips crashing into his. I instantly melt into him, our mouths moving in perfect rhythm. I feel the tension begin to ease and sigh into his mouth as goose bumps cover my body. He pulls away rubbing my arms up and down. "Are you cold?" he asks.

I shake my head no, feeling slightly stunned as I breathlessly look up at him. "What was that for?" I ask.

He chuckles, "For luck."

I grin and step back, my hands not shaking as much. "Making out in the parking lot for luck," I laugh. "It works. Thanks." My stomach flips inside out with his answering grin. I take a deep breath and stand tall, pushing my shoulders back like my mom taught me. I spin on my heel and stride with confidence towards the front door of The Pit. I feel Brady's eyes on me, so I wave to him over my shoulder, afraid if I turn around and look at him, I'll run right back to his arms.

I pull the glass front door open and step inside, my nerves immediately returning. "Mom, Dad," I murmur quietly, "I could really use your support right now." I clench my hands tightly together and anxiously scan through the restaurant to see if he's already here. I easily spot him in a corner booth rearranging the napkins and condiments on the table, helping me relax a little bit. "I guess he's nervous too," I mumble to myself. I take a deep breath and force myself to walk in his direction.

He looks up just before I reach the table. His hands freeze the moment his eyes land on me. He shakes his head slightly and pushes out of the booth, standing to greet me. "Samantha," he grins. "You're really beautiful," he murmurs, making me blush.

He fidgets with his hands, causing me to laugh quietly at the realization that neither one of us is quite sure what to do. "Thank you. Should we sit, hug, shake hands?" I ask throwing it all out there.

He chuckles and requests, "Is it okay if I hug you?" I nod shakily. He holds his arms out and I briefly step into his warm embrace as pinpricks stick me from the inside out, reminding me of the enormity of this moment.

I quickly pull away as my tears begin to surface. He immediately drops his arms, releasing me and sits down in the same spot he just occupied. "Sorry, I'm feeling a little overwhelmed and on display at the same time," I attempt to explain.

He looks around the small restaurant and laughs, "I know exactly what you mean." I slide into the booth across from him and set my purse down next to me. I pull my phone out and set it on the table between us to remind me Brady is close by if I need him. "Thank you for coming," he says. Then he quickly follows it by asking, "Is this okay?"

I nod my head and we spend the next few moments quietly assessing one another. The waitress steps up to our table with a welcoming smile disrupting the silence, "Good morning Mr. Scott! How are you doing this morning?"

"I'm good," he murmurs.

"How's your family?" she asks sweetly.

He answers nervously, glancing towards me and back to her again, "Um, they're all good."

She glances over at me and smiles, "Oh, sorry." She pulls out her notepad and a pen before asking, "Are you ready to order?"

I glance over to Lincoln and he nods his head towards me. "Um yeah," I murmur. "I'm just going to have some oatmeal, a bowl of fruit and some coffee," I tell her knowing I need something light and plain so I don't throw up on our table from my nerves.

I watch him as he orders, not really sure what I'm looking for, but I can't help it. The first day I met him is already such a blur, it's almost like it didn't even happen. He's a good-looking older man, probably about the same height as Brady, thin with broad shoulders covered by a white button down shirt rolled up to his elbows. He has a strong jaw and laugh lines along his mouth as well as by the corners of his eyes. He seems to still have all his dark brown hair. Hair the same color as mine, except his has some gray splattered throughout. The waitress retreats and he turns to look at me, his caramel colored eyes meeting mine. Eyes the same color as mine.

I take a shaky breath as he shakes his head and mumbles, "It's surreal." I glance at him in confusion knowing that statement could mean so much in this moment. He explains, "I think I told you this, but you look so much like her when she was your age. You have her hair, but hers was red and you have her nose and the shape of her eyes. I'm wondering if there's more I don't see yet. I found a picture," he informs me. I gasp and watch with wide eyes, as he pulls out a picture and holds it out for me.

The photo appears to have been taken in an open field somewhere and is centered on a beautiful woman a couple years younger than me. Her hair is auburn red with soft curls like mine. She's wearing a cute white sundress with spaghetti straps, fitted to her curves, flaring lightly around her at the bottom near her knees where it's slightly splattered with mud. She has a huge smile on her face with one of her arms up in the air like she's cheering. There's a crowd of people all around her, a few of them watching her with admiration, making me smile. I look closer at the guy standing near her in the picture and lift my head to look across the table at the same man, just a little bit older. "That's you?" I question.

He nods his head, "Yeah, that was the weekend I met her. We were at a music festival out in the country somewhere," he informs me. "I don't even remember exactly where," he admits.

I nod and acknowledge, "She looks happy." He nods in agreement. I bite my lip nervously and release it. "This is the weekend she got pregnant with me," I say, wanting confirmation.

He nods slowly and rasps, "Yeah." He pauses and clears his throat. "You can have it if you'd like," he offers.

"Thank you," I mumble.

He sighs and clasps his hands together on the table in front of him. "Look Samantha, you caught me off guard when you found me last week. I didn't know what to say," he stumbles over his words and releases an exaggerated sigh. "I guess I needed time to process the fact that you're really here. I'm sorry if I reacted badly."

I shake my head insisting, "You didn't. I get it was a shock to see me. I wasn't sure how else to get in touch with you, but I knew I needed to find you. It took me a while to even try, so I get it," I concede.

"You're welcome at my home anytime," he declares and my eyes widen in surprise. "I'm also at our store in town a lot," he informs me.

I nod my head wondering if I would ever feel comfortable enough to stop in and see him, wherever that might be. The waitress steps up to the table, setting our food down in front of us. "Thank you," we both murmur not taking our eyes off one another.

"I have a lot of questions," he states.

"So do I," I admit sheepishly.

He laughs and nods his head in understanding. He asks, "It feels kind of strange asking you this, but...where did you grow up?"

"In a small town outside of Chicago," I inform him. "Not nearly as small as this though," I laugh.

He chuckles and asks, "Do you still live there?"

I shrug, "Sort of, my parents' house is there and they left it to me, but I found a roommate here so I could look for you," I tell him, my voice becoming quieter as I go.

"You're living here now?" he asks surprised. I nervously take in his expression trying to decide how he feels about that when he answers my question for me. "That's wonderful!" he exclaims.

My body immediately sags with relief as I release the breath I didn't know I was holding. I didn't realize I was still hesitant to give him too much, afraid of being rejected again. "I thought...I thought if I found you maybe I could get to know you some if that's what you wanted," I stammer nervously.

"I would love that Samantha," he insists, smiling proudly at me. "What's your last name? You never told me your last name!" he asks suddenly.

I laugh, "Sorry, I guess I didn't even think about that. It's Voss, Samantha Ann Voss."

"It's a beautiful name," he murmurs. "Do you have any brothers or sisters?"

I shake my head, "No, but I have cousins I'm close to."

"Can I ask..." he hesitates, "Did you always know you were adopted?" he shovels a forkful of eggs nervously into his mouth.

I nod, "Yeah, my parents always told me how lucky they were that they were able to adopt me. They would say I was their greatest gift." I glance down at my oatmeal and begin stirring it with my spoon when my eyes well with tears.

"It sounds like they were good people," he tells me sincerely.

I nod and rasp, "The best."

"Good," he states vehemently. I take a deep breath and look up at him. "That's something I always worried about, but I had to assume you were with a good family." He shakes his head and clears his throat. He takes another bite of eggs before he asks, "So what do you like to do Samantha?"

"You can call me Sam," I inform him.

He smiles, "Okay, Sam."

I smile back and answer all his questions the best I can while he does the same for me. We continue to talk and talk, telling each other stories and sharing little facts. It's strange how I'm trying to compress my whole life story into such a short amount of time and there is no way I'm going to remember everything he's telling me, but I still keep asking. The waitress returns and asks, "Would you like me to get you some lunch too?"

"What?" I ask surprised. I glance at my phone and gasp in surprise at the 12:03 pm time. "I'm sorry, but I should go," I mumble, looking back at Lincoln as the waitress steps away. He nods his head and asks, "Do you need a ride?"

I shake my head, "No thanks." I quickly send a text to Brady, "Can you come get me? Come in if you want."

"My wife would really like to meet you," he informs me. "My son and daughter too, but I thought we could give you a little at a time if you'd prefer. I don't want to overwhelm you."

"Thank you," I reply gratefully.

"Maybe we could all have dinner together Friday night? You can bring someone with you if you want." He suggests.

"I think that will work. Can I call and let you know?" I ask wanting to talk to Brady before I agree to anything more.

He nods and pushes to stand, "Can I give you another hug?" he requests. I nod my head, unable to speak and stand up, stepping into his arms. I can't help but think this is going better than I ever expected it to, but I'm terrified to meet his family.

Chapter 43

Brady

I breathe a sigh of relief the moment I get the text I've been waiting for from Sam. I never expected her to be at breakfast for three hours. "I gotta' go," I mumble to my Mom on the way out the front door of the restaurant. My sister was working today, so she took her break early and had coffee with me. Then I came over to help at the restaurant, but no matter how busy I kept myself, I couldn't stop thinking about Sam. She was so nervous this morning that she actually made herself sick. I felt so helpless and I fucking hate feeling that way! Now she's been there for hours and finally says I can come in to get her. Is that a good thing? I have no idea, but I've never been so thankful to live in such a small town.

I pull into the parking lot moments later and park in the same spot I did this morning. I jump out of my truck and jog up to the door. I quickly pull the door open and survey the restaurant. I see a lot of familiar faces, but miss Sam's petite frame at first. I look again, my whole body relaxing as she steps out from behind one of the waitresses from the back corner, her smiling face walking towards me. "Hi," she whispers.

"Hey," I grin.

Mr. Scott steps up in front of me, holding out his hand to shake. "Hello, Brady. Here for lunch?"

"Hi Mr. Scott. Actually, I'm here to pick up Sam," I tell him gesturing towards her.

"You know Samantha?" he asks grinning.

The question immediately causes my whole body to tense, dreading the reason he knows her. "Yeah," I rasp. "She's my girlfriend," I inform him.

"Oh," he says, his eyebrows drawing together in surprise as Sam looks back and forth between the two of us, watching our interaction. "Sam and I just had a nice breakfast," he rasps nervously.

I think my heart completely stops beating as the blood drains from my face. My heart nearly punches through my chest as it restarts erratically; at the same time my stomach churns with mounting anxiety. She's going to flip out. I swallow hard and dare a look at Sam, eyeing me quizzically. "You're good?" I ask.

She hesitates before she answers, "Um, yeah. I um...I'm ready to go," she murmurs awkwardly.

I nod my head and turn back towards Mr. Scott, "It was good to see you Sir."

"You too and say Hi to your family," he tells me.

I nod and reach for Samantha's hand, immediately entwining our fingers together. Then I turn back around and walk out the door towards my truck with her in tow. When we reach the passenger side of my truck, I pull the door open for her and reluctantly release her hand. I press my lips to hers, desperately needing to feel her. She pulls away holding her hand firmly to my chest and whispers my name, "Not now Brady." I sigh and lift her up into the seat before she has a chance to climb up herself. I walk around to the back of the truck and wave to Mr. Scott still watching us. I jump in behind the wheel and start the truck, immediately backing out and turning towards our apartment building.

"So how do you think everything went?" I ask her, attempting to get her talking at the same time, delaying what I have to tell her.

"Good," she answers simply.

I grit my teeth and ask, "What did you talk about?"

She shrugs and sighs, leaning back in her seat, "I don't know...a lot...everything...it's hard to tell someone literally everything about you in a short amount of time. Where do you start? How much do you really tell?" she shakes her head and shrugs again. "It was kind of surreal. I don't know if I even remember half of what we talked about. He asked about my family and where I grew up. He asked what I liked to do growing up and what I like to do now. He told me about his family and he wants me to meet them," she says, making my stomach churn. "So, you know them?" she asks.

I swallow hard and nod my head. "Yeah," I rasp as my heartbeat picks up speed by the second. "Most of my life," I add.

"What are they like?" she asks nervously while pulling on a loose string on her jeans.

"Mrs. Scott is really nice," I begin as I park behind our building. I turn off my truck and turn to look at her, watching her reaction. She nods and bites her bottom lip. I reach across the console separating us and grab her hand, caressing the top of it with my other one. "He talked about his kids?" I ask, trying to sound calm, but I don't notice anything different in her demeanor. Maybe she doesn't realize? Or maybe it doesn't matter to her at least that's what I'm hoping.

She nods, "Yeah, but he kept asking so many questions, he really didn't tell me very much. What can you tell me about them?"

I look away and grimace. My palms become clammy and I clear my throat and begin with the easy part. "Frankie is a good kid. He loves sports. I don't really know what his favorite is right now."

"What about his sister? She's the same age as me," she states.

I nod and attempt to swallow the growing lump in my throat. "Yeah," I croak. I take a deep breath and exhale harshly, focusing on her hand in mine. "Sam, did he tell you her name? Do you know who she is?" I ask anxiously.

She clenches my hand a little tighter, her fingernails digging slightly into the back of my hand. "No," she declares.

I swallow hard and look into her eyes as I force myself to inform her. "His daughter is Jackie." Her eyes widen and her face pales as she leans slightly away from me, making me cringe. "It's no big deal Sam," I insist, hoping she believes it's true, at the same time wondering what she's thinking. She can't pull away from me because of this.

She nods stiffly, "Okay..."

"This doesn't change anything with us," I insist.

She nods again and quietly rasps, "I know." She pulls her hand away, leaving me feeling cold. "I'm just trying to process everything."

My chest tightens as I feel her pulling away, even though she's not moving. "Sam?" I question shakily.

She turns to me, her eyes welling and forces a smile, "We're fine Brady. We're good. I just need to think about how I'm going to deal with this." She reaches for the handle and jumps out of my truck.

I quickly grab my keys and scramble after her. We ride the elevator up, listening painfully to every creak and groan up to the 4th floor. I follow her to her door, my feet heavier with each step. I request, trying to keep the desperation out of my voice, "Can I come in?"

"Sure," she whispers as she unlocks her door.

I follow her to the couch where she flops down looking completely lost. I sit down next to her and pull her into my arms, without any help from her. "It's going to be fine," I tell her.

She laughs humorlessly, "She hates me...because of you."

"She doesn't know you!" I grit through my teeth.

"That doesn't matter," she mutters. "Now add this...None of them will like me," she grumbles.

"Samantha, I know them and they will all take time getting to know you. As you know, Jackie has her own issues. They won't take her word for it," I attempt to comfort her.

"Why not, he chose her over me once already. Why wouldn't he do it again?" she asks, her voice full of bitterness as tears slowly roll down her cheeks.

"Sam," I whisper, feeling gutted as my heart breaks for her. I want to help, but I don't know how. "Anyone who takes some time getting to know you can see how amazing you are," I tell her honestly.

"You barely know me either Brady," she tells me, staring intently at the floor.

My heart jumps into my throat and I grunt as if she punched in the stomach. I plead, "Don't do that Sam. Don't push me away. We can deal with this together. I was being completely honest when I told you I was falling for you. I want to be there for you. I can help them get to know you," I offer. I'm not about to let Jackie ruin what I have with Sam under any circumstances. We're just getting started. I can't protect her if I'm not there. I'm not letting her go now that I found her. I'm fighting for Sam, for us I admit to myself feeling a strong sense of determination. I just have to figure out how to get her to let me do that.

She sighs dramatically and informs me, "He wants me to have dinner to meet his wife, or his family, or both. I'm not really sure. He said I could bring someone with me."

"I'd love to go with you," I tell her and she huffs in annoyance. I grip her chin and tilt it up towards me until she looks me in the eyes. "Sam, please, don't push me away. Let me be there for you. I want to be by your side wherever that may be."

The intensity in her gaze is overwhelming, but I attempt to open myself up so she can see the truth in my soul. Her face softens and I lean in to kiss her, hoping our crazy chemistry will benefit me right now. I need to show her how strong we are together. I stop just before our lips meet wanting to tell her my heart is beating for her, that I love her, but I hesitate. I don't think she's ready to hear my whole truth, especially now. I close my eyes and drop my forehead to hers at my realization. I love her. My heartbeat speeds up and I stifle my gasp. I feel her warm breath on my face. I slide my hands to cradle her face and tell her what I hope she's willing to hear. I whisper with awe, "You are so beautiful. You are unbelievably strong. You inspire me to be more even if I'm not quite sure what that entails yet," I smirk. "You make me smile like no one has ever done before. Every single part of you inside and out is breathtakingly beautiful. You are truly incredible and you are *mine* Samantha Voss. I just want to be a part of all that's you. I'm not letting you go."

"You're too damn perfect," she mumbles, shaking her head.

I chuckle just before I brush my lips against hers. I'm barely able to taste her so I try again. I sweep my lips over hers again, letting my tongue trail along her lower lip and making her gasp. The sound alone makes me groan. I cover her whole mouth with mine, pushing my tongue inside to taste her sweetness. Our tongues playfully fight for dominance as she climbs on my lap and settles, straddling me. I love when she does that.

I quickly stand holding her in my arms, but I don't want to stop kissing her. I take a step towards her room and stumble. I break our kiss, wrap one arm around her supporting her head and the other in front of me to brace our fall, attempting to twist towards the couch. We bounce off the couch and I hit the floor hard with a rattling bang, "Shit!" I mutter.

She falls on top of me and bursts out laughing. "Ow," she grumbles as she laughs harder.

"Are you okay?" I groan.

She continues laughing and my mouth twitches in amusement, listening to her, watching her, holding her. This moment couldn't be more perfect. I laugh along with her believing everything will be okay.

When we both catch our breath, she smiles and softly presses her lips to mine. She pulls back and looks down at me still lying on the floor and tells me, "Brady, because of you, I'm smiling and laughing again. Let's figure this out together."

My heart breathes a sigh of relief as she kisses me again and I easily get lost in all that is Samantha.

To be continued...

Want to find out how Samantha and Brady's story ends? Read "Finding Home", book #2 in the Home Duet coming soon...

Acknowledgements

I have so many people I'd like to thank for this book; I almost don't know where to begin. First and foremost I'd like to say thank you to my family for their unwavering support! I wouldn't be able to do what I love without you by my side. Thank you to my friends who are there in so many different capacities. A special thank you is needed for Kelley and Nancy who go above and beyond, along with the rest of my beta readers who are always a tremendous help!

Thank you to Violette Wicik of Violette Wicik Photography for the beautiful cover photo. You knew exactly how to capture the perfect image for this story. I had so much fun working with you and it's no surprise that your creativity amazes me! https://www.violettewicik.com/ Thank you to Dominique as well for being the perfect model!

The rest of my thank you takes a little more explanation. Like Samantha in this story, I was adopted as a baby and found some of my birth family later on in my life. For that reason alone, this story was hard to write emotionally, although it's not really anything like my own. All the questions and fears that have gone through my head at one time or another would rush into my head as I was writing, knowing what Sam might be going through and knowing every single adoption story is different. Thank you to my sister Michelle and friends I have met over the years that have also been adopted. I will always be grateful for everything we're able to share and truly understand because of that special connection.

Thank you to my mom and dad who have always been there throughout all the ups and downs since the day they adopted me when I was only a few weeks old.

You both always supported and loved me no matter what. I couldn't ask for anything more and I wouldn't want to. I love you doesn't seem like enough, but I do with all my heart. I know you're still there watching over me from heaven Dad! Thank you for the rainbows!

Thank you to my birth mom who unknowingly helped with the inspiration of a part of this story with a special gift she gave me for my birthday not long after we met~ the second time. I'm grateful to her and every one of my "new" (or old depending on how you look at it) family that has come into my life. I also want to thank her for having me and giving me a chance at a good life by putting me up for adoption. I know you believed you weren't able to give me what I needed when you were so young. Thank you to my good friend Sarah. You gave me the final "push" to find my birth family and meet (some of) them in the first place. Without my personal experience, "Dreams Lost and Found" wouldn't exist. I'm thrilled to be able to share it with all of you!

Connect with Nikki A Lamers

Official Author Website
www.nikkialamers.com

Author Facebook Page
www.facebook.com/pg/NikkiALamersAuthor

Follow Me on Instagram
@NikkialamersAuthor

Author Goodreads Page
www.goodreads.com/author/show/8451774.Nikki_A_Lamers

Author Amazon Page
https://www.amazon.com/Nikki-A.-Lamers/e/B00NU1VU8M

Made in the USA
Middletown, DE
13 August 2021